THE FIRST WIZARD

DAWN OF WIZARDS
BOOK ONE

JEFFREY L. KOHANEK

D1707697

ALSO BY JEFFREY L. KOHANEK

Fate of Wizardoms

Eye of Obscurance

Balance of Magic

Temple of the Oracle

Objects of Power

Rise of a Wizard Queen

A Contest of Gods

* * *

Fate of Wizardoms Boxed Set: Books 1-3

Fate of Wizardoms Box Set: Books 4-6

Fall of Wizardoms

God King Rising

Legend of the Sky Sword

Curse of the Elf Queen

Shadow of a Dragon Priest

Advent of the Drow

A Sundered Realm

Fall of Wizardoms Boxed Set: Books 1-3

Fall of Wizardoms Box Set: Books 4-6

Wizardom Legends

The Outrageous Exploits of Jerrell Landish

Thief for Hire

Trickster for Hire

Charlatan for Hire

Tor the Dungeon Crawler

Temple of the Unknown

Castles of Legend

Shrine of the Undead

Runes of Issalia

The Buried Symbol

The Emblem Throne

An Empire in Runes

* * *

Runes of Issalia Bonus Box

Wardens of Issalia

A Warden's Purpose

The Arcane Ward:

An Imperial Gambit

A Kingdom Under Siege

* * *

Wardens of Issalia Boxed Set

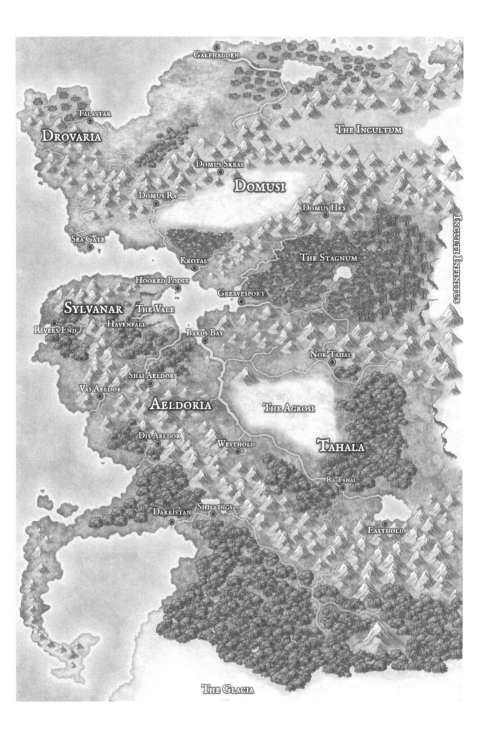

JOURNAL ENTRY

The first age was a time of balance, growth, and prosperity as the civilizations of man, elf, and dwarf evolved from crude savages to refined beings in pursuit of knowledge. But no age lasts forever, the first age ending when my brother found a way to tilt things in his favor. The balance of magic shifted, until the imbalance was beyond repair. Or so I thought, until a brilliant scheme came to me. One I spent centuries plotting. The complexities of such a device are beyond mortal comprehension, so I will not even attempt to share the intricate details. Suffice it to say that, when the plan was finally set into motion, it resulted in a series of events that brought the second age to an end. With that ending, a new age began.

The annals of history are seldom rooted in truth, and even if they prove accurate, the individuals who record such events omit the flair that makes a story compelling. History often features heroes who become legends. You may wonder about these heroes, whose deeds make them seem larger than life. I assure you that each is simply a person, be it man, elf, or dwarf, whom fate placed in a critical situation in which their actions influenced the course of history. Choices made during such events impact the result and perseverance against seemingly impossible odds, turning unknown individuals into legends.

The tale in the following pages centers around the rise of heroes destined to change their world and usher in a new era — an era where wizards rule and magic reigns supreme. These wizards, humans of magic, might, and mystery, did not always exist.

Before the third age could even begin, the world had to be gifted its first wizard. This is his story.

SOURCE unknown

PROLOGUE

Thick, black smoke filled the sky, blotting out the stars on a moonless night. The mutilated corpses of Drow, dwarves, and various monsters littered the ground. Patches of grass burned across the battlefield, the fires tainting the clouds an angry red, as if the blood spilled below had spread to the sky.

Arangar held his ancestral war hammer, Tremor, in one hand, his plate armor clanking with each step. When passing a downed dwarf who moaned while pressing a blood-soaked hand against his side, he called out. "Hilfagar! I found another one."

The flesh mender rose from a crouch as the dwarven warrior beside him sat upright. Hilfagar trudged past two dozen corpses and approached Arangar. His eyelids appeared heavy, his shoulders slumped. The battle might be finished, but the work of healing the wounded had just begun.

With a clap to Hilfagar's unarmored shoulder, Arangar said, "I know you are weary. We all tire of this endless fighting." Across the field, a dwarf roared while swinging a war hammer at a green-tinted creature thrice his size. Half a dozen other dwarfs rushed in with weapons flashing. They surrounded a lone ogre, the mindless beast flailing its massive, muscular and distended arms while the dwarves ducked and dodged the wild attacks. "Well, most of us are weary. My son and his crew behave as if they are engaged in a party rather than a battle."

"We were young when this all began. I recall you fighting with similar vigor during your first battle." Hilfigar wiped his brow. "Nothing against your son or the other newcomers, but I pray this is the last of it."

Arangar glanced toward the city a half mile away. "The Drow army has been soundly defeated. Talastar's fortifications will soon be breached. The city defenders have thrown everything they have at us, yet we still stand. When we capture the city, we will have nothing left to conquer. It will be time to go home. Even Gahagar will see the right of it."

The flesh mender knelt beside the injured dwarf, pulled the warrior's bloody hand aside, and pressed his own against the open wound. "Unless he decides to go on to Galfhaddon."

"The human city in the north?" Arangar had considered the idea and dismissed it for sound reasons, but he remained uncertain of how his king felt about it. "Why would he care? They are a backward lot, relegated to the fringes of society. They are uneducated, unsophisticated, and without magic." He shook his head. "No. My greater concern is that he may decide to betray the truce with the southern elves and seek to conquer Sylvanar." Arangar reflected on the topic while stroking his beard.

Being a warrior was in Arangar's blood, much like his ancestors. Born into it and trained from a young age, fighting was what he did best. As with his entire generation, war had become his way of life and was the source of his growing fame. However, Gahagar's campaign had consumed most of Arangar's adult years. *After fifty years of constant war, even I long for a respite.* And my son...he has grown into a mighty warrior, perhaps the best of his generation, and I missed all of it...until he arrived with the other new recruits. Only a week had passed since then and, while Arangar had done his best to spend time with his son in that span, they were still strangers with only one thing in common. Both excelled at fighting.

Focused on the current campaign, Gahagar had not given any indication of his future plans. Arangar had attempted to broach the subject on numerous occasions, but his concern that the high king might turn his attention toward Sylvanar after defeating the Drow kept him from doing so. That concern would linger until the dwarven army returned to Ra'Tahal, and Gahagar demonstrated his satisfaction with the new borders of his expanded empire.

"Be well, Hilfigar," Arangar clapped his old friend on the shoulder. "I am off to find the high king."

The flesh mender's hands glowed as he manipulated the wound, the gash easing shut in response. "May he live forever."

It was a common response when Gahagar's name or title were referenced. *Can he live forever? Not even elves live forever. Yet...* Decades of fighting at Gahagar's side left Arangar wondering if anything could kill him.

Cresting a rise, he spied a cluster of dwarven warriors at the northern edge of the battlefield. Among them, a massive sword burned with angry flames. Only one dwarf owned such a weapon...the only dwarf able to wield it. As Arangar descended the hillside, his gaze shifted to the gigantic corpse lying at the base of the hill. Standing fifty feet tall and weighing more than a house, rock trolls were terrifying creatures. Somehow, the Drow had captured one and convinced it to fight for them, just as they had done with more than a dozen ogres. To turn to such means, the dark elves must have been desperate to stop the Dwarven Army. They should have realized the truth by now. Nothing could defeat Gahagar the Impregnable.

Images of the battle flashed in Arangar's head, beginning with the towering giant stomping on dwarven warriors, crushing them as if each were no more than a child's toy. Gahagar, his flaming sword a streak of orange in the darkness, charged into the fray. The troll raised a foot and stomped as the high king launched an overhead stroke. The sky sword cleaved through the massive foot, toes landing all around Gahagar while dark blood coated his metal body. The troll howled in pain, fell to one knee, the ground shuddering at the impact. The giant swung a backhand blow. The swat struck Gahagar and launched him fifty feet – a blow that would have killed even the sturdiest of dwarves. Yet, Gahagar was far beyond sturdy.

Other warriors donned armor to protect them in battle, but not Gahagar. Centuries earlier, beyond any living dwarf's memory, a mysterious and powerful spell had turned the high king's own flesh to metal. Not only did this allow him to use his fabled, flaming sword, it also granted him protection far beyond the armor of any other warrior. Even those like Arangar, gifted with a helm, breastplate, and bracers made from dwarven steel, were nothing but brittle, fragile shadows of the dwarven high king.

After the troll's devastating blow, Gahagar had climbed to his feet, his hairless, metallic face on the brink of fury. The massive sword in his grip flared brightly, tongues of fire flicking along the length of the blade like an angry snake. The high king rushed toward the kneeling troll, leapt, and slashed. The troll raised a palm large enough to engulf a wagon, its fingers spread to block the attack. It failed.

The five-foot-long blade of fire sliced through two fingers and a thumb. The troll bellowed an earthshaking roar, yanked its wounded hand back, and toppled to its side. Pressing his advantage, Gahagar scrambled up the blubbery, gray-green body of the troll, leapt onto its shoulder, and spun the blade around so the point faced down. He drove the fiery sword into the creature's temple, not stopping until the hilt's crosspiece pressed against its flesh. The troll shuddered and fell still.

Now, an hour after the culmination of a long and hard-fought battle, the giant rock troll lay amid hundreds of much smaller corpses. Despite its size and fearsome nature, dead was dead and the rock troll had died no differently than the Drow, ogres, and dwarves surrounding it.

As Arangar rounded the bloody remains of the troll's half foot, Gahagar came into view.

Standing just over five feet in height, Gahagar was among the tallest of dwarves. His metal flesh was charcoal gray and made of bands that allowed him to bend, flex, and move. Stoutly built, he had the broad shoulders and barrel chest common among dwarven warriors. In contrast, his smooth, hairless appearance lacked even a beard, marking him as a rarity, for beards were greatly prized among dwarven kind. Stories whispered among the dwarven warriors said that Gahagar had once sported a thick, black beard that reached his waist, but none were old enough to have seen the high king in his youth. That beard, along with any other hair on his body, had been forfeited when his flesh turned to metal. How such a thing was accomplished, Arangar had no idea, but he supposed that foregoing a beard was the price paid to wield a weapon such as the Caelum Edge.

Arangar approached the group surrounding Gahagar, stopping between Fandaric, leader of the Clan Argent, and Kobblebon, leader of Clan Aeldor. All kept two or more strides from the flaming blade. Even then, its heat raged. Oftentimes, it made Arangar feel as if he stood beside a burning forge.

He bowed. "I am here to report, High King."

Gahagar nodded, his white, pupilless eyes on Arangar. "What word do you have, old friend?"

"Approximately three hundred Drow have been taken prisoner, including a Singer named Choridal."

"Very good," Gahagar nodded. "There is little sense in conquering a people if none survive to be ruled over. Send for Choridal."

"I ordered an escort to bring him to you. He should be along any minute." Arangar looked back as a group of six dwarven warriors crested the hill. The dwarves were arranged in two columns with a taller, leaner figure dressed in black robes, walking in between. The central figure had white skin and the points of elven ears stuck out from raven-black hair spilling over his shoulders.

The procession rounded the dead troll and came back into view.

Gahagar advanced to meet them, his officers parting for the high king and his massive, angry sword. "The battle is over, Choridal. Like all others, you were destined to fall to us eventually. While I commend your effort, the cost of so many lives saddens me."

Choridal spoke in a lilting tone, as if he were singing, his accent making him sound quite undwarvish. "We did not ask for you to invade our lands. Any lives you lost were a mere tithe paid for your presence. If I had it my way, your corpse would be among them. If my queen had hers, well, let us just say none of you would be standing."

"Tsk tsk. Is that any way to speak to your overlord?"

"Do you expect the Drow to bend knee to dwarves?"

"I expect obedience from my subjects. More importantly, I expect the magic that you and the other Drow singers wield to become assets to the Dwarven Empire."

"And if we refuse?"

"You will be executed."

Choridal shook his head. "You treat us like livestock. Would you do the same to the Sylvan?"

"Your cousins in the south will bend knee to me in time. The dwarves will rule this world from the western coast to the inland waste, from the polar cap to the north to the ice fields in the south."

"You are mad."

"Maybe so, but look at what my madness has wrought." Gahagar made a sweeping gesture, his gaze distant, his chest puffed out. "My empire already stretches beyond the borders of any nation that has come before. We stand on the brink of the greatest age, one where peace and prosperity replace petty squabbles over borders or belief. All will pray to the same god, will use the same coin, and will speak the same language. It will be a time of advancement, where the abilities of Drow, Sylvan, and even humankind augment the superior magic and craftsmanship of the dwarven race. Imagine what we could build together!"

As Gahagar spoke, the dwarven leaders standing behind him exchanged worried glances, and Arangar knew why. It had just become clear that the high king intended to continue his campaign. *How many more years must I endure?*

Choridal shook his head. "You are delusional, Gahagar. Should you force the world to bend knee to your crown, you will find it too large a pie to swallow. It takes weeks to travel from Galfhadden in the north to Darristan in the south. For an army, that number quadruples, and that does not even include the logistical issues of feeding such a force. Should a rebellion occur, it will take you too long to react. Face it, the lands are too vast to govern under one hand."

Arangar and other officers in the Dwarven Army had made the same argument, but Gahagar would not have it.

"It will happen, Choridal," Gahagar growled. "Now, kneel and plead fealty to me, and I will free you."

"And how would we live?"

"As you please, so long as you honor Dwarven Law, obey my commands, and send your singers with me to assist in our conquest as we ride north."

"We are a free people. No singer, me included, is going to help you continue this misbegotten conquest."

"Very well." Gahagar stepped toward the singer and thrust his flaming blade straight through Choridal's chest. The Drow's eyes bulged, he coughed crimson spittle, and collapsed. The high king stepped back, lifted the Caelum Edge over his shoulder, and laid it upon the metal scabbard on his back. The scabbard reacted, the plates clamping closed around the blade and dousing the flame. He then turned toward the hilltop where his soldiers were setting up camp. "It has been a long day, so I am retiring to my tent. Send someone with water. I am parched."

~

ARANGAR CROSSED THE ARMY CAMP, thick with exhausted dwarves. He passed a group of young warriors standing around an ale barrel with tankards in hand. Among them, his son, Arangoli, was laughing as an overweight dwarf acted out a scene from a recent battle. Their enthusiasm and camaraderie caused Arangar to shake his head and long for the carefree and fun days of his own youth.

As he approached the heart of the dwarven camp, he noticed Kobblebon, Fandaric, and a score of warriors huddled together and in an animated discussion. The two leaders both watched him as they spoke to their warriors and the sight sent a tickle of warning down Arangar's spine. But he had no time to dwell on it, not until he reported to his high king. He pulled the flap aside and ducked into the command tent to find Gahagar standing over a table with a map on it.

"Castle Umbra has been swept," Arangar reported. "Queen Liloth is missing and there are no other singers."

Gahagar frowned. "Choridal surely was not the only one stationed there, not after the magic we have faced during this siege."

"I agree. That is why I have sent in our stone shaper and a crew of engineers to search for a secret tunnel."

"Well done. We will find it and track them down." Gahagar reached for the jug of water on the barrel behind him and took a drink. Even a dwarf whose body was made of living metal required water and food to survive.

The high king set the jug down and leaned over the map. A moment later, he jerked as if struck by an invisible force. His eyes widened, and his hand went to his stomach.

"Ugh," Gahagar groaned and doubled over.

Concerned, Arangar rushed to his side and placed a hand around his back. "Your Majesty. What is wrong?"

"My stomach..." Gahagar fell to one knee, his metallic face twisted in pain. "It hurts."

Arangar rushed to the tent flap and stepped outside to shout. "A healer! The high king requires a healer!"

Kobblebon and a dozen guards had positioned themselves in an arc on the left, blocking that route. Fandaric and his men blocked the right.

The latter leader shook his head. "There will be no help."

"What is this?" Arangar demanded.

"We are finished fighting," Kobblebon declared.

The realization was like a slap in the face. Arangar staggered, his accusation emerging as little more than a whisper. "You poisoned your own king."

Silence.

A cry of agony came from the tent. Arangar spun and ducked inside. Gahagar lay on the ground, curled into a ball, moaning.

Kneeling at his side, Arangar spoke softly. "Did you hear what was said?"

Gahagar nodded. "I...have been betrayed."

Not knowing what else to say, yet fearing the answer he might hear, Arangar asked, "What would you have me do?"

The king tapped the golden band coiled around his metal bicep. "The Band of Amalgamation. You must take it when I pass. Hide it away. None can ever know where to find it."

"I don't understand."

"When donned, the band turned my flesh to metal. Without it, the Caelum Edge cannot be wielded."

"But the sky sword is the symbol of the high king. It is what binds the three clans together."

"I...know."

Suddenly, Arangar understood.

Gahagar convulsed. Foam and spittle shot from his mouth, turning from white to red. Then, he fell still. His charcoal gray flesh began to change, soften, and was soon the soft pink of the Tahal clan, the metal replaced with hairless skin. Arangar pressed his fingers to Gahagar's neck but felt no pulse. A tear tracked down his cheek and dropped to Gahagar's forehead. The high king was dead.

In silence, Arangar wept for a time before he remembered his king's last wish. *The Band of Amalgamation. You must take it when I pass. Hide it away. None can ever know where to find it.*

Arangar gripped the gold band, pulled one end away from the dead king's arm, and unwound it until it was free. He stood, grabbed a pack from beneath the table, and stuffed the magical artifact inside before heading toward the tent flap with the pack over his shoulder. After a pause to wipe his cheeks dry, he ducked outside. The other leaders and their soldiers remained in position, firm and resolute.

"He is dead." Arangar snarled, his tone making his feelings about their betrayal clear. "The high king is dead."

Fandaric sighed. "Then, it is over."

"My clansman and I can return to Shai Aeldor," Kobblebon said.

"And mine to Domus Skrai," Fandaric added.

The other two had been kings of their respective clans before falling under the high king's banner. "Clan Tahal now has no king," Arangar said in realization.

Fandaric strode up to Arangar and clapped a hand on his shoulder. "You must lead your warriors home. With their backing, you will assume the throne in Gahagar's absence."

"Me? I am a warrior. What do I know of ruling?"

"The same as any of us before we accepted the crown. At the least, I suspect you will do better than Gahagar. His ambition drove his people too far, something I suspect you know all too well. However, you may wish to give up your weapon when you take the crown. Your predecessor started a war that lasted a generation and cost much for all three clans."

Arangar nodded numbly. Decades of battle had worn on him. "I will gift Tremor to Arangoli." At least he still has enthusiasm for such things. He then recalled another weapon, one impossible for anyone to wield without the prize hidden in his pack. "What of the Caelum Edge?"

Kobblebon arched a brow at Fandaric. "He has a point. What do we do with the most famous weapon of our race when nobody can get near the thing unless it is sheathed?"

Absently, Arangar clutched his pack against his side. Nobody knew that the Band of Amalgamation had gifted Gahagar his metal flesh. Without it, the weapon of ages would be useless.

"I will take it and protect it for now," Fandaric said. "My hold is the closest, so that is the safest choice."

Kobblebon nodded. "Very well."

Arangar did not argue the point, for he was fighting his own internal battle. While he would never taint his honor by assassinating his own king, he found himself relieved to know that the conquest had come to an end, albeit a bitter one. Guilt for feeling such relief almost overwhelmed him.

The other two leaders turned and walked away, each heading in a different direction, much as they would do the following day, the day when the dwarven armies began the long journey home.

CHAPTER 1

CONFIDENCE

On a sunny spring morning, white, puffy clouds reflected in the still surface of Lake Shillings. The lake's name originated from the village on the south bank, a settlement consisting of a string of wooden structures clinging to the shoreline. As one might expect, the villagers rose every day with the sun, each person occupying themselves with the same mundane tasks as the day prior. Like a performance by an ensemble cast, every citizen portrayed a defined role, vital to the community. Whether one raised pigs, grew vegetables, caught fish, baked bread, tanned hides, shaped metal, or performed one of dozens of other jobs, all were valuable pieces of a large, but not particularly complex, puzzle. At least, that is how one teenaged boy viewed it. Even then, village life was utterly, depressingly dull.

Illian Carpenter stared out the window of his father's workshop, his mind wandering and his body imprisoned while the world outside remained free and full of possibility. Along the eastern lakeshore, below the scattered farmhouses, two fishermen in a small boat lowered a net into the water, ever so slowly. A flock of geese appeared in the sky to the north and descended as they neared the lake. Two dozen birds splashed down into the water, disturbing the tranquil scene, and sending ripples in all directions. Ian watched the ripples, which turned to small waves as they reached the shoreline. He imagined the waves continuing across the ground, a ripple running beneath the soil, slipping past buildings, trees, and continuing until they reached unknown lands far, far away – lands he longed to see and explore.

"Ian," a deep voice called, but the call went unheeded with him still lost in his musings.

"Ian," the voice said again, but Ian had turned his attention to the mountains north of the lake, the white peaks a reminder of winter, the season having yet to cede the higher elevations to the warmth of spring.

"Illian!" The shout echoed in the shop.

Violently awakened from his reverie, Ian spun around. "Yes, Pa?"

The man stood at a lathe, the blade in his hand pressed against the spindle of wood he was shaping while his foot pumped the pedal that spun its shaft. "If you do not pay attention, how do you expect to learn?"

A frown tugged on Ian's lips. *I do not want to make furniture*, he replied in his head, but aloud he simply muttered, "Sorry, Pa."

Ian approached the lathe and stood dutifully watching while his father carved the spindle. The blade ate away at the wood, forming ripples, lines, and details that made furniture more interesting. Yet, Ian could think of nothing of less interest. Soon, his gaze returned to the window, his mind miles away.

A hand clapped on his shoulder, startling him. Ian turned toward his father, who stood a few inches taller than him, his gaze intense. Like Ian, Perry Carpenter's eyes were emerald green, his hair the color of dirty straw. Unlike Ian, the furniture maker had broad shoulders and a body covered in the lean muscle of someone who performed physical labor for a living. A loose, stained tunic covered Perry's upper body, his sleeves rolled up to reveal muscular forearms.

"Your seventeenth Beltane approaches. You are no longer a child and must find something useful to do with yourself." Rather than scolding

Ian, Perry spoke in a compassionate tone. "I know how you feel about making furniture, but if you do not learn this craft, what will you do?"

"I like to draw..."

His father rolled his eyes. "That again? I don't deny that you have skill, but until you can explain how you can make a living that way, drawing pretty pictures does not make a career."

The conversation was one that Ian had lost on numerous occasions. With each attempt, his passion had dwindled until he ceased arguing his side. The realization depressed Ian, his gaze dropping to the floor until his father's hand gripped his shoulder in a comforting way.

"What if I told you that you could use that creativity to design furniture?" Perry said.

His interest piqued, Ian looked up at him. "How?"

"When you learn how various types of furniture are shaped and assembled, you will understand the potential and the limitations. Perhaps it will spark ideas. You are a smart boy, and with the understanding of what is and is not possible, you could utilize your skills to design something of value...something we can sell to others who find beauty in it."

Ian turned and looked toward the window again. He longed to flee from the subject and do anything but answer. But his father gripped his shoulder and even if he fled, he could not avoid the issue forever.

"Ian," Perry waited until Ian's gaze met his. "You are smart, of that there can be no doubt. However, unlike your brother, you are not strong enough for many of the other jobs. Your time at the smithy proved as much. Unlike shaping iron, woodwork requires skill more than strength, and the latter can be honed over time. It is a good, solid craft, and it has provided for our family for twenty years. If you make an effort and build something of value, the next time I visit Darristan, it could be sold with the furniture I have crafted this past winter."

"Darristan?" Ian had dreamt of visiting the city. "I could go with you?"

Perry shared a wry smile. "I cannot count the number of times you have asked me to go. This time, I will allow it...if you can focus and apply yourself. The weather has turned and summer approaches. In a few weeks, I will be making my first trip of the year. This gives you just enough time to build something of worth."

Ian sighed. "Very well. What would you have of me?"

Perry picked a three-foot birch branch off a pile and began mounting it to the lathe. "It is your turn. You will follow my instructions and shape a table leg to match the one I just finished."

Resigned to the task, Ian stepped up to the lathe, pumped the foot pedal, and the spindle began to turn.

HIS SKINNY CALF sore from pumping, his shoulders and forearms aching from holding the blade, Ian plopped down onto a stool.

Perry picked up the spindle and examined it. "This is fair work. You are improving."

The praise brought a smile to Ian's face and a newfound sense of pride puffed his chest up. While his parents had always been supportive, Ian rarely felt like his accomplishments mattered, especially when compared to Vic.

"That is the last of my lumber. Until your brother returns with more, I have nothing more for you to do." Perry gestured toward the door. "You are free to leave."

"Thanks, Pa!" The allure of freedom invigorated Ian, washing away exhaustion.

He stumbled out of the workshop and stopped on the gravel drive running between the building and the lake. The late afternoon sun warmed the left side of his body as he stared out over the lake. A girl in a long, blue dress was descending the hillside, a pole over her shoulders and an empty clay jug dangling from each side of it. Her golden hair shone in the sunlight, her gentle curves and narrow waist the marked signs of blossoming womanhood. Spurred into action, Ian headed down the hillside.

A path through long grass and shrubs brought him toward the lake, the route curving and leveling as it reached the rocky shore. The girl stopped beside the water, set the jugs down, and unhooked them from the pole.

"Would you like some help?" Ian asked.

She stood upright and turned toward him, her aqua blue eyes lighting as a smile bloomed. A warmth filled Ian's chest, and a smile stretched across his face. It was impossible not to smile when Rina smiled at you.

"Hello, Ian. I haven't seen you in days, and I worried something had happened to you."

Ian approached her and picked up one of the empty jugs. "My father had imprisoned me in his workshop. I was released early today only because he ran out of wood."

"So, you have agreed to be his apprentice?"

Ian shrugged. "After Master Kalvin dismissed me from his smithy...I was not given a choice."

"What else would you do?"

It was not the first time she had asked that question. "I don't know. I just feel like...there is something else for me."

She cocked her head. "Like what?"

He was reluctant to mention his drawings even though Rina had shown appreciation for them in the past. "In truth, I don't know."

Rina hopped out onto a rock jutting above the surface, squatted, and dunked the jug in the water, tipping it so water rushed in and bubbles flowed out. "When you figure it out, let me know. Until then, Mistress Cass has me fetching water for the wash. I had best not dally, or it'll only anger her."

"The wash..."

"The last load of the day." Gripping the jug with both hands, she stood and extended it toward him. "Take this for me."

Ian reached for it, and when she let go, his arm dropped under the weight and he stumbled. His foot slipped, and he fell forward, face-first into the lake. Ice-cold water enveloped him, its frigid temperature causing his torso muscles to contract. Gasping, he climbed to his feet. The water only reached his mid-thigh, but he was soaked from head to toe. The lake, fed by snowmelt from the mountains to the north, left him shaking, his teeth chattering.

Rina had the grace to cover her mouth and attempt to stifle her laughter. The other witness to Ian's blunder made no such attempt.

Standing twenty feet from shore was Ian's older brother, Vic. He clutched a hand against his stomach as he laughed heartily.

Ian hugged the full jug with one arm and climbed up the rocks, his foot slipping once again and nearly sending him back in. While his brother laughed, Ian fumed, his nostrils flaring in anger. Not at Vic. At himself.

Once on shore, he set down the full jug, scooped up the empty one, and held it out to Rina without saying a word. She flashed him a smile that eased his anger and embarrassment, but only slightly.

"Thank you." Rina squatted to fill the second jug.

Vic, his laughter quelling, walked down to the shoreline. "I was fortunate to arrive just in time to witness that. I must be blessed by the good spirits themselves."

Ian crossed his arms over his chest. He had often wondered if Vic was, indeed, blessed by the good spirits. While Ian suffered from numerous physical maladies – his stomach's poor reaction to many foods, his allergies, his frequent illnesses, his thin and frail build – Vic was quite the opposite. Standing a good four inches taller than Ian with a strong and athletic build, Vic was the image of perfect physical health. Moreso, he had a head of thick, brown hair, dark brows over his brown eyes, and chiseled facial features. Most would consider Vic handsome. Few, if any, would say the same about Ian.

Vic wove past Ian, hopped onto a rock jutting above the water, and accepted the other full jug from Rina with little apparent effort. He then extended his other hand, which she grabbed before leaping back to shore.

Ian gritted his teeth as he watched his brother flirt with Rina. Envy roiled inside of him. He knew it was an ugly response, but Vic had always been more engaging, more confident, and more capable than he ever could be. It was a fact of life that he had long since realized and reluctantly accepted, but it still stung to watch his crush laughing and giggling with his brother, who seemed to effortlessly charm her.

"Thanks for the help, Vic," Rina said, giving his hand a playful squeeze before letting go. "I should be going now." Rina slid the ends of the pole through the jug handles so each settled into a notch, ducked her head beneath the pole, and stood with it draped across her shoulders. "I will see you two later."

"Of course," Vic said smoothly, his eyes following her as she walked away. Once she was out of sight, he turned to Ian with a smirk. "Tough luck, little brother. Maybe next time you'll impress her."

Ian scowled at him. "Shut up, Vic. I don't need your help."

"Don't be like that," Vic said, clapping him on the back. "I'm just trying to give you some advice. You're never going to win her over if you're always moping around."

Jaw clenched, Ian turned away from him. He couldn't stand how easily Vic seemed to get under his skin.

"I'm just trying to help," Vic said, his voice softer. "I know you like her, but you need to show confidence. Girls like a man who knows what he wants and has a plan as to where his life is headed."

Ian looked back at him, his frustration melting into confusion. "How would you know? You've never had any trouble with girls."

Vic chuckled. "That's because I'm confident, I work hard, and I have an important role in the village. Without wood, there would be no furniture, no supplies to build or repair buildings, or fuel to feed the fires. Now that you are apprenticed to Pa, you are working toward two of those three things. Add in confidence and I am sure she will see that you are no longer the goofy boy she grew up with. Just try it out sometime."

Ian shook his head, unsure if he was capable of such confidence. As he walked back up the hill to his father's workshop, he considered Vic's advice. Maybe he did need to be more confident if he ever wanted to win Rina over. He just had no idea where to begin.

CHAPTER 2

CRAFTING

The scent of fresh wood and sawdust permeated the workshop. Repeated, rhythmic hammer strikes drove the chisel into the wood, eating away at it, and soon, shavings covered the floor at Ian's feet. With his tongue between his teeth, he focused on the work rather than allow his thoughts to stray. His wandering mind had cost him on numerous occasions over the prior weeks. The scabs and bandages on his hands were constant reminders.

Once the curve had taken a rough shape, Ian swapped the hammer and chisel for a planer, using it to shave away the rough portions. A swath of rough, scaly dogfish skin rubbed against the wood helped smoothen its surface. When finished, Ian stood back and admired his work. It was as he had imagined and he felt a sense of pride for turning an idea into something tangible. Remembering what day it was, he glanced toward the workshop window and noted that the western shore of Lake Shillings was blanketed in shadow. A hand rested on his shoulder, drawing his attention to his father standing beside him.

The man ran his fingers along the curved rail Ian had just finished. "Nice work, son."

The pride Ian already had toward the project further inflamed. "It is the last piece." He had been working on the bassinette for weeks, a piece of furniture he had designed himself...with his father's assistance.

Perry said, "Yes. Tomorrow, I will show you how to assemble it." The man lifted the freshly, carved rocker leg and placed it on a workbench with two dozen other components, all made by Ian. "While it takes you far too long to produce something, the quality makes up for it. You have skill, and in time, you will become more efficient, so and it won't take as long to finish a project."

"Do you think it will sell?"

"I've no doubt. In fact, this piece, along with the set of chairs I just completed, and the others I produced during the winter months, warrant a trip to the city."

His hopes rising, Ian asked, "I can come with you?"

Perry laughed. "Yes. I promised as much."

A grin spread across Ian's face. "When?"

"I will talk to farmer Wescott and see if we can borrow his wagon the day after tomorrow."

The trip to the city would come soon, but Ian had other, more urgent concerns. "Evening nears, Pa. Now that I finished this piece, I was hoping..."

Again, the man laughed. "I know what day it is. You can go and join your friends. I know how much you are anticipating it. I will clean up in here and then, I intend to enjoy the Beltane festivities as well."

Ian untied his apron, lifted it over his head, and tossed it toward the hook beside the door on his way out.

The weather had warmed, and despite the fast-approaching evening, he felt comfortable in his tunic. As Ian rounded the building, his gaze turned to the green in the center of the village, already thick with people. A longing to join them tugged at him, but when he lifted an arm and sniffed, the odor almost caused him to gag. *I need to wash and change*. So, he headed to the door at the front of the building, opened it and collided with Vic, who was on his way out.

"Hi, little brother," Vic grinned while gripping Ian's shoulder as he stumbled, steadying him. "Today is your day, and you are expected on the green."

Ian slid past him. "I'll be there after I wash and change."

"I will see you there. I might even save you a sweet cake."

"Might?"

Vic laughed as he stepped out. "I cannot make any promises."

The door closed, Ian turning from it to find his mother in the kitchen.

With brown hair and hazel eyes, Zora Carpenter was a pretty, petite woman who stood no taller than Ian's chin, and he was not considered tall. Beneath a stained apron, she wore her favorite yellow dress, a dress she reserved for special occasions. The scent of spiced potatoes filled the house.

"How was your day in the shop?" Zora slid on thick leather mitts and lifted a large, black roaster from the brick oven.

"I finished the last piece today." Ian headed toward the bedroom he shared with Vic while speaking over his shoulder. "Pa says we will assemble it tomorrow."

He hurriedly lifted his tunic over his head and tossed it in the woven basket in the corner of the room. On the vanity between the two beds sat a bucket of water, soap, and a washcloth. He wet and lathered the washcloth before scrubbing his armpits.

In a voice loud enough to hear in the other room, he said, "Pa is taking the bassinette to Darristan to sell. He said I can go with him."

After rinsing the washcloth, he wiped the soap away and turned to find his mother at the door.

She frowned in concern. "You are going to the city?"

Worry tainted his good mood. Ian could not allow her to talk his father out of taking him. "I will be fine, Ma. It's not like I will be alone."

He looked down at his bare, and far too skinny, torso. His lack of muscle embarrassed him and he did not like others seeing him unclothed, even his own mother. Hurriedly, he shuffled to the foot of his bed, opened the wooden chest, and dug out his best tunic, a deep green that matched his own eyes.

"When do you intend to leave for Darristan?" she asked.

With the tunic on, he turned toward her and began tucking it into his trousers. "The day after tomorrow."

"I see." She still did not sound pleased.

He walked up to her. "I am no longer a child, Ma. If I am old enough to work in Pa's shop, I should be old enough to travel to the city with him."

She cupped his cheek, her eyes sad. "You make a fair point. I guess I… have a difficult time not thinking of you as my baby boy."

Ian held her wrist. His mother had taken care of him his entire life. Considering how often he had been sick and in bed, such care required a considerable amount of attention. It was something they had both grown used to, and only of late had Ian made an effort to be more independent. If he relied on her for so much, others would never treat him as a man.

"I will be fine, Ma. Just because I am growing up does not mean I won't love you anymore."

Zora gave him a sad smile. "I know." She stepped back. "Now, you'd better hurry so you don't miss the fun with your friends, especially this year."

"What about the potatoes?"

"Your father will be here soon to help me."

That was all the assurance Ian needed. He rushed to the door. "I'll see you there." Opening it, he darted outside.

The sun hovered just above the forest to the west, the trees and buildings in town casting long shadows. Ian walked along the gravel road, toward the town hall and the crowded village green.

Shillings, including the surrounding farms, was the home of a hundred and twenty people, most of whom had gathered for the seasonal event. Tables had been set up on one end of the green, upon which people placed trays, bowls, and pots of food, each family bringing twice as much as they might consume on their own. Despite Ian's stomach problems, often finding that food disagreed with him, Beltane was his favorite day of the year. The feast was only one aspect of the day that signaled the beginning of summer.

Townsfolk sat on blankets spread along the hillside above the green. In the center of the lawn stood a twenty-foot-tall pole from which dangled dozens of colored ribbons that fluttered in the breeze coming off the lake. Children played near the pole, waiting for sunset. The air smelled of roasted pig, still lying in a bed of coals dug into the ground.

His brother stood among the other young adults with Owen, Rina's older brother, beside him. Tall with a lean build, Owen shared Rina's golden hair and blue eyes. Since his father's death two years earlier, Owen had run the riverside mill. Two young women, Jorna and Winnie, stood across from them, both smiling and laughing at something Vic said. While Jorna was thin with brown hair, Winnie had a voluptuous build and red hair. The way the two girls looked at Vic, Ian was surprised they did not tackle him and kiss him then and there. Ian knew Vic had dallied with each of them in the past and wondered if he would ever choose one and settle down.

He pulled his attention from them and continued scanning the green before spotting the four others who were his own age, all ready for the event that would change their lives. *Tonight, I become an adult.* He headed toward them, Rina's eyes lighting when she saw him approach.

"Ian!" She smiled. "I was worried you might work all night in that shop."

Poshi, the other girl of Ian's age, stood beside Rina. She was shy and hardly ever spoke, her posture poor and hands clasped at her waist. With green eyes, freckled cheeks, and a pudgy face to match her body, few would call Poshi attractive. Still, she had always been nice to Ian, which he appreciated.

Ian replied, "I would not miss Beltane for anything, especially not this year."

Terrick, a tall and thickly built farmer's son, clapped Ian on the back. "Even you get to become a man today."

The force of the blow caused Ian to cough. "Even me?"

Terrick crossed his arms over his chest. "It's not as if you look the part. Do you even have a craft?"

Ian frowned at the accusation. Terrick had bullied Ian since they were young and, if anything, it had gotten worse as they reached their teen years. He hoped Terrick would outgrow it, because he had never been able to deal with the issue directly.

"I have been working in my pa's shop," Ian said.

Brady, the one boy who was shorter than Ian, thrust his jaw out. A shock of messy, auburn hair covered his head, his hazel eyes flashing a challenge. "Leave him be, Terrick. You might be the biggest among us, but we are all the same age. Besides, furniture making is a craft just as valid as farming. It's not as if the girls are all lining up to watch you slop the pigs."

The taller boy made a fist. "How about I slop you up, you little runt?"

Despite his lack of height, Brady was not one to back down. He was strong for his size, and if things went poorly, he could run faster than anyone in the village. "You might try, but it'll cost you."

Terrick grimaced and glanced toward the crowded hillside. "Since it is Beltane, I'll let it pass. You just watch yourself next time, or you'll find a fist in your mouth."

Brady sneered and took a step toward the tall farm boy.

Ian stepped forward, placing himself between the two. "Come on, guys, we're here to celebrate. Let's not ruin it with a fight." He looked toward Rina and Poshi, the first watching the exchange with concern, the latter, with terror rounding her emerald green eyes. "It is growing dark. The music will begin soon." He gestured toward the globe in the sky, the full moon marking the new year. "Shall we go join the others?"

The two girls nodded, and the group made their way toward the pole, where a cluster of adults were preparing for the ceremonial dance. Anxiety and anticipation intertwined like a pair of snakes and Ian's stomach began to churn. After years of seeking respect, of wishing others would treat him as an adult, the day had finally arrived.

The village children, numbering close to forty boys and girls ranging from five to seventeen years old, formed a circle around the pole while the adults stood outside of them. Music began playing, consisting of a lute, a piccolo, and a drum. The surrounding crowd swayed to the beat with Ian joining in, feeling the rhythm in his bones. He was lost in the moment, as if nothing else existed outside of this circle, this music, these people.

As the dance progressed, he and all the others who were to advance this evening gathered around the pole, each taking hold of a ribbon. Ian's fingers wrapped around the smooth fabric of the blue strand, his heart pounding in his chest. He mimicked the other dancers, his eyes locked onto their movements, studying their every step. With the entire village watching, he didn't want to stumble or make an embarrassing mistake.

As the music picked up in tempo, the dancers moved faster, their steps becoming more intricate. Sweat began to bead on Ian's forehead. The dancers then began to weave in and out of each other, the ribbons becoming a twisting web of colors. Ian's ribbon became entangled with Rina's, but that did not bother him one bit. He smiled at her, feeling a sense of camaraderie with the girl who had been his best friend for most of his life.

The music slowed, and the dancers moved inward while wrapping the ribbons around the pole. Ian's heart swelled with pride as his ribbon was tied to the pole, signifying his transition into adulthood. He and his friends were now considered adults in the eyes of the village.

The last moments of daylight lingered in the western sky as the ceremony concluded. The music stopped and villagers flooded the green, many clapping Ian on the shoulder or ruffling his hair as they congratulated him. His mother hugged him, and his father told him that he was proud of the man he had become. Even Vic thumped Ian on the back welcoming him as a fellow adult.

Men with shovels scraped coals from the pig, then used thick, pointed stakes to hoist it onto a table, and Bostic, the village butcher, began to carve. The newly adorned adults gathered in the front of a line with the rest of the village behind them. With plates in hand, the line advanced along a row of tables covered in food, the plates filling while friendly chatter rattled in the air.

STARS DOTTED THE EVENING SKY, twinkling lights against a canvas of black. The full moon shone down on the green, its light added to that of the tall torches surrounding the tables. Although everyone had eaten, enough food remained to feed an entire village. Most of the attendees had eaten until they were about to burst, but not Ian. A lifetime of suffering for such choices had brought enough wisdom for him to avoid that mistake, along with doing his best to limit foods such as cheese and cream. He did not wish to spend the night in the privy.

As the evening wore on, the band gathered on a makeshift stage set up at the opposite end of the green and resumed playing. Couples and groups danced to the music, their laughter and happy chatter filling the air.

From his position on the outskirts of the festivities, Ian watched from afar and fought against a rush of jealousy as his friends danced and laughed. A hand touched his back, and he turned to find Rina standing beside him.

She flashed him a friendly smile. "Why aren't you dancing?"

Ian shrugged. "I don't know. I guess I'm just not in the mood."

Her smile fell away, replaced by a look of concern. "Beltane only comes once a year. This was *our* year, which will never happen again. We should join in, don't you think?"

Is she asking me to dance? Butterflies burst in Ian's stomach and fluttered against his ribcage. He swallowed hard, cleared his throat, and did his best to keep his reply restrained. "You are probably right."

"Come on," she urged, taking his hand.

He let her pull him toward the dance floor, and soon they were moving together to the music. Dancing with a girl felt awkward at first, but Rina's easy grace and infectious smile put Ian at ease. As they danced, a sense of joy came over him in a way he had never experienced before. He felt alive, free, and uninhibited. The music carried him away, and he lost himself in the moment, feeling as though nothing else mattered in the world.

The music slowed and Rina wrapped her arms around his shoulders. With her body pressed against his, he felt the warmth between them. He wanted to kiss her, to feel her lips on his, but he was too nervous to make the first move. They continued to dance, their bodies moving in perfect unison, until the music came to an end. The other dancers clapped, and Rina stepped back, smiling.

"That was nice," she said.

Ian found himself overcome, the words spilling out, "You are so beautiful."

Her face darkening, she turned and walked off, leaving him confused and alone.

Ian watched her retreat while contemplating what to do. Something he had said upset her, but he did not understand why. Finally, he rushed after her and slowed as he neared the lakeshore, well beyond the festivities. She stood facing the lake, hugging herself, her back to him while staring at the moon's reflection on the still surface.

He gripped her arm and gently turned her toward him. "I am sorry if I said something wrong."

She shook her head, but her eyes did not meet his. "It is nothing."

"Rina. We have been friends our entire lives. You can tell me."

She looked down at the ground and kicked a rock into the water, disturbing the tranquility. "It is how others look at me. I see them...the other boys with longing in their gaze, the older men leering, the women scowling. I hoped that you had avoided what infected them."

Ian blinked as he considered her perspective. He was used to the other villagers judging him by his obvious frailty. How Rina might have felt about others viewing her as an object of desire or as competition never occurred to him. "This is because of what I said," he realized.

Rina sighed. "Do not worry about it."

"Would you rather I lied and said that you resembled one of Terrick's hogs?"

She chuckled. "That might be going a bit too far."

Her laughter was akin to joyful music, easing the tension and his concern, but he still wished to soothe her worries. " I am the same boy you grew up with and that will never change. I promise."

"No." She shook her head. "You are no longer that boy. As of tonight, you are a man. Just try to be a good one."

"I will."

She turned from the lake and stared toward the torchlit green. "Let's go join the others."

They headed back to the party and came to a table occupied by a group of their friends. Terrick, already well into his third cup of ale, loudly entertained the others with a story from his father's farm.

Ian sat down beside Brady, the two of them quietly watching the other villagers dance. He considered trying a cup of ale but concerns over his body's reaction to it kept him from following through. Instead, he thought back to his dance with Rina and the short time when her body was pressed against his. He longed to hold Rina, to kiss her and not let go. Yet, he remained hesitant, not wishing to upset her further, not after her reaction to his comment about her appearance. *Perhaps another night*. He was determined to try, but not until the timing was right.

CHAPTER 3

DARRISTAN

Beneath a canopy of trees with freshly sprouted leaves, a wagon pulled by a pair of oxen rolled down a gravel road, heading south. The steady rumble of wagon wheels and the clopping of hooves drowned out all but the loudest of surrounding noises. Seated beside his father, who drove the wagon, Ian's rear had become numb from the constant vibration beneath it.

The excitement he had experienced while departing from Shillings the prior morning had long since faded, replaced by the boredom of traveling through redundant and mundane surroundings – the endless leaf trees bordering the road, the occasional glimpse of the river running parallel to it, the day passing ever so slowly while Ian willed the oxen to move faster, something they chose to ignore. Ian's boredom lasted until late afternoon on the second day out of Shillings, when the wagon crested a high rise, the trees parted, and the view expanded.

An open, grassy field, a mile wide and almost as deep, waited at the bottom of the hill. Trees bordered the southern and western edges of the open space. Beyond the trees, flat, blue waters stretched from horizon to horizon. Having grown up on the shores of a lake, Ian had never seen the ocean, and while others had explained that it was much larger than Lake Shillings, he never expected such a dramatic expanse of open water. Despite the impressive and majestic view, the ocean was not the central actor in this performance. That role belonged to the walled city on the eastern side of the field, nestled beside a bay where the river met the ocean.

"That is Darristan," Perry announced.

"There are so many buildings," Ian said in awe. "How many people live there?"

"Two or three thousand would be my guess."

The wagon rolled down the hill, following the gravel road as it curved along the edge of the hillside. To one side, sporadic oak trees spread broad, branching limbs above the grassy slope. To the other was a steep drop down to the river. At the same methodical and plodding pace they had kept during the rest of the journey, the oxen steadily towed the wagon toward the city.

As they drew closer, Ian determined that the fifteen-foot-tall city wall was made of thousands of head-sized stones held together by a web of mortar. In the middle of the western face of the wall was an arched opening with a pair of wooden doors that stood open. Two men in leather armor, their metal helms shaped to rounded points, stood outside the city gate. Each held a spear and watched the wagon's approach with heavy eyelids that made Ian believe they might fall asleep standing up.

When the oxen drew even with the guards, Perry pulled the reins, shouted a command, and the wagon came to a stop.

"Good afternoon." He tipped his brimmed hat.

"What is in the wagon?" One of the guards asked. The man was tall and lean, his facial features still reflecting the softness of youth.

"Ian. Show the man."

Ian climbed to stand on the wagon seat, gripped the stained, white tarp covering the wagon bed, and lifted it to reveal a dozen pieces of furniture, including the bassinette he had worked so hard to build.

Perry said, "We have come from Shillings to sell these wares at the market."

"Where do you intend to board while in the city?"

"The Hungry Boar."

"Ah." The guard nodded. "Wilkins and Agatha own that place."

"That's right."

The guard stepped aside. "Go on. Just don't cause any trouble."

After covering the furniture, Ian sat, and Perry snapped the reins. The wagon rolled into the city, and Ian gaped at his surroundings.

The streets – filled with people of all ages, shapes, and sizes – bustled with activity. The buildings were packed tightly together, their wooden frames leaning against each other in a precarious dance. As they made their way through the city, Ian witnessed merchants hawking wares, beggars asking for alms, and children playing in the dirt. It was a world unlike anything he had ever seen, stirring within Ian a sense of excitement and trepidation all at once.

Perry drove the wagon down the crowded streets, navigating the narrow passageways with skill. When they reached the city center, the street opened to a sprawling square thick with people crowded around tents and wagons positioned along the perimeter. The wagon turned and crossed to the edge of the square before rolling down another street.

"Wasn't that the market?" Ian asked.

"It was." Perry kept his attention on the street ahead.

"Why did we not stop there?"

"The day wanes and the vendors will soon pack up. It will be best to wait until tomorrow."

Eager to see how much someone might pay for the bassinette, Ian's enthusiasm quelled when he realized it would have to wait another day. "Where are we going?"

"To the inn I mentioned to the guard. We will stay the night and make for the market first thing tomorrow."

As the man said it, the wagon rolled past a building with its doors and windows open. Crowded tables filled the interior and the ruckus of many voices speaking at once came from within.

"That looks like an inn," Ian noted.

"Of that, there can be no doubt."

"Why don't we stay there? It is close to the market."

Perry shook his head. "The Dented Tankard is a bit wild for my taste. I stayed there once and won't make that mistake again."

"What happened?"

"Fights, one of which I almost got caught up in." At the next intersection, Perry turned the team and the wagon rolled onto a quiet street. "The Hungry Boar Inn is just up ahead."

"You've stayed there before?"

"Three times a summer for the past six years."

The wagon followed the street until drawing near the city wall. They passed a two-story stone building with an outdoor patio surrounded by a waist-high stone wall. A thick layer of ivy covered the wall and vines dangled down from the roof. A third of the patio tables were occupied, the patrons all adult and a mixture of men and women, often seated together. A middle-aged woman in a dark green dress and white corset emerged from the building with a tray of food and drink. Ian watched as she delivered the meal to a couple seated at a table. The scent of baked fish taunted him as the wagon rounded the patio and followed the narrow gap between the building and the city wall.

At the rear of the building was a gravel yard and an outbuilding Ian could only assume was the stable. A man strolled out of the shadowy stable interior, his thumbs hooked behind the straps of his suspenders. Brown curls graced his head, cheeks, and chin, his upper lip notably lacking hair. He was no more than ten years Ian's senior, but unlike Ian, thick muscle lined his bare arms and chest.

As the wagon came to a stop, the man smiled. "Welcome back to the Hungry Boar, Master Perry."

Perry climbed down from the wagon seat. "I trust you had a good winter, Orval."

"Good enough." His gaze shifted to the tarp-covered objects. "It looks like you have been busy."

"After half a year away, I should hope so. In addition, I now have help in the workshop." He clapped Ian on the shoulder.

Orval turned his gaze on Ian, who stood beside his father. "Is this your apprentice?"

"Apprentice and more." Perry patted the top of Ian's head. "This is my youngest, Illian."

The use of his full name irritated Ian. He did not need reminders of his illnesses. "Please. Everyone calls me Ian."

Orval extended a hand. "Pleased to meet you."

Ian shook the man's rough and callused hand.

"Take care to watch our wagon tonight," Perry said. "You can expect us to rise with the sun and head straight away to the market."

"Aye, Master Perry. You can count on me," Orval said with a firm nod.

"Good. As always, I'll be sure to share a silver piece with you when we are finished at the market.

The grin on Orval's face broadened.

Perry gestured to Ian. "How about we get a hot meal in before bed?"

"A hot meal would be welcome, especially after gnawing on bread and jerky for the past two days."

The man laughed and led Ian toward the Inn's back door. The moment he entered the inn, Ian was hit by the smell of roasting meat and a rush of heat. The small space was crowded with tables and chairs, half of them occupied by patrons of all sorts. The sound of chatter and clinking mugs filled the air. Perry led him to a small table in the corner. They sat as a plump, rosy-cheeked woman approached them.

"Good evening, Perry," the woman smiled and turned her gaze to Ian. "And who is this young man seated with you?"

Perry removed his hat. "This is my youngest son, Ian. He's joined me on this trip."

The woman beamed at Ian. "Well, welcome to the Hungry Boar, Ian. I'm Agatha. My husband, Wilkins, and I own the inn. Are you hungry?"

"Yes, ma'am." Ian nodded.

"Tonight, you've a choice between baked salmon and potatoes or mutton stew."

Ian had a difficult time with seafood and had discovered himself frighteningly allergic to shellfish, so he opted for the latter, thinking it the safer option. "Mutton stew, please."

Perry nodded in agreement. "And a pint of ale each, if you please."

The woman bustled away as the two of them sat.

"Ale for me?" Ian asked.

"You are a man now, aren't you?"

He grinned. "Yes, sir."

"Good. Just remember that when dealing with others. They will respect you if you give them cause to do so, but only if you give them that same respect."

Agatha returned to the table with a platter upon which rested two bowls, two tankards, and a quarter loaf of bread. She set the bowls and mugs before Ian and his father before placing the bread between them.

"I assume you are staying the night?" Agatha asked.

Perry nodded. "That we are."

"One night or two?"

He shrugged. "That depends on how quickly we sell our wares."

"In that case, a silver covers the meal, room, and breakfast."

Perry produced a pouch from below the table, poured out a silver piece and three coppers, and placed them into her palm. "Here is a little extra for the excellent service."

The woman's smile glowed with warmth. "Thank you, Perry. Be sure to wave me down if you need anything else."

She turned away, leaving them to their meals as they both dug in. Ian ate with vigor and even chanced the ale. It was bitter, the bubbles tickling his throat. By the time he reached the bottom of the tankard, his head buzzed and he felt good. They hadn't even begun to sell the furniture and the trip had already been a revelation.

And then, his stomach recoiled. Another quiver caused him to press his hand to his midriff. A cramp forced him to clench his teeth.

"I need to find a privy."

His father pointed. "Out back, near the stables."

Ian rushed out, praying he would find it unoccupied.

IN THE DIM light of dusk, Ian stumbled out of the privy, his insides emptied. The cramps had cleared, and he felt well enough, so he headed back to the inn.

"Are you well, kid?"

He turned toward the voice. Five men stood at the side of the yard, all older than him, none more than a decade. They were dressed in coats over tunics, their faces unshaven.

"I am fine." Ian then recalled his manners. "Thank you for asking."

Another man said, "The way you ran past us, we figured you'd been poisoned."

"I merely ate something that...didn't agree with me."

The first man asked, "We haven't seen you around before. Are you visiting?"

"Yes. My pa and I just arrived from Shillings."

The man arched a brow. "Shillings. That's two days away. What brings you here?"

Ian gestured toward the closed stables. "We have a wagon full of furniture we intend to sell at the market tomorrow."

"Furniture?" A third man said. "Do you have any chairs by chance?"

"Yes. Chairs, a wardrobe, a table, stools, and even a bassinette I made myself." Ian was proud of his work.

"Interesting." The first man rubbed his stubble-covered jaw. "We may have to stop by the market tomorrow morning. Perhaps you have just found your first customers."

Feeling hopeful, Ian grinned. "You had better come early. My pa tells me his works sell out fast."

"Thank you for the warning."

His companion waved. "Have a good evening."

"You as well." Ian stepped back into the inn, proud that he might have secured one or more sales.

Shouts from outside drew Ian from his dream. He blinked at the dark surroundings of their room at the inn as his father stood from the other bed. The man crossed to the window, pulled the curtain aside, and moonlight shone on his face.

Propped up by his elbows, Ian asked, "What is it, Pa?"

"Get up! Now!" Perry blurted in alarm. He spun from the window, rushed to the door, and darted into the corridor despite wearing only his smallclothes.

Ian froze in panic, his mind scrambling for reasons behind his father's reaction. A beat later, he hopped out of bed and went to the window. He peered down at the moonlit stable yard and froze again.

The stable doors stood open. The unmoving form of Orval lay against one of the doors. Five men – two working in a pair, the other three alone – carried wooden furniture out of the building and rushed down the alley. Even in the dark setting, he was certain it was the same five men he had spoken to after his urgent trip to the privy. His heart sank until it felt like a lump of lead in his otherwise empty stomach. *Oh, no.*

Alarmed, Ian grabbed his trousers, pulled them on, and held the waist with one hand as he descended to the main floor. As Ian emerged through the back door, he spied Perry kneeling beside Orval, his hand on the stable hand's neck. Ian's momentum carried him halfway across the yard before he staggered to a stop, his breath held in dread.

"He's dead," Perry said, his voice tight with anger.

Ian's stomach twisted. Had it not already been emptied, he would have vomited. *Orval died because of me.* The realization was paralyzing.

Perry stood, his eyes scanning the yard. "They took everything. All of our furniture...everything except the one piece you made."

Ian peered into the shadowy stable interior, the stall doors closed, the wagon empty apart from the bassinette. He croaked, "What are we going to do?"

"That furniture was going to put food on our table for the summer. Now..."

The man stood, his chin dropping to his chest as he shuffled back toward the inn. Ian looked down at Orval, his stomach twisting at the thought of staring at a corpse. He doubled over and retched bile, followed by raw, painful, dry heaves. The trip had turned into a disaster, and it was all his fault.

CHAPTER 4

DISASTER

Beneath clouds of pink, the setting sun hidden beyond the surrounding forest, Ian and Perry rode into their village, their wagon empty and their hearts heavy. The theft of their wares had left them with no choice but to return home, defeated. The sale of the single remaining piece, a bassinette crafted by Ian, had yielded three silvers, which covered the cost of the trip but left them with no profit.

The wagon rolled down the gravel drive running through the village. They passed the empty village green and approached their house, where Perry stopped the wagon. After Ian climbed down from the seat, his father rode off toward the Wescott farm to return the wagon and team.

Ian hesitated at the door for a long beat and sorted through his troubled thoughts before entering. He opened the door to his mother and brother seated at the kitchen table with forks in hand. The scent of roasted pork hung in the air, but it did nothing to encourage Ian's hunger. His stomach remained upset about the theft and Orval's death. He was certain that both were because of him, but he could not gather the courage to admit as much to his father. The thought of telling anyone was nearly enough to make him sick, yet the guilt dragged on him like a massive yoke draped over his shoulders.

"Ian," his mother smiled. "I am glad you made it back safely. How did it go?"

He shook his head. "I'd rather not talk about it."

She frowned in concern. "Dinner is still warm if you would like to join us."

"I cannot eat right now." He walked past them, went to his room, and closed the door.

With heavy feet, Ian stumbled to his bed and fell into it, face-first. Two minutes later, the door opened and closed.

His brother's voice came from behind him. "You are upset."

Still face-down in bed, Ian began to cry.

Vic sat beside him. "You'll feel better if you talk about it."

Ian lifted his head and wiped his eyes. "We were robbed."

"What?"

Sobbing, Ian said, "The furniture. It was stolen before we could sell it."

"What?" Vic pressed a palm to his forehead. "What is pa going to do?"

Tears still tracking down his face, Ian shrugged.

His brother sighed. "I realize how this affects the family, but why are you crying about it? It wasn't your fault, was it?"

"I..." Ian struggled for the words. When they finally came out, they were little more than a whisper. "I think it was my fault."

His brother frowned. "How so?"

"After dinner, my stomach forced an urgent trip to the privy. When I came out, I was met by a group of men. The conversation led to me mentioning the furniture in the wagon. Later that night, someone broke into the stables and..." Ian's tongue felt thick and unwilling to continue. Before he could do so, distant shouts from outside interrupted.

His brother rushed to the window and opened the curtain. The amber of fire flickered on his face. "Farmer Wescott's barn is on fire!"

"Wescott? Pa went there to return the wagon."

Vic ran to the door and tore it open.

A beat of hesitation later, Ian rushed out of the room.

"What is going on?" His mother asked as Vic grabbed a big, black kettle from a shelf in the kitchen.

"Wescott's barn is on fire." Vic darted out the front door.

Ian followed his brother outside, and as the two of them turned toward the lake, the scope of the situation altered dramatically.

Screams echoed as women and children ran from pursuers. Elsewhere, villagers fought with picks, shovels, hammers, and anything else they had handy. In all directions, Ian spied stoutly built invaders with long, black beards. The strangers all wore armor, often made of a combination of metal and leather, and wielded weapons ranging from swords to war hammers to cudgels. While none were even as tall as Ian's modest height, all outweighed him with thick shoulders and barrel chests. It took a moment for reality to connect with the legendary tales he had heard over the years.

"Dwarves?" Ian said, in shock.

Shouts came from the other direction. The two boys spun around as fisherman Issly rushed up from the lake, "Run! Hide!"

A trio of dwarves ran after the man. Fear clutched at Ian's throat and squeezed tightly. He turned to run into the house as four dwarves rounded the corner. Two held weapons ready, the others holding shackles made of black iron and thick chains. One of the dwarves shouted something in a strange language that almost sounded familiar.

Ian backed a step before his brother gripped his wrist and jerked him around. He followed numbly as Vic dragged him at a run.

Across the green, Brady wrestled an attacker in the grass and Brady's father, Grady, fought with a fire poker against an axe wielding dwarf. The man thrust and missed. The dwarf did not. The slash cut across

Grady's midriff in a spray of blood. The man cried out and collapsed as Ian and Vic ran past.

A woman raced toward the lake and screamed as a dwarf tackled her in the shrubs. Rina emerged from her house, eyes round in horror. Ian, concerned for her, yanked his wrist from his brother's grip and ran toward her. Before he could reach her, a dwarf rushed in and swung a cudgel, striking her in the back. Rina cried out as she fell and Ian slowed as the dwarf turned toward him.

"Dedi Tion!" the dwarf growled while thumping the cudgel into his palm.

Apprehension held Ian captive and unable to react. His brother had no such trouble. Vic raced past him and swung the heavy kettle at the dwarf, who dropped to one knee to avoid it. The kettle clanged off the dwarf's helmet, and the dwarf fell over. Before Vic could turn, an enemy swung a heavy hammer and struck him in the side of the knee. He cried out as his leg folded. The dwarf followed with a kick to the head and knocked Vic unconscious before turning his attention to Ian.

Rina climbed to her hands and knees, her gaze rising to meet Ian's. Her eyes reflected the terror gripping him. Someone struck him from behind, pain flaring in the small of his back and he collapsed. A knee pressed against his back as his hands were jerked behind his back. A shackle was clamped to each wrist and ankle. When finished with him, the dwarves shackled Rina and then his unconscious brother.

Screams echoed from Ian's house as his mother was dragged outside. She fell to her knees and the dwarf gripping her arm slapped shackles on her wrists. Her gaze met Ian's, and she shook her head, warning him not to do anything rash. He was too scared to resist and afraid of what might happen to him or the people he loved if he even tried to fight. Father! He then remembered the fire and turned toward the lake.

Across the bay, Wescott's barn burned. Silhouettes of humans fighting dwarves were visible in the firelight. The fire had spread, the flames claiming the tree between the barn and the silo, which was also on fire. The silo erupted in a bright burst of flames, the explosion rocking the night and sending flaming debris a hundred feet into the air. The flash of light dimmed, Ian staring toward the farm in hopes of seeing his father. The silhouettes were gone, the flickering flames the only movement left behind.

Ian began to sob. The world around him blurred through his tears as he lay there, crying. Around him, people screamed as they were tackled, beaten, and shackled. Fires consumed homes and businesses. The only things Ian had ever known were being destroyed around him, and he was helpless to do anything about it.

Moonlight shone down on Ian as he lumbered along the dirt road above the shoreline of Lake Shillings. Across the lake, orange flames flickered in the darkness, the last remnants of the fires that consumed most of the village he had called home his entire life.

Dozens of armored dwarves escorted captive villagers, guiding them north. Toward what, Ian had no idea. With each farm they passed, shackled people were added to the line. Most depressing were those who did not appear, including farmer Wescott. His body lay beside his wagon, or what remained of it. In the flickering light of the burning oak, it was clear that the man was dead. His was not the only corpse. Four dwarves lay dead not far from the man, all victims of the explosion. Then, Ian saw another body to the other side of the farmer's wagon. Like Wescott, blood covered his head and he lay unmoving. The sight made Ian's knees buckle.

"Father!"

His mother, further back in the line of prisoners, bawled a wordless cry and collapsed when she saw her husband lying dead.

A dwarf grabbed Ian by the arm and pulled him to his feet. Struggling to stand, he looked at the dwarf. A black braided beard, an embossed star in the corner of a shiny breastplate and eyes... In the moonlight, it was difficult to tell, but he thought he saw sympathy in those purple eyes.

"Ambulo a morta," the dwarf whispered.

While Ian did not understand the words, he knew the intent. The dwarf was warning him to keep walking.

After casting one last glance back at the farm, Ian resumed his march, his mother and brother trudging along further behind him. Now at the edge of the settlement, the line of prisoners was complete and totaled seventy people, not including fourteen children too young to walk. They rode in a cage on wheels, towed by a pair of oxen.

Ian lumbered along the trail lost in a haze of numbness, his mind unable to fully process the events of the past few hours. The only thought that kept repeating in his mind was the destruction of his home and the loss of those he knew. A mixture of anger and sadness welled up inside and threatened to overwhelm him. Deciding he needed to think of something else, anything else, Ian studied the dwarven soldiers escorting them.

The dwarves all had short and stocky builds, their small but muscular frames accentuated by the armor they wore, leather with metal panels tinted too warmly to be steel. Each had thick hands and feet wider than a human's. Their expressions were stern, and they moved with an air of efficiency and confidence that made Ian feel small and powerless.

He wondered what had led to the attack and why the dwarves had targeted their village. *Were they searching for something specific, or was it just senseless violence?* Ian couldn't imagine any justification for such destruction and cruelty. He feared he would soon discover that the worst was yet to come.

~

A soft kick to his shin woke Ian. He opened his eyes to pale predawn light. His brother lay on one side of him, Rina on the other, a chain binding them together. They both stirred as Ian sat up. A shadowy form stood over them, the pale light allowing Ian to get a better look at the dwarf's face. Beneath his metal helm were bushy eyebrows, purple-tinted eyes, a bulbous nose, and a thick beard braided in a way he had never seen before. The dwarf didn't say anything, but held out a bowl of gruel. Ian's stomach churned at the sight of it. Despite his hunger, he worried that it might make him sick.

"Vescora," the dwarf said.

Ian shook his head. "I am not hungry." He bent his neck from side to side, attempting to work out the kink from a night of sleeping on the ground.

The dwarf shoved the bowl at Ian. "Amusso Vescora."

"No eat," Ian shook his head.

The dwarf blinked. "You speak our language?" His eyes narrowed. "Why?"

Ian hesitated, unsure of how to answer.

"Tell me." The dwarf said a few additional sentences, but the words were unknown to Ian.

He considered what he had heard during the previous evening. Finally, he recalled part of a conversation. In Dwarvish, he said, "I...listen."

The dwarf pointed toward the surrounding prisoners, all of them stirred awake by the conversation. "Tell others, eat or die."

Ian blinked and turned to his brother, the next person in the chain of villagers. "He says that we must eat or they will kill us."

Vic frowned. "How do you know that?"

"I... I am not sure. Their language was strange at first, but the words somehow make sense to me."

Vic nodded. "Very well. You pass on the message to those ahead of you. I will deal with those behind us."

Ian relayed the message to Brady, who passed it on.

The dwarf spoke to another dwarven warrior. Both scrutinized Ian with suspicious, narrowed eyes before walking away. Deciding that being sick was preferable to dead, Ian began to eat the warm, mushy porridge. As he ate, he realized that he was famished. The gruel was plain, the consistency making him gag with the first few bites, but it was filling. He wondered why the dwarves bothered to feed them instead of letting them starve. *Perhaps they have more use for us alive than dead.* What that use might be...Ian shuddered at the thought.

Once dawn broke, they resumed their march into the mountains, methodically advancing north while the sun rose toward its apex. The road, little more than a trail consisting of two ruts with grass and weeds in between, wound through hills and valleys, often uphill and always surrounded by peaks still white on the northern slope. Ian's feet ached with every step.

Many hours later, with daylight waning, they arrived at a clearing with a brook running through it. There, the dwarves stopped the prisoners and forced them to gather while they set up camp with the captors stationed along the perimeter and the captives in the middle. The prisoners were allowed to sit and rest while the dwarves made a fire and prepared dinner.

With his wrists and ankles raw from the heavy shackles, Ian sat between Rina and his brother while watching the dwarves. He strained to listen as they spoke among themselves, attempting to discern if they were planning something, or if they were just making small talk. The conversation was difficult to follow, but Ian caught a few words here and there. The more he listened, the better sense he was able to make of the conversations.

As the night grew darker, the dwarves went about their business, settling in as if the prisoners were not even there. Still, Ian watched them and listened, but the noise of their armor clattering as they moved around the campsite, made it difficult to hear the various conversations.

Ian then noticed a dwarf sitting by himself, looking over a map in the firelight. It was the same dwarf who had whispered to him the prior evening. As if sensing his scrutiny, the dwarf looked his way, and Ian waved. The dwarf returned a scowl and continued studying the map for another minute before rolling it up, rising to his feet, and approaching him.

"What...you want?" the dwarf grumbled in Dwarvish.

"I want...talk," Ian attempted in the same language.

The dwarf eyed him suspiciously. "What about?"

Ian thought for a moment before pointing at his own chest. "My name is Ian." He pointed at the dwarf. "What is your name?"

With narrowed eyes, the dwarf stared at him while stroking his beard. Seconds passed before he said, "I am called Korrigan."

"Thank you, Korrigan." Ian held up his shackled wrists. "Why we... chained? What you want with us?"

The dwarf snorted. "You humans are always so eager to know everything. Be content that you live."

"Can you tell me...where are we headed?"

"We go to Ra'Tahal, home of my clan."

"Why?" Ian persisted. "Surely you can tell me."

The dwarf sighed heavily. "We need laborers for my people, for the mines."

"Mines?" Ian looked around. "You..." Ian struggled for the right word. "No expect women to work mines."

"No. They will work elsewhere. The need is plentiful and our people are not."

Ian tried again, using the words he had figured out thus far. "Why capture children?"

"You humans age rapidly. Soon, children become adults and work like the others." The dwarf gestured. "Sleep. Long days are coming. Try to escape, and you die."

The dwarf walked away and someone poked Ian's shoulder. He turned to his brother.

Vic whispered, "Did you just have a conversation with him?"

Ian nodded numbly, still concerned over his discovery.

"How do you know their language?"

"I can't say. It just…" He struggled to find the right words. "It comes to me almost like I knew their language long ago and simply forgot it until now."

"How is that possible?"

"I have no idea." Ian admitted.

"What did he say?"

If I tell him we are to be slaves, he will tell the others. Hope is all they have left. Ian decided to avoid the subject. "We are going to someplace called Ra'Tahal."

"Where is that?"

"I don't know."

Vic scowled at the dwarf, who was once again focused on the map in his hands. "We need to find a way to escape."

"That is the other thing." He swallowed the lump in his throat. "They will kill anyone who attempts to break free."

Vic fell silent, he and the other nearby captives all staring at Ian in alarm. He lowered his gaze, unable to look any of them in the eyes, afraid of them seeing the despair he felt inside.

CHAPTER 5
WILD

Victus Carpenter lay in the dark, in a forest glade, many miles from the only home he had ever known. A horrific, unpredictable series of events had left him stranded in unfamiliar territory. For the first time ever, he found himself dealing with an unfamiliar emotion. Doubt.

Even as a young boy, Vic had been confident in himself and his abilities. Strong, flexible, and blessed with natural dexterity, physical things came easy for him. Always had. As he grew into a teen and the old woodcutter, Jakes, became disabled, Vic leapt at the opportunity to apprentice to the man. Even with one arm, Jakes was an expert with his axe, showing Vic how to efficiently hew at a tree trunk, fell the tree, and remove the limbs. Vic learned to chop and haul wood, sometimes even stripping sections of bark, which his father would then cure and turn into a piece of furniture. In that physical labor, Vic found solace.

As Vic's teen years advanced, so did his strength and skill with the axe. Then, in his nineteenth winter, Jakes died of pneumonia, and Vic became the only lumberjack in Shillings. The village and the forest had become a part of him and, while he yet had to marry and have children, that was the only future he had ever pictured for himself. Now...all had been thrown in disarray, his life, his future, and his confidence all put into question. In the past, when he needed advice, he would go to his father. That had been taken away from him with the man's death, which left a void impossible to fill.

He rolled over and stared at the starry sky with his shackled wrists lying on his chest. Beside him, Ian slept soundly, curled up beside Rina. It was a rare moment where Vic envied his brother, not only because he was able to sleep, but because it was clear that in Rina, Ian had found his someone. The two had been close since they were young and Ian's crush on her could not be more obvious. Although Ian was as smart as anyone Vic knew, he couldn't seem to realize that she felt the same about him. Rina was the one village girl even near Vic's age that he had avoided in any romantic way, not because he didn't find her attractive. In truth, she was likely the prettiest girl in the village. Rather, knowing how Ian felt about her, kept Vic from making any advances toward her. Despite his dalliances with the other girls in Shillings, Vic had never found one in whom he held more than a passing interest or any depth beyond physical entertainment. *Maybe my someone awaits wherever we are headed.* The thought was meant to provide him comfort although he did not really believe it.

A howl echoed in the night, the sound sending a chill down Vic's spine and causing him to bolt into a sitting position. He peered across the glade, toward the moonlit half where dwarven guards gathered. The lack of alarm from the dwarves eased Vic's concern, until another howl rang out, this one far closer than the last.

A howl woke Ian, causing him to sit upright, his heart racing. In the darkness, it was difficult to see.

"What was that?" Rina whispered from his side.

Ian gripped her hand but remained silent. To his other side, Vic sat up, and stared across the glade. Along with two dozen other villagers, they huddled together in the shadows cast by the trees of the surrounding forest. Captive humans around him began to rise, those nearby masked in shadow while others stood out in the moonlight. All stared toward the forest, the night silent as a dozen armed dwarves eased toward the dark, shadowy trees. With terror causing him to shake, Ian peered into the darkness, waiting, hoping that there was nothing there.

A wave of furry shapes burst into the moonlight, swarmed past the dwarves at the edge of the glade, and charged toward the prisoners. *Rock wolves.* While Ian had heard tales of packs attacking humans, they had always felt removed from reality, like distant memories and not something that could ever happen to him. Then, he realized they were coming straight for his mother.

Vic, burst to his feet, straining against his chains as he shouted, "Mother! Look out!"

Kalvin, the village blacksmith stepped in front of Zora. He was a big man with brawn built up from decades of forging weapons, his mass easily eclipsing the petite woman. Although no wolf was more than half his size, the man was engulfed as five of the beasts attacked him simultaneously.

Ian and the other captives reacted by bolting to their feet and backing away from the fight. Bound together by chains, flight was impossible, but nobody wanted to remain on the ground, unable to defend themselves. With taller people in the way, it became difficult to see what occurred.

Through the gaps between people, teeth flashed in the moonlight. The wolves growled, barked, and tore at the blacksmith while the dwarves rushed in. More wolves burst from the forest, two of them attacking Issly. Moonlight glinted off weapons and armor as the dwarves fought back. Screams of terror rang out, but Ian remained silent, unable to move or even breathe.

The fracas was chaotic, the silvery fur of the wolves mixing with dark blood splatter. Yelps echoed in the night as the dwarves fought, wounded, and killed the beasts. The remaining wolves abruptly bolted toward the trees and faded into the shadows. The whimpers of frightened or wounded and the panting of dwarven warriors were the only sounds breaking the silence left behind.

Ian gasped the first air he had drawn since the attack began. His armpits were damp, his heart racing as if he had run a mile although he had not even moved.

A rustle behind him caused him to spin toward the forest. Four silvery shapes burst out from the trees and darted straight toward him and Rina. Terror and instinct caused Ian to step backward. He tripped over the chain linking them together, and he fell. A wolf leapt toward him with its jaw open wide.

A GROWL from behind caused Vic to spin around. A wolf charged his brother, teeth flashing. As Ian fell to the ground, Vic reacted.

He yanked on the chain secured to his shackles, causing it to flip up. The chain caught the charging wolf across the chest, the momentum of the beast yanking on Vic's arms and causing him to stumble. The beast flipped over the chain and landed on its back next to Ian.

Instantly rolling back to its feet, the beast flashed its fangs about to lunge at Ian again, but Vic was already moving. He kicked hard, his boot toe striking the wolf's snout. The beast yelped, and backed away, shaking its head.

IAN SHIED AWAY as Vic kicked the attacking wolf. He then rolled and rose to his feet beside Rina, who appeared frozen in shock. Still facing the backing wolf, Vic did not see the other charging at him from behind

"Vic!" Ian shouted, but even then, he realized any reaction by Vic would be too late.

Suddenly, Korrigan was there. The dwarf swung an overhead attack. His mace struck the wolf on top of the head. The creature crashed into Vic's legs, sending him sprawling, the chain connecting to him pulling taut and yanking Ian forward. Ian fell to his stomach and looked up as the first wolf turned and bolted.

The night fell quiet.

Ian scrambled to his feet and eyed the wolf on the ground. It lay still, its head bloodied.

Between ragged breaths and over the noise of his pulse thumping in his ears, Ian asked Vic, "Are you alright?"

Vic stood and dusted himself off. "I am fine."

"Thank you,"

"It was nothing."

Ian glanced at Rina and saw her staring at his brother. *Once again, Vic is a hero, and I am a mess.* It was no wonder the girls from Shillings doted over Vic while Ian stood in the shadows. *He just saved your life.* He reprimanded himself. *Stop with the jealousy.* Then, he remembered seeing his mother caught up in the attack and turned to see if he could find her.

Long, tense moments passed as dwarves wove among the prisoners. Through the crowd, Ian hoped to see a sign of his mother. He then spied a silhouette with hair tied in a bun, the moonlight on her face revealing a look of horror.

Women around him began to cry, the males hugging them. Ian, Vic, and Rina remained still and silent until the other villagers began to lower themselves to the ground, opening the view. What Ian saw made him wish he had turned away.

Kalvin, Issly, and two other male villagers lay on the ground, covered in blood and unmoving. Four dwarves lay beyond them, also dead. All had their throats torn open.

A gasp at his side caused Ian to turn as a tear tracked down Rina's face. He wrapped his arms around her, and she buried her head in his neck, sobbing.

"Why are they doing this to us?" she whimpered.

"I wish I knew."

He silently stroked her hair, unable to tell her the truth.

CHAPTER 6
RA'TAHAL

The days wore on like a bad dream with Ian unable to wake. From dawn until dusk, he and the surviving villagers were led along a winding path through white-capped mountains and thickly wooded valleys. The nights were cold, forcing them to huddle together like beggars. While those nights offered Ian the opportunity to be close to Rina, something which he had long dreamt of doing, exhaustion and a cloud of melancholy kept him from enjoying even that.

Korrigan and the other dwarven captors soon got used to communicating with Ian and using him to interpret commands to his fellow villagers. Each day, Ian learned new Dwarvish words, expanding his ability to speak and understand what was expected of him. While the other captives were as exposed to the dwarven conversations as he, none displayed his ability to adapt to a new and foreign language.

Eight long days after departing from Shillings, the mountains opened to an expansive basin, where they descended into a forest dominated by sturdy, aged oaks. The next two days had them walking beneath a thick canopy of leaves before emerging on the bank of a raging river. The river flowed in from the east, its origin lost somewhere beyond a wooded bend. In the other direction, the water abruptly dropped out of sight, disappearing into a valley a thousand feet down. The roar of the falls drowned out the other noises of nature, demanding everyone's attention yet losing to a sight that could not be natural.

A bridge of stone spanned the river, its size, ornate design, and flawless workmanship instantly astounding. Ian had never suspected such marvelous works existed. The prisoners and their captors climbed the bridge, and as they crossed over the water, an even more impressive sight came into view.

A massive, sprawling citadel stood at the edge of the bluff, overlooking the valley and the falls. Towering walls, a hundred feet tall and made of gray stone, surrounded the fortress. Multi-tiered, rectangular stone structures and blocky towers rose above those walls.

Crossing the bridge with Korrigan walking beside him, Ian asked, "Is the fortress our destination?"

"Aye."

"What is it called?"

The dwarf replied in a proud voice, "Ra'Tahal. It is the home of my clan."

Ian frowned. "Your clan?"

"There are three dwarven clans. We are of the Tahal Clan. Gahagar the Impregnable was Tahalian before he united the three clans. Unfortunately, when he died, the clans again became divided."

Ian had no idea who Gahagar was but it seemed a good idea to feign interest. "When did he die?"

"Five years hence." Korrigan shook his head. "Even after three years of fighting at Gahagar's side, it was a sad day. One I will never forget."

Ian eyed the dwarf. While his age was difficult to determine, Ian would have guessed that he was no more than twenty-five years old. "I did not think you were old enough to have been a warrior for so long."

The dwarf snorted. "You humans view time differently than we dwarves. In my forty-three years, I have seen things you could not comprehend."

With blocky towers jutting above walls made of dark, carved stone, the citadel loomed like a vigilant sentinel monitoring their approach. Upon reaching the end of the bridge, the prisoners and their escorts descended to a gravel road that led toward the city gate. As they approached the massive, black iron portcullis, a sense of dread washed over Ian. He knew something of the future awaiting his people and it was as dark and foreboding as the fortress itself.

The guards standing watch at the gate were heavily armed and armored, eyeing the group of captives suspiciously. Korrigan and another dwarf approached the gate and spoke to the guards on the others side of the bars while gesturing towards Ian and the other prisoners. After a brief exchange, the guards shouted and a portcullis began to rise. Korrigan bellowed a command and the dwarves began marching through, escorting Ian and the other captives inside.

The interior of the fortress, bustling with dwarves going about their daily business, was just as impressive as the exterior. The citadel's outer walls were thirty feet thick, with homes and shops built right into the foundation, utilizing the space in a way that was both practical and efficient. Everywhere Ian looked, intricate carvings and impeccable stonework displayed the dwarves' crafting skill.

Korrigan and the other dwarves escorted the captives through the citadel, past outdoor markets and open shop doors, through narrow alleys and across catwalks over pools of water. They eventually arrived at a large courtyard, where they were met by another group of armed warriors. Korrigan spoke to them in Dwarvish, and the overseers nodded curtly before taking the captives to a nearby building.

The windowless room, a hundred feet square, had only one door. The shackled captives were pushed inside, and the door was locked behind them. A single torch mounted to the wall flickered and cast shadows across the otherwise dark room. There were no beds, blankets, or furniture, the room empty apart from a few wooden buckets filled with water in each of the corners.

The chained villagers sat on the cold stone floor with their backs against the wall. Like Ian, everyone appeared exhausted, hungry, and scared. No one spoke, and the only sound was the occasional sob from one of the children.

Across the room, Ian's mother stared in his direction, her appearance ragged, her eyes at half-mast. He glanced to his right, where his brother sat beside him with his back to the wall and eyes already closed. To his other side, Rina sat in silence. Her eyes were red and puffy, and she looked like she had been crying for hours. He reached out, took her hand, and offered a small smile. She grasped his fingers tightly. While Ian wished to reassure her, he could not find words that would do so without lying. He leaned back and lifted his gaze to the arched beams supporting the ceiling. As with everything else in the citadel, the workmanship was impeccable.

Despite the dire circumstances, he marveled at the architecture of the fortress. The precision and skill involved in constructing such a grand structure were beyond his comprehension. He wondered how long it took the dwarves to build the citadel, and what other marvels were hidden within their walls.

His thoughts turned back to their captivity and the concern that he may never see his home again. Clearly, he was not the only one with such worries. He squeezed Rina's hand, wishing he had the words to comfort her, but in that moment, there was nothing to be said. They were prisoners and at the mercy of their captors. Rina leaned against him, and he slid his arm around her as she snuggled in and rested her head on his shoulder. While the contact was pleasant, his own exhaustion soon overwhelmed him. He drifted off to a heavy, dreamless sleep.

~

"GET UP!" a gruff voice said, waking Ian. He opened his eyes to a stout dwarf standing in the open doorway and guards visible just outside of it. "We are removing your chains, but you are to behave or suffer for it."

Rina lifted her head from his shoulder and rubbed her eyes. "What did he say?"

"They want to take us somewhere." With reluctance, Ian pulled his arm from around her and climbed to his feet. In a loud voice, he said, "Everyone up. They are removing our irons."

A quartet of guards entered the room, each holding a ring of keys. The dwarves began opening shackles, moving from prisoner to prisoner while chains and iron rings fell to the floor. When it was Ian's turn, he stood patiently with his wrists out. The irons fell to the floor with a clang. He rubbed the raw, bruised and scabbed skin, thankful to be free of the weight and chafing.

Once everyone was freed, the dwarf at the door said, "You are all to follow me. Try to escape and you will die."

Ian again translated, "We are to follow. Do as he says."

The others stood. While some appeared weary, many displayed signs of fear and anxiety – wringing hands, flicking eyes, quivering lips. Ian could not blame them. Their lives had been turned upside down and half of the townsfolk had died. Those who had survived thus far now worried about what their future might bring, and Ian was among them.

A hand clapped his back, drawing his attention to his brother, who stood beside him.

"You have shown more strength than I thought possible."

Ian shrugged. "I have done nothing anyone else would not do."

"The fact that you can understand them and have taken the initiative to interpret for the rest of us, well...father would have been proud."

The statement reminded Ian of his father's death, reopening the fresh wound. Tears blurred his vision. He turned and rubbed them away, while following the others out the door.

An escort of dwarven warriors brought them down a narrow street illuminated by morning sunlight. They came to a daunting structure, two hundred feet high and five times as wide. They passed through a twelve-foot-tall doorway, which was ironic since Ian had yet to see a single dwarf taller than five feet. Murals marked the walls of the entrance hall. Beyond it, they entered what could only be a temple dedicated to the dwarven god, whoever that might be.

The prisoners walked along a twelve-foot-wide catwalk, toward a dais at the far end of the chamber. Recessed areas filled with empty benches stood along each side of the catwalk. Columns bracketing the edge of the catwalk supported second story lofts with additional seating. An arched cathedral ceiling stood high above and sunlight filtered through stained glass windows in the walls at each end of the temple.

The catwalk came to a sprawling platform stretching the entire width of the temple. In the center of the platform was an opening in the floor, fifteen feet across. Heat rose up from the opening, and when Ian neared it, he peered down and saw an amber glow far below. In shock, he realized that molten lava bubbled at the distant bottom of the pit.

Beyond the pit was a dais upon which thirteen occupied thrones stood in a row. Twelve were made of carved stone and one in the center was coated in glimmering gold. A fifty-foot-tall statue stood behind the thrones, shaped into a robed male figure with his hands spread as if blessing his worshipers. The sculpture's face was smooth, featureless, and unknowable. Instantly, Ian knew that the statue represented the god for which the temple was built.

He lowered his gaze and turned his attention to the thirteen male dwarves seated on the thrones. All had a beard of white except the dwarf on the center throne, his black beard peppered with gray.

Ian and the others stood in a long cluster between the pit and the dais while those guarding them positioned themselves along the platform's perimeter. When everyone was settled, the dwarf on the golden throne, the only one wearing a crown, spoke.

"As you all know, Gahagar's campaign to extend dwarven rule came at a great cost. Over the course of decades, the Tahal clan suffered many casualties, and now, we find ourselves drastically short of servants and healthy males to perform the more strenuous tasks. This is why we now resort to the long-time practice of our elven cousins. For the first time in clan history, the Tahal must resort to using human slaves to augment society. Today, these newly acquired slaves stand before the council of elders, awaiting disposition." The dwarf gestured. "Captain Korrigan. Bring the first prisoner forward."

Ian's heart sank as he realized he would have to watch as each of his fellow captives was assessed and judged. While not responsible for their fates, he knew he would have to deliver the news to each person. On numerous occasions during their journey, Ian had attempted to avoid this moment but was unable to convince Korrigan to free them. In response to each attempt, the dwarf stated that such a decision was not his to make.

Listening to the dwarven king helped Ian understand the motivation behind his capture. He now understood that he and his fellow villagers had become victims of a war that had powerful repercussions on the Tahal Clan, leaving the dwarves desperate for laborers. While that was both wrong and unfair, at least it helped him to make sense of why he and his people were being forced into slavery.

As each captive was brought forward, Ian translated his or her name and occupation to the council of elders. He watched as each villager was scrutinized and his or her fate decided. It was a soul-crushing process, and, with some, Ian could barely bring himself to speak the words and inform them of their assignment. Then came his brother's turn. Like Brady, Terrick, and the other young men, Vic was designated to work in the mines. Vic accepted the sentence with his chest full and chin thrust, his determination evident as he refused to give in to despair. While Ian did not wish to be separated from his brother, he worried that his fate would be the same – a life he did not know if he could endure.

With all other men given their assignments, the dispositioning advanced to the women, including his mother. All were assigned as cooks, seamstresses, and maids, some remaining in Ra'Tahal, others to be taken elsewhere. His own mother was to be sent away to work as a cook in another citadel, where or how distant, Ian had no idea. Before she turned away, he caught her attention, their gazes meeting. Sadness almost overwhelmed Ian when seeing her eyes empty of the spark that had guided him through life.

Finally, besides himself, only one villager remained.

Korrigan brought her forward. "This pretty young thing is named Rina."

Ian stared into her eyes for a long beat, considering what he might say about her. He could not imagine Rina living the life of a slave, but if it was to happen, he would do his best to ensure her situation was as comfortable and pleasant as possible. He turned toward the council, stood tall, and spoke as clearly as he could muster.

"Rina has been training as a personal servant and was to soon move to the city and begin working for a wealthy mistress."

"A personal servant?" the king said.

"That is correct."

The king stroked his long beard while narrowing his eyes. "In that case, she shall join my personal staff. Queen Pergoli could use another servant. With her comely appearance, she would be a fine bauble to parade before visiting dignitaries."

Rina whispered. "What did he say?"

Ian said, "The king has made you part of his staff."

"What?"

"You are to be a servant for the dwarf queen."

She crossed her arms. "I don't want to be a servant."

His heart sank. "I was only trying to help. Would you rather be a cook or work in a bakery?" When her lips pressed tightly together, Ian sighed. "I am sorry. It was...the best I could do."

Although she remained quiet, she flashed him a spiteful glare before stomping off to the side of the room. *She is angry with me.* While he preferred otherwise, he had done his best to protect her.

Korrigan gripped Ian by the shoulder and turned him to face the council. "This is Ian, the last of the captives. As proven today, he knows something of our language and has been translating between my crew and the captive humans."

The dwarf king leaned forward in his throne and narrowed his eyes at Ian. "How do you know our language?"

"Well, mister..."

The king smiled. "My name is Arangar, King of Clan Tahal."

"Well, King Arangar, I learned your language by listening to Korrigan and the others."

"During a ten-day journey?"

"Yes."

"Most impressive." King Arangar sat back and stroked his beard while staring down at Ian. "I have made my decision," he said, his voice echoing through the hall. "Ian will apprentice to Chancellor Devigar. If he can learn one language, he likely can learn others. At the least, he will be of use when dealing with humans from the south." The king turned to the group of males who had been assigned to the mines. "Work hard and your sentence may be shortened. In the meantime, should you attempt to escape, know that your mothers and sisters are in our control. Their servitude will take place here and in other holds, where they will remain under control of the Tahal Clan. I assure you that they will remain safe and will be treated well but, should any of you attempt to escape your duty, you will place their lives in jeopardy."

Ian gasped at the implication, the shock of it causing him to hesitate before he translated. While doing so, he watched his brother closely. Vic's eyes widened as he realized the same fact – their mother and many others would be held hostage to ensure their compliance.

The king dismissed them, and the escorting guards began ushering the humans out of the chamber. As Ian joined the trail of captives, he glanced at Rina and realized that the two of them had not only both avoided being sent elsewhere, opening the possibility that they might see each other in the future. He had lost his father in the attack, his brother to the mines, and his mother as a servant in another dwarven settlement, but at least he had something from his former life to which he could cling.

Although relieved to avoid the harsh conditions of the mines, the burden of being the court translator settled heavily on him. He worried that it would be a challenging job, and he had no idea how many languages he might be required to learn. *Will any come as easily as the Dwarven dialect? Will the dwarves treat me well, or will they act as if I am a dog for them to mistreat?*

As he was escorted out of the hall, he caught Rina's attention and gave her a small smile. Despite the disappointment in her eyes, he hoped to find a way to make her situation better. He might be a slave the same as her, but he felt a sense of responsibility towards her.

A pair of dwarf guards grabbed him by the arms and ushered him away from the others. They took him to a door in the citadel wall, opened it, and shoved him into a small room occupied by a bed, a desk, a chair, and a vanity. His escorts locked the door, and their retreating footsteps faded to silence. Ian turned to the room with a sigh. With nothing else do to, he lay down on the bed and stared up at the ceiling. Questions about what his new life might entail occupied his thoughts. Rather than answers, he found only an empty, nebulous vacuum.

CHAPTER 7

LOST IN TRANSLATION

A knock on the door woke Ian just before it opened. A pair of squat female dwarves entered, one holding an armful of clothing, the other a tray of food. Both had long braids draped over one shoulder, their round faces smooth and features softer than the males he had met. Since he wore only his smallclothes, Ian held the covers up to his chin to hide his scrawny frame. Thankfully, their stay was brief.

After placing the food on his table and plopping the clothes on the foot of the bed, the two females headed out the door and closed it behind them. No instruction had been given, but the intent was obvious, so he hopped out of bed and hurriedly dressed. Rather than a tunic and trousers, as he was used to wearing, they had delivered amber colored robes and sandals. It felt odd to wear loose clothing, even after cinching the sash around his waist. The sandals were startlingly comfortable and, given the moderate temperature he had experienced since arriving in Ra'Tahal, he suspected the toeless shoes might be particularly nice during the hot summer months.

The meal turned out to be an odd cake with a savory flavor and bits of meat inside it. However, it was far more food than he could fit in his stomach, so he stopped with the cake halfway finished and chased it down with a glass of milk, hopeful that it would not send him racing to the privy. As the thought crossed his mind, a knock came from the door.

He stood as the door opened.

Korrigan walked in. "You are dressed. That is good. I trust you slept well."

Ian shrugged. "As well as can be expected."

The dwarf drew in a deep breath before stepping into the room and closing the door. The troubled look in his eyes had Ian worried.

Korrigan said, "I am to escort you and the others down to the mines."

"Me?" *I thought I had avoided life in the mines.* "Why me?"

"Do not worry. Your visit will be brief. Once you have translated instructions to the others, we will return to the upper hold." Korrigan said, "Before we leave, I wanted to offer my condolences."

Ian blinked. "What happened?"

"Nothing you are not aware of already." Korrigan turned away, as if unwilling to meet Ian's gaze. "Desperation led King Arangar and the elders to turn to slavery. While the elves had long practiced it, we dwarves considered ourselves too honorable to stoop to such measures. Honor is important to us, but if we no longer exist, honor means nothing."

"Why are you telling me this?"

Korrigan covered his eyes. "The quest to find and capture humans to become slaves fell on me. I never intended for it to lead to murder, but when the other villagers fought against my warriors, they reacted as warriors do." He turned back toward Ian, lowered his hand, and looked into his eyes. "I am sorry for the loss of your father and the others. It was never what I intended."

Since his father's death, Ian had spent hours crying for his loss, mourning and missing him. The pain of that loss slowly numbed, settling in as bitter acceptance. He never expected any of the dwarves to care, let alone to offer condolences. Yet, Korrigan was clearly troubled by it. When thinking back to the dwarf's behavior during the journey, Ian had attributed Korrigan's terse behavior toward him as mere grumpiness, but he now realized that the dwarf had been struggling with the deaths of the villagers and his role in their capture.

Finally, Ian said, "Thank you for caring."

Korrigan grimaced and gave him a sidelong look. "I am a warrior. There is little room for caring during war. The others...they would not understand."

"Well, I understand."

Although he still appeared troubled, Korrigan stepped to the door. "Come. I need you to translate to the other humans. Their new jobs begin today."

The dwarf opened the door and led Ian down the corridor. Once outside, they returned to the building where Ian and the other prisoners had first been held captive. Dozens of dwarves stood outside the building, armed and alert. One of them unlocked the door, opened it, and led Korrigan and Ian inside.

The captives were spread out across the room, many sitting with their backs against the wall, some lying down, others standing in clusters. All eyes turned on Ian.

"Tell them that those with the red wrist bands are to come first," said Korrigan. "I need them all to line up at the door. The others will wait until their turn."

After Ian explained what they were to do. The villagers lined up with Vic in the lead, standing just a stride from Ian.

"Are you well?" Vic asked in a hushed tone. "Where did they take you?"

A wave of guilt washed over Ian. He had spent the night in a private room and slept in a soft bed, while the others had been treated like livestock locked in a pen and awaiting slaughter. Despite all of that, his brother remained concerned about Ian's welfare.

"I am fine, Vic." Ian waved it off. "Do not worry about me. Just take care of yourself."

Vic frowned. "You are my little brother. It sounds like the dwarves are sending mother off to some other hold. With pa gone as well, I am responsible for you."

Again, guilt twisted Ian's stomach. His brother was off to begin a hard life in the mines, a far more difficult job than his own assignment. Unable to look Vic in the eye, he turned toward Korrigan.

The dwarf said, "Tell them to remain in line and not to try anything. It would be a shame for them to die for a stupid mistake."

After relaying the message, Ian nodded to the dwarf. "They are ready. Let's get this over with."

"Tell them to follow." Korrigan walked out the door.

"Come along, Vic." Ian said before trailing the dwarf.

The two of them led the line of thirty-eight villagers, all male, the youngest in his early teens, the oldest north of fifty. The escort of dwarven warriors marched alongside the captives, each wearing a fierce grimace and gripping a weapon.

At the first intersection, Korrigan turned and led them west with the rising sun at their backs. A five-minute walk brought them to a hundred-foot-tall wall split by a bulky tower. At the foot of the tower was a raised portcullis a dozen feet wide and twice as tall. They passed through the opening, beneath the sharp, metal spikes of the gate, and beyond the wall. The view opened to a tongue of stonework jutting out from the top of a thousand-foot-tall escarpment. Forest-covered, flat land stretched out below, split by a winding river. In the distance beyond the forest was a vast expanse of grassland and a solitary peak jutting up from the hazy horizon. At the foot of the cliff was a walled area consisting of plowed fields and clusters of stone buildings. Smoke rose from some of those buildings and the distinct sound of hammers striking iron rang from below. Five hundred feet to the south of where Ian stood, water spilled over the cliff edge and tumbled down into a pool at the bottom, just outside of the lower hold wall. The river led from the pool and flowed northwest. The stunning vista held Ian speechless. Then, he saw something that obliterated all other thoughts.

In the distance, a massive, orange-tinted creature emerged from a cloud and flew across the sky.

"What is that?"

Korrigan grunted. "A dragon." It was a word that did not require interpretation.

Ian looked at his brother, the two of them exchanging wide-eyed glances.

The dwarf laughed. "Do not worry. It is not headed this way."

The idea had not even occurred to Ian. He had enough difficulty comprehending that the creature was real, let alone thinking it might cross the expanse and attack. Dragons and other magical creatures had long been the subject of fireside tales. Ian had never suspected that those stories were rooted in truth. The sight left him stunned. Judging by the expression on the faces of the other villagers, they felt the same way. The dragon crossed behind the distant mountain and faded from view, dispelling his trance.

Korrigan gestured toward the staircase to the side of where Ian stood. "We go down."

Following the dwarf, Ian began descending a stairwell carved into the cliffside. A hundred feet below the citadel, they reached a landing where they turned and continued their descent. Again and again, flights of stairs brought them down the cliffside. The earth and fortress above cast them in shadow and a mist swirled around the falls, the breeze blowing the mist toward them and coating Ian's skin. The air grew colder and wetter as they descended.

Halfway down the cliffside, the stairs abruptly ended at the entrance to a tunnel and Korrigan led them inside. Shadows thickened and threatened to blot out all light until a warm glow appeared ahead.

The tunnel opened to a massive chamber with tiers and ledges surrounding a pit that dropped so far down, Ian could not see the bottom. Ten-foot-tall columns burning with amber light stood on many of the levels and illuminated the cavern. Straight ahead was a stone column with a platform jutting out from it. A bronze panel mounted to a pedestal stood in the center of the platform.

Korrigan stepped onto the platform. "Tell your people that half are to board the lift. The others must wait until it returns."

Ian shared the instructions and climbed on. Vic and eighteen others joined them, along with half of the guards. The platform soon filled up with humans and dwarves crowded within its railed edges. Korrigan pressed his hand to the panel, a hum arose, and the lift began descending. A shaft of rock walls surrounded them, its depths unknown.

As they descended deeper into the earth, the temperature grew hotter, and the air thickened with the scent of molten rock. Heat radiated off the shaft walls, making them feel as if they had been kissed by the morning sun despite being underground. A distant clang came from below, the sound repeating and gradually growing louder as the platform continued its descent. A palpable tension gripped the humans on the lift, who stood in silence, unsure of what to expect and unable to do anything about it.

Finally, the platform ground to a halt, and the group disembarked. A short tunnel then opened into a vast underground chamber, with forges and smelters lining the walls. Intense heat emanated from the forges and sweat began to bead on Ian's forehead. The dwarves led the captives to a section of the chamber where metal carts were waiting. Each cart was piled high with platinum-colored rocks. A massive assembly of gears, rods, and heavy plates, all made of metal, stood over them.

Korrigan pointed. "Count out eight men. They will begin working in this location."

Ian asked, "What kind of rock is that?"

"Vartanium. It is extremely rare and is a critical element of dwarven steel." Korrigan warned, "Tell them that they must not attempt to take any ore from the mines. It is an act punishable by death."

The dwarf's stern demeanor made it clear that the warning was serious, so when Ian told the others, he took care to ensure they understood.

After instructing the group to split up, Ian turned back to Korrigan. "What are they to do here?"

Korrigan pointed at a track fading into darkness. "These carts of ore must be loaded into the crusher. This is done by rolling the rocks down the chute. When more carts of ore roll in, those are to be emptied in the same way. The dwarf up there," he pointed above the strange mechanism, "Is named Gidli. He will operate the crusher, which is designed to pulverize the rock. What comes out the other end will go on to be turned into workable metal. I need a few of the men assigned to this location to act as transports between here and the forges. I suggest they rotate in shifts, moving from one operation to another." He gestured to Ian. "Once you have this explained, the rest of us will move along."

Ian did as bidden, and when ready, he and the remaining captives followed Korrigan down a tunnel leading away from the forges. Flickering torches provided light in the otherwise dark space. As the forges and lava grew more distant, the air cooled and turned dank. The tunnel opened to an irregular shaped chamber fifty feet wide and a hundred feet deep. Alcoves surrounded the room and the ceiling stood ten to twenty feet high, depending on the location in the chamber. The cavern was empty other than racks of tools and a cluster of carts sitting in the middle of the space. Veins running through the wall shimmered with the same silver sheen as the rocks in the carts.

Korrigan stopped and turned toward Ian. "The rest of you will start working here, cutting away at the walls and filling carts with ore. This deposit of Vartanium is the latest we have located, and there is no telling how extensive it might be."

As Ian relayed the message, Korrigan approached the rack and selected a pick from it. He walked over to a wall, gripped the pick with both hands, and swung. The sharp point bit into the wall and sent shards of rock spraying out to tumble across the cavern floor. The clang of metal on stone rang throughout the space. He swung again, yielding a similar result. With the third swing, a chunk broke free. Korrigan bent, picked up the section of rock and tossed it into an empty wooden cart.

Turning toward Ian, he said, "While they can figure out what to do by watching me, I want to ensure there are no lingering questions.

Ian explained, and while nobody appeared pleased, none had any questions, either.

"Well done," Korrigan patted Ian on the back and headed back down the tunnel. He then stopped and looked backward. "Say goodbye to your people. I do not know when you will see them again."

Ian turned to his brother. "I am to leave."

Vic walked over to the rack and pulled out a pick. "It appears I have work to do." He hefted the tool, his jaw set in determination. "Swinging a pick is not so different than an axe, so I am capable of holding my own." He gave Ian a nod. "Take care." Turning away, he wound back and swung at the wall.

The other townsfolk followed Vic's example, but more than one cast Ian an angry look, including both Brady and Terrick, the latter shoving Ian, who went sprawling to the floor.

Terrick stood over him, scowled, and made a fist. "You will pay for this, twerp."

Vic, who was facing the wall and swinging his pick, did not see the exchange, nor did Korrigan, who stood in the exit tunnel, talking to the remaining six guards. As Ian climbed to his feet, Korrigan looked back at him.

"What happened?" the dwarf asked.

Ian cast a quick glance toward Terrick, who flashed a fist before turning to grab a shovel. "I...tripped."

Korrigan nodded. "The floor is uneven. You must watch your step."

They followed the tunnel back to the crusher and then to the lift room, where the last nineteen villagers waited with another cohort of guards.

"Now, tell your people to follow," Korrigan said. "We have another stop to make and little time to do it."

Eager to be away, Ian called for his fellow villagers to follow. He slipped past the wall of guards in the tunnel mouth and followed Korrigan, the two of them walking in silence. Although one was bound by duty, the other held against his own will, neither of them liked the arrangement. Yet, what could they do?

CHAPTER 8
APPRENTICE

The peal of a hammer on metal resounded off the tunnel walls and grew louder as Ian, Korrigan, and the last nineteen villagers drew closer to the forges. Intense heat emitted from a river of molten lava along a deep crevice beside them. The odd duo in the lead – Korrigan stout and powerful, Ian lean and weak – approached a recessed area with a dozen stairs leading down to the forge floor. A huge well stood in the center of the recess, filled with orange, bubbling lava. A ring of anvils, each as tall as Ian's midriff and likely weighing thousands of pounds, surrounded it. Dwarves dressed in heavy leather worked in the area, pounding and shaping glowing metal.

Standing at the lip of the top step. Korrigan pointed. "This is Valas Fornax, the forge where the greatest weapons and armor in existence are crafted."

Curious about the process, Ian watched a dwarf hammer a disk of metal into a shield. The metal had a warm color tone even when cooled, making it appear as much like bronze as steel, the sheen matching that of the Vartanium rocks. Then, the smith paused and held a hand over the shield, causing it to glow with white sparks.

"What is he doing?" Ian asked.

Korrigan said, "You are watching a metal wright. Those born with the gift are able to manipulate metal. The incredible hardness of Vartanium requires the magic of a metal wright to shape it and maintain elasticity. Without such magic, the shield would shatter the first time it was struck by a weapon. When the magic is added to the hardness of the metal, it becomes indestructible." The dwarf gestured. "Come along. I have something else to show you as we head to the boarding house."

A dimly lit side tunnel brought them to a small chamber with yet another platform with a pedestal mounted to it. The dwarven warriors and the remaining humans climbed onto the platform. Korrigan pressed his palm to the bronze panel, and the entire thing began to rise. Dark, rock walls slid past as they climbed a shaft with light at the top. The lift rose into a cavern with a tunnel leading to daylight. They followed the tunnel, the rock ceiling soon giving way to the pale blue sky.

They stood at the base of the cliff with the roar of the falls coming from Ian's left. Fortifications surrounded a space a mile wide and half as deep. Buildings made of seamless stone surrounded the broad, gravel yard where they stood. Armored dwarves moved between the buildings, often in pairs. Small piles of shining, silver rock stood to both sides of the tunnel entrance. Farther away, beyond the nearby buildings, were plowed fields with sprouts of green crops growing in perfect rows. As in the upper hold, the wall of the lower portion of the city was lined with doors and windows, which were likely homes for the dwarves who worked those fields.

"What is this rock?" Ian asked, pointing to the pile beside the tunnel entrance.

"Chromium. It is mined in Westhold and delivered here for use in the forges. As when iron is forged into steel, chromium is married with vartanium to make dwarven steel." Korrigan set off across the gravel yard.

Ian and the other villagers trailed the dwarf, the group heading straight for a multi-tiered building with angled walls. A short staircase at the front brought them to a tall door bracketed by thick stone columns.

"Tell them to wait out here for a minute."

Ian relayed the command and turned back toward the dwarf. "Now, what?"

"Come in. I want to show you something." Korrigan opened the door and led Ian inside. "This structure is called the enchantorium."

The interior was a mirror image of the exterior, the floor shaped in tiers descending to the lowest level in the center. Sunlight shone through the highest ceiling, which was made of a milky-white, semi-transparent material. The upper two levels of the building consisted of an elaborate storage system of tubes and chutes.

Korrigan led Ian down a set of stairs and the two of them approached a rail with a drop beyond it. There, they leaned over the rail and peered down at the lowest level. Workbenches on the floor surrounded a vat with bubbling, silver liquid. Six elderly dwarves, some with gray tinting their black beards, others with beards of white, sat at the workbenches with their backs to the vat. Each had a metal object resting on the bench in front of them, including an ax, a hammer, a sword, a helmet, a breastplate, and a shield. While the building and arrangement were interesting, those elements were lost to what held Ian's attention.

The dwarves were bent over the workbenches in intense concentration. With hands held above the object before them, each waggled his fingers. Threads of silver slowly flowed up from crucibles, arced through the air, and descended toward each weapon. The flowing silver reacted in concert with the finger movements of the dwarven enchanters. As the silver met the metal objects, it turned to script burned into its surface. All the while, white sparks sizzled in the air around their hands.

"What magic is this?" Ian muttered.

"Aye. Magic, indeed." Korrigan said, "You are witnessing spellwrights. Their magic enables them to imbue objects with enchantments. It is a difficult and time-consuming craft." He gestured for Ian to follow before turning away and ascending the stairs.

Once they were back outside, Korrigan waved for the prisoners to follow while he marched toward a large building with a metal reinforced, oak door. A pair of armed guards stood outside the door, but Korrigan walked past them and opened the door without discussion.

Standing to the side of the door, Korrigan gestured toward the interior. "Everyone inside. This is your home."

Rather than translate, Ian asked, "What do you mean?"

"This is the boarding house. Miners used to live here when not working. Since we lack the dwarves to dig in the mines, these humans are taking their place. Tell them that they are to rest during the day and will head to the mine at nightfall to relieve the others."

As requested, Ian told the men to file inside. He climbed the stairs last and peered through the doorway. Torches mounted to pillars down the center of the room provided light. Bunks stood along the outer walls while empty tables and benches occupied the middle of the chamber.

Ian frowned at the dark interior. "It does not look like a place someone might live."

"The lack of windows and doors makes the building easier to defend, and the lack of sunlight makes it easier to sleep, regardless of the time of day," Korrigan noted. "When it comes to holding slaves, the design makes it easier to keep them penned in."

"Like a prison." Ian allowed his tone to take on an edge.

Korrigan frowned. "As I told you, I am no more pleased about it than you are." The dwarf descended the stairs and headed back toward the cliffside.

Ian caught up to him. "Then, why do it?"

"Because. We are fighting for our existence."

His brow furrowed, Ian asked, "What do you mean?"

Korrigan gestured. "I assume you have noticed the stonework in our buildings, bridges, and other structures."

"Of course. I would be blind to ignore such craftsmanship."

"Yet, we will build no more unless something changes."

"Again, I feel like you are speaking in riddles."

Korrigan glanced from side to side. Dwarves roaming about the area stared in their direction. Ian assumed it was because of him. Dressed in orange robes, it was difficult not to notice him.

The dwarf spoke softly, "Let's head back to the fortress. I will explain once we are on the lift."

They returned to the tunnel, the surroundings darkening the moment they stepped inside. After the bright sunlight, Ian walked with his hand extended in front of him, concerned that he might stumble right into a wall. Dim light ahead drew him forward until he reached the chamber with the main lift. The shaft stood empty, the lift nowhere to be seen. Korrigan pressed a panel on the wall, and a low hum filled the silence as the lift climbed from the lower depths and slowly approached their level. When it stopped, the dwarf and young man climbed on board, Korrigan pressed his hand to the panel, and the platform began to rise again. Only once they were in the privacy of the lift shaft and surrounded by walls of smooth stone did Korrigan speak.

"Our buildings and these tunnels were crafted by dwarves known as stone shapers. They possess an innate ability to manipulate stone with their bare hands. We have others who are able to sense, locate and shape precious gems. And then, there are dwarves who are born with the talent to mend flesh. All of these, along with the metal wrights and spell wrights, make up the core of dwarven culture. Those among us who do not possess such abilities become warriors or fill other roles one might expect to find in any society. Our race is male-heavy and only one in six births yields a female. Our women often take up crafts that help society, ranging from bakers to tailors and farmers. Unlike you humans, who repopulate rapidly, our births are few and far apart."

Ian listened intently. Whatever Korrigan was trying to tell him was important, of that, he was certain. However, it was a puzzle he had yet to solve. "I am with you thus far, but I still don't understand why you are telling me all of this."

Korrigan's gaze appeared distant despite the narrow shaft of rock surrounding the lift. "Decades of constant war came with a cost few understood. After Gahagar died five years ago, the dwarf clans split apart, each returning to their hold. That is when we realized the gravity of our situation.

"For decades, every male old enough to fight, yet not too old to hold up to the rigors of the campaign, had been forced into the army. Since our crafters were not warriors and not used to battle, most of them died in the war. Worse, with the males in their prime away, very few births occurred over that span. As a result, we were left with very few crafters, and those were all aging. Most will be too old to work or dead within the next twenty years. Who will take their place? Our people age slowly, and it takes thirty to forty years for our young to reach the point where their magic begins to manifest itself. It takes another twenty years for them to become proficient with their abilities."

The lift reached the top and came to a stop.

Ian stepped off. "If you are seeking my sympathy for your plight, you are asking too much. My father is dead, my brother, my friends, and I are all being held as slaves, forced to work for your people without pay or the freedom to do as we please, and you hold my mother and the other women hostage to ensure our compliance."

"I do not desire your sympathy. I simply seek to inform you. Knowing my people will help you in your role as a translator. Understanding our motives will help you better glean our intentions moving forward."

Ian nodded. "I think I understand."

"Just watch and learn. We dwarves are complex in some ways, but quite simple in others. I might be able to teach you a few things, but your own eyes and ears will teach you others. Now, let us go and meet your mentor. He will be another source of knowledge, but I suggest you remain wary. He functioned as the court chancellor for over a hundred years. If anyone in Ra'Tahal has mastered the art of court intrigue, it is him."

"Thank you for the warning." Ian followed the dwarf up the stairs. "What is this dwarf's name?"

"The chancellor is called Devigar. He is Gahagar's nephew. Watch him closely. I worry that he does not always have King Arangar's best interests at heart."

THE LONG CLIMB up the cliffside, covering hundreds, if not thousands, of stairs, left Ian winded and exhausted. His legs shook as he walked through the gate and returned to the upper hold. While Korrigan asked Ian if he was well, he refused to display any more weakness than he had already shown.

After a trio of turns amid the narrow streets, they came to a squat, cylindrical tower near the center of the complex. Korrigan knocked on the tower door. To Ian's surprise, it opened to reveal a familiar face from his village.

Ian shifted to his native tongue. "Winnie?" The girl was a year older than Ian and had pursued his brother for years. While Vic had spent time with her, some as more than a friend, he had thus far avoided anything serious with her or any of the other girls in Shillings. "What are you doing here?"

The young woman stood at Ian's height with red hair, pale skin, and sparkling green eyes. She wore a simple brown dress with a white apron, her plentiful chest and hips straining against the fabric. Her ginger braid rested on her collarbone and she absently ran her fingers along it, as Ian had seen her do dozens of times before.

· · ·

HER EYES FLICKED TO KORRIGAN, her response little more than a timid whisper. "I was assigned as Master Devigar's servant."

Ian smiled. "I am to apprentice to Devigar."

In return, Winnie flashed a nervous smile and stepped back from the door. "In that case, come in."

Korrigan arched a brow at Ian. "You obviously know this girl."

"Our village was small. Everyone knows everyone there."

"This is good. Her presence will make you feel more at home."

"I suppose." Ian stepped inside.

The inside of the tower's main level was dimly lit, the only source of light coming from flickering candles placed intermittently throughout the room. The scent of old parchment and ink hung in the air. Rows of ancient books lined shelves that reached the ceiling, the leather bindings worn and weathered with age. The sheer amount of knowledge contained within those walls felt intimidating to Ian, as if the books themselves judged him for how little he knew of the world.

Winnie led them past a sitting area with a sofa and three chairs, toward a staircase at the side of the room. They began an ascent that wound its way up the perimeter of the tower. A four flight climb later, the stairs ended at an open doorway at the top. Beyond the doorway was a chamber Ian instantly assumed was the chancellor's study.

Morning light illuminated the chamber, streaming through five windows, evenly spaced along the wall of the circular room. Bookshelves spanned the gaps between each window and ran from floor to ceiling. Those shelves were packed with books, the thick, dusty tomes teasing Ian with the knowledge they held and leaving him wishing he knew how to read.

A large oak desk stood to one side of the room, behind which sat an old dwarf with a bald head and a thin, pointed, white beard. With purple eyes, sharp and calculating, the elderly dwarf studied Ian with a shrewdness that made him uneasy.

"Master Devigar," Korrigan said, bowing deeply, "I have brought your new apprentice, a human named Ian."

Gripping a staff leaning against the desk, Devigar rose from his seat, his movements slow and deliberate, as if every action was calculated. "You are late, Captain Korrigan."

"Before I could deliver Ian, I required his skills to translate to the humans assigned to work in the mines."

"Ah," Devigar kept his sharp gaze on Ian the entire time he spoke. "They tell me you learned our language in a matter of days. Is this true?"

"I suppose, sir."

"How is this possible?"

"In truth, I do not know."

"You speak it well enough, but can you read it?" Devigar lifted a parchment from his desk and held it out to Ian.

The sheet was covered in strange runes and symbols unfamiliar to Ian. He stared at it and felt as if he should know what it said, but nothing came to him. He had heard that some of Darristan's wealthier citizens were able to read, but he didn't know anyone from Shillings that had been taught to do so.

"I have no idea what this says," Ian admitted.

"So, our prodigy has a weakness." The old dwarf tossed the parchment to the desktop with disdain. "Can you even read in your own language?"

"I... was never taught to read, Master Devigar."

The chancellor snorted. "Pity." He glared at Korrigan. "Am I truly saddled with this illiterate oaf?"

Korrigan narrowed his eyes. "King Arangar wishes for him to become a translator. He already knows two languages, and you will not live forever."

"I may be old, but my mind is sharp."

"Some might say it is too sharp."

Devigar's nostrils flared. "What is that supposed to mean?"

Rather than reply, Korrigan said, "Ian is smart, but he is young, even for a human. I suspect he will learn quickly enough. Teach him what you can. Hone his abilities. Make him useful to the clan. Those are the orders I was instructed to deliver even if you demanded otherwise."

The old dwarf glared at Korrigan before his lips turned up in a forced smile. "I will do what I can to mold this lump of clay. I just hope he holds his shape and doesn't melt when pressed into service."

"You do that." Korrigan nodded to Ian. "I will likely see you soon." He turned and descended the stairs, leaving the mentor and apprentice alone.

Ian immediately disliked Devigar, but he did his best to bury such feelings. Any display of disrespect towards his mentor would only make his situation worse.

"What would you like me to do first, Master Devigar?" he asked calmly.

The dwarf leaned forward, his sharp eyes scanning Ian's face. "First, I want to know what you've learned about our language and culture so far."

Ian took a moment to collect his thoughts before responding. "Well, I've discovered that your language is complex, and includes nuances that don't exist in my own language. I've also learned that your culture is deeply rooted in tradition and honor, and that you place a high value on craftsmanship and hard work."

Devigar nodded, seemingly pleased with Ian's answer. "And what do you think sets us apart from humans?"

Ian thought for a moment before responding, fearing that the question might be a trap. "I think the main difference is that dwarves prioritize the clan and the greater good over individual desires or ambitions. You work together as a community to achieve common goals, whereas humans tend to value individual achievement and success above all else."

Devigar's eyes glinted with amusement. "Do you truly believe that?"

"I..." He shook his head. "I don't know what to believe. I can only go by what Korrigan has told me and what my own eyes have seen over the past few days."

"Good," the old dwarf nodded. "At least you are smart enough to doubt what you see. Watch. Listen. Question. Seek to not only hear what is said, but what goes unsaid. This is as important for our role as anything else. When a foreign representative visits our court, you must attempt to determine his or her motives while also watching for signs of subterfuge. The silent threats are often the greatest."

The lump in Ian's throat was difficult to swallow. "I did not realize so much responsibility fell upon us."

"Few do. Being underestimated is among the advantages you can leverage. This is your first lesson."

Ian dipped his head. "Thank you, Master Devigar."

"Now, pull up a chair and sit." The old dwarf hobbled around the desk and settled in his seat. "I will begin by teaching you how to read and write in our language. It will be difficult, but I have faith in my skills as an instructor."

As bidden, Ian picked a chair up from below a window and carried it over to the desk. "Yes, Master."

CHAPTER 9

SOLACE

Vic considered himself a hard worker. Although he had only recently reached his twentieth year, he was stronger and more capable than most men his age. Four years spent as a lumberjack, cutting down, splitting, and hauling trees from the woods to his home village of Shillings had added sculpted muscles to his already athletic frame. While others might have wished to avoid such a strenuous profession, Vic had discovered that the monotonous nature of the work allowed his mind to wander, and he often found peace and clarity in those moments. He had never imagined he might one day work in a mine, but when circumstances forced him into the role, albeit against his will, he discovered that same sense of solace.

Each day was the same as the last – he and those in his crew waking with the sun, eating a fair breakfast, and then going off to the mining tunnels to relieve the night shift. His time there was divided between breaking rock with a pick, loading chunks of vartanium into carts, pushing those carts to the crusher, and loading the massive machine. The work was difficult, and while the other men often complained to one another, he did not. Instead, he sank himself into the work and pushed his body while allowing his mind to settle into a sort of mindless meditation. Often, his thoughts turned to his mother and younger brother, wondering if both were safe and well. While one was somewhere distant, Ian lived in Ra'Tahal, so Vic expected an occasional visit. Yet, days passed and those days became weeks of him working in underground tunnels without sight or word of Ian.

It was on a day like any other, some six weeks into his enslavement, that Vic swung his pick, the tip striking the dull rock adjacent to a metallic vein. Again, he swung, driving the pick into the wall. The rock cracked, split, and a chunk tumbled to the floor, forcing Vic to dance backward. Early on, he discovered the pain of having toes crushed in such situations.

He leaned his pick against the cavern wall, squatted, and lifted the watermelon-size chunk of rock. Straining at the weight, he carried the rock over to a nearby cart and placed it on top of the heaping pile.

"This cart is full," he said aloud. "I'll push it to the crusher."

Terrick set his pick down and wiped his brow with the back of his hand. Like many of the others, Terrick had lost weight since their capture. Where he once was just a big person with as much softness as muscle, his stomach had slimmed and his arms showed definition they had lacked before.

"Do you need help?"

"No. I can do it." Vic pointed toward the tunnel ceiling. "Just remember to set a beam and posts in place every twelve feet. We don't need another incident like the one we had last week."

Just mentioning the event caused a shadow of sorrow to darken the chamber. None of the crew needed the reminder. Like Vic, nightmares and concerns had plagued them all since that frightful day. Deciding he would rather be away from the room than attempt to reignite the conversation, Vic leaned into the cart. Its wheels squeaked as it began to roll.

He pushed it past the six dwarven warriors positioned at the cavern entrance and entered the dark tunnel leading to the crusher. The tunnel opened to the massive chamber with the crusher positioned along one wall. Pushing hard to gather momentum, he rolled the cart up the ramp and onto the lift platform. The dwarf manning the lift pressed a hand against the panel, and the lift began to rise toward the rock shelf where the crusher was to be loaded.

In Dwarvish, Vic said, "Good day," and gave a nod.

The dwarf scowled and said something Vic did not understand. While he had picked up a few words, most remained gibberish to him and to everyone except for Ian. *How does he do it?* Although Vic had kept such thoughts private, some of the other miners had questioned it aloud more than once, along with them mentioning how unfair it was that Ian had avoided conscription to the mine. Vic did his best to ignore their complaints. Jealousy was an ugly emotion people resorted to when they refused to take responsibility for themselves. Normally, he would defend his brother, but since Ian was safely away from those who complained about him, he chose to let it go, hoping they would tire of blaming Ian for something he had no hand in creating.

When the lift stopped, he pushed the cart off the platform and across the flat rock shelf, three stories above the cavern floor. He slowed as he approached Brady, Cassel, Owen, and Sven, all of whom had been assigned to the first shift of loading the crusher that day.

"I've another load for you," Vic said.

Brady eyed the heaping cart. "Since you are here, I'll deliver an empty one back to the others. It is time for a shift change, anyway."

"My shoulders are sore from swinging a pick, so I'll not argue."

As Brady pushed another cart back to the lift, Vic and the others began unloading the full one. Hoisting the chunk on the top, Vic lugged it a half a dozen strides, stopped at the chute, and dropped the rock. It slid and tumbled down the chute while the dwarf seated up in the control room activated the strange machine. Gears whirled and the trap began to open and close. The chunk of rock slid into the crusher, and the massive metal teeth grinded it into bits.

He turned and stood behind Sven, who was the last in line, waiting while the others each lifted a chunk of stone with metallic veins from the cart. Then, he heard a cry.

Vic spun around as Owen fell head-first into the chute. Alarmed, Vic dove and tried to grab the man's ankle, but he was too late. A terrified scream echoed in the chamber as Owen tumbled toward the massive, gnashing, metal teeth.

"Stop the crusher!" Vic bellowed before realizing that the dwarves did not understand him.

The crusher's teeth caught Owen and tore through his flesh, sending blood spurting. The dwarf in the control room reacted, shutting the machine down, but it was too late. Vic turned away and cringed as Owen's cries fell silent. The other two surviving members of the crew wore horrified expressions. The tunnel collapse had been bad enough, but to witness this...

At that moment, Vic realized he needed to find a means to escape. But with his mother and the other women at risk, he worried about what might happen to them if he did. Trapped and disheartened, he fell to his knees and his chin dropped to his chest. *What are we to do?*

AT THE END of their shift, the eighteen surviving men followed an escort of dwarven warriors along the tunnels leading outside. Light at the end of the tunnel called to Vic, taunting him with the false promise of freedom. Emerging, he squinted in the light of late afternoon, a stark difference from the dark confines of the mine.

As Vic crossed the outer yard and headed toward the lodge where he and the other miners slept, he spied an old dwarf and a thin young man crossing the grounds. Both wore robes, the dwarf in white with red trim, the young man in amber. Dressed in the unexpected garb and with his hair slicked back, it took a moment before Vic recognized his own brother.

"Ian!" he shouted.

Ian turned toward him, a smile appearing on his face. He then spoke briefly to the elderly dwarf before walking over. Some of the miners shot Ian angered looks, but most just trudged on in exhaustion, leaving Vic behind.

"How are you, Vic?" Ian stopped a stride away and fidgeted with his hands.

Vic frowned. "You are worried about *me*?"

Ian's gaze dropped to the ground. "I feel...bad for you and the others working in the mine."

He feels guilty. Vic could not blame him. He likely would have felt the same had he been in Ian's shoes, but at the same time, their roles would have been miscast if reversed. Ian was unfit for such hard labor, and his mind would have been wasted with such an assignment. *At least the dwarves were wise enough to get that right.*

"I would be lying if I claimed that it was an easy life. In fact, it has turned out to be a dangerous one." Vic admitted. "Last week, we had a small collapse that killed Corbin Thatcher and Will Baker."

The news caused Ian to raise his gaze, his eyes filled with concern. "Were you injured?"

"No. They both worked the night shift. I was safe in the bunkhouse and sleeping at the time. However, there is more."

"What?"

"Owen Miller died today." The image of Owen's bloody, ravaged body flashed before Vic's eyes. His screams rang in his ears like a faint echo that would not stop repeating. The incident was bound to conjure fresh nightmares.

"Rina's brother?" Ian's brows shot up. "He was only a year older than you."

"The crusher does not care what age you are."

"He died in the..." Ian covered his mouth. "That is horrible."

"Be glad you were not there to see it."

Ian shook his head. "After losing her father a few years ago, Owen was Rina's only family. She is going to be devastated when she finds out."

Vic set his hand on Ian's shoulder. "She needs to know. If you see her..." One of the dwarves escorting the miners grabbed Vic by the arm and urged him along. He spoke over his shoulder, "Be well, Ian. Do not worry about me. I can take care of myself."

The dwarf guided Vic to the bunkhouse before shoving him inside. The door slammed behind him, followed by the thud of the bolt on the outside being set.

Vic paused in the doorway, allowing his eyes to adjust to the dim interior. He then walked over to his bunk and sat with a sigh. Leaning forward with his elbows on his knees, he rested his head in his hands. Concerns for Ian and his mother warred with a growing need to escape his incarceration.

The sound of footsteps approaching preceded a pair of scuffed boots coming into view. He looked up to find Terrick standing over him.

Vic sighed, lacking the patience for any nonsense. "What do you want, Terrick?"

"I want to know what Ian said to you."

"He wanted to know how I was doing. I told him about what happened to Corbin, Will, and Owen."

Terrick scowled. "Aren't you worried you might be next?"

Of course, the thought had crossed Vic's mind, but dwelling on such things would do no good. "I think we can learn from what happened to them and take precautions so it doesn't happen to us."

"What about Ian?" The big man scowled.

"What do you mean?"

94

"While we labor and risk our lives, he lives a lavish life of robes and sunlight and court antics," Terrick snarled.

Vic grimaced. "Lavish? You know nothing of his situation."

"I know that his robes were clean and his hands appeared as soft as ever."

Anger stirred inside Vic. He rose to his feet and locked his gaze with Terrick's, who stood a few inches taller than him. "I suggest you worry about yourself. If anyone should be concerned about Ian, it will be me."

Terrick thrust a finger in Vic's chest. "I think your brother sold us out. He traded us away so he could live like a prince while we labor all day in darkness."

Vic swatted the finger away and pointed toward the door. "If you think yourself clever enough, go find a way to impress the dwarves. I suggest you try a dress and a high voice. Maybe they will take you for a serving maid and set you up in a palace as well."

A meaty fist came at Vic, who hastily raised an arm to block the blow. He followed with an underhand thrust to Terrick's gut. Weeks earlier, it would have been a softer target. Still, the blow caused Terrick to exhale and double-over. Vic followed with a double fist to the bigger man's upper back, driving his upper body down while lifting a knee to his face. The blow snapped Terrick's head back and sent him tumbling to the floor.

When Vic took a step toward Terrick, Brady rushed in to stand between them. "Stop! Now!"

"He started it," Vic said.

"I don't care. We shouldn't be fighting amongst ourselves. Our enemies are not locked in here. They are outside, holding us hostage."

"You are right," Vic nodded. He looked down at Terrick, who wiped the blood from his nose. "I am sorry."

Terrick climbed to his feet and grimaced before walking away.

When the area was clear, Brady said, "Terrick is frustrated."

"He is not the only one." Vic lowered his voice. "This life...is no life at all."

"What can we do? We are outnumbered and have no weapons, so fighting is a poor option that is likely to leave most of us dead. Worse, they hold our mothers and the other woman captive."

"I don't know what to do yet, but I will think of something. If we remain here, we will all eventually end up like Corbin, Will, and Owen."

"Well, if you think of something, count me in. I'd rather risk my life trying to escape than work in that blazing mine for the rest of my life."

Vic nodded. "Good. Watch for opportunities and keep an ear peeled for others who are of a similar mind. Just be sure to keep this to yourself until I am ready to do something about it."

"I can do that." Brady walked away, leaving Vic alone with his troubled thoughts.

CHAPTER 10
COURT ENVOY

The ancient tome before Ian smelled of must, mixing with the scent of the ink in the open well beside it on the desk. He finished recording one line, dipped his quill in the ink, and moved on to record the next.

At first, the strange runes and symbols had bewildered him, but days of Devigar's tutelage and Ian's own studying had taught his mind to perceive them in another manner. Once he understood what each symbol stood for and how their meaning changed when they were arranged in different ways, something clicked. Like a peg slipping into a drilled hole, everything suddenly fit just right.

Working from dawn until dusk, the next three weeks were spent proving to Master Devigar that he had mastered not only the audible aspects of the Dwarvish language but writing and reading it as well. Although the terse old dwarf refused to praise Ian, the satisfaction in his eyes said enough. Then, he saddled Ian with the task of learning a new language. While differing from Dwarvish, this new language was obviously related but with an elegant, lilting flair that made it both more beautiful and more complex.

The door to Ian's room opened and Devigar walked in, dressed in white robes with a gold and red stole – something Ian had never seen him wear before.

"How are your studies coming along?"

"I have been recording these Elvish proverbs all morning." Ian gestured toward the pile of freshly written parchment.

The old dwarf picked up a sheet and looked it over. "Your penmanship is improving. Weeks ago, it was hardly legible. Now, I might even be willing to show it to others without complete embarrassment."

In six weeks of his tutorship, that was the closest thing to a compliment Ian had heard from the grouchy dwarf.

"May I make an observation, Master?" Ian asked.

Arching a bushy, white brow, Devigar said, "Go on."

"Whoever wrote these proverbs was both arrogant and judgmental."

To Ian's surprise, Devigar chuckled. It was a strange sound and the first time he had heard it. "That is because this was written by a Sylvan elf. Most of them are insufferable people who think themselves superior to all others."

Ian had heard the sentiment before but chose not to mention it. "I am almost finished with this book, Master. What would you have of me next?"

"That is why I am here. A visitor arrived at Ra'Tahal this morning. An audience between this envoy and the council is to take place within the hour. As court chancellor, I am to join the assembly to translate and mediate. King Arangar requested that I bring you along, so you may observe."

An unexpected excitement arose in Ian's chest, his heart thumping as if to get his attention.

"However," Devigar held up a gnarled finger. "You are to only listen. Unless I give you leave, you are not to speak a single word. In fact, I warn you to take care to hide your emotions and reactions. The envoy is Drow and they are a devious, perceptive lot."

"Drow?"

"Yes. A dark elf from the north."

Ian's excitement level doubled. His studies had given him some insight into elves, but having never even seen one, they remained a strange, nebulous concept lacking the solidity of reality. "I will get to meet an actual elf?"

Devigar raised a finger and a bushy white brow. "A *dark* elf, but yes. Just remember to remain silent. Watch. Listen. You may learn something." He gestured toward the bowl of water on the vanity. "Now, wash up and dress in your finest robes. Tame that mop of hair on your head. I will return shortly to escort you to the throne room."

THUMP, thump, thump, Devigar's staff struck the paved street in time with his deliberate stride. Ian walked alongside his mentor as the old dwarf headed toward the citadel's central structure. It would be Ian's first visit to the building, and the anticipation of the experience had his stomach churning and his heart aflutter. As he approached the Hall of Ancients, Ian stared up at the multi-tiered building. Towering columns crafted of sparkling white marble stood along the hall's facade. The beauty of the columns created a stark contrast to the stern, gray stone from which the rest of the keep was built.

Lifting the hem of his best robes, white with gold piping along the hem and sash, Ian climbed the stairs and approached the towering entrance doors. A quartet of dwarven guards stood outside, their scrutinizing gazes affixed on Ian as he followed Devigar inside. While the building's exterior reflected the practical nature of dwarven culture, the interior was lavish and embellished.

They stood in an entrance hall encircled by gilded pillars. Tapestries of golden threads weaved in intricate designs hung from the walls. A massive, elaborate chandelier of sparkling crystals dangled above the center of the room. Strands of gold wove in between the pillars and were draped to the chandelier overhead. Marble staircases rose along both sides of the room. Polished marble tiles stretched across the hall, the marble a deep black with gold and white striations. Across the hall stood a set of ornate gold doors bracketed by armored warriors holding pikes barring the way.

Devigar and Ian crossed the room, the thump of the old dwarf's staff echoing throughout the chamber. The guards drew the pikes back toward themselves, opening the gap between them. The doors opened of their own accord, and the old Chancellor and his apprentice entered the Hall of the Ancients.

Sixty feet up, murals of legendary battles adorned the coffered ceiling. Marble columns rose to support a balcony three-quarters of the way around the room. A short run of stairs formed into half-circles rose to a round floor made of black and gold marble tiles.

A raised dais curving to match the circular chamber stood at the far end of the room. A line of twelve ornate chairs with red velvet padding stood on the dais. In the center of that row of seats, with six to either side, was an ornate, golden throne much like what was found in the citadel temple. The chairs were occupied by the elderly dwarves of the council, all wearing black robes trimmed in gold. On the throne sat King Arangar, dressed in a gold doublet with red panels and black stripes. Upon his head rested a golden crown encrusted with a single ruby at the front. The ruby itself was the size of a chicken egg and was worth more than Ian could imagine.

The tapping of heels on marble and the thuds of Devigar's staff dominated the otherwise silent room as the chancellor and his apprentice climbed the stairs and approached the open center. Five strides in front of the dais, Devigar stopped and Ian settled at his side, his hands clasped at his waist.

Bowing, Devigar said, "I am here to serve, my king."

Ian bowed, mimicking his master's actions as was instructed.

King Arangar nodded. "Welcome, Chancellor. I notice that your apprentice has joined us today."

"As you requested."

"And it is appreciated." The king glanced up and down the line of seats while the council members shot scrutinizing glares at Ian and Devigar. "Before we begin, do you have anything of concern to share?"

"Only that you remain wary for any signs of treachery or deception."

The king grimaced. "Our history with the Drow is well known. None of those seated before you need to be reminded of what has transpired in the past."

"In that case, let us begin."

Arangar motioned to the guards at the side of the room. "Deliver our guest."

The guards headed out the door and silence fell over the room. Tense minutes passed before the guards re-entered, escorting a tall male figure draped in dark robes. An ominous aura emanated from the newcomer, a darkness that seemed to absorb the light around him. Ian's heart quickened as he realized that this was the Drow envoy. Even while masked by a hood, this strange newcomer was unlike anything he had ever seen. Rather than walk, the dark elf seemed to glide, the hem of his robes fluttering along the tiles, his footsteps silent.

The Drow stopped a few feet in front of the dais and bowed, his face masked in the shadows of his hood.

In Elvish, the guest spoke, his voice lilting and musical in nature. "Greetings, King Arangar. My name is Rysildar. I have been sent by Queen Liloth to represent the interests of the Drow nation."

Devigar translated the elf's words into Dwarvish.

"I would see your face, so I may better judge your intentions," Arangar said.

Again, Devigar translated.

The Drow reached up and pulled the hood back. Ian gasped.

White hair spilled down Rysildar's shoulders, the color matching his strikingly pale skin. Long, pointed ears stuck up at the sides of his head. Angular eyes with red irises glared at the dwarven king. Strange symbols were tattooed around the dark elf's neck.

"Does my appearance meet your expectations?" Rysildar asked.

Rather than say the exact words, Devigar translated, "As you wish, Your Majesty."

Ian frowned, wondering why his master had altered the sentence rather than translate it as it was spoken. He was not the only one to turn his mouth down, for the king and most council members scowled at the remark. If they understood the words, Ian was unsure. The tone of the elf, however, had been obvious in its derision.

"Your presence is noted." Arangar spoke in an even tone, his voice echoing in the spacious room. "I assume you have come bearing a proposal?"

After Devigar translated, the Drow replied, his voice low and smooth. "Difficult times plague dwarf and elfkind alike. Thus, my queen proposes an alliance."

When translated, one of the council members spat, "Our kingdom has no need for alliances with treacherous races such as yours."

"Cease!" The dwarven king held a palm toward the member who had spoken, a gesture with clear intentions, warning the dwarf and his fellow council members from another outburst. He lowered his hand. "Allow us to listen before passing judgement."

Rysildar seemed unfazed by the council member's aggressive response. Instead, he took a step forward and continued speaking. "Three years have passed since the combined Dwarven Armies assaulted Drovaria. Our people have suffered much hardship due to that vile act. Thousands died, both warriors and innocents. Many of our cities lie in ruin. Our greatest citadel, Talastar, still stands, but her walls remain damaged, and we struggle to defend our people from creatures that roam the wild."

The dark elf paused while Devigar relayed the statement.

When finished, Arangar snorted. "While we sympathize with your situation, what does that have to do with us?"

If the king's reply bothered the elf, it did not show. Instead, once the translation was complete, the elf said, "Dwarven artisans are known for their craftsmanship. Queen Liloth seeks assistance in returning Talastar to its former glory. Send us a team of stone shapers, so they may rebuild her fortifications. In return, Queen Liloth is prepared to offer the Tahal Clan an exclusive trade center in Talastar." Rysildar said, "The trade center would enable you to sell or trade goods with the Drow people. This is unprecedented. As you know, our people have never allowed a foreign entity to establish themselves within our cities."

"Why have you approached the Tahal Clan with this proposal? Talastar is a great distance from Ra'Tahal, while our cousins in Domus Skrai reside just south of your lands."

Devigar spoke with the Drow and then voiced the reply, "We have spent the better part of the past two years negotiating with Fandaric, King of Clan Argent, but he refuses by stating that he has no stone shapers to spare."

Arangar shared a look with the council members. Nobody spoke, but Ian knew what they were thinking. Clan Argent was not the only one lacking stone shapers.

The Drow spoke again, not waiting for a reply.

"To sweeten the agreement, Queen Liloth has also agreed to provide you with the magic of the greatest surviving Drow Singer. So long as your craftsmen are away from Ra'Tahal, this singer will dedicate his abilities to the good of Clan Tahal, beginning with a gift so unique and powerful, it will forever altar the fortunes of this great citadel."

When Devigar finished translating, the council members murmured among themselves, some nodding while others scowled. Ian sympathized with them, for an unease squirmed in the pit of his stomach. His studies of elves and their culture had mentioned singers as beings of mysterious and powerful magic.

Arangar stroked his beard thoughtfully. "I would be lying if I claimed your offer was not intriguing. However, given the lack of precedence, we require some time to consider the implications. You may remain in Ra'Tahal as my personal guest tonight. At mid-day tomorrow, we will reconvene, and you will have your answer."

The Drow dipped his head. "I appreciate your consideration in this matter, and I look forward to your response." Rysildar turned and glided down the stairs and out of the room.

The moment the door closed behind him, the council erupted into a cacophony of voices, each dwarf vying for his opinion to be heard. Curiosity and intrigue tugged at Ian as King Arangar calmly listened to each member, his expression unreadable. Devigar climbed the dais and stood at the king's side, occasionally leaning close to whisper something in his ear.

After several minutes, the king held up a hand and the room fell silent.

"Martagon," Arangar said. "How many members of our clan are true stone shapers?"

The council member seated to the far left leaned forward and replied, "Three, Sire, including myself."

"And the other two?"

"One resides at Westhold, the other at Nor'Tahal. Like myself, both were too old to join Gahagar's campaign."

The king stroked his beard while frowning in thought. "We have no young shapers to offer?"

"There are some youths we hope might soon demonstrate the ability, but, even if the magic began to manifest today, it will be years before they are proficient."

Another council member asked, "What of stone masons?"

Martagon replied, "Two dozen reside here in Ra'Tahal, and half that number live at each of our other holds."

The king, again, stroked his bearded chin. "If we were to send an elderly stone shaper and augment him with masons, I suspect Queen Liloth will not know the difference. Even lacking the magic of a stone shaper in his prime, the skill of a single dwarven stone mason far outstrips that of a Drow craftsman."

Ian whispered to Devigar. "Is this true?"

"Yes," his master whispered back. "Now, hush."

Again, the council members began throwing out objections, forcing the king to raise his hand and still the room.

When the others fell silent, Arangar said, "While I understand your concerns, we must consider the potential benefits of this alliance. The rebuilding of Talastar would be a gesture of good faith between our peoples. The ability for us to trade and sell crafted items in the Drow capital with no other foreign competition would be a boon and it could bring the clan great wealth. In addition, access to a Drow singer's magic could be invaluable in times of crisis."

The idea of a magic user living in Ra'Tahal created conflict within Ian, one side intrigued by the opportunity to witness what wonders the singer might conjure, the other filled with unease of what might come of the dark and mysterious magic they wielded. The histories he had studied under Devigar's tutelage included numerous accounts of past Drow treachery, and singer magic was said to be powerful but unpredictable.

"However," Arangar continued, "we must also be cautious. Gahagar's campaign ended not so long ago, and the Drow are unlikely to forget what transpired. Worse, we cannot be certain of their true intentions. I ask you all to weigh both sides of this proposal. Return here after breakfast tomorrow, and I will hear the arguments from each of you before coming to a decision." Arangar stood. "Until then, you are dismissed."

The king descended the dais, crossed the flat area, and continued down, toward the doors, where the waiting guards escorted him out of the chamber. The council members followed, the old men moving slowly, some holding the small of their back with one hand while gripping a staff with the other. Soon, the room was empty with only Devigar and Ian remaining.

"When the Drow asked if the king approved his appearance, you translated something else. Why?"

Devigar arched a brow. "Why anger the king and council with a meaningless comment such as that? Would it not be more prudent to ensure that each of them listens with an open mind rather than with the tainted perspective of someone already angry? As it stands, many of them harbor prejudice and resentment against the dark elves. I saw no need to inflame the bias that already exists."

Ian nodded, admitting that his mentor's explanation made sense.

Devigar went on, "Sometimes, translating requires adjustments to ensure emotions do not get in the way of progress. Yet, there are times when emotions are demanded. It is up to us who stand in between the two parties to balance the two. In the end, the best outcome for the clan must be achieved."

Ian had to ask, "What is the best outcome from this proposal?"

The old dwarf smiled. "You will soon find out."

CHAPTER 11
SAFRINA

S afrina Miller climbed the central keep's stairs, crested the landing, and opened the door leading outside. She emerged to afternoon sunlight, the breeze catching stray golden hairs and whipping them about. The rest of her hair remained tied back in a bun, as demanded by her mistress. While her duties required her to rush, the attraction of the view tugged her in the other direction. Her slippered feet silently crossed the keep rooftop, taking her to the waist-high wall at the western edge. With her hands resting on the wall, she gazed out over the citadel.

As the home of the king, his family, the council, other clan leaders, their servants, and their personal guard, the keep was the largest building in Ra'Tahal. Twelve stories up, the rooftop provided a rare view of the region beyond the citadel's fortifications.

While staring out over the vast lowlands stretching out toward the western horizon, Rina dreamed of the freedom to venture into those wilds. *What delights lurk in the forests, the grasslands, and the mountains, just awaiting my discovery? How distant is the sea? Which ports await on its shores and where might its ships take me?* Such thoughts were destined to remain nothing more than nebulous wishes. Few in Shillings understood, but she had been trapped there as if in a prison lacking walls. She thought to escape it through her apprenticeship, training as a servant with the dream of living in Darristan. The dwarven attack on Shillings changed that, and while Rina ended up in a city of sorts, she again found herself imprisoned in a helpless position leading toward endless misery.

She longed to return to her childhood, back when her life was simple and filled with joy, before her mother died, before her father began to beat her. The man always had a temper, one that grew far worse when he turned to wine, something that became frequent after the loss of his wife. As Rina matured, the situation worsened until her brother, four years her elder, had enough. When others asked, Rina and Owen claimed her father's death had been an accident. It was easy enough to believe that the man had slipped and fallen into the millstone. In reality, Owen had caught him standing over Rina, her dress torn, her face bloodied. In a rage, Owen struck his own father over the head. The man fell onto the millstone and the waterwheel driving it had done the rest. Only the two of them knew the truth. It had become a burden that darkened both of their souls, but at least neither Rina nor her brother had to endure the abuse any longer.

The situation had forced Rina to find work. In a village with few options, she apprenticed to the local washer woman, Mistress Cass. Thus, she traded in a life of abuse for one of mundane, redundant tasks of washing clothing and bedding for others in the village. The job did not pay well, but it left her with a skill she might take with her to the city. Two years into her apprenticeship, her lot changed with her capture, but not for the better.

Thinking back to the dwarf attack on the village felt surreal, as if it had been a bad dream rather than reality. The events following the attack seemed to happen too swiftly for her to fully comprehend. In a bewildering twist of fate, Rina found herself many hundreds of miles from home, living in a fortress keep and working for a dwarven queen.

Pergoli displayed little patience toward Rina and was obviously irritated by her inability to speak the language. How many weeks had passed since she began her new life, Rina could only guess. Despite being surrounded by others speaking Dwarvish, she only understood the words most closely tied to her expected duties. The rest remained gibberish, often spoken too rapidly to even attempt to decipher.

She then recalled the reason for climbing to the keep roof, turned from the wall, and crossed the rooftop.

White sheets clipped to thin lines across the rooftop fluttered in the breeze. Rina touched the fabric and decided it felt dry, so she began removing the clips and dropping the sheets into a woven basket. When finished, she lifted the basket, returned to the stairwell, and descended to the keep's top floor. A dimly lit corridor brought her to the royal sleeping chambers. Thankfully, they were empty. She crossed the sitting area, made straight for the bedroom, and began making the bed. Before she finished, the chamber door opened and someone walked into the neighboring room. Voices, one male, one female, speaking Dwarvish filled the silence. Neither dwarf sounded pleased although Rina did not understand what was said. Hurriedly, she completed the task, scooped up the basket, and headed back to the main chamber.

King Arangar and Queen Pergoli stood across the room, talking to one another in an apparent argument. Without trying, because she did not wish to snoop, Rina caught a few words but not enough to make sense of the conversation. The queen was angry about a decision he had made. He insisted it was the best thing for the clan. The rest was lost on Rina, the conversation ending when the king noticed her, his mouth clamping shut. The queen followed his gaze and scowled at Rina.

Rina approached them and bowed. "Finished." It was one of the few words she knew.

"Good," Pergoli said, followed by a bunch of words Rina did not understand. "Blah, blah, blah, blah," is all she heard. Then, the queen added, "Blah blah blah blah, go."

Go was a familiar word, and one she was happy to obey.

After a bow, Rina opened the door, pulled it closed, and passed the quartet of guards standing outside it. She descended six floors and began down a corridor toward her own room. When she reached the room, she found the door open. *Who is in my room?* Anxiety caused her breath to come in gasps, terrified of what or who she might find inside.

She eased close to the door and peered past the frame. A male figure in amber robes stood in her room, facing the other way. The person was both too tall and too lean to be a dwarf. He turned and her heart leapt.

In a flash, Rina closed the distance, her arms wrapping about him, her momentum causing him to stumble backward. He regained his balance, leaning into Rina while hugging her back. She buried her face in his shoulder and began to cry.

He stroked her hair, "Please, don't cry."

She stepped back and wiped her eyes. "It is just so good to see someone I know."

"Someone?" He appeared hurt.

"Well, you are more than someone, Ian. You know that."

His gaze dropped to the floor. "I am sorry. I...should have found a way to come sooner."

"Do not be sorry. You have as little control over your situation as the rest of us."

Ian lifted his head, his eyes meeting hers as he smiled. He had a nice smile and a way about him that made her feel better about herself. "I am glad to see you, too. How have you been?"

Rina turned toward the open door and swung it closed. In a hushed voice, she said, "Queen Pergoli is awful. She demands much and I don't understand half of it, which causes even more conflict. I do my best, but she never smiles and often makes me do something I just finished all over again."

He nodded. "My master, Devigar, is difficult as well. I don't know if it is cultural or if it is something else. The citizens are on edge, and they worry about what is to become of them. You, me, and the other villagers are victims of their desperation."

"Still, that does not make it right."

"No, it does not," he agreed.

Rina smoothed her skirts when she realized that she must look a wreck after a day of cleaning the royal chamber. Reaching behind her head, she pulled at the end of the ribbon holding her hair back and it came free. A shake of her head sent her hair swinging from side to side and then settling.

Ian stared at her with longing in his eyes. She dropped her gaze, not wishing to encourage him. It wasn't that she didn't like him, rather she did not wish to lose his friendship by complicating it. She desperately needed to keep that friendship. It was among the last things of her child-hood to which she could cling.

"Did you come here just to say hi?" she asked.

"I..." Ian cleared his throat. "I came with some bad news."

Her head snapped up and she looked into his green eyes, filled with sadness. She asked in a whisper, "What happened?"

He turned to the narrow window as if to stare outside. "I saw my brother yesterday. An accident occurred in the mine. He told me that... Your brother...is dead."

Rina covered her mouth with her hand and plopped down on her bed. Owen had raised her after her father died. In fact, he had raised her in the two years preceding the man's death, after the loss of their mother. Without Owen...she was truly alone.

Tears clouded her vision, joined by a whimper. Ian turned toward her, bent, and wrapped an arm around her back. She leaned her forehead against him as she sobbed.

Rina considered Ian her best friend. They had grown up together, shared everything from their meals to their secrets, and while things had become more complicated as they grew into young adults, she valued that friendship greatly and never more than she did now. Other than

Ian, Owen had been her only steady source of support in a world that had not been kind to her. Now, he was gone and she was alone...except for Ian.

"I'm so sorry," Ian whispered, his hand rubbing soothing circles on her back. "I wish I could take your pain away."

Rina shook her head, unable to find words through her grief. All she could do was cling to him, grateful for his presence and the comfort it brought.

After a few moments, Ian pulled back and took her hands in his. "Rina, I know how hard this is for you. But we must persevere. We have to find a way out of this situation, for ourselves and for Owen's memory."

Rina stared up at him with a furrowed brow. She knew she must look a mess with her eyes red and face swollen from crying. "How can we do that? We're trapped here, with no way out." The situation had seemed hopeless from the start. Owen's death only made it worse.

Ian's grip on her hands tightened, his expression fierce. "We'll find a way. We'll make a plan, we'll work together, and we'll get out of here. I promise you that."

"What about your mother and the other women? Didn't King Arangar threaten to hurt them if we tried to escape?"

"He did, but there must be a way to deal with that. So long as he does not think we intentionally escaped, he would have no reason to take such drastic measures."

Rina looked at him, hope stirring in her chest. Ian had always been resourceful and determined, despite his physical shortcomings. If anyone could find a way out, it was him. "Very well," she said, her voice shaky with emotion. "I trust you."

Ian smiled at her, his eyes shining with determination. "Good. However, I need some time to figure it out. In fact, we may have to act quickly if an opportunity presents itself. Just be ready to act if I tell you that the time has come. For now, you should rest. Again...I am sorry about Owen."

Rina nodded, grateful for his concern. She lay on the bed, curled on her side, and watched him as he made his way to the door. "Ian?" she called out softly.

He turned to look at her. "Yeah?"

"Thank you. For everything."

Ian smiled at her. "Anytime, Rina. You know that."

With that, he left the room, leaving Rina to her thoughts. She cast her mind back to her childhood days, when life was simple and her older brother watched out for her.

CHAPTER 12
SHAME

Ian opened the central keep's front door, passed the two dwarf guards posted outside it, and strode into the street. In the failing daylight, he paused and looked up at the window to Rina's room. He hated having to share such bad news with her, but right was right, and she needed to know what had happened to her brother. Somehow worse, he felt guilty about his unintentional response to Rina hugging him. Her body pressed against his had sent his pulse racing and parts of him reacting in far more obvious ways. If she had noticed, she did not say anything, for which he was grateful. Thoughts of her occupied him as he walked down a narrow corridor, on his way back toward Devigar's tower.

Due to the late hour, the streets of Ra'Tahal were quiet, the path ahead of Ian empty until a tall, cloaked figure emerged from a doorway and glided down the street in the opposite direction. In a city of dwarves and female human servants, there was only one inhabitant who fit the profile of the cloaked person – tall, lean, and male. *Rysildar.* Like an itch demanding to be scratched, Ian's curiosity raged. *Devigar gave me leave for the evening.* The realization was all he needed to talk himself into following the dark elf.

Rysildar turned at the next intersection, heading east. The moment the dark elf was out of sight, Ian quickened his pace. He reached the corner and slowed, glancing to the side as he crossed the intersection. A hundred paces away, Rysildar's back faced him, seemingly headed toward the citadel's outer wall. Ian turned to follow at a measured pace, hoping that the Drow would not look backward.

His heart thumping and his palms slick with sweat, Ian trailed Rysildar as the dark elf approached the wall. *What is he doing?* He had no business following Rysildar other than to be curious about the dark elf's movements, but the nagging feeling that the Drow had ulterior motives in their new alliance was too great to ignore.

Rysildar paused at the base of the citadel's outer wall, his head tilted upward as if studying the sunlit stones. Ian held his breath, pressing himself against a nearby building while hoping he was masked in shadow. The dark elf raised a hand to the wall, ran it along the surface, and stopped. A faint click came from that direction. A narrow section of the wall slid open, revealing a narrow doorway with darkness beyond it. Rysildar slipped inside, and the wall closed behind him.

Ian's mind raced. *What is happening here? Is Rysildar up to something nefarious?* He knew he should turn back and report to Devigar, share this discovery and what had led him to it, but curiosity got the better of him. He had to know what was inside that passage. Ignoring the part of him that warned of danger, Ian approached the wall and examined it closely.

Made of the same gray stone as the rest of the citadel, the seams between the blocks all but imperceptible, there was nothing unique about the section of wall other than it was at the midpoint between two doors, each positioned twenty feet away. Ian ran his fingers over the seemingly solid stones, but he couldn't find the switch that Rysildar had used. He tried to push against the wall in different places, but it wouldn't budge. As he was about to give up, his finger felt a cool spot on the otherwise warm stone. When pressure was applied, an unseen button sank into the wall. A click preceded, a section of the wall pivoting in to reveal a dimly lit staircase leading downward. Just inside the doorway, a metal lever stuck out from the wall, and Ian instinctively knew he was looking at another means to open it.

He hesitated for a moment while considering the consequences of what he was about to do. Caution screamed for him to turn away, but curiosity won out. Determined, Ian stepped into the shadowy interior and pushed the door closed. Impenetrable blackness crashed in and left him blind. With his hand against the cool, stone wall, Ian slid his foot forward until he found the first stair. Wrapped in a blanket of gloom, he began his descent.

The staircase was narrow and steep, the air musty and damp, the depth of the stairs unknown. After what felt like an eternity, he reached the bottom. Two strides ahead, a thin strip of amber light ran along the floor. Arms extended as he advanced, his fingers touched a wooden door. He located the handle and eased it open to reveal a narrow corridor illuminated by torches mounted on the wall. The corridor was empty and silent.

Ian crept down the corridor, the scuff of his sandals on the stone floor making more noise than he wished. The torches flickered and cast unsettling shadows on the walls. The air was thick with must. The faint sound of a lilting chant came from somewhere ahead. He followed the sound to the end of the corridor and found himself standing in front of a heavy wooden door. The source of chanting, along with something causing a strange humming sound, waited on the other side.

With his hand hovering over the doorknob, Ian hesitated. He knew he shouldn't be in that tunnel and that Devigar had warned him of how dangerous the Drow Singer might be, but the curiosity that had led him down the secret passage was too powerful to resist. He took a deep breath, turned the knob, and eased the door open just enough to peek inside.

What he saw made his blood run cold.

A circular chamber waited beyond the door, its ceiling domed, the rock walls carved with smooth perfection. An open stairwell waited on the opposite end of the room, rising into darkness. In the center of the chamber stood a stone pedestal with a crystal globe mounted to it.

Rysildar stood before the pedestal, his back facing Ian. With his hands extended toward the crystal, the Drow sang a song of strange, unknowable words, his voice high, warbling, and inhuman. In time with the song, a purple glow pulsed within the crystal. The power emanating from the chamber, a raw energy that made his skin tingle, was terrifying.

Ian took a step back, unsure of what to do. He knew he should leave and report what he had seen to Devigar, but the sight of the Drow singer and the pulsating energy of the crystal were too mesmerizing to abandon. He watched in awe as the singer's hands moved in intricate patterns, the glow of the crystal intensifying with each passing moment. The dark elf abruptly stopped singing and turned around.

"Who is there?" Rysildar demanded, his voice sharp and piercing.

Ian froze for a beat, unsure of what to do. Panicked, he briefly considered giving himself up before deciding to flee.

He yanked the door closed and sped down the underground corridor. Just before he reached the far door, the one behind him opened.

The drow belted a high-pitched note. The air around Ian wavered and drew hotter as he opened the door. He dove into the stairwell as the door burst into an inferno. Flames splattered off the rock walls and set the hem of his robes on fire. Urgently, Ian tore the robes off, stripped down to his smallclothes and sandals, and raced up the staircase, which was now illuminated by the fire below. A cry of rage came from the Drow. Driven by terror, Ian pushed past his physical weakness and ascended the four-story staircase faster than he would have thought possible. As he reached the top, he glanced back to find the Drow at the bottom, his white face and red eyes flickering in the firelight. It was the most frightening thing Ian had ever seen. Please, don't let me die here.

The plea was directed to the good spirits as he pulled on the lever sticking out from the wall. The hidden door swung open, and Ian darted outside.

Down the narrow citadel streets, Ian ran. The few dwarves he passed stared at him with shocked expressions, but none tried to stop him or even ask why he was unclothed. When he reached Devigar's tower, he tore open the door, hurried in, and closed it behind him. Leaning his head against the door, he panted to reclaim his breath.

"Ian?" A female asked.

He spun around to find Winnie standing in the entrance hall.

Her eyes widened in alarm. He followed her gaze, looked down, and discovered that he had torn his smallclothes, exposing his private parts. He urgently covered himself with his hands and backed toward the stairs. "I...um..." *How do I explain this?*

Finally, he gave up, turned, and leapt to run up the stairs but tripped, tearing his smallclothes even further in the process. With the tatters of what remained of his dignity gripped in his hands, he ran up the stairs, wishing to retreat to his room and never come out.

A KNOCK at the door woke Ian. He sat up in the darkness and glanced toward the window to gauge the time. Through the curtain, he saw no sign of daylight, making it clear that the sun had not yet risen.

"Come in," Ian rubbed the sleep from his eyes.

The door opened to reveal Devigar. The old dwarf set a lantern down on Ian's desk and stood over his bed.

"I believe you have some explaining to do," said his mentor.

Ian groaned. "Winnie told you. It was not on purpose. I would never expose myself that way if..."

The old dwarf held up a palm, stopping Ian. "If something occurred between you and Winnie, I am not aware."

Furrowing his brow, Ian said, "She didn't tell you?"

"I need you to tell me what happened last night. Numerous citizens reported you racing through the citadel half naked and behaving as if an angry dragon was giving chase."

"They reported that?" Although Ian worried about Devigar's reaction, he needed to tell someone of what he had witnessed. Bracing for punishment, he went on to explain that he had followed Rysildar and how the Drow had disappeared into the hidden passage. He then did his best to explain what he saw underground and how the singer had attacked Ian with his magic, destroying Ian's robes in the process. "When back outside, I ran until I reached your tower. That's when I happened upon Winnie."

Devigar stared into space while smoothing his thin, white beard. The silence caused Ian to worry more than if the old man had shouted at him.

Unable to contain himself, Ian asked, "Are you going to punish me?"

The dwarf arched a white brow. "For curiosity? Hardly. Besides, I suspect that your brush with death was a teaching moment in of itself. Would you ever go down in this secret chamber again?"

Ian shook his head. "No, sir."

"Good...assuming that there is a chamber and it was not something conjured by an overactive imagination."

"It was real, I..."

Again, Devigar stopped him in mid-sentence. "Be at peace. Give me until morning to arrange it, but you and I are going to investigate this secret door together."

Relieved, Ian grinned. "You believe me."

"I believe you saw something. You are young and impressionable, but you are too smart for someone to have manipulated you into believing in something that does not exist, unless you were either drugged or the target of magic that has affected your mind."

Ian frowned. He knew little of magic and never suspected that it might be possible to affect his perception of reality.

The dwarf continued, "If this hidden passage is real, it could compromise the citadel's defenses, especially if it offers a secret means for invaders to get into and out of fortress walls. As chancellor, I must investigate and report my findings to King Arangar." Devigar exited the room, stopped outside the door, and looked back at Ian. "Rest for now. You are safe here. We will resolve this in the morning."

The door closed, the room falling dark and leaving Ian alone with his thoughts.

A knock came from the front door, the sound carrying up to the second level, where Ian ate his breakfast.

"That would be our escort." Devigar set his fork down, gripped his staff, and stood.

Almost finished with his meal, Ian took one last bite of sausage before chasing it down with a long drink of apple juice. He wiped his mouth clean, rose to a stance, and followed his master down the curved staircase along the tower's circumference.

As the main level came into view, so did Winnie. The red-haired girl wore a tan dress with a white apron, her hair tied back in a tail, her corset too tight for her chest, causing her breasts to heave. Ian's eyes bulged at the sight, and when she looked at him, he looked away, fearing to be caught staring. The embarrassment of his unintentional self-exposure remained firmly affixed in his mind and left him wondering if he could ever look her in the eye again.

Winnie opened the door and stepped back. Devigar wobbled past her, followed by Ian, who nodded thanks while sneaking one last glimpse of the soft, pale flesh of her cleavage. While he couldn't meet her gaze, he also found it impossible to not appraise her distinctly female assets.

Six dwarven warriors waited outside, the morning sun glinting off their armor. Standing among them was Korrigan, whom Ian had not seen since the beginning of his apprenticeship.

"Good morning, Chancellor. Hello, Ian." Korrigan nodded to each of them.

Devigar nodded to Korrigan. "Thank you for coming, Captain. I must say I did not expect you to be leading this inquiry. I thought you were still away from the hold."

"I returned from Westhold last night." Korrigan glanced at his soldiers. "If you are ready, I prefer to get this over with. I am to report to Arangar before his mid-day session with the Council."

Chancellor Devigar said, "Yes. Let us go visit our resident Drow."

While Devigar and the dwarven warriors began down the narrow citadel street, Ian stood rock still. His stomach roiled so strongly that he thought he might vomit. He never expected Rysildar would be involved. *Will he use his magic against me?* His heart began to race, his breath coming in gasps as panic set in. Ian longed to rush back into Devigar's tower and find a dark corner where he could hide. Even facing Winnie was preferable to staring into Rysildar's red eyes.

Devigar paused and looked back, his mouth turning down in a grimace. "Apprentice! You requested this inquiry, so you are bound to participate."

Korrigan and the other five warriors stared at Ian, watching him, waiting for him...judging him. Ian's gaze dropped to the ground, unable to face those stares and knowing they would see the terror in his eyes. He drew in a deep breath, gathered his resolve, and set his jaw before lifting his face.

With purposeful strides he crossed the open space between him and the group of dwarves. "Let's do this." Thankfully, his voice remained firm despite the quiver of his spine.

"Good." Devigar turned and hobbled down the street with the six guards and Ian in his wake.

As he walked, Ian thought to himself. *Maybe he won't recognize me. If he does, he wouldn't do anything to me with the dwarves present, would he?* He tried to convince himself all would be fine, but it was difficult when he knew nothing of singer magic and what might or might not be possible.

They reached the same door Ian had seen Rysildar emerge from the prior evening. Lifting his staff, Devigar thumped the butt of it against the door. Tense, quiet moments passed before it opened. A hooded figure in black robes lingered in the shadowy doorway.

A lilting voice came from inside, speaking in Elvish. "It is early, Chancellor."

Devigar replied in the elf's language. "Pardon our interruption, but we have need of your presence."

The Drow stepped into the doorway to examine the group. When his hooded gaze landed on Ian, it lingered. That stare left Ian unable to breathe.

Finally, Rysildar turned back to Devigar. "What is this about?"

"My apprentice claims he had a run in with you last night."

His composure disintegrating, Ian gasped. The Drow looked at him again. Although Rysildar's hood kept his face blanketed in shadow, Ian felt an intense hatred emanating from the dark elf.

"I am sorry," Rysildar crooned. "The only time I recall seeing this young man before now was during the meeting with Arangar after my arrival in Ra'Tahal."

"That is a relief," Devigar said. "However, we must ensure this situation is resolved. If you would join us for a brief stroll, we can clear up the issue in short order."

The Drow glanced backward, hesitating before nodding. "Very well." He stepped out into the sunlight and pulled the door closed behind him. "Lead the way."

Turning toward Ian, Devigar nodded. "Ian. The rest is up to you."

Drips of sweat tracked down Ian's ribs as the entire party turned toward him. He swallowed the lump in his throat, spun on his heel, and headed down the street. At an intersection, he turned toward the east wall, taking the exact same path as Rysildar had when Ian followed him. The sun, a quarter of the way into the sky, forced Ian to squint and lower his gaze until he drew near the city wall, where the fortifications blocked the sunlight and cast him in cool shadows. Without pausing, he walked straight up to the wall and stopped at the midpoint between the two doors, just as he had the night before. He reached up and ran his hands along the wall, searching for the release. Unlike the prior evening, when the west-facing wall was still warm from an afternoon of direct sunlight, the stone felt cool to the touch. He pressed against various spots in the wall, hoping to trigger the hidden door. Each attempt yielded no result. Minutes passed with Ian shuffling along the wall while trying to find the release.

Rysildar snorted. "Why am I being subjected to this? What does he expect to find?"

Devigar said, "My apprentice claims that a secret passage lies hidden in the wall."

"Even if that were true, I only arrived in the city weeks ago. How would I know of something like that when dwarves who have lived their entire lives here do not?"

Ian glanced back at the Drow with a furrowed brow. Devigar scratched his chin while the dwarf warriors looked on.

"He does make a good point, Ian," Devigar said.

"I know what I saw."

"Then, please, reveal the door, so we don't appear like fools."

Turning, Ian tried again, but the stone all felt the same and pressing on it did nothing, no matter where or how many times he tried. Finally, he stopped with his palms pressed against the wall and his gaze drifting far beyond it. Without turning around, he spoke over his shoulder in

Dwarvish. "The wall was warm last night after being in the sunlight all afternoon. In contrast, the release was cold. That was how I found the trigger."

"Come now, Ian." Devigar did nothing to hide his irritation. "You don't expect us to wait all day for the sun to cross the sky and warm the wall, do you?"

Defeated, Ian dropped his hands to his sides and his chin to his chest. "No," he croaked as he turned around.

Devigar turned to the Drow while shifting to Elvish. "I must apologize, Rysildar. My apprentice has a powerful imagination. It comes in handy at times, but in moments like this, it is a terrible distraction. Thank you for your time. You are free to go."

The Drow dipped his head. "Thank you, Chancellor."

Turning, Rysildar glided down the street, toward his apartment while Ian drowned in a vat of shame, frustration, and failure.

CHAPTER 13

SHRIA-LI

Shria-Li climbed onto the portal stone, crossed the rune covered surface, and took position beside her father, Fastellan. Although he was nearly a century older than her, strangers sometimes made the mistake of assuming he was her brother. Like her, Fastellan's hair was so fair, it was almost white. His angled eyes sparkled like the sky, his skin flawless, his features perfection. In all of these ways, she took after him, yet their personalities clashed with a frequency that drew her mother mad, which left Shria-li surprised that she was allowed to join him on this trip. Having recently reached her majority, she had yet to travel outside of Sylvanar. Thus, her heart raced with anticipation as he raised the Staff of Life and placed the staff's butt in the recessed center of the portal stone.

Light flared from the staff, and the runes etched into the surface of the stone began to glow. The surrounding forest shimmered and brightened until white light enveloped both the portal stone and the twelve elves standing on it. The light faded, and the area around the portal stone came back into view. Rather than a forest of golden trees, oaks with green leaves and brown bark surrounded them.

"Where are we?" Shria-Li asked.

Fastellan lifted the staff from the hole, the light in it dousing. "We are deep into dwarven lands, roughly five miles southwest of Ra'Tahal." He climbed into the palanquin resting on the portal stone's surface. "Come. Join me. We will talk during the short journey to the citadel's gate."

She parted the curtain and sat back on the pillows. Six brawny Sylvan, whom other races would still consider lean and lithe, lifted the litter to their shoulders. Another four Sylvan warriors climbed off the portal stone and began down a forest trail at an easy jog. The elves hoisting the palanquin followed, the trees rushing past while Shria-Li and her father relaxed in plush luxury.

Conversations with her father had always felt disjointed, as if the two of them struggled for the right thing to say. Yet, Shria-Li was trapped in a small space with him and the thought of traveling five miles in silence felt odd, so she broke it.

"Thank you for allowing me to join you this time."

A nearly imperceptible shrug later, he said, "You are an adult, now. It is time for you to learn something of the world."

"I have been studying the world for forty years," she countered.

"Studying is not experiencing."

The shortness of his reply caused her to frown. *He makes it sound as if it was of my own choosing to not leave Havenfall until now.* "Then why could I not have come with you during your last visit?"

He drew the curtain back a few inches and stared outside. "That was twelve years ago, and Gahagar was still in power."

"Yet, he was away from Ra'Tahal."

Fastellan dropped his hand, the curtain closing. "He was *always* away from the city. Chancellor Devigar and the council governed Ra'Tahal for decades. When Gahagar died, the war ended, and Arangar returned to claim the throne in his stead."

She frowned. "After experiencing a taste of ruling, does Devigar hold any resentment toward Arangar now that he is a mere chancellor again?"

Fastellan smiled. "Very good. For you to ask that question makes me believe you have taken your studies of court intrigue to heart."

Shria-Li's pride swelled at the rare compliment.

"However," he continued, "dwarven societal norms would require Devigar to remain steadfast. While the dwarves are often uncouth and unrefined, they hold only one thing in higher regard than pride. Honor. Still, with the two ideals battling against each other, one would think that Devigar teeters between loyalty and betrayal. It is among the things we must measure during this visit. If anything appears amiss, it becomes another thread we can pull, should it suit the needs of our people."

The constant manipulations and machinations of court made Shria-Li uncomfortable. She had been taught to seek out motives and personal agendas in every conversation, and oftentimes, she found it all exhausting.

She and her father sat in silence, the conversation dried up and neither inclined to resume it. Lacking a common interest was a common theme between them. He enjoyed the contentious nature of life as king. She longed for a simpler existence, but more than anything else, she desired freedom – the freedom to be herself, the freedom to explore the world, the freedom to mold her own future. Instead, she felt like a prisoner, chained to a life not of her own choosing.

When the rhythmic jostling of the palanquin slowed, she drew back the curtain again and the sunlit walls of Ra'Tahal came into view. The citadel appeared imposing, and despite the undeniable craftsmanship, distinctly functional in comparison to the elegance of her home city. As the palanquin drew near the gate, the towering walls consumed the view, blotting out all else.

She sat back. "We approach the gate."

Her father leaned forward and pulled the curtain aside as the palanquin came to a stop. He spoke to someone in the chopped, terse language the dwarves used. A gravelly voice replied in the same language. The gate opened, and the palanquin was carried through it.

Shria-Li only understood a small slice of Dwarvish. Her lack of effort in learning the language was one of the many ways in which she had disappointed her father. It wasn't that she was incapable of learning Dwarvish, rather that she just did not care. The human language, however, intrigued her greatly. She found humans and their culture interesting and wondered what it might be like for one's life to pass so quickly, as it did for them. Most humans died by the time they reached her own age of seventy-two, yet she was barely an adult by elven standards.

After a few minutes of jostling, the palanquin stopped and was lowered to the ground. Fastellan climbed out and Shria-Li followed.

They stood in a small courtyard with streets intersecting in all four directions. A large, blocky building loomed to one side, a structure with quartz columns to the other. An old dwarf with a thin, white beard leaned against a gnarled staff, his purple eyes watching her every move. Beside the old dwarf stood a taller and far younger figure in amber robes hanging loosely on his lean frame. It was immediately obvious that the younger one was not a dwarf, and with the lack of pointed ears, Shria-Li knew he must be human, the first human she had ever seen apart from the slaves working in her home city.

"Welcome to Ra'Tahal, Your Majesty," the old dwarf said in Elvish, while dipping his head in respect.

"Good afternoon, Chancellor," Fastellan replied. "It has been too long since our last visit."

"Seven years, I believe."

"And much has changed in the span since then." Fastellan arched a brow. "How is King Arangar?"

If the statement caused any irritation, Devigar hid it well. He smiled. "The king, the queen, and the council are well. I sent word of your arrival, but they are currently occupied. A formal dinner will take place later this evening, at which you will be the guest of honor. Until then, you may rest in the guest chambers. I suspect you are exhausted from your journey."

The last statement caused Shria-Li to narrow her eyes at the chancellor. She watched him closely but was unable to determine if he was intending sarcasm. *Do they not know of the portal stones? Even if not, it was clear that my father and I rode in the comfort of the palanquin. How exhausting can that be?*

"Very well," Fastellan nodded. "Tell me, who is the human at your side?"

The old dwarf gestured to the young man beside him. "This is my apprentice, Ian."

Her father tilted his head. "A human apprentice?"

"It is uncommon, I will admit."

"Does he understand our language?"

Devigar arched a brow while glancing at the young man. "Ian?"

"I do understand, Your Majesty," the human apprentice replied in fluent Elvish.

"Interesting."

"And I am assuming this beauty is your daughter?" Devigar asked.

"Yes." Fastellan placed a hand on her shoulder. "This is Shria-Li, my daughter and heir to the Sylvan throne. She is young and often impertinent, but I hold hope that she will mature before it is her turn to rule."

Shria-Li wilted at the embarrassing statement. *Why would he say that to the chancellor?* She knew enough not to ask the question in public, but she also was aware that her father did nothing without intention. *Is he attempting to manipulate me, or is he purposely lowering the chancellor's opinion of me? If the latter, why?* These were the types of questions she had learned to ask herself. It was the only way for her to deal with her father's machinations without her emotions ruling the moment.

Devigar gestured toward the dwarven warriors waiting in the courtyard entrance. "These guards will escort you into the keep. My apprentice will be at your disposal should you require anything. Although he is young, he is fluent in both of our languages as well as his own. While you are here, enjoy the meager comforts we can provide. Until the assembly, I bid you a good afternoon." With that, the chancellor climbed the stairs in front of the neighboring building, passed the massive columns, and faded inside.

Shria-Li followed her father and the guards into the keep, trailed by the chancellor's human apprentice. The stone walls, dimly lit by torches, were cold and unwelcoming after the warmth of the sun outside. She shivered and wrapped her arms around herself, wishing she had brought a cloak. The differences between the dwarven architecture and that of her own people leapt out at her. The dwarves seemed to build for function and durability, while the elves preferred grace and beauty. She wondered if their different approaches were a reflection of their respective societies.

A series of ascending staircases and winding corridors brought them to the guest chambers. While quaint compared to what she was accustomed to, the space consisted of three adjoining rooms, those on the ends both bedrooms while the one in the center included a table, six chairs, a desk, a small sitting area before a stone fireplace, and a window that overlooked the courtyard where they had met with Devigar. The dwarven escort and her father's guards all stopped in the corridor, along with Devigar's apprentice.

Her father waited until the door closed before turning to her. "I know you're not fond of courtly affairs, but it's important that you pay attention to everything that happens here."

"I know, Father," she replied, rolling her eyes. "You've told me a thousand times."

"Good. And remember to be on your best behavior."

"I always am."

Fastellan gave her a doubtful look. "If you have done your best to behave, I do believe Sylvanar is in deep trouble when your mother and I pass."

Shria-Li huffed, crossing her arms. "I know how to behave, Father. I just don't see the point in all this political posturing."

He sighed. "It's not just posturing, Shria-Li. It's about maintaining alliances, negotiating trade deals, and seeking opportunities at every turn. These are the responsibilities of a leader."

"I understand that, but I don't see why we must waste so much time and energy on it. Can't we just focus on making our own kingdom better?"

Fastellan gave her a patient smile. "It's not that simple, my dear. We live in a world where actions in one region can affect nations and people who live a thousand miles away. What happens in one corner of the realm can have ripple effects across the world. We have to be aware of what transpires around us and act accordingly."

Shria-Li scowled, but she knew her father was right. It was frustrating, but she couldn't deny the truth of his words. "Fine. I'll pay attention and behave, but I don't have to like it."

He chuckled. "Honestly, I don't care if you like it or not, just as long as you do it." He headed toward the bedroom. "I am in for a nap while we wait. I wish my head to be clear for dinner."

He closed the door behind him, leaving Shria-Li feeling quite alone. She crossed the room and opened the glass door leading to a balcony. Standing eight stories up, the citadel sprawled out around her with only the outer walls and a handful of buildings rising up above her elevation. She leaned over the rail, the heat of the afternoon sun pressed against her cheek. After a few moments of silence, she decided she preferred company, so she entered the chamber, passed the sitting area, and opened the door.

The guards, ten of them lean and lithe elves, another four squat and stout dwarves, all turned toward her. The last to turn was the one human present.

The young man blinked. "Princess."

She smiled. "You may call me Shria-Li."

"Yes. Of course...Shria-Li." He held his hand to his chest. "My name is Ian."

"I know." she glanced at the guards, all watching and listening. "Would you please come in? I have some questions."

"As you wish, Your Highness." He walked past her.

Shria-Li closed the door and spoke in a soft voice, "My father is sleeping." She crossed the room, heading toward the balcony door. "Let's step outside, so we don't wake him."

Ian joined her outside, his hands seemingly seeking a place to go as he wiped his palms down his robes, then clasped them together at his waist. *This boy is nervous.* She wondered at his age and decided to ask.

"How old are you?"

"My seventeenth Beltane came earlier this year."

She had never heard of Beltane, but the number seventeen was no surprise. Humans aged notoriously fast. To her, it felt as if they raced through life. At the same time, legends said that they stomped through the world with an intriguing flair that her kind would call reckless.

"Tell me, Ian. How did you come into this role? Were you recruited, or did you come here seeking a new life?"

His green eyes flicked toward the southern horizon. "I grew up far from here, in a village named Shillings. At the start of summer, the dwarves attacked our city. A quarter of the villagers died that day. The rest of us were captured, brought to Ra'Tahal, and forced into slavery. Most of the other captured males were assigned to work in the mines. I was fortunate enough to evade such a grueling sentence when King Arangar decided to make me Devigar's apprentice."

Human slaves existed throughout Sylvanar, but she had never heard of dwarves taking slaves. "Why were you spared from the mines?"

"Arangar saw promise in my ability to speak Dwarvish."

"And to speak Elvish, as you are now."

"That came later."

In human, she said, "I know something of other languages."

He smiled and replied in his native tongue. "Where did you learn?"

"Among my various tutors was a human slave. She taught me."

His smile faltered, his eyes and lips tightening. "A human slave?"

She looked down, ashamed. Having grown up surrounded by slaves, she had taken them for granted. However, those men and women had been born into it and lived their entire lives in servitude. Here, she was talking to one who had known freedom until his recent capture. Her own desire for independence now seemed both selfish and trivial in comparison.

Ian broke the uncomfortable silence. "How long did it take for you to travel here?"

"We left just..." Although unaware if the dwarves knew about the portal stones, she knew her father's preference that they remain a secret. Recalling her lessons on geography, combined with the fact that they traveled by foot, she replied, "Two weeks ago."

His brow furrowed. "I did not see any packs or provisions."

She shrugged while looking off into the distance, her mind scrambling for an answer. "We elves are attuned to nature." That much was true. "It is simple for us to find water and sustenance while traveling." That part was a stretch, but she assumed he would not question it. He did not.

"Ah," he nodded. "I must admit, I am intrigued by your people. I have only met one elf before now, and he is quite different."

"How so?"

"He is a dark elf." His voice cracked as he said it.

It sounds like he is afraid of this elf. "Our cousins to the north," she said, allowing her tone to show her derision.

"You do not like them?"

Dislike would be an understatement. "The Sylvan and the Drow have been at odds for centuries. This is no secret." She glanced at him, her brow furrowed. "You met one this far south?"

"Yes. He now lives here as part of a recent alliance."

"What is this alliance?"

Ian's eyes widened. "I...should not say."

Shria-Li's years of training in court intrigue screamed for her to know more. "Is there anything you can tell me?"

"I...don't know."

"This Drow. What is his name?"

Ian frowned before saying, "Rysildar."

The name was not unfamiliar to her. "I have heard the name. He is a singer of some renown."

"I suppose." Ian looked back at the open door. "I should go back to my post."

She reached out and gripped his hand. It was soft and lean, with long fingers, and could easily have belonged to one of her kind. "Please. Do not leave. I won't press you any longer."

"Very well."

"Tell me something of your people, of your home."

"I suppose there is no harm in that. However, if I am to share with you, I would ask you to do the same with me."

Shria-Li smiled. "I agree to that bargain."

Thus, Ian began describing a simple life in a small, far away village. Shria-Li allowed herself to imagine such a life, giving her a taste of the escape she longed to make. As he continued, she found herself becoming more and more captivated by his words. The peaceful fields, the humble homes, and the warm smiles of his people became images in her mind, soothing her anxiety. It was a stark contrast to the political intrigue and power struggles she had grown up with. She was so distracted by it all, that she didn't notice when Ian's words trailed off.

"Is something wrong?" he asked, noticing her distracted state.

She shook her head. "No, I'm sorry. I was just lost in thought."

Ian smiled. "I understand. It's easy to get lost in memories of home."

"You are obviously fond of your memories. I find myself jealous of your simple childhood."

"Didn't you grow up in some elegant palace?"

"I did, but that does not mean it was easy."

She began telling him things she had never shared with others. The more she said, the less weight seemed to press down on her. He asked poignant questions and appeared engaged in her every word. Soon, it felt as if she had found a long-lost brother. As an only child, having a brother was among her greatest unfulfilled wishes. So, she allowed herself to enjoy the cathartic nature of the conversation, oblivious to the darkening skies until a knock sounded at the door.

CHAPTER 14
CONFLICTING EMOTIONS

I an climbed a torchlit stairwell, keeping pace with Devigar, while trailed by King Fastellan, Princess Shria-Li, and a half dozen armed elves. Upon reaching the top floor, the procession followed a torchlit corridor lined by tapestries. The hallway ended at a square chamber occupied by a dozen armored dwarves bracketing a pair of ornate doors stained black. Devigar gestured as he approached the guards. Two of them responded to the wordless command, each opening a door and standing aside.

The chancellor paused in the doorway and announced Fastellan's arrival. Ian followed Devigar into a dining hall with a high, coffered ceiling supported by dark-stained oaken beams. Colorful murals of past battles covered the recessed, flat surfaces between the beams. Paintings and sculptures decorated the walls on three sides, the fourth covered in diamond-paned windows facing west. Outside, the setting sun painted an awestriking picture with pink and orange clouds contrasting a deep blue sky.

In the heart of the chamber was a long table surrounded by chairs to seat twenty. Warm light emanated from torches mounted to pillars at the edge of the room, and the massive, multi-tiered chandelier made of dark beams and black iron positioned directly over the table. Dark blue marble tiles with gold and white striations covered the floor, completing the scene.

Arangar stood arm in arm with a female dwarf at one side of the room. The king wore a white coat with red panels and gold buttons down the front, matching the golden crown resting on his bald head. The female wore a tiara in her black hair and a red gown on her stout frame. Although Ian had yet to meet Queen Pergoli, he knew it must be her.

The twelve council members stood along both sides of the table. All wore black robes with golden trim, some gripping staffs, others leaning on canes. Following Devigar's lead, Ian took position between Devigar and the council members.

Fastellan approached Arangar and dipped his head before speaking in Dwarvish. "Greetings, Arangar. Thank you for accommodating us despite the unannounced visit."

"Well met, Fastellan," Arangar dipped his head in return. "We welcome you and your daughter to Ra'Tahal."

"I offer my condolences for the loss of King Gahagar," said Fastellan. "He was...a force of nature."

Arangar's smile faltered. "He was the best of us. I miss him every day."

A brow on Fastellan's face twitched. "Well, the past is best left there, so rather than dwell on it, I congratulate your elevation to the throne."

"I...thank you." Arangar turned away. "Come. Let us sit, eat, and enjoy the evening."

The king walked to the far end of the table with his wife on his arm. A pair of servants emerged from the shadows, one a dwarf dressed in a stiff, black coat, the other a young blonde woman with a black dress fitted for her lean figure. Ian gasped, *Rina!* While he could not recall her ever looking less than beautiful, in that moment, she was particularly striking. His gaze clung to her as she and the other servant each grabbed a chair at the end of the table, pulled it out, and waited for the king and queen to slide in. They then pushed the chairs for Arangar and Pergoli as they sat.

Fastellan and his daughter approached the table, drawing Ian's attention away from Rina. He noticed the man's sparkling blue eyes affixed on Rina as she rounded the table and pulled out the seat opposite from Pergoli's. The elf king stopped before Rina, his hand lifting to stroke her cheek while she stared into his eyes.

"Who is this?" Fastellan asked in a distracted tone.

Pergoli said, "That is my handmaid, Safrina."

"She is a beauty. You must be proud." The king appeared reluctant to turn away, but did so before sitting while Rina pushed his chair in.

During this exchange, Shria-Li stood before the chair at Fastellan's side, her brow furrowed at him until the male servant behind her pushed her chair in, bumping the back of her legs and causing her to sit. Rina seemed to have remained rooted behind Fastellan, staring at the back of his head, until the male servant harshly tapped her on the arm, causing her to jerk in reaction. The two of them then moved down the table, pulling out chairs and pushing them in as the council members claimed their seats. They worked their way around the table until only Ian and Devigar remained. The chancellor sat beside Queen Pergoli and Ian beside him.

"Drinks!" Arangar proclaimed.

The two servants flitted out of the room, and Ian caught Fastellan watching Rina again. The way he stared at her gave Ian a creepy feeling and left him wondering why. Those seated at the table began to carry on with small talk, Arangar conversing with Fastellan, the council members among themselves, and Pergoli asking questions of Shria-Li, who frequently requested translations from Ian. Rina, the male servant, and two other female dwarves returned with carafes and began to fill the goblets on the table. Ian waited while the dark red liquid was poured into his goblet. He had only tried wine once and was reluctant to do so again. The last time had him drinking too much and the hangover had scarred him, leaving him sick for two days. Ironically, Rina had been with him at the time, the two of them getting so drunk they could barely walk. The memory caused him to smile and look up at her as she poured wine into Fastellan's goblet. Her eyes met his, and a smile flickered at the corners of her lips. He lifted his goblet and drank, the bitter liquid warming his throat and insides.

Baskets of baked bread and fresh fruit were set on the table, allowing the guests to pick at the food while chatting. The servants left and soon returned with plates occupied by cuts of steak, steaming potatoes, and green beans. A plate was placed before each guest, and the party began to eat. The clinking of cutlery against plates, tapping of goblets against the table, and smacking of lips echoed in the dining hall while everyone ate. Soon, the plates were emptied, all except for Ian's and Shria-Li's, which both remained half eaten. When the plates were taken away, King Arangar cleared his throat, drawing everyone's attention.

"While the Tahal Clan is honored by your presence, Fastellan, I assume you have come this far for more than a meal with a foreign king."

Fastellan sat back, his sapphire-like eyes intense. "As you know by now, nothing occurs between leaders for no reason." He paused as Arangar nodded. "Although the Sylvan were spared during Gahagar's quest to rule the world, we do not find ourselves free of strife. The creatures that roam the vale have become increasingly aggressive, and we now frequently find them in the southern highlands. They hunt our hunters, besiege our farms, and invade our cities. Even Havenfall endures attacks.

"As you know, our people replenish slowly, even compared to dwarves. We have lost ten percent of our population in the past decade, and if this continues, a mere fraction of the Sylvan will remain by the time a single generation turns."

Ian had studied the Sylvan language and culture enough to know that a generation covered eighty to a hundred years. Despite these studies, he understood little of the conversation. *What is the Vale? Where is Havenfall? What creatures does he speak of?* Knowing that his job was to interpret rather than inquire, he stifled those and other questions despite his raging curiosity.

"We sympathize with your plight, Fastellan," Arangar said, "But what does that have to do with us?"

"As you know, our kind cannot wield steel, its mere touch causing us pain. Wood is useful but is often too weak when dealing with monsters. We seek armor and weapons crafted of Dwarven steel. It is the lightest and strongest of metals, which is why other races value it so. To us Sylvan, who can wield it without pain, it is vital to our survival."

"Surely you must have armor and weapons already."

"Our armories were raided during Gahagar's campaign. Little remains of items crafted of Dwarven steel."

Arangar grimaced. "Our production slowed greatly over the past few decades. Only recently, after acquiring human slaves to work in the mines, have we even come close to our previous output. Even dwarven metal is susceptible to dragon fire and singer magic, both of which we encountered in heavy measure over the tail end of Gahagar's campaign. We seek to replenish our own armories."

The elf king narrowed his eyes. "I can offer cultivators to encourage your crops to grow and your fruit trees to flourish."

"Which would be greatly appreciated, but we are not in position to offer armor or weapons at this time."

After a brief pause, Fastellan adjusted tactics. "Our primary concern lies with protecting our people. With additional fortifications, Havenfall would become more defensible. If we could make a different sort of exchange, that might be achievable."

"Such as?"

"Send your stone shapers with me. Allow them to live and work at

Havenfall for one year. In exchange, I will not only supply you with cultivators, but I will allow a storm dancer to relocate to Ra'Tahal during that
span. Having influence over the weather can be useful for growing crops
and for defending your hold, should the need arise."

Arangar stared at Fastellan, the silence deafening. Finally, he said, "I
am surprised you have come to the Tahal clan with this proposal. Clan
Aeldor's land borders Sylvanar."

Fastellan shrugged. "I would be lying if I said that Kobblebon was
not approached first. However, he has no direct access to dwarven steel,
and when asked about stone shapers, he claimed there were none to
spare."

The dwarf king leaned back and stared at his empty plate. "Your
offer is most intriguing. I wish I could accept."

"Then do so, Arangar, for the good of both of our peoples."

"I cannot. Not even six weeks back, we sent the last of our stone
shapers north for similar reasons."

"North? To the dwarves in Domus Skrai?"

"No. To Talastar."

"The Drow?" Fastellan exclaimed. "Have you learned nothing from
history? They are not to be trusted."

"That was a concern, but Liloth offered certain reassurances. In fact,
a Drow singer now lives here and has taken an oath to obey my every
command during his stay. He is working on something special, something that will greatly benefit the clan."

The elf king grimaced and turned to his daughter before speaking
softly in Elvish, his voice barely loud enough for Ian to hear. "It is time
for us to leave." He stood and looked down at Arangar. "I have come here
to offer an alliance that would have benefitted both of our peoples, but
you have made your decision. When you side with the Drow, they are
certain to betray you. It is just a matter of time. We will depart first thing
tomorrow. Should we meet again, it will be you coming to me, begging
for help to repair the destruction laid upon you by a poor decision. I just

pray that the path you have chosen does not lead you and your people to ultimate doom." Fastellan turned and stormed toward the door.

His daughter stood, looked at Ian, and whispered in his native language. "I am sorry."

Before he could reply, she sped after her father. The elf guards joined them as they marched down the corridor, their fading footsteps echoing in the silent dining hall.

Pergoli snorted. "Elves are a haughty lot. They think themselves better than everyone else."

Arangar sighed. "That might be true, but, in this case, I worry. What if I made the wrong decision? Had we waited a few weeks and Fastellan had come to us before we committed to Queen Liloth, I suspect we would have gone another route." He rose to his feet. "This dinner is over. I wish to retire for the evening. We will convene in the Hall mid-day tomorrow."

The queen stood, took her husband's arm, and they headed to the corridor, where they were joined by a quartet of dwarf guards. The council members filed out, and soon, Ian sat alone with Devigar.

When everyone was beyond earshot, Devigar turned toward Ian. "Were you able to gain the confidence of the princess?"

A pang of guilt accompanied Ian's reply. "Yes."

"What did you learn?"

Ian had established a connection with Shria-Li, and by the time dinner began, she seemed like the sister he never had. He had shared with her, and she had done so in return. While he had never promised to keep her inner thoughts and feelings a secret, repeating them to Devigar felt as if he were betraying her.

"Ian," Devigar's tone hardened. "You are to tell me what she said. Now."

Trapped between friendship and duty, Ian hesitated a moment more before responding. "She does not get along well with her father."

The old dwarf nodded. "I suspected as much. Can you tell me why?"

"I believe she resents him and the fact that she is being groomed to take the throne should anything happen to him and her mother."

Devigar pressed his tented fingers to his lips. "Interesting. What else did you learn?"

Ian continued, spilling out every bit of information she had shared while hoping that the elf princess would not hate him for it...if he ever saw her again.

CHAPTER 15
A BAD SITUATION

Rina stood in the doorway at the far side of the dining hall, looking over the head and shoulder of Bucklegon, the head of the royal servant staff. Holgan and Guston, two of the keep staff servants, both of whom were dwarves, stood beside her, waiting. The dining hall had emptied some time earlier, except for the two robed individuals still seated at the table, their conversation too quiet and too distant to hear. She longed to enter the room, approach the table, and talk to Ian, but so long as he sat beside Chancellor Devigar, she had been strictly forbidden from doing so.

Devigar picked up his staff and leaned into it as he stood. He began toward the door, and Ian rose to follow. The moment the duo moved away from the table, Bucklegon gestured and crossed the room. Rina and the other two servants followed, the four of them spreading out while quickening their pace, so they arrived at the table at the same time. Rina stacked two plates on top of each other, lifted them with one hand, and scooped up a pair of empty goblets with the other. As she turned, she found Ian standing in the doorway and facing her while Devigar continued down the corridor.

"Hi, Rina," Ian said.

She glanced back at Bucklegon, who grimaced.

"Hello, Ian."

"Can you talk?"

Another backward glance found Bucklegon and the other two servants heading back toward the kitchen. She turned back to Ian. "Just for a minute. I am supposed to be working."

"I was surprised to see you tonight. It has been weeks." He gave her a shaky smile. "How have you been?"

She shrugged. "I am adapting. I understand enough of the language by now and what is expected of me, so I get by."

"Maybe Devigar will allow me to visit you from time to time? I could help to teach you Dwarvish."

"I..." Rina missed connecting with others, and Ian remained her best friend. "I would like that very much."

"Good." An unforced smile stretched across his face. "I will ask him first thing tomorrow. I believe I have earned his confidence enough to make it happen."

She longed to hug him but worried that she would cry if she did so. "I should be going."

His smile wilted. "I hope to see you soon."

"I do as well." Rina turned and headed back to the kitchen, having to pause as the other three emerged through the doorway, ready to gather another load.

"Festina!" Bucklegon blurted in a harsh whisper as he passed her.

She sighed, knowing that the word meant she was to hurry.

Two hours later – the dining room cleared, the dishes washed, dried, and put away, and the queen's clothing prepped for the next day – Rina returned to her chamber on the keep's third floor. She lit the candle, closed the door, and plopped on her bed with a sigh.

Her days had begun to blur together, each consisting of a monotonous series of menial tasks that left her sore and exhausted each and every evening. Life as a servant for a queen was not as grand as she once imagined. While Rina had longed to leave Shillings and employ herself as a servant for some wealthy woman in Darristan, she now wondered if such a life would have been any better than her current situation – a situation she despised.

Rina recalled her conversation with Ian and the pain in his eyes. While she didn't want him worrying about her, it was clear that he did so regardless. She wondered if he could really visit her with some frequency, and even if he was allowed, if she would be allowed to adjust her schedule to accommodate those visits. Either way, she found herself reluctant to place hope into the idea. Hope had become a rare and elusive commodity, and she feared being disappointed.

Rising to her feet, Rina stepped up to the vanity, picked up a wash-cloth, and dipped it into a bowl of clean water. She bent in front of her small mirror and began washing her face, as she did every evening. Consumed with the task, she did not hear the door open.

A flicker of motion in the mirror caused her to gasp and spin around as the candle was snuffed. A powerful hand clamped over her mouth, stopping her scream just before it emerged. She grappled with her attacker, but another pair of hands gripped her wrists and yanked her arms behind her back. Desperate, she kicked, her toe finding a target and eliciting a grunt. The hand covering her mouth pulled away, allowing her to catch a deep gasp. A strip of cloth wrapped around her head and slid into her mouth as she tried to scream. Someone picked her up and slammed her on the bed, face first. A heavy knee pressed against her back while securing the gag. A trio of moonlit silhouettes stood over the bed. Her wrists and ankles were bound before the attackers wrapped her in the covers from her bed. She felt herself hoisted up, a shoulder pressing into her stomach as her body was draped over an attacker. Heavy jostling shook her as she was carried down the stairs. Suddenly, she was out the door with cool night air seeping through the ends of the blanket wrapped around her.

Panic turned to terror. Someone had abducted her. She had no idea who, why, or what horrific intentions they had in mind. Tears flowed freely, her breath coming in ragged gasps as she was carried away.

CHAPTER 16
MYSTERIES

The balconies surrounding the Hall of Ancients were empty, the thirteen chairs on the dais full. On the side of the floor before the dais stood Ian and his master, Chancellor Devigar. The only other individual in the hall occupied the center of the floor, shadows clinging to his black robes despite the sunlight streaming in through the windows high above.

King Arangar sighed. "I will ask you again, Rysildar. Summer draws to an end, and you have yet to display any benefit to our city or our people, as was promised when we agreed to this alliance."

As Devigar translated for Rysildar, Ian recalled what his mentor had stressed before the meeting, Devigar's voice echoing in his head. *Remember to maintain a stoic expression. I cannot have Rysildar, Arangar, or the council members inferring something unintended because of your reaction.* What went unsaid in the discussion was that Devigar might adjust the messages between the two parties to ensure his intended result.

The Drow drew in a breath, the air around him shimmering like heat coming off a stone on a steamy summer day. "I have not been sitting idle. Singer magic is unique and often takes time to fully manifest. I assure you that my efforts will soon yield significant results."

After translated, Arangar asked, "How soon?"

"Within a cycle of the moon, I would expect."

A council member said, "What can we expect from these so-called efforts?"

Rysildar smiled, the action sending a chill down Ian's spine. "I'll not spoil the secret, but I assure you that it will change things in Ra'Tahal forever."

When Devigar finished translating, Arangar arched a brow while staring down at the Drow. After a moment, he said, "Very well. Another four weeks it is. At that time, I expect you to return and share your secret project with the council."

The dark elf dipped his head. "And you will have it, Your Majesty."

The hall doors opened, and Queen Pergoli stomped in. She positioned herself at the foot of the stairs and pressed her fists against her hips, her face a thundercloud.

The king frowned. "You are excused, Rysildar."

Before the message was even translated, the dark elf singer turned, glided down the stairs, and slipped out the door. When the door closed, Pergoli climbed the stairs and shot Ian a scowl, causing him to flinch.

"To what do we owe the pleasure, my Queen?" Arangar asked.

"Don't *my queen* me, Arangar," she snapped. "I want my handmaid back."

The king frowned. "What do you mean?"

"The human girl, Rina," Pergoli's voice climbed an octave. "She is nowhere to be found."

"Have you checked with the guards?" His tone was hopeful as he attempted to quell her anger. "Has she been seen out in the city? Did she go down to the lower hold?"

The queen threw her hands up. "Nobody has seen her. Considering her striking appearance, it would be unlikely for her to pass any male without notice. The guards assure me that no human has crossed in or out of the citadel. I have a squad combing the upper hold and another has been sent to the lower hold. However," she pointed at Ian. "I suspect *he* is hiding her."

"Me?" Ian blurted.

She strode toward Ian and waggled a finger at him. "It is no secret that the two of you are close."

Devigar spoke in an even tone. "Ian slept in his room last night and has been with me today since rising."

"Did you inspect his room?"

He blinked. "No. There was no cause to do so."

"There is cause now. In fact, I have guards doing so even as we speak." She thrust a finger at Ian again. "If she is found before you confess your involvement, I will have you flogged. In public. Naked."

Ian swallowed the lump in his throat and waved his hands, desperate for her to believe him. "I swear, I don't know what you are talking about."

Her eyes narrowed. "You and she shared a private conversation last night after dinner, as three witnesses have already confirmed."

"Um...Yes." His eyes flicked around the hall. Everyone's attention was on him, the intensity in their gazes burning into him like sunlight through a magnifying glass. "We spoke briefly, and then I returned to Devigar's Tower. I have not seen her since."

The queen crossed her arms over her plentiful chest. "We shall see."

Devigar turned to the dais. "My king, if you are finished with my apprentice and I, it might be best if we addressed this issue directly."

Arangar nodded. "I agree. That is why I am assigning the two of you with the task of tracking the young woman down. You have full reign to go wherever needed and to interrogate anyone who might lead you to her location. In fact, I will have an official writ drafted as soon as I return to my chambers. Do not come to me again unless you have tangible leads or have my wife's handmaid in your custody."

The briefest of scowls passed over Devigar's face before he smiled and bowed. "As you wish, Your Majesty."

The old dwarf spun, walked past the disgruntled queen, and descended the stairs leading to the entrance hall. Ian cast one last glance toward the king before rushing to catch up to his master. Once outside, neither of them spoke until they were beyond earshot of the guards posted near the outside door.

Devigar stopped and turned toward Ian. "Do you promise you had nothing to do with this?"

"I promise." Ian shook his head. "In truth, I am worried about Rina."

"Good. You have a sharp mind, Ian. It is time for you to put it to use." Devigar resumed walking as he headed toward his tower.

Ian caught up to him. "How so?"

"Figure out what happened to her. Since the queen wishes to place blame on you, that should provide motivation even if you did not already care about this missing girl."

While Ian was eager to find Rina, he instantly felt overwhelmed by the responsibility of conducting the search for her. Should he fail, he would fail her, his master, and King Arangar. He sought to free himself of burden, his mouth working but no sound coming out until he asked, "What about you?"

Devigar stopped and turned to Ian. "I have other issues that require attention, so I am leaving this one up to you." He gave Ian a level gaze. "Your search begins now. Do not disappoint me." The old dwarf walked off, leaving Ian alone beneath the midday sun.

A PAIR of dwarf guards trailed Ian and Bucklegon, the head of the keep staff, as they climbed a staircase to the second floor. The four of them approached Rina's bedroom, the closed door and silence giving Ian chills. Bucklegon dug out a ring of keys, sorted through them, and slid one into the lock. A turn and a click later, he opened the door. Ian walked past him and looked around the room while squashing his feelings toward Rina. He needed to keep an open and clear mind if he was to find her.

The only chair in the room lay on its back. An empty bowl and a used washcloth lay on the floor beside the chair. The bed was unmade, and the red quilt that normally covered it was missing.

Ian wandered around the chamber, looking for anything that was unfamiliar or unexpected but found nothing. He turned to Bucklegon. "This is exactly how you found the room this morning?" He squatted and felt the carpet near the bowl. It was wet.

"Yes. When Rina didn't appear for the morning dispositions, I filled in for her by serving his and her majesties breakfast. Once the king had gone off to meet with the council, I visited this room, seeking her. The door was not locked, and Rina was nowhere to be found. So, I locked the door and headed straight for the royal chambers to inform the queen. That is when the guards became involved."

Ian stood and rubbed his jaw. Soft hair covered it, but the growth was spotty, leaving short patches amid longer ones. It was an odd feeling he was still growing used to, as was the image he saw when looking in a mirror.

He considered everything in the room while recalling his last visit and how the chamber should appear. The clues slid together to form a clear image, one that caused a shiver of dread to snake down his spine.

Pushing his feelings aside, Ian spoke as if reading from a report written by another, "Someone broke in this room when she was washing, causing her to spill the water and drop the washcloth." He turned to the bed, covered only in a sheet. "They used the quilt somehow, either to bind her or to hide her, and then snuck out."

Bucklegon frowned. "Even if this were true, who would do this and how would they escape the keep? Guards are posted at all entrances, night and day."

"That requires more thought," Ian admitted. "However, until I come up with something, I will assume she is still in the keep. Somewhere." He drew a deep breath, resigned to the task. "That is why we will now conduct a search of every room in the building."

"This is a twelve-story structure," Bucklegon warned. "It will take some time."

"Then, we had best get started."

THE SEARCH of the keep consumed the entire afternoon. Despite his attempt to seek out any possible clue to Rina's whereabouts or who might have been involved, Ian found no answers.

He then moved on to question the guards who were on duty the night before. Not one of them saw anyone leave the keep after Ian and Devigar, at least not until early morning when King Fastellan's guards exited, visited the stables, and returned with the palanquin. About an hour later, Fastellan, his daughter, and two more Sylvan warriors exited the keep. The king and the princess climbed in and the palanquin was carried off toward the gate. The next time anyone left the building was mid-morning when the council members headed off to the Hall of Ancients. The king left shortly after, and then Rina's disappearance was realized.

Ian recorded the timeline and noted all comings and goings in a journal. Pieces of the puzzle had been found, but others were missing. Worse, how they fit together was yet a mystery. The only three ways in or out of the keep were guarded day and night. *How could someone pass by without notice?* Since he could not come up with a practical answer, he chose to pursue a mystical one. *Magic.*

He turned to the two guards who had been accompanying him all day. "It is time to go visit Rysildar."

Vargan grimaced. "The Drow singer?"

The other dwarf, Ipsegar, blanched. "You think he had something to do with it?"

"I don't know. Can singer magic turn someone invisible or make them disappear altogether?"

The two dwarves shrugged, Vargan responding, "We know little of Drow magic."

"What do you know?" Ian asked.

Ipsegar snorted. "To stay away from it."

In truth, Ian felt the same way. However, Rina was his friend, and he was determined to pursue the truth. He looked up at pink clouds over the city. "The sun is setting. Let's go there right now. I would rather not visit him in the dark."

"If you are determined to do talk to him, I agree. In the dark would be worse." Vargan nodded. "Let's go see the Drow." .

The three of them set off down the street and came to the building where the singer lived. The main floor consisted of four shops: a bakery, a butcher, a tailor, and a cobbler. Each of the three upper floors contained two apartments. Ian and the guards climbed a stairwell, turning at each level before reaching the top floor. Choosing the door on the left, Vargan knocked. A long silence followed before the door opened to reveal a dark interior and a figure in black standing in the doorway.

In Elvish, Ian said, "Good evening, Singer." He coughed as his throat tightened. His heart thumped like it wanted to leap out of his chest, his stomach churned, making him afraid he might need to run to a privy. The worst was the sweat, leaving his armpits damp and his hands sloppy with it. "I have come as part of an inquiry."

"An inquiry?" Rysildar spoke in a derisive tone. "What have you come to blame me for now, you little cretin?"

"I...I am sorry about the last time." Ian still believed he had not imagined what he saw, but as time passed, his conviction had waned. Now, his greatest concern was finding Rina. "A girl has gone missing. A human girl."

"What does that have to do with me?"

Ian pressed forward. "The girl was the handmaid to Queen Pergoli. She disappeared last night. I need to know where you were between sunset and your appearance today at the Hall of Ancients."

The Drow waved a long, pale finger. "I spent the night as I do every night, focusing my magic on the gift I am preparing for King Arangar and the council. I then slept until mid-morning, waking in time to appear in the hall before the king, as requested."

Ian frowned. "Do you have any proof?"

"I work alone. How could I prove my presence without a witness?"

Without a reasonable answer to the question, Ian turned to frustration. "The girl could not exit the keep without the guards being aware, so we suspect magic. Singer magic seems capable of such a feat."

"Ah. I see. Your ignorance about magic has you applying guilt to one who uses it, regardless of you possessing any proof."

The conversation was not going as Ian had hoped. "I did not say you were guilty. I said that your magic seems capable."

Rysildar nodded. "That it is. In fact, I can think of five different ways I might secretly sneak someone out without notice. However, in this case, I have no cause to do so. In fact, I do not even know this girl you seek."

Ian clenched his fist. It felt like he was going in circles.

"However," Rysildar said, "I was not the only magic user in the city last night. Another visited the city and slept in the keep. He carries a staff known to contain great power."

Blinking at the accusation, Ian asked, "Fastellan?"

"Were I you, I would focus my efforts there. Now, be on your way. You have wasted enough of my time." The Drow closed the door.

Ian turned toward the dwarven guards.

Vargan asked in Dwarvish, "What did he say?"

"He claims himself innocent and instead implicated King Fastellan."

Both dwarves snorted, and Vargan replied, "I am not surprised. The Drow and the Sylvan have been at odds for centuries."

"What if he is right?" While Ian had not originally considered Fastellan, the idea that the elf king might be responsible now seemed more than possible. *He was in the keep when Rina disappeared and then left the citadel early the morning of her disappearance.* The facts clicked into place and the elf king became the most likely culprit.

Vargan glanced at Ipsegar, who grimaced. "The king did leave in a rush this morning. As I hear, he was out of the city at first light."

"He was angry after dinner and said as much," Ian noted. "Would he resort to abduction as a way to get back at Arangar and Pergoli?" While it seemed too childish for the aloof, regal elf king, the dots connected too easily to ignore.

Rubbing the soft whiskers on his jaw, Ian began down the stairs. *Pergoli is angry about Rina's disappearance, and that anger has spilled over onto Arangar. Would the king of a rival nation steal a slave servant just to spite another king?*

He reached the street level and stared up at the darkening sky. Hundreds of stars were visible, soon to become thousands. *Rina, wherever you are, I pray that you are safe.*

Fourteen Hours Earlier

"SHRIA-LI!" her father's voice stirred her awake.

She rolled over in the bed and sat up to the dim light of predawn seeping through the bedroom window. The unfamiliar setting gave her a moment of pause until she recalled the trip to Ra'Tahal and the tense dinner the prior evening. "What is happening?"

"Get dressed. We are leaving." His tone was gruff. Urgent.

Rubbing her eyes she asked, "Why so early?"

"Don't ask questions. Just do it. Now." He pulled the door closed, leaving her alone.

She rolled out of bed, picked her breeches off the floor, and slid them on. Moments later, she was fully dressed and opened the bedroom door. Her father stood in the sitting room with the Staff of Life in his grip. He opened the door and led her into the keep corridor, where a pair of guards waited.

"Where are the others?" she asked.

In a whisper, he said, "With the palanquin. Now hush. We don't wish to disturb anyone."

The four elves descended to the main level, passed the guards posted at the door, and emerged in a dark courtyard still in the grip of evening shadow. The faintest hint of light graced the eastern horizon, beyond the citadel's outer wall. Following her father, Shria-Li approached the palanquin, where six of their warriors stood, waiting.

As Fastellan reached for the curtain, he held a finger up in Shria-Li's face. "Make no noise. Do you hear me?"

"I..." She recognized the gravity in his voice, filling her with alarm. She didn't understand why, but he was worried about something. In a hushed tone, she said, "I will be silent."

He drew the curtain back and gestured. "Get in."

She ducked and climbed in the dark interior, gasping when she felt the warm skin of someone's arm.

Her father climbed in, "Hush, now." In a whisper he said, "I want to hear nothing from you until we are far from Ra'Tahal."

Shria-Li shied away from the person hidden amid the pillows. The palanquin was hoisted onto the elves' shoulders and it began moving through the narrow citadel streets. Soon, they came to a stop. Fastellan stuck his head out and spoke in Dwarvish. A city guard replied and the clanking of chains disturbed the quiet of morning as the portcullis opened. Soon, the palanquin was again moving, this time at a jog. All the while, Shria-Li wondered who was in the palanquin and why.

The sun edged over the horizon and sunlight shone through a gap in the curtains. In the light of that gap, she spied a soft, young face with sparkling blue eyes and hair of gold. Her mouth was gagged, her wrists and ankles bound.

"The queen's handmaid?" Shria-Li did not even attempt to hide her surprise.

"Yes," Fastellan said.

Her tone turned accusatory. "You abducted her."

"I did."

"Why?"

"I am king. You should not question my actions." He held a finger at her face before lowering it. "However, if Arangar will not help our people, he will suffer for it. In this case, the suffering will come from his wife as she complains about the loss of her personal servant."

"Stealing a slave to make a rival ruler's life more difficult?" Shria-Li frowned. "That is awfully petty."

"True, but she will make a fine servant in Havenfall palace...for you."

"For me?" The slave woman who had acted as Shria-Li's servant and tutor had died earlier that year.

"I thought you would be happy."

She crossed her arms and glanced down at the bound woman, her eyes wide in horror. The abduction and his reasoning for it were out of character for her father, leaving her certain there was something he was not telling her, but she could not fathom what that might be.

Minutes later, the palanquin stopped and slowly sank to the ground. She emerged to a shadowy glade surrounded by tall oaks. Fastellan stood and nodded to his captain. "Put the palanquin on the stone but leave the woman inside. We will free her bonds after the translocation."

He climbed onto the portal stone and Shria-Li joined him. They both crossed to the center while their escort lifted the palanquin onto the platform. When everyone was in position, he inserted the staff into the hole in the center of the stone's surface. A bright light bloomed, the runes on the stone glowing as a white light blotted out the surrounding trees.

CHAPTER 17

HAVENFALL

Bound, gagged, and out of tears from a day of crying, Rina lay curled on her side, her body shaking to the rhythmic jostling of the palanquin.

The day had dragged by agonizingly slowly. Three times, the elves had stopped to rest. During each, her gag was briefly removed and the girl elf would pour water down her throat. Shria-Li was the name she had given. To Rina's surprise, the female elf spoke her language. Despite providing reassurances that Rina would not be harmed, the gag was put back in place and the journey resumed.

The palanquin stopped, causing Rina to roll onto her back as it was set down. The curtains opened and the elf king climbed out. His voice echoed as he spoke to someone. Other male voices responded, their conversation in the elegant, flowing language of elves.

Shria-Li leaned over Rina. "I am going to untie your gag. Do not scream. It will only make him angry. Do you understand?"

Rina nodded. Her fear would have held her silent even without the warning.

When the gag was removed, Rina breathed in deeply and worked her jaw. She froze when she saw Shria-Li holding a dagger.

"Do not worry," The female elf said. "I am going to cut your bonds."

The elf princess rolled Rina onto her side and sawed at the ropes around her wrists. The ropes securing her ankles came next. Freed, Rina sat up and rubbed her wrists, the skin raw from chafing.

"You are to follow me." Shria-Li pulled the curtain aside and climbed out.

Anxiety tinted with a shade of curiosity stirred in Rina's empty stomach. She crawled out of the palanquin, rose to her feet, and looked around. Her swirling emotions settled, the anxiety and curiosity replaced by awe.

She stood in a courtyard illuminated by golden light coming from a massive, towering tree in the center. Light glinted off the tree leaves, as if they were made of metal...golden metal. The lowest branches were a hundred feet above her, the tree's pinnacle ten times that height. High above the tree, stars dotted the night sky.

Walls with twenty-foot-tall arches bordered three sides of the courtyard, the fourth open to a city made of arches, domes, multi-tiered buildings, and elegant, narrow towers capped by cone-shaped roofs. Just as in the courtyard, trees with golden leaves stood among the buildings, each emitting a soft glow that staved off the darkness of night. It was the most beautiful sight Rina had ever seen. Transfixed, she turned slowly while drinking in the stunning vista.

"Where are we?" Rina muttered.

"Welcome to Havenfall, your new home."

Rina spun toward the girl elf. "My home? Why?"

"I...do not know, exactly." Shria-Li's golden green eyes stared into Rina's. "I suspect you are hungry."

"Famished."

"Good. We shall eat, and I will attempt to answer your questions." She arched a brow. "You do have questions, yes?"

"I...yes."

"Come along."

The elf slid a graceful hand with long, elegant fingers against Rina's back. The soft pressure urged her forward, toward a waiting arch. They passed beneath the arch and crossed a shadowy area with a high ceiling. Another arch waited ahead. As they approached the opening, the view beyond it expanded to reveal another tree even larger than the last. This tree stood on an island in the center of a pool. A garden of flowers, arches, trellises, shrubs, and meandering paths bordered the pool. A palace consisting of buildings with pointed arches for roofs and towering spires overlooked the tree, the pool, and the garden.

The two of them followed the path through the garden, the sweet scent of flowers thick in the air. White, purple, blue, pink, red, and yellow petals stood out among the green foliage. The garden, the tranquil pool, and the golden tree, combined to create a sense of peace unlike anything Rina had ever experienced. The path turned toward the palace, the impressive structure looming over the two females like a mountain. They climbed a flight of stairs, passed beneath another arch, and began down a broad corridor tiled in white marble.

Shria-Li led Rina through the palace's grand archways and halls, each decorated with intricate carvings and embellishments that must have taken years to complete. The sheer scale and beauty overwhelmed Rina, causing her to gasp and drop her jaw again and again. She had never seen anything like it.

Finally, they arrived at a small dining room, where a table was set with an array of foods that Rina had never seen before. There were fruits and vegetables she couldn't name, cuts of various cheeses and slices of meats that looked like they belonged to strange animals. Despite her hunger, she hesitated.

Shria-Li noted her reluctance as she sat down at the table. "Do not worry, Rina. None of it is harmful. In fact, you might find it quite delicious." She picked up a red, egg-shaped fruit and took a bite.

Rina settled into a seat and, with some trepidation, picked up a slice of cheese. It was slightly bitter with a spice that tantalized her tongue. She moved on to sample the fruit, some sweet, some sour, all juicy and delicious. The meats were even more surprising. The food was unlike anything she had ever tasted before. The flavors were rich and complex, and every bite made her taste buds come alive. She ate with fervor, her stomach eager after a full day of fasting.

As her hunger quelled, her pace slowed to match that of Shria-Li, who stared across the table at Rina. Finally, Rina's need for sustenance was sated, but she still hungered for answers.

She swallowed a piece of fruit and looked across the table. "You said that I could ask questions."

Shria-Li wiped her mouth and set her napkin aside. "That, I did."

The day had been frightful, confusing, and as traumatic as any Rina had experienced. Thus, it took her a moment to sort through her churning thoughts, trying to decide where to start. "Why did you take me from Ra'Tahal?'

A distaste turned the elf's mouth to a frown. "I did not. My father did. As for why...he claims that he wanted to cause Arangar some difficulty and thought that angering Queen Pergoli would spill over on the king."

At Pergoli's name, Rina grimaced. "The queen is an insufferable, cruel harpy."

Shria-Li laughed. "She would not be the first in her position to develop unreasonable expectations and find pleasure in mistreating her help."

"Well, I can't say that I am sorry to be freed from the weight of her thumb. However, there are others I already miss..."

Thoughts of Ian, Vic, and the other villagers still in Ra'Tahal came to Rina. *I am alone*, she thought. Another voice in her head replied, *You were alone before. Only Ian came to see you and only twice in an entire season.*

Shria-Li, reached across the table and rested her hand on Rina's "Is that why you look so sad?"

"In part." Rina once again found herself in a foreign place, not of her own volition and worried that she had simply exchanged one prison for another. She asked the question she feared to have answered, "Am I free to go where I wish?"

"I am sorry," the elf princess shook her head. "You are to live in the palace as my attendant."

Her lips tightened. "I see. Will I be paid?"

"No."

"So, I am a slave." *Again.* Anger sizzled, the heat burning away the fear and sorrow.

"We have many human slaves."

"Does that make it better?"

Shria-Li's gaze dropped to the table. "It is the way of things and has been for many centuries." She lifted her face, her eyes meeting Rina's. "This does not mean you will be treated poorly. If you do as commanded, all will be well. Havenfall is a special place."

Rather than dwell on the word *commanded*, she followed her curiosity. "Havenfall? I have never heard of it."

"We are in the capital city of the Sylvan, located in the heart of Sylvanar and a thousand miles west of Ra-Tahal."

Rina jerked back at the statement and then furrowed her brow. "Unless I was unconscious and missed it, we traveled only a day from Ra-Tahal."

A wry smile appeared on Shria-Li's face. "A day of travel is what you experienced, but I can assure you, we covered a thousand miles since departing this morning."

"How is that possible?"

"Magic, of course. Ask no more about it, for I cannot share details. Some things must remain a secret, even from my own people."

Magic. It was a mystical term that elicited the sensations of possibility and fear in equal measure.

"You speak my language," Rina said. "Is that common among your kind?"

"Not at all. As princess and heir to the throne, I am required to learn all languages. Yours was the most intriguing, particularly since my prior nursemaid, Katarina, was human and spoke it as well as Elvish."

"So, if I am to fit in here, I will need to learn your language as well." Just when Rina had learned enough of Dwarvish to get by without causing problems, she had a new language to master.

"You will, but do not worry. I will teach you. In return, you will share your knowledge with me when requested." Shria-Li stood. "Now, come. We can retire to our rooms. I am exhausted."

The corridor, lined by paintings of colorful vistas, elegant cities, and trees of golden leaves, led them to a stairwell. Ascending to the third floor, they followed a catwalk bordered by round columns. Arches spanning from column to column supported a high ceiling. A garden with a fountain waited below to one side, the tree on the island to the other. The catwalk took them to a tower, where they climbed once again. Three more flights up, Shria-Li opened a door and led Rina into a chamber with six walls, five of which included a single door. The sixth was covered by windows and a glass door leading to a balcony, beyond which shone the golden aura of a giant tree. A divan, a pair of lounge chairs, and a round table with wooden chairs occupied the room.

"These are my quarters," Shria-Li said as she led Rina around the room. At the first door, she gestured. "This is my study." Soft, golden light coming through the window revealed a desk, two chairs, and a wall of shelves covered in books. As she passed the next room, the princess said, "This is my bedroom." A four-poster bed surrounded by sheer drapery occupied the chamber, along with a nightstand, a vanity, a wardrobe, and a chest large enough for Rina to fit in. "This is the bathing room." A marble dais stood in the center of the room, the middle of the dais recessed and filled with water. Towels were draped from a rack near the window. "A privy resides in the small chamber in the corner. The golden rope hanging above it releases water into the privy. Pull the rope when you are finished." She moved on to the next room, this time entering the chamber. Waving her hand over a globe on the nightstand near the door caused the globe to glow with golden light. A bed for one, a vanity, and a wardrobe completed the chamber's furnishings. "This is your room. I know it isn't much. My last attendant lived here for fifty-eight years before she died."

Rina frowned. "Fifty-eight years? Aren't you my age?"

Shria-Li laughed. "Hardly. This was my seventy-second summer."

The statement caused Rina to blink in disbelief. "How is that possible?"

With a smirk, the princess added, "My father is a hundred thirty-five and is still considered young among my people."

"So, in sixty years, when I am graying, you will look like he does now?"

"I suppose."

The idea shocked Rina. "You have so much time...you could do anything with your life."

A cloud darkened Shria-Li's face. "I do not have such freedom."

"You are a princess. Can't you do whatever you wish?"

"Duty requires otherwise." She walked out the door. "It is late. We should sleep. Tomorrow, we will see about getting you suitable clothing. Rest well, Safrina." The princess closed the door, leaving Rina alone.

She sat on the bed and glanced around the room. It was twice as large as her chamber in Ra'Tahal, which was already bigger than her room back in Shillings. Thoughts of her simple life in the village brought her to the realization that she had been raised without any knowledge of the world. In the passing of fifteen weeks, her life had been turned upside down and inside out. Here she sat, in a palace halfway across the world, living with the princess of a race she didn't believe even existed just a season ago. Destiny had swept her up in a storm and dropped her into a completely different life. After her brother's death, she had no family, and now she had even been taken from Ian, her closest friend. Regardless of her actions, she found herself helplessly caught in a heavy current, sweeping her toward something unknown. She prayed that the unknown would not become a frightening plummet to an ugly end.

CHAPTER 18

HIDDEN TREASURE

Dust swirled in the air and clung to Vic's sweat-covered skin. He swung the pick repeatedly, eating away at the wall as chunks of earth broke free and tumbled to the cavern floor. Dim lighting gave shape to the narrow tunnel where he worked. Alone. Perspiration ran down his forehead and into his eye, the sting forcing him to take a break and wipe his brow. Beyond the rasp of his breaths, noises of the other miners on his shift echoed in the adjacent chamber. When asked why he chose to branch off and carve his own tunnel, Vic had replied that he wanted to make something himself. In truth, he needed it as a form of personal fulfillment. Rising each day with the goal of advancing his tunnel deeper into the earth had given him purpose, and in that purpose, he found a sense of accomplishment that would keep him sane.

He downed a long drink of water from the skin on his shoulder, regripped the pick, wound back, and swung. Again and again, he struck the wall, the rock chipping, cracking, splitting. And on the next swing, the pick broke through all the way to the shaft.

"What the...?"

He yanked the pick free. A chunk of stone came with it and fell to the floor, leaving an opening in the wall, a soft glow emanating from it.

Vic bent and peered through the opening into a neighboring cavern. Warmth radiated from the opening. Inspired by the discovery, he stood, wound back, and drove the pick into the wall, breaking another section free. He set the pick down, squatted, and stuck his arms through the opening. His head and body followed. With his palms firmly placed on the cavern floor, he walked them forward and pulled his legs through. Rising to his feet, he dusted off his hands and looked around.

Warm light shimmered from a crevice at the far end of the cavern and shone on the domed ceiling sixty feet above. The floor consisted of descending tiers leading toward the crevice, beside which stood an object eliciting a curiosity inside Vic unlike any he had ever known. Drawn like a moth to firelight, he climbed down to the next tier, crossed it, and climbed down again. The air grew hotter as he neared the crevice and the object beside it.

Sitting upright, amid a nest of gray rock, was an egg taller than Vic's six feet. The egg's surface shimmered with an iridescence of swirls that seemed to shift and flicker in the warm light. As he circled the egg, he glanced down into a pool of red hot, bubbling lava. When he looked up, he discovered a round shaft rising up from the cavern. Dim light outlined a circular opening at the far end of the shaft, hundreds of feet above him. *That must be why I can breathe*, Vic realized. The shaft allowed fresh air in while expelling some of the heat.

Turning his attention back to the egg, Vic put his hand against it. The surface was hot, nearly too hot to touch. When in contact with the egg, he felt something unexpected. A heartbeat. Enthralled, Vic circled the egg while running his hand along the smooth shell, stopping with the egg between him and the heat radiating from the pool. There, he leaned against the egg, his palms and forehead pressed against it. The heartbeat in the egg thumped like a drum calling to him. Something alive lurked inside the egg, something big.

Vic stood there for a time, listening to the heartbeat like an echo of his own. He longed to remain but the day was waning, his shift ending soon. Concern settled in, drawing him away from the egg. *I cannot allow anyone else to find this.* He swiftly ascended the rocky shelves, returned to the hole in the wall, and crawled through it. Once on the other side, he picked up the last chunk of rock and fit it back into place. The next piece blocked most of what remained of the hole.

Vic stepped back and admired his work, unable to see any of the warm light from the cavern beyond. Satisfied, he began to lift chunks of rock off the ground and set them into the waiting cart. When finished, he pushed the cart along the tunnel and emerged in the chamber where the other miners worked.

To one side, Brady, Paulson, Chaz, Rodrick, and Fez swung picks at the wall, chipping away chunks of rock striped with metallic layers. To the other, Terrick, Wes, Nells, and Matlock bent, lifted, and stacked chunks into carts.

The ring of a bell echoed down the tunnel connecting the chamber to the rest of the mine. As one, the picks stopped, the men dropping them to the floor and wiping their brows. Those loading carts began pushing them down the tunnel, toward the crusher.

Brady walked up to Vic, eyeing the cart. "Your load seems a bit light today."

Vic shrugged, doing his best to appear nonchalant. "I reached the end of the vartanium veins. I'll have to work on expanding the tunnel width starting tomorrow."

The others lumbered out of the cavern and down the tunnel.

"What if we all ran out of vartanium?" Brady mused. "Do you think the dwarves would let us go?"

"I have no idea," Vic admitted. "I'm beat. Let's go get some food."

The two of them headed down the tunnel as men from the night shift came toward them. Vic watched closely, seeking Danrick, who like him, had taken the lead for his shift. When Danrick approached Vic, he intercepted the man and informed him that he had reached the end of the vartanium deposit, ensuring that he understood that going any deeper would only be a waste of time. Danrick thanked Vic and sent him on his way.

A five-minute underground walk, including a ride on the lift, brought Vic and Brady outside. As had become his habit, Vic paused beneath the open sky and took a deep breath, savoring the moment.

To the west, beyond the buildings and walls of the Lower Hold, the sun licked the treetops. It would soon set and bring night with it. By then, Vic would have cleaned up, eaten, and be lying in his bunk.

They followed the gravel path toward the bunkhouse. As they rounded a building, a pair of dwarf guards came into view. With them was a taller, thinner figure in tan robes.

Vic forgot his hunger and exhaustion. "Ian!"

Ian nodded as he approached. "Hi, Vic. Hi, Brady. I was hoping I might run into you guys."

Vic said, "Where have you been? It has been weeks since I last saw you."

"I have been busy. Summer has come to an end, and with the new season, Devigar has given me additional duties."

The statement was a shock to Vic. "We have been here an entire season?"

"I am afraid so."

Brady asked, "What are you doing down here today?"

"Investigating."

Vic frowned. "Investigating what?"

A sadness softened Ian's gaze and a hint of desperation sank into his tone. "I am looking for Rina."

His gaze going to the citadel perched on the cliff above them, Vic asked, "Isn't she somewhere up there?" He turned back toward Ian. "I thought she was working for Queen Pergoli."

"Until two days ago, she was. Now..." Ian looked like he might cry.

An unease settled in Vic's stomach. "What happened?"

Ian swallowed visibly, his lip quivering as if he were afraid to say the words. "Rina has...disappeared."

"What? How?"

"Since Rina arrived in Ra'Tahal, she did not leave the keep, not without the queen's leave, which was never given. Yet, she is not there. The building is always guarded, but the dwarven warriors who man those posts insist that Rina never left. I conducted a thorough search of the keep, the city, and now the lower hold. Nobody has seen her and no clues to her whereabouts have been found. I even searched the chicken coups, barns, and every other building in the lower hold. The only area in the citadel that remains unsearched is the mine."

Vic shook his head. "I know those tunnels as well as anyone, Ian. She is not there."

Ian's shoulders slumped, his chin dropping to his chest. "Then, she is truly gone." Tears tracked down his cheeks. He wiped them away and sniffled.

Brady asked, "How could she have gotten out of the keep in the first place?"

Lifting his face, Ian sniffled again before making a fist. "Magic."

The response earned him a snort from Brady. "You cannot be serious."

Vic nudged him. "Consider where we are, Brady. Do you still think that magic is merely the stuff of fireside tales?"

The boy's smile slid away. "I suppose there might be some truth to those stories."

"I suspect that the truth outstrips the stories," Ian replied. "I also believe that some arts deal with a darkness that is best to avoid."

The way Ian responded gave Vic the impression that something had affected Ian. "Have you seen magic used in the citadel?"

"I have, by a dark elf."

"A what?" Brady sounded incredulous.

"Believe it, Brady. This elf is the creepiest person I have ever seen. He lives in the citadel and is up to something, but I have yet to figure out what." Ian pressed his lips together, his nostrils flaring. "But he is not the only elf that has been to the city. Fastellan, king of Sylvanar, visited just a few days ago and left the very same morning Rina disappeared."

Vic said, "Maybe this king had something to do with it."

"That is what I am afraid of. The thing is, why? Even if I could come up with a motive, how do I prove it? As I understand, he lives a thousand miles west of here."

Vic rubbed his bearded jaw. He hadn't been able to shave since his capture, and he was still getting used to the beard. It had filled in well, a dark brown that framed his jawline and made his brown eyes pop. Although he could think of nothing to help Ian with his search for Rina, Vic's own recent discovery begged to be shared with someone. He did not trust any of the miners, not even Brady. Ian was another matter.

"Why don't you go eat, Brady." Vic pointed toward the bunkhouse. "I need a moment alone with my brother."

"Be well, Ian," Brady nodded. "I hope you find Rina."

"So do I," Ian replied.

When Brady was out of earshot, Vic glanced toward the two guards waiting for Ian. Both stared in their direction but stood far enough away. Quietly, he said, "I found something."

Ian frowned. "Something? Where?"

"In the mine. Today, I broke through to an underground cavern. A fissure with a lava pool at the bottom heats the cavern. Beside the fissure, nestled among rocks, is an egg."

"An egg? By itself?"

"Yes. And this egg is big. Really big." Vic held his hand above his head. "This tall." He held out his arms. "And this wide."

"Maybe it is petrified or something?"

"I felt a heartbeat coming from the egg." The excitement Vic had felt upon his discovery returned in force. "Something is inside it. Something alive."

Ian's eyes widened. "How could this be?"

"I don't know." Vic's eyes flicked to the guards again. There were other questions he longed to have answered. Ian was the smartest person he knew. More importantly, he had access to information few others could equal. "Your master has books, doesn't he?"

"Devigar? He has more books than I ever imagined even existing. That is how I learned to read in the first place."

"Could you, do some research for me? Maybe one of those books can tell us what is in the egg."

Ian nodded. "That is an excellent idea."

Not only did Vic desperately want more information, he also hoped that the new objective would take Ian's mind off Rina's disappearance. He glanced toward the sun, now hidden behind the treetops.

"I should get going, or there won't be any food left." Vic gripped Ian's arm. "Take care of yourself."

"You, too, Vic."

The two brothers walked in opposite directions, Vic returning to the bunkhouse he shared with the other miners, Ian to Chancellor Devigar's tower in the upper hold.

As he approached the building, Vic thought back to Ian's behavior during the conversation. He exhibited distrust of the dark elf, and that left Vic worried. *Please, Ian, don't go seeking trouble.*

CHAPTER 19

BARGAINS

The sound of a door opening behind him caused Ian to turn as Devigar entered. Ian set his quill down, leaned back, and stretched.

Devigar approached the desk, lifted a sheet of parchment covered in runes, and examined it. "This is impressive." He shook his head. "One would never believe that you did not know how to read or write just a season ago."

The compliment had Ian beaming. "Thank you, master."

The old dwarf eyed the stack of paper Ian had already finished and then picked up the book from which Ian had been recording. "You will soon be finished with this one."

Ian nodded. "I should finish tomorrow."

"For your next subject, I may need to give you something more challenging to focus your efforts upon."

Ian bit his lip while gathering his courage. "Master?"

"Yes?"

"I was hoping I might choose the subject for my studies. I am weary of dwarven genealogy, Sylvan culture, journals describing the construction of cities, and treaties with foreign powers."

Arching a bushy white brow, Devigar asked, "What would you suggest?"

"I wish to know more about magic and about the strange beasts that roam our world."

"Beasts?"

"Various texts have mentioned magical creatures such as rock trolls, griffins, unicorns, and dragons."

"Ah." Devigar smiled. "You are curious about the world outside these walls."

"I am curious about the world outside of any walls."

The old dwarf rested a finger against his pursed lips. "It makes sense. Your village is so far south, so distant from the Vale, you are unfamiliar with magical creatures."

"The Vale?"

"It is a lush valley in Sylvanar, where magic feeds life. The creatures you speak of originate there, and while they have spread and exist across the midlands, few would choose to venture so far south. Those few, such as rock wolves, frost wolves, moarbears, and werecats, are better equipped for your harsh winters."

"Rock wolves are creatures of magic?" Ian recalled a hungry pack raiding the Wescott farm when he was young. The townsfolk had gathered to discuss how to deal with the creatures should they return. Traps were set, and when they did, a half dozen wolves were captured and slaughtered. And then, there was the attack during the journey from Shillings to Ra'Tahal – a traumatic event he preferred not to dwell on. "I have been warned of encountering those animals in the wild but did not realize they were magical beasts."

"Finish your recording. When you are through, come to my study. I will then give you your next task."

"What of my..."

Devigar stilled Ian with a gnarled hand in front of his face. "The tome I have in mind is quite comprehensive and should take you longer to record than the others. The title is The Vale: The source of Monsters, Myth, and Magic."

Ian grinned. "Thank you, Master Devigar."

The old dwarf turned and lumbered toward the door, leaning into his staff with each step. He slipped out and pulled the door closed behind him, leaving Ian alone once again.

Eager to finish, Ian lifted his quill and resumed writing, the runes on the page an exact match for those in the book beside it.

Hours later, with Ian recording faster than ever before, he finished and cast a glance toward the window to find only the faintest hint of daylight remaining outside. Eager to begin reading from the book he was promised, he climbed the stairs to the top floor of Devigar's tower. The door to the study stood open, the room dark and the interior empty. Too determined to be dissuaded by the empty study, Ian descended one level and visited Devigar's bedroom. It was empty as well. Still unwilling to give up, he continued his search, checking each floor for the chancellor. The upper three floors were empty. On the second floor, he found Winnie in the kitchen, preparing dinner.

"Hi, Winnie."

She looked up and smiled when she saw him in the doorway. "Hello, Ian. Did you need something?"

"I am looking for Devigar."

Her smile faltered. "I haven't seen him in hours."

"Thank you." Ian turned from the kitchen and descended to the main floor.

The shadowy silhouettes of furniture occupied the otherwise empty and dark room. Ian sighed. He did not wish to wait another day, not with a belly full of anticipation too powerful to deny, so he stepped out into the night and prayed for a bit of luck that he might find Devigar somewhere nearby.

The narrow citadel streets were quiet and dark other than torches illuminating intersections, the nearest a hundred feet away. Then, Ian heard whispers. He peered into the night, seeking the source of the whispers but saw only darkness. With careful steps and draped in shadow, Ian snuck along the tower wall. Beneath the pillar-supported awning of the Hall of Ancients, he spied two robed silhouettes standing in the darkness, one short and stout, the other tall and lean. The whispers were in Elvish and Ian was now close enough to hear them.

"...a few weeks and all will be ready."

The voice was familiar. *Rysildar!* Ian realized.

"If I were not patient, I would not have held my position for so long," Devigar replied.

The singer whispered, "Watch for the sign as we agreed."

"The Tahal Clan shall return to greatness, and you will have my gratitude." The old dwarf's voice was thick with pride.

"Do not forget our bargain," Rysildar hissed.

"I will honor our agreement. Of that, you have my word. You will have what you wish and more."

The Drow turned and walked off into the night. Ian remained still until he realized that Devigar would return to his tower. Fearing discovery, Ian scurried around the tower as fast as he dared move while remaining quiet. He ran around the tower base until reaching the front door just before the old dwarf was in sight. He ducked in, eased the door closed, and dashed up the stairs, not stopping until he reached his room. There, he sat on the bed, panting for air while his mind raced. *Why was Devigar meeting with the Drow?* Whatever the reason, Rysildar needed a few weeks. Ian then recalled the singer telling the council he required another moon cycle before his gift was ready. The last portion of the conversation then replayed in Ian's head, with Devigar saying, *"The*

Tahal Clan shall return to greatness, and you will have my gratitude." Most chilling was the Drow's reply, *"Do not forget our bargain."*

THE NEXT MORNING found Ian tired after spending the night tossing and turning, his own mind at war with itself and unable to relax. Part of him remained suspicious of Devigar and the dark elf. *If they were not up to something nefarious, why meet at night in a quiet alley?* Another part of him gravitated toward the statement about the Tahal Clan finding greatness and owing gratitude to Rysildar and his people. That part insisted that Devigar was a good master and cared deeply for the good of Ra'Tahal and her citizens. Then, there was the tantalizing promise of the book Devigar had agreed to share with Ian.

When light finally seeped through the window of Ian's room, he rose, washed, and dressed himself. Pushing thoughts of the prior evening aside, he ascended to the top floor and approached the door to Devigar's study. It was closed, so he knocked. When Devigar called for him to enter, Ian opened it and found the old dwarf seated at his desk.

Devigar looked up. "I suspected you might rise early and come here straight away."

Ian froze. "You suspected?" His stomach recoiled in apprehension. *Did he see me last night?*

The old dwarf smiled. "You seemed eager to learn about the Vale."

Relieved, Ian said, "Oh. That. Of course."

"Did you bring the last book."

Ian held it out. "The Reign of Talfagar, first king of the Tahal Clan."

"And what did you learn?"

It was a typical question after Ian finished with a book, one he had learned to consider carefully rather than dismiss, even if the material bored him to tears.

"King Talfagar earned the love of his people by conquering the human tribes who occupied this region and then by constructing this citadel. While he ruled well for many years, his mistake was to isolate his people and resources rather than trading openly with others. As time advanced, both of the other clans advanced, as did the elves, while the Tahal clan remained stagnant. When the king died, his nephew, Gahagar took over and immediately opened trade with other nations. It did not take long for Ra'Tahal to return to a thriving trade center."

"Very good," Devigar crooned.

"I have a question, master." It had stuck with Ian like a sliver of wood hidden in his smallclothes, too irritating to ignore but impossible to resolve.

"Yes?"

"Talfagar died many hundreds of years ago. Gahagar is mentioned as his replacement."

"True."

"This could not be the same Gahagar who died just five years past."

"Oh, but it is."

Ian frowned. "But that would make him..." He did the math. "Seven hundred eighteen years old."

"Ah," Devigar leaned back and nodded. "While you humans live brief lives compared to dwarves, no other of my people has lived as long as Gahagar. In fact, he was over five hundred years old when I first met him."

"How is that possible?"

"Suffice it to say that Gahagar was unlike any other dwarf, but that is a tale for another time." Devigar gestured toward the massive book at the corner of his desk. "Claim your prize. Leave the other behind."

Ian put the old book on the desk, gripped the new one with both hands, and hefted it to his chest. He then backed to the door. "Thank you, Master Devigar. If you no longer need me..."

"Go," Devigar waved him off. "Enjoy your studies. I will send for you if I need your expertise."

Turning, Ian opened the door and darted out, happy to be away. He paused in the corridor as another wave of concern over last night's secret meeting tugged at him. Dismissing the thought, he raced down the stairs, tantalized by what he might discover in the massive book clutched against his chest.

CHAPTER 20
THE VALE

Morning light streamed through the window, the diamond-shaped panes casting a matrix of shadows across the bright sunbeam on the floor at Rina's feet. She raised the pump handle and pushed it down. Water spilled from the spigot and splashed into the wooden bucket positioned below it. When filled, she turned toward the tub recessed in the floor and poured the water over Shria-Li's head. Soap bubbles tracked down the elf woman's flawless, bare skin. Like Rina, Shria-Li had a lean, willowy frame, except the elf princess moved with unmistakable grace.

Shria-Li stood and water tumbled off her gentle curves before splashing into the knee-high water. She gestured. "My towel, please."

Rina lifted a towel off a hook and spread it wide. The fabric felt soft and luxurious against her fingertips. She knew quite well how nice it felt to wrap around herself. However, her baths were to be taken when Shria-Li did not require her services. Like it or not, it was the way of things in her new life, a life much like the previous ones. If Rina would ever find true freedom, she did not know, but she could dream of it.

She wrapped the towel around the elf woman, lifted another towel from a hook, and began drying her hair. "What would you have of me today, Your Highness?"

Shria-Li sighed. "I told you to call me by my name when we are in private."

"We are always in private. Nobody comes here, and I do not get to leave." A week had passed and Rina had yet to step outside of Shria-Li's chambers.

The princess pushed the towel and the hands gripping it away before turning toward Rina. "You are unhappy."

"Would you be happy being trapped in a tower without the freedom to come and go as you wish?"

"I am trapped in the palace and have been for most of my life."

"The palace is much larger than your chambers."

The steel in Shria-Li's gaze softened. "True. However, you have only just begun learning our language. Given more time..."

"I realize that I am to attend to you, to honor your needs and your wishes, but you promised to treat me well."

The challenge struck a nerve, causing Shria-Li's face to tighten. "I did, and I meant it."

Seeing her opening, Rina gripped the elf woman's hands. "I long to explore your city. Would it not be helpful for me to better understand your people? Seeing how they live would do more than dozens of hours of instruction. Is that not as important as me learning your language?"

The princess frowned. "You may have a point, but I was warned by my father to..."

Rina's tone shifted to pleading. "Please, Shria-Li?"

She nodded. "Very well. I have not been requested to attend court today, so you and I will spend some time together beyond the palace grounds."

A smile bloomed on Rina's face as joy bubbled inside. She released a squeal and wrapped her arms around Shria-Li. With the princess' damp, naked body pressed against her, Rina suddenly realized the awkwardness of the situation.

She let go, backed away, and looked down at her dress, covered in wet splotches. "Thank you, Princess."

The princess shook her head and smiled "You are welcome."

"When do we leave?"

"Breakfast is due to arrive soon. We will eat on the balcony and then depart."

For the first time since her arrival in Havenfall, Rina found herself looking forward to something. It was a small thing, but she was tantalized by the beauty she had seen thus far and excited to see what other wonders awaited her discovery.

Sunlight warmed Rina's exposed arms, shoulders, and upper chest. She wore a dress given to her by Shria-Li after breakfast, the princess claiming that it would be improper to be seen out in the city while wearing her servant dress. The new dress was pale green with straps over the shoulders and hugged her hips in a way that made Rina feel self-conscious. Having a slim frame, her breasts were modest at best, yet the plunging neckline undoubtedly drew attention to them in a way she preferred to avoid. Despite her feelings about the dress, she remained eager as she circled the garden outside Shria-Li's room.

The elf princess walked at Rina's side, appearing as graceful and regal as ever. A circlet of golden leaves rested upon her head, instantly reminding others of her royal heritage. A yellow dress with white ruffles on the collar and skirts framed her lithe, willowy figure. As always, she moved with a fluidity and ease Rina envied.

They approached the wall of arches that surrounded the half of the garden not bordered by the palace. Beyond the wall, the view opened to a city made of narrow spires, elegant buildings, and a myriad of terraces.

Trees much smaller than the one in the palace gardens grew among the buildings in perfect, beautiful synergy. Sunlight danced along the edges of golden leaves shimmering in the breeze.

Shria-Li led Rina down a short staircase to a circular plaza paved with white stone tiles. Trees of golden leaves surrounded the plaza. In the heart of the plaza was a ring of pillars surrounding a fountain. A column taller than the others stood in the center of the fountain. Water gushed from the top of the center column and splashed into troughs mounted to the top of each of the eight pillars with additional water spilling over to rain down into the pool below. From each pillar, a series of arches stretched in eight directions, reminding Rina of the spokes of a wagon wheel.

"What is this," Rina asked.

"Many centuries ago, a team of dwarves helped to construct Haven-fall. Although the city is on an island in the middle of a river, getting fresh water to all parts of the city is not as easy as it seems. This fountain taps into a hidden stream hundreds of feet underground. A magical device pumps water from that stream up to the top of the center column. The water flowing out of the column fills each of these eight aqueducts, which then carry fresh water across the city." Shria-Li stood with her hands clasped behind her back, strong and proud. "From this well origi-nates the water we drink and the water used for my baths, which are just two examples among hundreds of uses throughout the city." She crossed the plaza, followed the path between two trees, and led Rina down a hillside path beneath one of the aqueducts.

The trees parted to reveal another paved square, this one surrounded by buildings. Citizens dressed in browns and greens crisscrossed the open space, some carrying baskets, some carrying sacks, others unladen. Elves worked beneath the shade of awnings sticking out from each of the buildings lining the plaza exterior.

Shria-Li led Rina to a building with an open front, the interior occu-pied by a trio of elves tending to a variety of herbs and spices. The smell was overwhelming, consisting of a mélange of sweet and savory scents. Plants growing from pots occupied the shelves and tables, arranged in a way that seemed haphazard yet was undoubtedly planned.

"This is the apothecary," Shria-Li said, gesturing at the shelves. "Each of these plants has a specific purpose." Touching one, she said, "This one is good for headaches." The princess pointed to another. "This one for stomach troubles, and so on." She turned to Rina. "Do you know about herbs and their uses?"

Rina shook her head. "I know very little about anything. My village was small, and our local healer was a secretive, grumpy old woman."

"Then this is an excellent opportunity to learn something new."

Shria-Li turned to a female elf whose hand hovered over a plant with shiny, smooth leaves. The leaves wiggled and a fresh bud sprouted in seconds, as if the world stood still while the plant advanced at a quickened pace. The female elf stood and bowed to the princess, who said something to her in Elvish. It sounded like gibberish to Rina other than the word, *friend*.

The princess shifted to Rina's native language. "Rina, this is Miral. Having lived in Bard's Bay for a time before Gahagar's campaign, she is able to speak your language."

"Before who's campaign?"

"Gahagar was the dwarven king who sought to rule the world. He captured each of the free cities, and once under his control, forced the citizens to learn Dwarvish. This is why Dwarvish is now the most common language in the world."

"Oh."

Shria-Li added, "Miral specializes in herbs but is also a highly skilled cultivator."

Rina had heard the term cultivator before but did not know what it meant.

The princess turned to the other elf. "Miral, this is Rina. She is my new attendant. I thought it might be useful for her to learn about herbs and their uses. Can you show her around?"

The elf, Miral, bowed. "Of course, Your Highness." She gestured to a nearby shelf. "We'll begin with these herbs. They are commonly used for cooking, to add flavor to dishes." Rina followed Miral and listened intently. Learning new things was something Rina truly enjoyed, and to learn about herbs from someone skilled seemed a unique and special opportunity.

A cornucopia of colors and smells greeted Rina as she meandered the shop, and she soon discovered that each herb was unique from the others, be it by appearance, taste, smell, effect, or any combination of those things. Miral showed her how to identify the different herbs and explained their medicinal properties, which ranged from treating minor ailments to more serious conditions. One hour turned to two, which soon became three. All the while, Rina's admiration for the elves and her appreciation of their knowledge of the natural world increased. They seemed to have a deep understanding of the plants and the environment, something she found impressive and vital.

After they finished the exhaustive tour of the apothecary, Shria-Li led Rina through the bustling streets of Havenfall. The city was a marvel of architecture and design, with buildings made of white stone and grayed wood, many of them adorned with intricate carvings and colorful mosaics. The streets were filled with elves going about their daily business, dressed in elegant clothing that seemed to flow effortlessly in the breeze.

A sense of wonder had Rina's head buzzing as she walked through the elven city. It was unlike anything she had experienced before, and she couldn't wait to see what else it had to offer.

Finally, after a day of meandering, they drew near the outskirts of the city with pink clouds gracing the sky above them. A powerful rushing sound came from ahead, and a line of towering, branchless trees spaced hundreds of feet apart seemed to mark the edge of the island. Beyond that line of trees, Rina saw nothing but the sky.

"What is that way?" She pointed northeast.

"It is, perhaps, the most wondrous thing I can show you."

Rina arched a brow. "After everything else we have seen today, I find that difficult to believe."

The princess narrowed her eyes in thought while staring in that direction. "I am supposed to stay away from it, but if father does not know, it should do no harm to show you."

Now, Rina was twice as curious. "I promise not to tell."

Shria-Li smiled. "I trust you." She grabbed Rina's hand and pulled her down a path bordered by bushes thick with purple berries.

The path turned to stairs, forcing them to climb. As they drew nearer, Rina realized that the trees were even taller than she had guessed. The base of each was at least a dozen feet in diameter, and the trees thrust up toward the heavens like an arrow lacking feathers.

"Why do they not have branches or leaves?" Rina asked.

"These trees were grown for a specific purpose."

"Which is?"

"To provide a barrier."

The strange responses caused Rina to frown. "But the trees are so far apart."

"I will explain."

The path crested a rise and the scene opened to a broader vista that beckoned Rina toward it like the scent of freshly baked bread would tempt one dying of hunger. The trail wound down a hillside and came to a barren, rocky shelf sixty feet deep and running the width of the island. Amid the rock, the branchless trees stood in a line no more than a dozen feet from the edge of a tremendous drop. Beyond the drop was the most awestriking view Rina had ever seen.

The river that split and flowed around the island city of Havenfall became a pair of gushing waterfalls a half mile apart and she positioned at the midpoint between them. The falls spilled down over a thousand feet to splash into a lake at the base of the sheer, rocky cliffside. A river flowed from the lake and meandered along the floor of a lush, green valley that stretched many miles to the east and west. To the distant north, a broad stretch of water spread defined the horizon. With the scattered clouds above the valley turned pink and orange from the setting sun, the entirety of her view painted a dramatic and breathtaking picture.

Shria-Li stared into the distance. "The land below Havenfall is called the Vale. This land is special and extremely dangerous. Creatures of magic originate from the Vale. It is where they breed, hunt, and thrive." She pointed north. "It stretches north a hundred miles until it reaches the shores of the Inner Sea. The valley's width is thrice as long as that."

With her head still buzzing with the awe of the view, Rina spoke in a detached tone, "What sort of magical creatures live down there?"

"Everything from brownies to dragons call the Vale home."

She turned toward the elf woman. "What is a brownie?"

A female voice came from behind, speaking in Elvish. Rina spun around and spotted a trio of elves, two males and a female, standing beside the nearest tree. All three wore armor made of dwarven steel, the sheen appearing even warmer than normal in the light of sunset. On their heads were helms that came to a peak and had wings on the sides.

Shria-Li and the warriors exchanged words, all in Elvish and all beyond Rina's understanding. The elf princess then spoke to Rina. "These are Valeguard Warriors. They warned me that it would not be safe to be near the barrier at night."

"Why not?"

"The creatures below have been restless of late. Some have even attempted to attack the city."

Rina turned toward the Vale. "We must be a thousand feet up, and the cliffside looks too steep to climb. How do they..." she frowned as she noticed dark dots in the sky over the valley. "What is that?"

Shria-Li turned and peered north as wings became visible. "I think... those are griffins."

"What is a griffin?"

"They are vicious creatures, part eagle and part werecat and larger than both put together."

The shapes grew more pronounced as the creatures grew nearer. They flew above the treetops, giving Rina an idea of their size, the wingspan as broad as any tree they passed. The monsters reached the edge of the forest and sailed out over the lake. They flapped their wings mightily and began to rise, drawing closer, and Rina was finally able to see them in detail.

The feathers on their massive wings and necks were brown and white, their bodies covered with gray and black spotted fur. Each was as big as a wagon, leaving Rina amazed that something so large could fly. As the creatures ascended and drew closer, she found herself entranced by their grandeur.

One of the three Valeguard warriors shouted something.

Shria-Li grabbed Rina by the hand and pulled her backward. "We must move beyond the barrier."

As they backed from the edge, the griffins faded from view. Soon they were forty feet beyond the line of branchless trees and nearing the area where the rock ended and shrubs began.

For a few tense moments, Rina stood still, waiting to see what would happen. Then, the first griffin crested the edge and came into view. Its head appeared to be like that of an eagle, as did its wings and tail. The body was muscular with its front legs ending in the talons of a bird of prey, the rear paws clawed and each large enough to wrap around her slim waist. Two other monsters appeared behind the first, all three coming directly toward Rina. Fear climbed her spine, wrapped around her throat, and squeezed out all other thoughts.

CHAPTER 21
THE BARRIER

As the griffin's came at them, Shria-Li, backed toward the city, dragging Rina with her. The three Valeguard warriors positioned themselves between them and the oncoming monsters. Each held a shock lance ready, the charged tip pointed toward the beasts.

The lead griffin reached the invisible barrier and sparks enveloped its body. It crashed to the ground with a heavy thump and tumbled to a stop just strides before the warriors. The second beast struck the barrier a beat later. Electricity sparked, shocking the monster and sending it crashing to the ground. As it settled beside the first downed creature, the third griffin reached the barrier. It passed through unharmed and came at the three guards with its wings spread and talons extended.

The warriors split up, the female guard darting left, one of the males darting right, and the third male standing firm. He thrust the shock lance as the creature struck. The griffin twisted one talon and gripped the lance a few feet down the shaft while sparks flickered off the lance's tip, which remained too far from its flesh for the shock to affect it. The creature's momentum and grip on the weapon lifted the warrior off his feet and tossed him into the shrubs. The lance broke from his grip and spun off to the other side of the trail. Shria-Li and Rina ducked as the monster flew overhead, toward the city. The griffin spread its wings, tilted, and banked. Then it dove at them with talons extended.

"It's coming for us. Run!" Shria-Li, still holding Rina's hand, ran along the rock, parallel to the greenery, heading west.

As the monster veered toward Shria-Li, the female Valeguard ran in. She leapt high into the air and thrust at the flying beast. At the last moment, the griffin banked hard to avoid the attack. The guard missed and tumbled to the ground. The monster turned again and came around until it eclipsed the setting sun. Shria-Li stopped, turned, and fled in the other direction with Rina at her side. The creature rapidly closed the gap, bearing down on them. Just before it reached them, Shria-Li yanked Rina toward the shrubs and dove in with her. Branches snapped, leaves brushed against her, and twigs tore across her skin as she landed.

A heavy wind struck, shaking the shrubs and the two females as the griffin flew by, its massive, dark shadow briefly passing over them.

Shria-Li crawled to her hands and knees while glancing over at Rina, who's arm was scratched, and dress torn. "Are you well?"

Rina touched her scrape and nodded. "Well enough."

On her knees, Shria-Li stuck her head up as the griffin banked. "It is coming back."

"Why won't it leave us alone?"

"I don't know." She spied a glint in the shrubs beside her and realized it was the shock lance lost by one of the Valeguard during the initial strike.

Shria-Li crawled through the shrubs and reached for the lance. With it in her grip, she rose to a stance while the griffin spread its wings, extended its talons and came at her. The monster, eight times her size, bore down on her with terrifying speed. Just before it struck, Shria-Li dropped to her knees while thrusting the lance above her. Talons swept past her, tearing through the shrubs and sending leaves spinning through the air. The lance struck the monster's werecat torso, and sparks sizzled. The creature's back leg struck the lance, the impact knocking the weapon from her grip. The griffin flew another dozen feet before crashing into the shrubs, snapping branches and sending leaves twirling into the air. It tumbled and settled to a stop some thirty strides from where Shria-Li knelt.

She climbed to her feet as the female Valeguard rushed toward the beast. The warrior reached the downed monster, detached a large shackle from her belt, and clamped it around one of its bird-like front legs. A red aura pulsed from the shackle, the magic disabling the beast.

The guard turned toward Shria-Li. "It is safe, now, princess."

Spinning around, Shria-Li found each of the other two Valeguard warriors standing beside the other fallen griffins, each of whom wore a similar, enchanted shackle.

Satisfied, Shria-Li extended a hand down to Rina. "It is safe now. You can stand."

Rina stood and slid a fallen dress strap back up over her shoulder. "Why didn't the barrier stop the third monster?"

Shria-Li shook her head. "I don't know, but I intend to find out."

THE TRICKLE of water from a bubbling fountain echoed in the quiet hall. Cascading water flowed down a multi-tiered sculpture and spilled into a pool surrounding the trunk of a small tree. The tree's bark, branches, and leaves, all glowed with a golden aura that illuminated the hall with soft light. Through nearby arches, the last moments of daylight bathed the palace courtyard in a purple haze soon to turn black.

Shria-Li waited with feigned patience while staring through another doorway with Rina at her side. Beyond the doorway, two trees twice the size of the one in the entrance hall illuminated the throne room. The branches of those glowing trees extended toward the other and wove together to create a pair of seats elevated above the ring of benches surrounding the trees. On one throne sat her father, Fastellan. On the other was her mother, Tora-Li. Before them stood Chavell, Captain of the Valeguard.

The trio in the throne room spoke softly, their voices all but drowned by the running water. The captain then dipped his head, turned, and walked out.

As he passed Shria-Li, he dipped his head. "I am glad you are unharmed, Princess."

"As am I, Captain," she replied. "Had it not been for the quick actions of the Valeguard, things might have gone differently."

Chavell frowned. "That is not the way my guards reported it."

Shria-Li did not wish to cause the guards any trouble. Had she not placed herself in harm's way, they wouldn't have had to protect her in the first place. "In that case, I suspect your warriors are being modest."

He stared at her for a long beat before replying. "Perhaps."

"I must know," She pressed him with an intensity in her eyes, "How did the griffin break beyond the barrier?"

"I..." Chavell glanced toward the throne room. Inside, the king and queen stood, squeezed each other's hands, and the queen walked off. "It is a question not mine to answer."

She suspected as much. "Very well. I will ask my father."

The captain gave her a small smile. "Thank you, Your Highness. Have a good evening."

"You as well, Captain."

As Chavell walked off, her father crossed the throne room and approached the arched entrance.

"Shria-Li," Fastellan said as he drew near. He then looked at Rina. "Safrina." His attention lingered on her as he spoke. "I am glad you two are well after tonight's scare."

"How did it happen, Father?" Shria-Li asked.

He appeared reluctant to tear his gaze from Rina but did so anyway. "The barrier is...failing."

"What? How?"

"The trees that form it are two thousand years old. Without branches and leaves, those trees struggle to survive and have done so only because of our cultivators' caring attention. As the magic in the trees recedes, the resilience of the barrier weakens. Chavell worries that it will outright fail in a few years. When that occurs..."

She finished the statement for him. "There will be nothing to protect us from the monsters who call the Vale home."

"We do have the Valeguard. Among them, there are still a handful of tamers."

The tamers. Few had been born in the previous five hundred years. Why, nobody knew. Cultivators were common, as were trackers, but tamers and rain dancers had become rarities, even more so than healers. Thus far, Shria-Li had proven to have no special gifts, but she had only just reached the age where such gifts usually bloom.

"Is there nothing we can do?"

"I will speak with the lore keepers. Perhaps the methods used to grow the barrier trees lie hidden somewhere within the great archives. If the barrier is going to fail, we might regrow a new one."

There was another, far more controversial answer, an answer Shria-Li chose to voice. "Evarian has long claimed that we should hunt the creatures in the Vale and destroy them before they can harm us or anyone else."

Fastellan snapped. "Evarian is a fool. Those innocent creatures have a right to exist, no different than us. We Sylvan have long believed in being one with nature. To hunt for sustenance is in harmony with nature. To slaughter for any other reason is not. He would have us exterminate creatures viewed as risks purely because they exist. The griffin attack tonight was nothing more than them hunting and choosing the wrong prey. It was neither out of spite nor intentional. If Evarian had his way, those creatures would be exterminated, and the world would never know the grip of their talons, the thrust of their wings, or the cry of their young. Griffins would fade to memories, and when those memories died, they would be viewed as nothing but legends. Two thousand years from now, even those legends would be forgotten, and it would be as if the creatures had never existed."

Shria-Li had heard the argument before, and while she did not disagree, she feared for the safety of her people. "I pray to Vandasal that a solution will be found."

"As do I." He placed his hand on her shoulder. "Have you eaten?"

"No. Not yet." The hollowness in her stomach wanted to scream the words.

"Good. I was hoping that you and Safrina would join me for dinner."

It was not unusual for him to invite her to dinner. Inviting her personal servant was another matter. *Katarina never ate with us. Why Safrina?* Shria-Li suspected he felt some modicum of guilt for her abduction. Yet, it left another question unanswered.

"What of mother?" Shria-Li asked.

"Your mother is to dine with rain dancers. She believes we are due for rain and wishes to ensure it does not interrupt the ritual she has planned."

"Ritual?"

He rested a hand on her shoulder and looked her in the eye. "It is time to determine your gift, daughter."

Shria-Li blinked in realization. "She wishes to conduct a testing?"

"It will force your ability out. You know this."

Anxiety caused her heart to flutter and sweat to trickle down her ribs. "But if we just waited..."

"We have waited long enough." His voice was firm, his decision made. "It is time to determine your skills. As much as anything else, it is your duty to your people."

Her stomach began to churn, and she found herself thankful it was empty. "Very well."

"Come. Let us dine together." He moved his hand to the small of her back and led her across the room.

"Where are you going?" Rina asked.

Shria-Li stopped and turned toward her and replied in the human language, "We are to dine with my father."

Fastellan added. "Do not worry. We will keep the conversation in your native tongue for tonight. In the meantime, you must continue to practice our language."

Rina curtsied. "Thank you, Your Majesty."

"Please. When we are alone, call me Fastellan."

The king walked toward an arched doorway with Shria-Li and Rina following. All the while, troubled thoughts occupied Shria-Li's mind. The barrier failing, her testing trial, and her father's strange behavior toward Rina battled one another for her attention, but all three issues were questions without answers.

CHAPTER 22

INCUBATION

The weeks passed swiftly once Vic had found a new purpose, one that consumed his thoughts at every available moment.

Each morning, he would rise with the men in his bunkhouse, eat, and march off to the mine to relieve the night shift workers. He did his best to act nonchalant and sometimes expressed frustration about their situation as slaves conscripted to a life of working underground. The truth he hid was quite the opposite.

Whenever away from the mine, he longed to return to it and retiring to the bunkhouse at the end of each day only with reluctance in his heart. While in the mine, he operated alone in his private side tunnel, chipping away at rock, expanding the tunnel width, and working extra hard to produce as much vartanium as before despite his long breaks. During those breaks, he would sneak to the rear of the tunnel and remove the rocks blocking the opening to the hidden chamber. Once inside, he would go straight for the egg, touching it, feeling the heart-beat while caressing the surface. He talked to the egg, telling it stories of his childhood, of his hopes, his dreams, and the desire to be freed of his enslavement. Whether anything heard what Vic said was not of his concern. Rather, it felt good to share his past, his feelings, and his private thoughts. Those moments with the egg ended sooner than he wished, but since he was afraid of discovery and desperately wished to keep his prize a secret, he took care to spend no more than half an hour in the cavern at a time before returning to work.

At night, Vic would lay in his bunk and stare at the ceiling, listening for the heartbeat in the egg despite the distance. The thumping sound visited his dreams and seemed to settle in the back of his mind, so he heard it even when working, eating, or talking to another miner.

Outside, the weather cooled, the heat of summer replaced by the fresh chill of autumn. He had been told that it rarely snowed in Ra'Tahal, the guards claiming that it had not done so in over twenty years. Still, winter evenings were said to be cool enough where one could see their breath swirl in the air when exhaled. Having grown up in Shillings, where snow fell every year, sometimes deep enough that Vic would sink to his crotch when tromping through the forest, he had little concern.

On a cool morning while on his way to the mine, Vic found Ian standing near the tunnel entrance with a pair of dwarf guards. He rushed ahead of the others to speak with Ian, knowing that he only had a few minutes before he was expected in the mine.

"Ian," Vic said as he slowed. "It is good to see you."

Ian gripped Vic by the arm and drew him aside. In a hushed voice, he said, "I have been studying a book about the Vale."

Vic frowned. "The what?"

"It is a distant region where magic flows like a river through a lush, jungle valley. The book describes many things, including how magic creatures reproduce."

"The egg...Did you find out about the egg?"

"Yes. The only creatures that lay eggs are avian and reptilian. The only ones that lay eggs even approaching the size you mentioned are rocs and dragons."

Vic frowned. "What is a roc?"

"Rocs are birds reputed to be as large as a house."

"A house?" Vic shook his head. "How could a bird be so large?"

"I told you. Magic." Ian gripped him by the shoulder. "It may also be a dragon egg. However, dragon eggs hatch a full clutch, ranging from three to thirteen creatures at a time. Legends say that those eggs lay dormant for a thousand years before they hatch. It also says that they require great heat to gestate."

"So, you think it is a dragon egg?"

"I think you had better be careful. If this thing hatches and you are there, a massive bird or a clutch of dragons might emerge. Either way, they are monsters who are said to eat humans, and they are likely to be very hungry." His tone was one of warning.

"What are you saying?"

"Stay away from it, Vic." Ian grabbed his arm.

Vic jerked away. "I can take care of myself."

"Against a bird large enough to eat you in one bite? Against dragons?" Ian sounded worried, his words coming out with an edge of urgency. "Nobody knows how to kill a dragon, Vic. Many have tried. None lived."

Night shift miners began to emerge from the cave mouth. "I have to go."

Ian stared at him while taking a deep breath. "You aren't going to listen to me, are you?"

"I..." Vic struggled to explain his feelings. "I need to do this, Ian. I need it." He backed toward the cave. "Take care of yourself. Don't worry about me. I will be fine."

Determined to continue visiting the egg, Vic jogged down the dark tunnel, heading to the underground warrens where he spent his daylight hours.

～

IAN and the two guards escorting him climbed the stairs built into the cliffside overlooking Ra'Tahal's lower hold. They remained quiet during the climb, all three gasping for air while concerns for Vic occupied Ian's thoughts. Regardless of Ian's warning, his brother was determined to continue visiting the egg. Ian worried that a monster would emerge hungry and view Vic as a tasty morsel. The bestiary had included numerous examples of both rocs and dragons attacking and eating humans, dwarves, and elves. Those tales, along with the drawings in the book, were enough to bring Ian nightmares.

Upon reaching the top of the plateau, the two guards returned to their post at the gate and joined the other dwarves on duty. Ian thanked them as he passed back into the upper hold, the rising sun still masked by the surrounding buildings and the citadel's outer wall. He followed narrow streets draped in shadow while enjoying the fresh, cool autumn air. When he reached Devigar's tower, he stepped inside as the old dwarf rounded the stairs along the main floor's outer wall.

"There you are." The old dwarf hobbled down the stairs with his staff in hand. "Where have you been?"

"I wanted to visit my brother. Two of the dwarves at the gate agreed to escort me down to the lower hold, and I was able to catch him on his way to the mine, before his shift began."

Devigar harrumphed. "It is good you got that out of the way."

"Why do you say that?"

"I just received word from the king. Rysildar sent an announcement to Arangar and the council. He is prepared to reveal his gift to them today."

"Today?" Ian was of two minds about the announcement, torn between dread and anticipation. He doubted Rysildar's motives and was afraid of what the singer's magic might produce. At the same time, his promise of a vast boon for the clan held tantalizing possibilities.

"Yes. At noon." Devigar eyed Ian's robes, his expression one of displeasure. "You and I are to be present, so I need you cleaned up and wearing your best robes."

"Yes, master." Ian only wore those robes on special occasions, but a visit to the king's court certainly qualified.

"Have you broken your fast?"

"No. I rose before dawn, dressed, and left straight away."

"Go find Winnie. Eat, clean up, and meet me down here. I wish to brief you on Drow magic, so you understand what might occur."

Ian's eyes widened. Devigar had explained little of magic to him, regardless of the form or race. It all seemed so mystical and unknowable and undeniably enticing all at the same time. "Yes, sir!"

He raced up the stairs so fast, he stepped on the hem of his robes, tripped, and fell onto his hands and knees, smacking his shin in the process. While it hurt, his enthusiasm masked the pain. Lifting his robes, he limped up the stairs, seeking Winnie.

CHAPTER 23

POWERFUL MAGIC

With the sun at its apex, Ian walked at Devigar's side. The two of them entered the Temple of Vandasal for the first time since Ian was assigned to be the chancellor's apprentice. They strode along the raised catwalk, the recessed seating to either side of it empty. In fact, the entire building stood empty.

A sunbeam streaming through the glass dome high above painted a circle of light between the pit and the dais. Devigar and Ian strode the length of the catwalk and rounded the pit, the heat rising from it warming Ian's shoulder. They then stopped at the side of the floor, just beyond the circle of light. As during his last visit, twelve chairs and a throne of gold were lined along the dais. Impossible not to notice, a statue loomed above it all, each extended hand large enough for him to sit in.

"Vandasal," he muttered.

"What?" Devigar glanced at him. "Oh. Yes. Our god."

Ian frowned. "How come I don't ever hear you mention your god?" Gods were a curious thing to Ian. His own people relied on the spirits of their ancestors for guidance, although he had never heard of such spirits actually appearing before someone, at least not during his lifetime. "I know little of gods, and I know even less of Vandasal other than brief mentions in the texts I have studied."

"What is there to know?" Devigar shrugged. "Gods are unknowable. It is not as if Vandasal watches over us, gives us his blessing, or even cares."

"Why do you say that?"

"What god would allow his people to dwindle as we have? We are struggling, Ian." He looked up at the statue and snarled. "If Vandasal ever were real, he gave up on the Tahal Clan long ago."

Ian was taken aback, having never before heard such anger from Devigar. The old dwarf's distaste for his god left him disturbed and at a loss for words.

The side door opened. King Arangar emerged, trailed by a line of elderly dwarves. The king was dressed in red and black with gold trim to match his crown. Black robes with gold piping, as Ian was now used to seeing them wear, covered the elderly dwarves who made up the council. As the middle-aged king and his retinue crossed the room and claimed their chairs, Ian and Devigar stood still and remained silent.

The king stood before the throne and waited while the council members settled into position. When all were standing before their individual seats, Arangar sat, as did the council members.

Devigar bowed. "Welcome, Your Majesty."

"Thank you, Chancellor." Arangar glanced around the chamber. "Where is the Drow?"

"A cohort is escorting the singer and his creation. They should arrive..." The temple door opened. Devigar glanced back as Rysildar entered. "Ah. Here he is."

The Drow, hooded and robed, glided across the catwalk. Eighteen dwarven soldiers trailed him. The door opened again, and a pair of stout dwarves pushed a cart covered in a tarp through the doorway. Rysildar continued, rounded the pit, and stopped just shy of the sunbeam. The guards split into two groups, nine of them bordering each side of the temple floor, their watchful eyes on the Drow. Lastly, the two dwarves pushing the cart crossed the chamber, the squeaks emitted by the cart's wheels echoing in the spacious temple interior. The dwarves guided the cart past Rysildar, stopped in the heart of the sunlit circle, and then retreated, leaving the cart behind.

Ian stared at the cart and the object hidden beneath the tarp. It was roughly the size of his head and stood a few feet above the top of the cart. Something about it made him uneasy and caused him to fidget.

Devigar turned to the dais and spoke in a firm voice. "My King and Council, I present to you the Drow singer, Rysildar."

King Arangar nodded. "This moment has been much anticipated, singer. I trust you are prepared to reveal your gift to Ra'Tahal?"

After Devigar translated, Rysildar spoke. "As promised and after many weeks of diligent effort, I have produced the ultimate tool for the Tahal clan." He stepped forward, gripped the tarp, and yanked it off the cart with a flourish. Upon the cart stood an object of beauty and wonder.

A pedestal made of bronze and covered in strange runes rose up three feet above the cart's tabletop. Mounted to the pedestal was a crystal of untold worth. Perfectly cut, its facets glimmering in the sunlight, the crystal sparkled like an oversized diamond. Without a doubt, it was the same crystal Ian had seen when he followed Rysildar down the hidden passage in the citadel's eastern wall. As time had advanced, Ian's conviction about that night had waned until he found himself believing that it had only been a dream. Now, he knew with certainty that the experience had been real. With the realization came a renewed fear of betrayal.

The council members muttered amongst themselves while the king eyed the object. Finally, he said, "While this is a thing of splendor, it appears to be nothing more than a bauble my people can admire. How will this help the Tahal Clan return to greatness?"

Once Devigar finished translating, Rysildar replied, "This object has been attuned to my voice. When my magic is applied, this crystal opens a rift in space, creating a portal to a sister crystal, two thousand miles distant. With this ability, the Tahal Clan can travel a great distance in an instant, enabling open trade with my people."

Ian's brows rose in surprise, and he whispered, "Is that possible?"

"Hush," Devigar chided quietly before raising his voice and translating for the king and the council.

The murmurs returned, this time with a fervor. Arangar raised his hand, stilling the room before speaking. "Such a tool could be powerful, indeed. Whether for trade or for battle, the ability to leap great distances in an instant, presents tantalizing possibilities." He leaned forward in the throne. "However, we require proof."

Upon hearing the translation, a smile appeared within the shadows of Rysildar's hooded face. "I would be happy to perform a demonstration, Your Majesty. Please, allow me a moment."

Devigar translated, and Arangar agreed. All eyes were on Rysildar as the Drow stood before the crystal.

Rysildar opened his mouth and song came forth. Wordless, wavering, singing echoed in the temple. In response, a purple glow bloomed in the crystal. The glow grew brighter and brighter until Ian was forced to squint and Rysildar's form appeared as nothing more than a dark silhouette standing before a star come to life.

A tremendous thump tore through the temple, followed by a ripping sound as reality was torn asunder. A line of light appeared on the opposite side of the crystal from where Rysildar stood. That line began to spread, creating a frame ten feet tall and not stopping until it was twenty feet wide. Like peering through a window, a completely different scene waited beyond the frame.

The flat rooftop and low, merlon-lined wall of a fortress lurked just on the other side of the opening. Beyond the wall, the view stretched out to a distant horizon. A seemingly endless body of water encompassed the view with only two small islands of land visible. Ian knew they were far from any sea or ocean, yet, here he was, staring at one as if he stood on a tower overlooking the shoreline.

The king burst to his feet and gaped. "I know that vista. It is Talastar, on the southeast bank of the Arista Sea."

Rysildar nodded. "Very good, Your Majesty."

Ian frowned. *I didn't know that he understood or spoke Dwarvish.* If anyone else noticed, none said a word.

Arangar said, "Can one truly pass through this doorway, or is it just an illusion."

"I assure you, this is no illusion." Rysildar shouted in Elvish, "Come, Letalis!"

Dark elves dressed in dark leather armor appeared on the other side of the rift. First, it was just a handful, but more joined until the number was north of two dozen. Most of them gripped weapons with a nasty, two-foot-long blade attached to each five-foot-long shaft. The others held bows carved of ebony black wood. Those with the bows, drew arrows, nocked, and loosed. Held in the grip of stunned shock, nobody in the temple moved until it was too late.

Three arrows plunged into the king's body, knocking him back into the throne. Others found council members in rapid succession. Dwarves with arrows sticking out from their chest jerked and slumped in their chairs or slid to the floor. In mere moments, all thirteen citadel rulers were dead. A silent beat followed and then, chaos ensued.

Dark elves poured through the rift and met the dwarven warriors who had escorted Rysildar. In the span of a breath, the invaders outnumbered the city protectors. Shouts, screams, and the clash of metal on metal echoed in the cavernous temple.

Terror held Ian frozen in place. Helpless to act, he watched in horror as the scene before him unfolded. The once peaceful temple had become a battleground, filled with the sounds of clashing weapons and screams of agony. Weapons flashed, blood spilled, and warriors died. His mind fumbled as it attempted to process what was happening and how he should react. Through that chaos, one clear thought solidified, giving him guidance. *I must escape the temple and warn the citizens of Ra'Tahal.*

He ducked past a Drow and dwarf engaged in battle, their weapons clashing furiously. Through the fracas, a path opened, and he spied the temple entrance at the far end of the catwalk. Ian gathered himself to run when his body lurched. A sharp pain flared in his side as he stumbled and regained his balance. Looking down, he saw an arrow protruding from his skin. In shock, he staggered and fell to his hands and knees. He gasped for air, each breath like a knife thrust into his side as he tried to come to terms with what had occurred.

The hem of a black cloak swirled into his sightline. He looked up to see Rysildar standing over him. The singer wore a sinister smile on his face.

"Well, well, well," Rysildar said in a mocking tone. "I see that my little spy has been injured. I heard that you were smart, but intelligence lacking wisdom is often wasted, as proven by your actions. You should have known better than to cross me."

Ian gritted his teeth, the pain in his side intensifying. He tried to speak, but no words came out. The battle around him raged with dwarves and dark elves falling to one another's weapons. Another wave of Drow burst through the rift and rushed over to Rysildar's side.

Rysildar chuckled before leaning down to whisper in Ian's ear. "Don't worry. I won't kill you... yet. You still have some use to me, as does your master."

With that, Rysildar stood and glided toward the temple entrance. Sixty dark elf warriors followed him out while a handful of others fought the last of the surviving dwarves.

Ian remained on his hands and knees while blood tracked down the arrow shaft in his gut and dripped to the tiled floor. Terror and uncertainty battled inside him, but through the haze of pain, one clear thought remained. He had to get out. With the arrow still in his side, he crawled toward the temple's exit, only to see a pair of sandals blocking his route. He looked up to find Devigar standing there.

The old dwarf shook his head. "I am sorry, boy. I never wished for you to get hurt."

Ian fought through the veil of pain. "You knew?"

Devigar nodded, his expression pained. "The council was bad enough before the war ended. When Arangar returned to take the throne, the situation only grew worse. Those blind fools would have destroyed the clan, even if it was to be a slow, painful death."

Anger brewed in Ian's stomach. "And what do you get out of this?"

"I will return to rule, as I did before Arangar returned. However, this time I will not be restricted by the council and will have the strength of Queen Liloth to back me." The old dwarf extended a hand. "Come. I will bring you to a flesh mender."

Ian refused the offer, rising on his own, one hand pressed against his knee, the other against his stomach at the base of the arrow. The wound hurt so bad that tears blurred his vision, but he remained steadfast. "I cannot stomach betrayal."

Devigar looked around. Only a handful of dwarves remained standing, outnumbered by the Drow warriors. "I cannot either. It is the sacrifice I make for my people."

Ian lunged and snatched the staff from Devigar, causing the old dwarf to stumble.

"What are you doing?" Devigar reached for the staff, but Ian staggered back a step.

"The only thing I can think of." Ian wound back, took aim, and launched the staff over Devigar's shoulder. The effort cost Ian, the pain causing him to stumble and fall to the floor.

The staff sailed across the chamber and struck the crystal, knocking it from the pedestal. The crystal fell onto the cart and rolled off while the staff flipped off and fell into the pit. The crystal crashed to the stone tiled floor and shattered with shards skittering in all directions. The rift shuddered and collapsed in on itself.

A tremendous concussion burst from the destroyed rift, the force of it catapulting bodies in all directions. Devigar, standing and facing the blast, was launched over Ian. The thump of the released energy struck Ian in the side like a hammer and sent him sliding across the floor with the arrow in his side pointing toward the ceiling. His ears rang and head swam. He tried to climb to his hands and knees, but the ground shook and shuddered while the room spun around him. The glass ceiling shattered. Shards tumbled to the floor and into the pit as Ian staggered to his feet. Another quake rattled the temple, the floor beneath Ian's feet rippling like a wave of earth. He stumbled and fell face-first to the tile. Spots danced before his eyes before blackness crashed in.

CHAPTER 24
A BROKEN SHELL

V ic worked alone, as he always did, while the other miners opened a new tunnel parallel to his. He finished loading broken rock into a bin, leaned into the cart, and began pushing it toward the central chamber. An hour had passed since he last visited the egg, yet the strange and alluring object firmly occupied his thoughts. A small part of him railed against those desires, insisting that his obsession with the egg was unhealthy, but that voice was drowned out by one declaring that he had nothing else good in his life. He would continue spending time with the egg regardless of what Ian said.

He crossed the spacious, empty chamber where his crew had worked for many weeks before branching off to a side tunnel. As he entered the tunnel leading to the crusher, the ground shook, causing him to stagger and grip the cart, lest he fall. Another tremor tore through the mine, the second one even more violent than the first. Chunks of stone, dirt, and debris rained down from the cavern ceiling. Vic dove over to the wall and pinned himself against it while squeezing his eyes shut and covering his nose and mouth. When the debris settled, he opened his eyes to dust swirling in the dim light coming from the neighboring chamber. The cart and floor were coated in dirt. Chunks of stone lay strewn about.

As the noise settled, screams came from deeper in the mine.

Alarmed, Vic ran back into the central chamber and discovered the new tunnel entrance partially blocked by a fallen beam. He ran to the tunnel mouth. Only darkness waited within.

"Can you hear me?" Vic shouted.

Brady's voice came from the darkness, his tenor strained. "Vic! Help!"

Vic spun, raced for the nearest of the five torches lighting the chamber, and lifted it from its sconce. He returned to the tunnel and held the torch over the fallen beam. He saw Brady's face just ten strides away. A rock half the size of a wine barrel lay across Brady's leg. Farther back, Colby lay on the floor, his forehead bloodied. A pile of rock blocked the way just beyond where Colby lay.

Adrenaline and concern overcame Vic, allowing him to toss caution aside. He climbed over the beam and wedged the torch between two fallen boulders. Squatting beside Brady, Vic gripped the bottom edge of the boulder lying across his leg and lifted. His muscles strained, the veins in his neck and forehead bulging as he tipped the boulder up.

"Pull your leg out," Vic groaned between clenched teeth.

Brady pulled himself backward, sliding across the tunnel floor. His lower leg emerged bloodied and ravaged. When it was clear, Vic released his hold on the rock. It fell with a heavy thud.

"My leg..." Tears made Brady's eyes glassy.

"I need to get you out of here. We will worry about your leg later." Vic squatted beside Brady, wrapped an arm around him, and helped him stand on his one good leg. "You hop while I help you."

The two of them hobbled to the fallen beam. Vic helped Brady over and into the central chamber before lowering him to sit with his back to the far wall.

"Remove your belt," Vic said. "Secure it around your thigh just above the knee to slow the bleeding."

Brady nodded numbly as he began undoing his belt.

With Brady safe, Vic hurried back to Colby, putting his cheek to the downed man's face. When he felt breath, he sighed in relief. *At least he is still alive.* After sliding his arms beneath Colby, he sat the unconscious man up, bent low, and lifted until Colby was draped over his shoulder. Beneath the dead weight, he returned to the tunnel mouth, climbed over the fallen beam, and set the man down.

He then returned and grabbed a shovel lying on the floor. With it, he began working at the pile of debris blocking the tunnel, digging at the top of the pile until he broke through to a cavity.

"Can anyone hear me?"

From the other side of the rock pile came Terrick's voice, thick with angst. "I am trapped."

"Stand back." Vic used the shovel to push and dig, making the opening larger. He then bent and lifted the torch. Ten feet away, on the other side of the pile, he saw Terrick's dirt-coated face.

"Crawl through."

Terrick whined. "I can't."

"Why not?"

"What if another quake hits? I'll be buried alive."

"You'll die if you remain. Now, crawl!"

Terrick climbed up the other side and lay on the pile, squirming through the opening. When his extended arms were within reach, Vic gripped his wrists and pulled with all his might, dragging Terrick through the gap. He let go and Terrick rolled down the rock pile. Cuts and scrapes were visible amid his torn clothing.

As Terrick climbed to his feet, Vic asked, "Is anyone else alive back there?"

"I don't know."

Vic cupped a hand to his mouth. "Hello! Can anyone hear me?"

Silence. A pang of loss settled in Vic' stomach. Sixteen men had set out that morning. Five had been sent to work at the crusher. That meant seven were missing.

"Come on," he lifted the torch while leading Terrick back to the main chamber.

When they got there, Colby was awake, his face bruised and covered in blood from his wounded forehead. "Can you walk?" Vic asked.

Staggering to his feet, Colby nodded. "I will be fine."

"Good." Vic squatted beside Brady and slid his hand around his back. "We are getting out of here." With a grunt he helped the shorter boy stand.

The four of them headed for the tunnel still occupied by Vic's cart. They passed the cart, navigated past fallen rock, and emerged in the crusher chamber, where they found their five companions along with a trio of dwarves.

In Dwarvish, one of the guards asked, "Where are the others?"

Vic understood enough to get by. He shook his head and said, "Dead."

The dwarves waved and headed toward the mine exit, making it clear that Vic and the others were to follow. However, the object of Vic's obsession tugged at him.

Vic turned to Terrick. "You need to help Brady get out of here."

"What about you?"

"I am going back. I have to know..." he couldn't reveal the truth. "That nobody else is alive back there."

Terrick shared a doubtful look with Colby, but said, "All right."

Once Terrick had an arm around Brady, Vic turned and ran back down the tunnel. He emerged in the torchlit chamber and grabbed another torch, leaving just one burning behind as he entered his own tunnel.

Rocks ranging from pebble-sized to waist-high boulders littered the tunnel floor, but the path was navigable. Dim, warm light waited at the tunnel's far end, the rocks he had placed to hide the opening now shifted and fallen. He reached the tunnel end, squatted before the opening and pulled a heavy chunk of stone aside as another quake struck.

The shockwave passed beneath his feet, causing him to fall to one knee. The tunnel ceiling cracked, split, and massive pieces of rock began to fall, one three times the size of his head just missing him. Driven by urgency, Vic dove through the opening, into the neighboring cavern just as the tunnel roof collapsed. The shaking eased as Vic climbed to his feet and surveyed the chamber.

Boulders, rocks, and debris now covered much of the multi-tiered chamber. A chunk tumbled down from the shaft in the cavern roof and plunged into the lava pool. When the boulder hit the water, glowing, molten rock splashed in all directions, some of the splatter landing on the egg.

Vic gasped, suddenly worried about his precious prize. He leapt down to the tier below and ran across it, dodging fallen rocks while focused on the egg. When but one tier away, he froze.

A crack ran across the egg's iridescent surface. The crack spread and split, and split again, until the entire upper third of the egg burst open into a dozen pieces that tumbled to the ground around it. A twisted mass of dark, wet something jutted up from the remaining two thirds of the egg. Vic stared at it, trapped between shock and wonder.

Then, it moved.

A wing raised up and stretched. Another appeared, followed by a head. Damp, scaly skin and webbed wings were joined by a head and neck with a crest of spikes running down the length. It had a long snout with a blunt end and amber eyes with slits for pupils. The creature crawled out of the egg. Iridescent, dark purple scales cover its head and neck while its body, tail and wings were a dark red.

"A dragon!" Vic exclaimed as he stumbled backward.

Then, another dragon emerged from the egg, this one with a dark green body and purple head and neck. A third followed, its body orange.

Then came a fourth, its body black, and although each dragon had a different coloring, all had a neck and head of purple and each was larger than Vic, leaving him wondering how all four had been packed into that single egg.

The dragons all turned their snake-like eyes toward him. The one with the red body then released a roar, revealing a jaw filled with sharp, white teeth. Three of the dragons suddenly stormed at Vic. In his panic to retreat, Vic's heel caught on a rock and he fell backward. He rolled over and scrambled to his feet to find the dragons surrounding him with the red one standing between him and the opening to the neighboring tunnel. Even if the tunnel was navigable after the collapse, he was trapped. The word *Hungry* kept echoing in his head, the monsters salivating as they edged toward him. His heart thumped in alarm, and his mind screamed, *Please don't eat me.*

The dragons all stopped, several of them tilting their heads as they stared at him. His breath came in gasps, and he was unsure what to do. The body of each dragon matched his own size, excluding the massive wings and long tail. While he might be able to fight one, he could not face all four and hope to survive. He gathered his courage, hoping his voice would remain steady.

"Easy," Vic crooned. "I am your friend. I have been visiting you, talking to you every day."

All four dragons tilted their heads from side to side. None advanced on him.

"I suspect you are hungry, but you don't want to eat me." He pointed toward the opening in the cavern ceiling. "If you fly out, you can find food. Maybe a nice cow, or some chickens?"

The dragons glanced at each other and then back to Vic. In his head, he urged, *Go on. Fly out. Be free.*

As one, the dragons burst into action, more than one coming toward Vic, who recoiled and raised an arm in protection. Instead of attacking, the creatures scrambled past him, hopping down to the tier below while following their brethren. Just before reaching the broken eggshell, the red one leapt into the air, spread its wings, and pumped them mightily. It streaked up toward the cavern ceiling and disappeared up the shaft.

In rapid succession, the other dragons took flight and sailed up the shaft, leaving Vic alone. The awe and fear that had dominated his thoughts faded away. He realized that he was alone and trapped underground. The tunnel collapse had left him with no way out.

CHAPTER 25

FLIGHT

A void of blackness surrounded Ian, pain the only thing tangible. He hurt, an ache radiating from his side like a horrible spasm timed to the beat of his heart.

"Ian," a voice called in the void, but it was distant and the source undefined.

"Ian," the voice called again.

His body shifted, and light appeared before him.

"Ian," the voice called. "Come to me."

Was this the afterlife? Was he being drawn to a place where pain was nothing but a distant memory? He stretched toward it and pain struck again, this time in the face.

He blinked his eyes open and lifted a hand to his cheek, still stinging from a slap. The blurred image of a giant, black beard hovered over him. Squinting, his eyes came into focus, and he saw the face attached to the beard.

"Korrigan?" Ian groaned.

"You are alive," the dwarf said.

Ian then remembered Rysildar presenting his gift to the king and council. *The Drow betrayed the king. I must warn others.* Pain flared from his side when he tried to sit up, causing him to cry out.

"Don't," Korrigan said. "Let me help you up. We will find a flesh mender."

The dwarf went behind Ian, slid his hands under his arms, and lifted him to a standing position. Ian pressed his hand against his wound, his fingers around the base of the arrow sticking out from his side. With shuffling steps, he slowly turned as he surveyed the temple.

Broken stone, shattered glass, and bloodied corpses lay everywhere. Among the dead were twelve dark elves, fifteen dwarven warriors, the council members, King Arangar, and finally Devigar. The old chancellor lay beside a pillar, his head cracked open, his eyes staring into space.

"They are all dead," Ian muttered.

Korrigan nodded gravely. "All except for you."

"What of Rysildar?"

"He and his Drow warriors have taken the city. Some fought against dark elves, but the singer's magic incinerated them. Others hurriedly threw down their weapons." Korrigan shook his head. "I have never been so ashamed of my people."

"But you are warriors."

"Our greatest warriors, at least those who survived Gahagar's endless war, are away from the city. Some are stationed at other holds, but many chose another life altogether. Only the less skilled and unexperienced ones are assigned to guard Ra'Tahal, for its walls are impenetrable." He looked at Ian. "How did they get into the citadel?"

"Rysildar's magic. He used it to tear a hole in reality and open a gateway to someplace called Talastar." An image of the crystal and the rift it produced remained firmly fixed in Ian's mind. It was both the most wondrous and terrible thing he had ever seen.

"How can that be?" The dwarf's brow furrowed. "Talastar is thousands of miles away."

"That is what King Arangar said, right before he was murdered."

A monstrous cry echoed in the temple, startling both Ian and the dwarf. A second later, a purple and red winged creature sailed up from the pit opening, shot toward the temple ceiling, and disappeared through the broken dome. Another set of cries came from the pit just before a string of three more monsters emerged. Streaks of orange, green, and black sailed past and were gone in an instant.

"What was that?" Ian asked, stunned.

"Dragons. Young ones." Korrigan crept toward the opening in the floor and peered over the edge. "The better question to ask is how they got down into the pit in the first place."

Ian's eyes widened as he remembered his brother's discovery. "It was the egg."

Korrigan spun toward him. "What egg?"

"My brother...he found an egg near a lava pool in a hidden cavern connected to the mine."

"He what?" the dwarf exclaimed. "I heard nothing of this, and I am captain of the city guard."

The secrecy with which Vic treated the issue struck Ian. "He...did not wish to tell anyone."

Korrigan sighed. "I suppose a fresh clutch of dragons is the least of our issues right now."

A distant cry came from the pit, this time as a male voice. In Ian's native language, the person cried, "Help!"

Ian gasped, recognizing the voice. He limped over to the opening, taking care to avoid stepping on any bodies, glass, or debris. At the edge of the pit, he stopped, the air wafting up from below warming his face.

Drawing in a deep breath, Ian gasped and winced, the pain in his side flaring. With as much force as he could muster, Ian shouted, "Vic? Is that you?"

Vic's distant voice called back. "Ian! I need help. The tunnel collapsed. I am trapped."

It took a beat for the situation to sink in. The lava pool was easily five hundred feet down, perhaps twice that distance. In that hot environment without access to water or food, Vic would not last more than a day or two.

He spun toward Korrigan, who stood a few strides away with a furrowed brow. "My brother is down there. He says that he is trapped and cannot get out."

The dwarf approached Ian. "How did he get there in the first place?"

Ian recalled Vic's story. "He discovered the cavern with the lava pool when mining a tunnel adjacent to it. That tunnel collapsed, so the way he entered cannot be used to leave. I need your help to save him."

Korrigan nodded. "Tell him we need some time. We will get him out, but first, I need to get you to a healer."

THE ROCK VIC sat on was hard, uneven, and uncomfortable, but it offered a respite from standing. Covered in dirt, sore, and sweating, he remained as far from the lava pool as possible. During his four weeks of visiting the cavern, it had never felt so hot. He suspected the quake had disturbed the molten rock and released more heat than ever. Fumes filled the chamber. Despite the shaft acting as a chimney and a vent, releasing bad air and replacing it with good, the balance had been shifted and breathing the tainted air made him feel sleepy. He worried that if he had to wait much longer, he would succumb to his exhaustion and never wake.

Then, he heard Ian's distant call, "Vic!"

Vic stood and stared up at the opening in the chamber ceiling, uncertain if his mind was playing tricks on him.

"Vic!" the voice carried down from the shaft again.

After climbing down a tier, Vic staggered across it, cupped his hands to his mouth, and shouted. "I am still here."

"We are sending down a rope. Shout before it reaches the pit. We will then swing it to you."

His thoughts clouded and spots dancing before his eyes, Vic tried to make sense of his brother's words. "Help me, Ian!"

Staring up at the opening in the ceiling, Vic swayed, his weight shifting from foot to foot, trying to remain awake while also not collapsing. Moments later, a large, black cauldron appeared from the shaft opening. A thick rope was tied to the kettle's handle. The cauldron twirled slowly as it descended toward the pool of molten rock. Vic watched it, his thoughts bogged down in the thick haze clouding his mind. *I am supposed to do something.* He could not recall what until it was almost too late.

"Stop!" he shouted.

The cauldron stopped just above the lava. The rope jerked and the kettle began to swing. Again and again, the rope waved. With each movement, the sway of the kettle increased. Vic stumbled over to the rock pile where the egg had once been, the broken shell pieces the only things remaining. The kettle swung toward him. He reached out to catch the handle, but his vision had doubled. Between the two images he now saw, he tried for the wrong one. With the next swing, Vic reached for both images of the cauldron. His hands passed through both handles and met in the middle, where they found something. He clamped one hand around iron and pain flared, the metal hot enough to burn him. Vic instantly let go but swiped with the other hand, latching onto the rope just above the handle. Even that was hot, but not so much as to burn.

Ignoring the pain of his burning hand, Vic leaned back, pulling the rope taut before he shouted. "I have it!"

The rope went slack, causing him to stumble backward and almost let go, but he caught himself and held on. The cauldron bounced on the ground and settled. Vic's head swam, and he knew he was running out of time. He had no knife to cut the rope, so he stepped into the cauldron with one leg to either side of the handle. After wrapping the rope around his wrist once, he gripped it with his good hand and placed the other above it.

He drew a deep breath and shouted. "Lift me up!"

The rope tightened. It lifted him off the ground and swept him toward the lava pool. Intense heat enveloped him as he swung over the lava and past it. The cauldron swayed back as the rope continued to rise. Sweat covered Vic's entire body, his palms slick, the thick, stifling air burning his lungs. It took every ounce of concentration he could muster to maintain his grip and remain conscious. The cavern floor grew increasingly distant while the top of the domed ceiling drew closer. Finally, Vic entered the shaft, the kettle slowly rotating as it rose higher. The heat receded to a tolerable level.

Up, and up he rose, the shaft walls gradually sloping inward, time trickling while he fought to hold his grip and remain conscious. When he was fifty feet from the top, the kettle struck the side of the well, bounced off it, and hit it again. Soon, it scrapped and bounced along the wall as he ascended. When the shaft lip drew near, Vic unwound the rope from his wrist, freeing it and allowing him to slap a hand up onto the floor. Thick fingers gripped his wrist. He reached up with the other hand and that was grabbed as well. Two dwarf faces appeared as they lifted him up and over the edge, Korrigan and another whose name he did not know.

When they let go, Vic lay on the floor, surrounded by broken rock and shards of glass. He rolled over and stared up at the blue sky through the broken temple dome. Sweet, blessedly fresh air filled his lungs, the cloud in his head receding.

Ian knelt beside him. "You look horrible. Are you hurt?'

Vic opened his palm. It was red and blistered. "I burned my hand. Otherwise, I think I'll be fine."

"Can you stand?"

"Yeah."

He rolled to his hands and knees, placed one foot beneath him, and the room spun. His innards cramped and he vomited. Once, twice, three times he wretched, emptying the meager contents of his stomach.

Ian chuckling caused Vic to look up at him with a frown.

"Why are you laughing?" Vic asked.

"Sorry. It is just a funny turn from our past. How many times have you rescued me? How often have you looked on while I emptied my stomach?"

Despite the situation, Vic chuckled. "I see what you mean." He stood, looked around and was stunned by what he saw.

Bloody corpses lay in all directions, amid rubble of stone, wood, and glass. The rope used to hoist him out of the pit ran to the side of the chamber and around a pillar. A third dwarf stood by the pillar, the rope at his feet, a bow on his shoulder, and his eyes toward the temple entrance while he stroked the pommel of the short sword at his hip.

Vic asked, "What happened here?"

Ian's smile slid away. "Something horrible."

Korrigan gripped Ian by the arm and said something in Dwarvish. The only word Vic understood was *hurry*.

"What's wrong?" Vic asked.

"We need to leave. Korrigan wants us to follow him and remain quiet." Ian gestured toward the other two dwarves. "The one holding the axe is Vargan and the one with the sword and bow is Ipsegar. They are coming with us."

Vic followed their lead. "Where are we going?"

"We need to escape the citadel."

"Why?"

Ian stopped. "Ask questions later. For now, do as we tell you and remain quiet."

Taken aback, Vic paused for a beat. He was unused to Ian giving orders. To see his brother taking charge and keeping a level head in such a precarious situation caused him to reassess his opinion and acknowledge that Ian had changed since leaving Shillings.

With a shake of his head to clear his thoughts, Vic hurried after the others, stepping over and around corpses on his way toward the exit. While many of the dead were dwarves, there were others dressed in dark leather, their skin pale, their ears long and pointed. He spied a weapon on the floor, squatted and picked it up. The weapon appeared much like a pick, but the opposite face was flat and square. The weapon shaft was wrapped in leather, the head stamped with a bronze symbol. A guard working in the mine used a similar weapon, and in curiosity, Vic had asked him about it one time. That dwarf had referred to the weapon as a mattock, its weight, the shape of the head, and length of the handle all of a slight but important difference from those of a pick.

"What are you doing?" Ian asked.

"Getting a weapon. From the looks of what happened here, I thought I might need it."

Ian opened his mouth, as if to say something but just nodded before turning and hurrying after Korrigan. Just inside the doors, the three dwarves each grabbed a full pack leaning against the wall and hoisted it to their shoulders before Korrigan opened the door. The group gathered behind Korrigan as he peered outside. A beat later, he waved and stepped out with Ian, Vic, Vargan, and Ipsegar following.

Shouts and cries echoed in the citadel streets. A string of four dwarves ran past, a few intersections away. A line of warriors in black chased after them, each holding a blade on a pole, the afternoon sunlight reflecting off the metal edges.

"Who are they?" Vic whispered to Ian.

"Dark elves. Now, hush."

Korrigan waved, and the group took off at a run, toward the south gate. They turned a corner, and the gate came into view. Dwarven warriors and dark elf bodies lay strewn about the ground. Eight dark elves stood beside the closed gate, holding their weapons while scanning the area. One stared right at Vic, pointed, and shouted something.

When Korrigan shouted and bolted east, Vic followed, not needing any translation. He would have run anyway.

They turned at an intersection, raced down a narrow alley, and turned again. Another hundred strides, they ducked into a shaded alcove, where they stood, panting.

Vic furrowed his brow while sorting through the situation in his head, promptly reaching a conclusion. "The dark elves have taken the city."

Ian nodded. "Which is why we are trying to get out."

"What of the other villagers? What of the women the dwarves held captive and threatened to harm if we should flee?"

"I asked Korrigan the same thing. He said that none of that matters now. The king and council are dead, and the surviving dwarves have much bigger issues to deal with than a pair of escaped slaves."

While Ian's explanation made sense, it did not address the bigger question. "If they hold the gates, how do we get out?"

Ian blinked and glanced down the narrow street, toward the eastern wall. "I think I know a way." He spoke to the dwarves, gesturing emphatically toward the wall while doing so. Vic understood a few of the words as Ian claimed he knew another way out. His gaze lowered and he noticed a crimson splotch on Ian's robes and sash.

Vic gasped. "Ian. You are bleeding."

Ian looked down at his side. "No. That was from before. I am good, now."

"What happened?"

He shrugged. "An arrow got me."

The nonchalant response to such a dire event said as much as anything else. Ian had grown up and had done so in quick fashion.

After a brief conversation with the dwarves, Ian gestured toward Vic. "Follow me."

With Ian in the lead, the five of them ran toward the eastern wall, not slowing until they were right upon it. Ian then ran his hands along the sunlit stone. Just when Vic was about to ask what his brother was about, a click resounded, and a door hidden amid the stone blocks swung inward. Darkness waited beyond it.

"Come on," Ian darted inside.

Vic followed, the sunlight seeping through the doorway revealing a staircase with Ian already a dozen stairs below and descending. As Vic followed, so did the dwarves, the last of them closing the door. Darkness crashed in, making it impossible for Vic to even see his own hand in front of his face. He pressed his burnt palm against the stone wall, the cool surface soothing the pain as he continued downward. Torchlight became visible below, beyond the silhouette of his brother. At the bottom were the remains of a doorway, the frame nothing but blackened coal.

"What happened here?" Vic asked.

Ian glanced backward. "This is where I almost died." He gestured toward the frame. "The Drow singer turned the air to fire, incinerating the door and setting my robes ablaze. I raced up and ran back to Devigar's tower where..." He blinked and jerked as if realizing something. "Winnie. She is still there."

Korrigan grunted and spoke in a broken way. "We no go back."

Ian replied in Dwarvish, "What if they kill her?"

Korrigan shook his head and replied using words unfamiliar to Vic, but his meaning was clear. They could not go back for Winnie. The dwarf pushed past Ian and headed down the tunnel. Vargan and Ipsegar followed, leaving the two brothers alone.

"What did he say?" Vic asked.

Ian, appearing unhappy, shook his head. "He said this is too dangerous to bring a girl unless she is strong and brave. If it had been Rina, I'd have argued to get her. Winnie, on the other hand..."

Vic nodded. "I agree. Winnie is a fine woman, but she is neither of those things."

"Let's keep going."

They rushed down the corridor and came to a circular chamber, empty apart from a flickering torch on the wall. On the far side of the chamber was a staircase.

"This is where Rysildar, the Drow singer practiced his magic," Ian said. "Here, he crafted a crystal into an item of tremendous power. He used that crystal to create the doorway that brought the other Drow to Ra'Tahal." He closed his eyes, his shoulders slumping. "Had I known, I could have stopped him."

Vic stared at Ian with a frown. He appeared weary and defeated. *Ian blames himself, but how could he expect to have stopped this dark elf?* He clapped his brother on the shoulder. "We know nothing of magic, Ian. We are just simple townsfolk from a small village. We did not ask to be here. It was not our fault that we were thrown in the middle of this mess, and you can't blame yourself for what happened."

Ian shook his head. "We used to be those things, Vic, but our lives have changed. We cannot blame our own ignorance or stand aside when bad things happen to good people around us, be it humans or dwarves. To do so makes us culpable."

Korrigan snatched the torch off the wall and entered the second stairwell with the other dwarves following.

"Come on," Ian said.

"Where does this lead?" Vic asked.

"I don't know, but we are certainly beyond the citadel walls already. Hopefully, there is a way out at the other end."

They climbed a flight of stairs just as long as the one they had taken down. At the top was a landing with a boulder blocking the way. When Korrigan pushed against the boulder, it slid outward with apparent ease. Daylight shone through the opening. The three dwarves squeezed through with Ian and Vic coming last. They emerged from an outcropping of rock, pushed past a cluster of bushes blocking the opening, and turned to look backward.

Across a field of stumps and yellowed grass stood the citadel walls, a few hundred feet away. The rock outcropping stood halfway between the fortress and the edge of a forest blanketed in leaves turned to the yellows and reds of autumn.

"We go," Korrigan said in the human language.

"Where?" Vic asked.

"Get help. Find Arangoli."

"Who?"

Ian said, "I have heard of Arangoli. He is reputed to be the greatest warrior of his generation. He is also son of Arangar, the king who was just slaughtered."

Ian pushed through the forest, following the other two dwarves. After a backward glance at the walls of Ra'Tahal, Vic followed, feeling very much like he had lost all control over his own life while having no idea where it was headed.

CHAPTER 26
FUGITIVES

The climb down the cliffside consumed much of the afternoon, and the effort left Ian both mentally and physically exhausted after what had already been a difficult day. The dwarf healer who had mended his wound warned that the act would sap his energy, and the aftereffect was undeniable. But Ian, his brother, and the three dwarven warriors were in flight mode. Stopping to rest before sunset was not an option. So, following Korrigan's lead, the party climbed down boulders and narrow shelves in a zig-zagging pattern. Upon reaching a broad shelf, Ian paused and gazed south.

The afternoon sun shone brightly on the towering escarpment. Three miles away, the walls of Ra'Tahal stood at the edge of the cliff while the lower hold bulged out into the broad field at the foot of the cliff. Both appeared lonely and abandoned with no movement visible. The Drow occupation of the citadel troubled Ian far more than he would have anticipated. It wasn't until he was forced to flee that the realization came to light: Over the past two seasons, Ra'Tahal had become his home, and he felt a connection to it and her people despite the circumstance that had brought him there. A part of him recoiled at his feelings of loyalty toward the Tahal Clan, the same part that held a grudge about the death of his father and many other villagers from Shillings. The internal struggle was just one of many, including his mixed emotions about Devigar. The old dwarf had helped Ian adapt and his mentorship had been invaluable, but Devigar's actions had led to the city's downfall, even if his intentions had been well placed. In the end Devigar got what he deserved, at least, that is what Ian told himself. *If that is true, why am I saddened by his death?*

"Ian." Vic's voice drew him from his musings.

He turned to find his brother standing thirty feet below and Korrigan twice that distance.

"Are you alright?" Vic called up.

"Yeah. I was just...thinking."

"Well, you can think when we make camp. If you want to avoid falling and injuring yourself or worse, it might be best if you paid attention to your surroundings."

"Yeah." Ian nodded numbly. "Good idea."

The next section was too steep to descend like stairs, so Ian turned to face the cliffside, lowered himself to his knees, and backed over the edge. With care, he placed a sandaled foot on a knob of rock, found a foothold lower down, and continued, lowering himself step by step until reaching the next ledge, which he walked along as it descended at a gentle slope. He stepped onto a boulder, hopped to another one, and lowered himself down to another ledge. This process continued for another fifteen minutes before the ground leveled. Weary from the effort but relieved to have reached the bottom, Ian stood at the cliff base and surveyed the area.

Long, yellowed grass stretched out between their location and the lower hold while a forest of leaf trees blotted out the view to the west and north.

Korrigan approached Ian and held out a waterskin. "Drink."

Eager to do so, Ian took a long swig.

"Easy," Korrigan touched Ian's arm. "We have to conserve until we can refill the skins."

Ian handed it to Vic and waited for him to drink before turning back to Korrigan. "Where are we heading?"

"Nor'Tahal. It is a modest sized hold, but that was where I last saw Arangoli."

"When was that?"

"This past spring." Korrigan accepted the waterskin from Vic and slid the cord over his shoulder.

Ian frowned. "We are deep into autumn. That was two seasons ago."

"I know," the dwarf admitted, "But we must start somewhere."

"How long will it take to get there?"

"The ground is level, so we should have little trouble keeping a good pace, especially once we reach the northbound trail. I expect it to take five days, but only if we travel from sunrise to sunset." Korrigan turned toward the other two dwarves. "If everyone is ready, we should keep moving and find a place to camp at sunset."

With Korrigan leading, the three dwarves pushed through the undergrowth and headed deeper into the trees, their path angled to the northwest.

Vic sidled up beside Ian and spoke in their home language. "I heard him mention Nor'Tahal. Is that where we are headed?"

"Yes and..." Ian frowned. "You keep asking me to repeat things Korrigan says. Surely, you must know something of their language by now."

Vic furrowed his brow and tilted his head. "Not everyone has your skill with language. I know enough to get by, but they speak so fast, I have a difficult time keeping up."

"Well, we have days of travel ahead of us, so I will teach you what I can." Ian followed the trail of trampled grass and bent undergrowth carved by the three dwarves. "Let's start with something simple. Repeat after me. *Sitio*."

Vic repeated the word. "What does it mean?"

Ian pushed a branch aside while stepping over a fallen log. "Sitio means *I am thirsty*. Now, say it again."

After Vic repeated it, Ian tried another. "Let's try *I am hungry*. The word for that is *esurio*."

Thus, they continued as the day went on with Ian testing Vic's memory and attempting to speak to him in Dwarvish to see if he understood. All the while, the shadows amid the trees thickened.

IN A QUIET GLADE surrounded by trees, Ian, Vic, Korrigan, Vargan, and Ipsegar sat around a crackling fire. The heat radiating from the flames balanced the chill of night. Weary, Ian stared into the flames and dreamed of a solid, hot meal rather than the trail rations he had been relegated to since breakfast early that day.

The mood among the group was sullen and subdued. Nobody mentioned what had occurred in Ra'Tahal, but Ian was certain that it weighed on everyone's mind. Thus, he sought to engage in conversation to break the tension and give everyone something else to think about.

"What can you tell me about this Arangoli?"

Korrigan glanced at the other two dwarves, who both shrugged. "Vargan, Ispegar, and I all grew up with Arangoli in Ra'Tahal. At the time, his father was a warrior in Gahagar's Army, and while Arangar was a captain and leader, he had not yet been anointed as King. That was Gahagar's role. Rather than being a prince, Arangoli was like us, just another youth dreaming of fighting for our people. When we were young, we pretended we were warriors, battling in the square with sticks rather than using true weapons. Even then, it was clear that Goli was the strongest and quickest among us.

"When we were of age, we began official training under the guidance of Captain Shookle. We each claimed a weapon. Following in Arangar's footsteps, Goli selected a war hammer. Ipsegar went with a short sword. Vargan chose the axe. Following the footsteps of my deceased father, I took up his mace, a weapon that had been in my family for three generations.

"The four of us trained hard and rose through the ranks together. Six years ago, we graduated and were sent to join Gahagar and the army up north, in Drovaria. Only weeks after we reached the front, Gahagar died. The circumstances of his death remain suspect, but the truth is, without him to hold the clans together, the war could not continue. Those of us who were new to the army argued to continue the campaign. After only a taste of battle, our desire to prove ourselves remained unsated. Despite Arangoli's attempts to convince his father otherwise, it was too late. The other clans returned to their own lands, reducing our army to one third. The war was over, so the Tahal clan began the long march home.

"When back in Ra'Tahal, the army leaders backed Arangar as king, with only Devigar as possible opposition. With the backing of the military, which the chancellor lacked, Arangar's crowning was a simple formality. The responsibility of rule and decades of fighting combined to force Arangar to give up his prized, legendary weapon. He gifted it to Arangoli with the intent that his son would stand at his side and help defend the city. Goli thought otherwise.

"He and other young warriors left Ra'Tahal, seeking an enemy to fight. Goli begged me to come with him, but Arangar promised to raise me to captain if I remained and agreed to lead the warriors who would call the city home. Loyalty to my city and king, along with that opportunity, kept me in Ra'Tahal. I also convinced these two to remain with me, and the rest...well, you know fairly well by now." Korrigan shook his head. "I just wish we had never turned to enslaving humans, regardless of the circumstances. Had we not, you two would still be in your village, safe and far from here."

Ian had listened closely, and questions came to mind as Korrigan relayed the story. "You mentioned a legendary weapon."

"Yes. The war hammer, Tremor. It belonged to Arangar's father before he bequeathed it to Arangoli. It was crafted in Valas Fornax by a metal wright and enhanced by a spell wright." Korrigan lifted his mace, an oddly shaped weapon, a foot and a half long handle connected to a boxy-shaped chunk of metal formed with flared edges that came to a point at the end. Runes and silvery script marked the head and shaft of the mace. "As was my weapon, Skull Crusher."

"And you think Arangoli can help us?"

Korrigan sneered. "Those dirty, dark elves have taken my city. We have to reclaim it and crush them, so they never try something like this again. Arangoli may have had issues with Arangar, but he will not allow his father's death and betrayal to go unpunished. He will help us, and with him and the other Head Thumpers on our side, we will find a way to win."

"Head Thumpers?"

The dwarf shared a wry smile. "That is what Arangoli's team call themselves. They are a wild lot, but they are skilled and each is worth more than three other warriors."

Ian knew nothing of the Head Thumpers, but Korrigan was far more experienced with such things, so he decided not to pursue that line of questioning any further. He then considered what waited in Ra'Tahal and what they might face. Even if they, somehow, found a way into the citadel and were able to overwhelm the Drow warriors, one daunting issue remained unsolved.

"What about Rysildar's magic?" Ian asked.

Vargan said, "We will find a way, singer or not."

Both Korrigan and Ipsegar grunted in agreement, the latter saying, "And we will make them wish they'd never betrayed our clan."

The vehement response made it clear how the dwarves felt. There would be no way to talk them out of it, and Ian had nowhere else to go. He glanced over at Vic, who had remained quiet the entire time, listening. But whether he understood, Ian wasn't sure.

"Enough chatter for tonight," Korrigan declared. "It is late. We have a long day tomorrow, and I intend for us to depart at first light. You should get some sleep." He dug into his pack, pulled out a cloak, and tossed it to Ian. "Use this to stay warm."

Ian caught the cloak while Vargan tossed one to Vic. The three dwarves all lay down, the crackle of the fire the only sound remaining as the camp fell still.

Weariness wore on Ian, so he was not about to argue about sleeping. He wrapped the cloak around himself and curled up on his side, using the hood bunched up as a makeshift pillow for his head. Just two feet away, Vic lay on his side, facing him.

"What did you talk about?" Vic whispered.

In a hushed voice, Ian explained, "I asked about Arangoli and why we were trying to find him. Korrigan made it clear that he will stop at nothing to retake Ra'Tahal and he views Arangoli as the one dwarf who can help him achieve that goal."

"Why do we care what happens to the dwarves? Look what they did to us, what they did to pa."

It was like Vic was voicing the internal battles Ian had already fought. "I know. Yet...what else can we do?"

"We could return to Shillings," Vic offered.

Ian had considered the idea many times since being abducted. Over the course of two seasons, the answer had slowly changed until the truth squashed his childhood desires. "There is nothing there for us, Vic. Pa is dead. Our house and his shop both burned to the ground. Our friends are gone. Heck, I think everyone is gone. And mother is still out there, somewhere. Maybe she is in Nor'Tahal. If not, there are only a few other holds. We could look for her."

"And if we find her?"

Ian was unprepared for the question. "I...don't know."

"Hush, you two," Korrigan growled.

Ian sighed. "Korrigan is correct. We need to sleep."

After a silent beat, Vic said, "Very well, but we will need to decide on a path for the future at some point."

"I suppose, but the answers seem impossible to determine right now. I just hope that, so long as we do not give up, something will happen and the future will figure itself out."

The camp fell quiet. Ian's eyes grew heavy, and sleep soon claimed him.

.

CHAPTER 27

THE AGROSI

Before daylight could mask the starry sky, the dwarves broke camp with Vic using the flat end of his mattock to scoop dirt onto the smoldering coals of the fire. Korrigan again led them northwest and within twenty minutes of walking, they reached the forest's edge. Vic strode out of the trees through yellowed grass that reached his knees and stared out at the new vista.

Vast, rolling plains stretched out to the west and north. Yellowed grass dominated the scene in all directions other than the forest behind them. Winds blowing from the west caused the grass to dance in waves, reminding him of a mountain breeze stirring the surface of Lake Shillings. The thought brought a pang of loss. He missed his home and the peace and simplicity of his prior life, but Ian was right. They could not go back. It would not be the same. Nothing would ever be the same.

To the distant northwest, a single, lonely peak stood tall above the open plains. Even farther away, masked by the haze of the great distance, mountains defined the horizon everywhere Vic could see. No more than fifty strides away, a dirt road ran parallel to the tree line.

The party of two humans and three dwarves walked through the grass and turned north when they reached the road. Their pace then quickened, the forest rolling by on their right, the expanse of grass to their left. Ian asked Korrigan a question, Vic staring into the distance rather than attempting to translate it in his head. The dwarf gestured toward the plains as he responded.

"What did he say?" Vic asked when Korrigan was finished.

Ian replied, "The dwarves call this open land the Agrosi. He claims that beasts roam this land, some harmless, others dangerous. Nor'Tahal resides at the foot of those mountains, north of the plains." He pointed down the road.

"It will take four more days to reach the hold?"

"More or less, depending on our pace and the weather. If it rains, it will slow us down."

They continued walking at a fast pace.

Ian added, "There are two way-stops between here and our destination. Korrigan hopes to make the first one tonight."

"How far is that?"

Ian winced. "Thirty miles away."

"Ugh," Vic groaned. It was a good distance to walk through a land filled with strange beasts.

Vic found himself wishing he had a harness for his mattock. It did not weigh that much, and he was strong, but gripping it with both or either of his hands all day long proved to be exhausting. Doing so left his fingers cramped and his forearms stiff.

In contrast, the three dwarves carried their weapons with ease – Korrigan's mace on a loop secured to his belt, Ipsegar's sword in the scabbard at his side and short bow over his shoulder. Even Vargan, whose axe was strapped to his back, left Vic envious. The dwarves also seemed tireless, their pace steady and quick despite their shorter strides.

They did appear to need to stop to rest and ate only the same meager trail rations he and Ian were given. When he considered complaining and realized that even Ian had avoided doing so, Vic remained silent, determined to avoid being the first. *I am the older brother and the stronger one. If he doesn't complain, I certainly cannot.*

Thus, he walked and walked, his only words the dwarven translations that Ian continued to make him recite. Vic had to admit, he had learned more in the course of a day with Ian than he had after twenty-some weeks of working in the mine.

And so, the day wore on and the miles slipped past. It was mid-afternoon when they stopped for the third time, allowing him to set his mattock down and sit on a rock between the road and the tree line, while he gazed out over the grasslands and the wind whipped his hair. It was a peaceful, restful moment until a distant rumble arose above the noise of the rustling of leaves and swishing grass. Vic listened closely. Without a doubt, the sound was drawing nearer.

"What is that sound?" he asked.

Ian shrugged and glanced at Korrigan.

The dwarf held up his hand and said something in Dwarvish. Vic understood two words. *Quiet* and *Danger.*

The rumble grew louder and louder until motion appeared on the plains as a herd of horses crested a hilltop. Brown, black, grey, patched and piebald steeds raced over the hill and down the other side, coming straight toward the party. At their lead was a glorious white stallion, but it was not a mere horse. A three-foot-long, spiral shaped horn thrust up from the top of the steed's head. Sunlight glinted off the silvery horn, making it impossible not to notice.

Ian whispered, "A unicorn."

Vic shook his head. "I don't believe it."

Vargan hissed something in Dwarvish.

His voice barely audible, Ian said, "Do not move."

The horses raced toward the party and, just before reaching the road, slowed to a stop. The unicorn turned slowly, eyeing Vic and his companions while positioned between them and the herd. The horses began to graze, seemingly unconcerned. A tense, yet silent, moment passed as the unicorn stared warily at them and the others chomped on the grass. A branch behind Vic snapped, causing him to flinch and the unicorn to shift its head slightly. Ever so slowly, Vic turned toward the trees.

Thick trunks, orange, red, and yellow leaves, and green undergrowth filled his view while shadows lurked deeper in the wood. Amid those shadows, something moved. Terror tightened his chest, causing him to freeze. Pushing past the fear, he eased his hand down to his side and wrapped his fingers around the mattock handle. The shadow burst forward and barreled through the trees. It was not alone.

Three massive, cat-like creatures burst from the forest, one of them leaping right toward Vic, forcing him to dive out of the way. He hit the ground, rolled, and scrambled to his feet with the weapon held in front of him, ready for an attack.

The cats, each thrice the size of a man, were covered in gray fur with black stripes. They stood on the road, facing the herd, their massive, razor-sharp teeth flashing as they snarled. The cats charged at the horses. Rather than turn and bolt, the entire herd stood rock still. The unicorn lowered its head, dug at the turf with its hoof, and a burst of silvery light shot out from the horn just as the middle, charging cat leapt toward it. The light struck the feline full on, the blast altering its path and sending it crashing into the cat to its right. Both fell in a heap, the first behaving as if frozen in a block of ice, its limbs, tail, and expression locked in place.

The third cat raced past the unicorn and made straight for the herd. The unicorn spun toward it and another beam of silvery light burst forth, striking the feline. It tumbled, rolled, and came to a stop just shy of the herd. Like the first, it lay there, frozen stiff.

The only unparalyzed cat climbed to its feet and shook its head, as if to clear it. It released an angry snarl, and the unicorn turned toward it.

Rather than attack, the cat turned and sped toward the forest. Again, Vic braced himself for an attack, but the cat angled to avoid him and his companions, burst into the brush, and faded in the forest shadows.

The unicorn reared back, rising on its hind legs as it released a mighty whinny. It then turned and galloped north. The herd of horses burst into a run, following the magical steed as it crested a hilltop. The unicorn disappeared over the other side and the herd of horses followed. Soon, only the fading rumble of their hooves remained until even that was gone.

Korrigan hoisted his pack. "We must go."

He and the other two dwarves took off at a jog. Vic and Ian followed as they ran north for a full mile before the dwarves slowed.

Vic glanced back but only saw empty fields and the bordering tree line. "What was that all about?"

Ian asked Korrigan, who went into a detailed explanation, his hands waving and his expression serious.

When the dwarf finished, Ian said, to Vic, "The unicorn leads the herd. It has dangerous magic, which it used to paralyze the attacking werecats. Crossing either creature can be deadly. To be caught in between them...Korrigan says we were lucky that neither decided we were a threat."

While that made sense, one obvious question remained unanswered. "Why did we run after the herd left?"

Ian explained, "The spell will soon wear off and the werecats will be angry. It is better to be far away when that happens."

Vic glanced back, now glad to be holding the mattock. Whether he would survive an attack, he had no idea, but he felt better knowing he had some way to fight back.

CHAPTER 28
WAYSTOP

With the sun melting into a dark cloud along the horizon, Ian crested a hill and stopped beside the three dwarves. His legs shook, causing him to wobble with the wind. He had never been strong, and although the past year had improved his endurance, walking at a fast clip from sun up to sun down wore on him.

"There's the first waystop." Korrigan pointed.

Then, Ian spied it. Two hilltops away, likely a mile distant, stood a structure made of brown stone. The building stood above the grass-covered hills like a rodent on its hind legs, startled and alert. The road appeared to run between the waystop and the forest.

"Daylight wanes. Let's keep going, so we make it before dark," Korrigan resumed walking "I prefer not to be out here at night this far from a hold."

Ian could hardly argue the point. He wished he could will himself to the building rather than walk, but such abilities were beyond him. If he had been asked even a week ago, he would have steadfastly insisted nobody could do such a thing. The gateway opened by Rysildar had altered that opinion and left him wondering what magic could not do.

Unwilling to ask anyone to carry him and having no other means of traveling the remaining mile, he forced himself into a walk. The sandals on his feet had never felt so heavy.

At Ian's side walked Vic. Quiet, with his jaw set. Other than the Dwarvish Ian was teaching Vic little had been said since the werecat attack. Ian's thoughts shifted back to the incident. The werecats had moved with frightening quickness and power. The thought of facing three of them left Ian terrified. The unicorn's majesty brought on entirely different feelings.

In his entire life, Ian had only seen a handful of horses. The wild herd must have numbered at least sixty, perhaps even eighty steeds in total. He knew little of horses, but he could understand why the herd followed the unicorn. The sight of the legendary creature had left Ian compelled to follow it, and he would have done so if not for the presence of the three werecats.

They reached the bottom of the hill, followed level ground for a bit, then climbed the next rise. At the top, the waystop came back into view. Although the distance was half that of the prior sighting, the sun was hidden behind a storm cloud, bathing the Agrosi in the dim light of dusk. Down that hill, across another low area, and up the next had them approaching the building as shadows thickened and dusk prepared to give way to night.

The ground around the waystop had been shaved away, leaving a flat top to the hill where nothing grew. The building was shaped like a cube built upon a base of square pillars. Wooden fencing connected the pillars, making a pen of sorts beneath the structure.

Korrigan approached the gate, pulled a lever, slid a bolt aside, and opened it. The party filed inside before Korrigan closed and secured the door.

Once inside, Ian realized that a column much thicker than the others stood beneath the center of the structure. In that column was a wooden door, reinforced by metal bands and studs. As they walked beneath the building, heading toward that door, Ian noted a long trough at one side of the yard. It smelled much like the Wescott farm.

"What is this space for?" he asked.

"Riders leave their horses in this pen. The trough is so they can drink." Korrigan pointed. "Try to avoid stepping in the manure. The waystop can be a bit stuffy, and we don't need any additional odors inside with us."

As Korrigan reached the door, he held his hand to a bronze panel beside it. The door clicked and swung open. "After you," he said.

Vargan and Ispegar entered while Ian glanced at Vic, who shrugged. Following, Ian found himself in a stairwell with only half a dozen ascending stairs before reaching a landing. To one side was a wall, to the other, a hole in the ground. He began climbing while looking over the interior railing, into the hole, but found only darkness below, which left him wondering how deep it ran. The air smelled dank and musty.

Upon reaching the landing, they turned ninety degrees and climbed six more stairs before turning again. After three such turns, they reached another door. Beside the door was a bucket tied to a rope running over a pulley. Ian realized that a well existed in the center of the stairs, the mustiness a hint of the water waiting far below.

Vargan opened the door and led them into a dark room with only the faint light of dusk seeping through the narrow slits on the western wall. The dwarf fumbled for a moment before warm light bloomed from a quartz column in the middle of the room.

The space was roughly thirty feet long and half as wide. At one end were shelves filled with crates, barrels, and sacks. A stack of wood and a brick oven stood near the shelves. To the other side were a table, six chairs, and more shelving filled with supplies and even a few weapons, including four bows, eight quivers, a handful of spears, and the largest wooden bolts Ian had ever seen – each four feet long, thicker than his wrist, and sharpened to a point on one end. To either side of the stairwell were open doors leading to a pair of rooms with four bunks in each.

Like the chamber in which they stood, the two bedrooms had a quartz column in the center with a brass lever sticking out from it.

"Welcome to your first waystop." Korrigan walked over to the first set of shelves and began ruffling through the crates. "First things first, we find something to eat. We will drink our fill of water here and then refill our skins and packs with provisions before we leave in the morning. Since nobody else is here right now, you two can take one room, Vargan, Ipsegar, and I will take the other." Korrigan reached into a sack, pulled out something, and spun around with a grin, holding oval, brown objects in his hand. "Who wants a baked potato?"

A THUMP SHOOK Ian's bed, waking him. He sat up in the darkness and struck his head on the bunk above him. The pain made him wince and press his palm to the bump on his forehead as he swung his feet off the bed. The stone floor felt cold beneath his bare feet. He lifted his gaze to the narrow window as a flicker of light flashed outside.

Vic's voice came from the bunk above him. "Ian? Are you feeling well?"

"I am fine. That storm we saw on the horizon is upon us. Its thunder woke me and I bumped my head."

"I felt it when..." A thump shook the room, interrupting Vic. "What was that?"

Ian stood and walked to the window. Clouds blanketing the sky masked the moon and stars, leaving the plains thick with shadow. Another thump shook the building. Vic jumped down and stood at Ian's side, the two of them staring out into the night. Lightning flashed, lighting up the plains. Ian gasped.

A few hundred feet away stood a massive creature, fifty feet tall and weighing more than a house. It walked on two, thick, meaty legs, its body bare other than a loincloth the size of a tent. The creature took a step, the thump of its footstep shaking the waystop despite the distance. Thunder rumbled and darkness returned, engulfing the creature in the gloom of night. Although Ian could no longer see the monster, the sight of it remained affixed in his mind and left him frozen in shock. Panic squeezed a tight grip around his throat.

In a hushed tone, Vic asked, "Did you see that?"

"Yes," Ian croaked.

"What was it?"

In Ian's studies of the bestiary of creatures originating from the Vale, only one matched the description of what he and Vic had just seen. "I think it was a rock troll."

Thump. Thump. Thump. The monster's footsteps shook the building again. Lightning flashed to reveal the troll standing much closer. With a bald head, a big nose, black eyes, and a thrusting jaw with an underbite, the troll was as ugly as anything Ian had ever seen. Two sharp teeth, each the size of a man, stuck up over the monster's upper lip. Lightning flashed again as the behemoth opened its massive mouth. It looked at the waystop and released a mighty roar, the volume loud enough that Ian felt it vibrate in his chest.

Terrified, he backed from the window. "What do we do?"

The door flung open, causing Ian and Vic to spin toward it. In the warm light of the central column stood Korrigan with his mace in both hands.

"We have trouble," the dwarf growled.

"A troll," Ian said.

"Yes." He gestured toward Vic's weapon leaning against the wall. "Grab your mattock, Vic. You are coming with me and Vargan."

Ian glanced at Vic before asking, "What about me?"

Korrigan gestured with the weapon in his hand. "You can help Ipsegar, on the roof."

Ian blanched. "The roof?"

"He is manning the ballistae. Grab two bolts off the shelf, climb up, and help him reload. Vargan, Vic, and I are going down to the pen."

Ian glanced at Vic and translated what he was to do, just to be sure he understood.

"What about you?" Vic asked.

"Don't worry about me." Ian had spent his entire life having others care for him. During his time in Ra'Tahal, he had learned to fend for himself, and he was not about to revert to his old self.

He rushed out into the common room, and found two wooden bolts, the shafts thick enough that his fingers could not touch his thumb when wrapped around them. He cradled them in one arm, gripped the ladder beside the stairwell door, and climbed up. Upon reaching the open trapdoor at the top, Ian wrapped his free arm around the ladder pole, gripped one of the bolts, and held it while placing the other on the flat roof. The second bolt followed before he climbed up and out.

Ipsegar stood just a stride away, staring out into the night. Beside him was the dark silhouette of a war machine mounted to the roof. Lightning flashed to reveal the troll standing a hundred feet away and staring in Ian's direction. The monster's eyes widened and it thumped its chest with a fist big enough to crush him. Lightning flashed again as the creature stomped toward the waystop, its heavy footsteps shaking the structure and causing Ian's courage to quake.

The dwarf turned the ballista, took aim, and pulled the release. A heavy thwap sang out and the bolt sped toward the charging behemoth, striking it in the blubbery stomach. Despite the four-foot long, three inch in diameter shaft sticking out from it, the monster did not slow.

With urgency, Ipsegar cranked on the lever sticking out from the ballista, a series of ratcheting clicks coming from it as the launch arm slid backward.

"Slide a bolt in," Ipsegar urged.

Ian placed a bolt into the channel running down the center of the ballista, his gaze then rising to the darkness, seeking the troll while wishing he could flee. Lightning flashed, the flicker of light revealing the troll thirty feet away and advancing far too quickly. As darkness crashed back in, thunder rolled, joining the heavy thumps of the monster's stomping footsteps.

Ipsegar tilted the ballista up and launched again. The bolt struck the troll in the shoulder, the force of the blow causing it to twist and stumble a step. The monster roared in anger and pain.

"By Vandasal's beard, I missed!" Ipsegar swore.

"You hit it," Ian insisted.

"I aimed for the throat." Ipsegar urgently cracked the launch lever back. "Another bolt. Hurry."

Vic, Korrigan, and Vargan stood in the fenced-in pen beneath the waystop. Taking care to do so quietly, Korrigan opened the gate and slid out with Vargan and Vic following. The trio edged along the wall of the pen and rounded the corner. The troll, standing outside the rear of the building, released an enraged roar when a bolt plunged into its shoulder. After a stumble, it swept a hand over the rooftop. A body flipped through the air, arced across the cloud-covered, night sky, and plummeted to the ground fifty feet away.

"Ian!" Vic screamed and raced out toward the still, shadowy shape lying in the long grass.

CHAPTER 29
BEHEMOTH

Moments Earlier

Ian bent to grab another bolt as the monster lunged. A humongous arm swept over the building grazing him and sending him sprawling across the rooftop, his momentum stopping with his head and an arm dangling over the edge. The dwarf was not so lucky.

The troll's hand struck Ipsegar, knocking his helmet off and launching him into the night.

Suddenly alone on the rooftop, Ian froze, afraid that if he moved, the troll would react and crush him.

A roar came from below as Korrigan and Vargan burst out from beneath the building. The dwarfs ran over to the troll's foot, wound back, and attacked. Korrigan's mace smashed into the troll's big toe, shattering the toenail. At the same time, Vargan attacked the small toe, his axe chopping deep into it. The troll roared and yanked its foot back.

Since Vargan continued to grip the shaft of the axe, still stuck in the troll's toe, the dwarf was thrown onto his back.

With the troll's attention on the two dwarves, Ian scrambled to his feet and spun, searching for the dropped bolt. There. Right at the foot of the ballista. He darted over to the war machine and began cranking the launch arm back. The crank was difficult to move, requiring all of his strength and causing him to wind it far slower than Ispegar had. The entire time, he watched the troll while praying it would not come for him.

VIC FELL to his knees beside the still form, his heart breaking at the mere thought of losing Ian. In the darkness, he reached out to roll the person over and felt armor, realizing that it was Ipsegar. Pulling, he rolled the dwarf to his back. Lightning flashed and revealed an empty gaze staring into nowhere, and a neck bent at an unnatural angle.

Rising to his feet, Vic turned toward the troll, which now stood thirty feet from the building with Vargan and Korrigan at its feet. Lightning flashed, the brief illumination revealing Ian on the rooftop beside the ballista. Vic reacted, unwilling to allow the monster to kill his brother. With his mattock firmly in his grip, he charged toward the giant monster.

Korrigan ran between the troll's legs as the troll's fist drove downward. It struck the ground just behind the dwarf, who circled to the back of the monster's leg and swung. His mace struck the creature's heel. The monster roared in pain and frustration.

Vic came at the monster from behind and made for its other foot. As he drew near, he wound back and leapt with an overhead swing. The pick side of the mattock drove into the tendon above the troll's heel. The moment it sank in, red light flashed from the weapon's head and azure sparks sizzled up and down the troll's leg. The monster roared and lifted its foot. With Vic still gripping the shaft of his weapon, he was lifted with it. Dangling fifteen feet above the grass, Vic snorted at the insanity of the situation. He had just attacked a monster hundreds of times his size.

The troll stomped its foot into the ground, driving Vic downward. The force of the impact tore the mattock free and sent him tumbling into the long grass.

IAN FINISHED CRANKING the launch arm, lifted the bolt off the rooftop, and placed it in the slot with the butt against the launch arm. He stood behind the ballista, the wind whipping his robes while he stared up at the towering, shadowy silhouette of the troll. Lightning flashed, thunder boomed, and in that light, Ian was able to see his target clearly. Tilting the ballista up, he took aim, and when the troll turned his way, he pulled the launch release.

The bolt sped toward the troll and plunged into its throat. The beast wavered and grappled for the bolt. It staggered toward the building with its other arm outstretched. Ian backed away in dismay, weaponless and helpless. It was too high for him to jump and there was no place to hide. A hand large enough to squeeze the life out of his entire body reached for him. Ian hopped backward as it came at him. His feet slid through the open trap door, and he dropped out of sight.

VIC ROSE to a stance with the mattock in his grip. The troll towered above him, its back facing him as it stomped toward the waystop. A flash of lightning revealed Ian on the roof, backing away from the monster, unarmed and alone.

Desperate to help his brother, Vic raced toward the troll. Korrigan rushed in from his right, Vargan from his left. They all converged on the troll's heel, a track of dark blood running down it from Vic's earlier attack. Again, Vic leapt and drove his pick into the tendon. He lost his grip and fell to the ground with the weapon still in the troll's skin and a fury of sparks dancing around it. From one side, Korrigan came in and smashed his mace into the monster's heel, from the other Vargan swept his axe around and sliced deep. The tendon ruptured, skin splitting and blood spurting out. The troll bellowed and toppled backward, right toward Vic, who darted off to the side as fast as he could move. Like a felled tree, the troll's body came down and Vic made a desperate dive to avoid being crushed.

The troll's arm just missed Vic as the monster crashed to the ground with a heavy boom, causing the earth to shudder. Vic rose to his feet and backed from the monster as it lay in the grass, coughing and spurting fountains of blood. A ballista bolt stuck out from its throat, another from its shoulder, and a third from its stomach.

The troll coughed, convulsed, and fell still. Lightning flashed, thunder boomed, and it began to pour.

Korrigan appeared at Vic's side and clapped a hand on his arm. "Bene fecisti."

In his head, Vic translated, *good job*. When he realized that the dwarf was praising him, he thanked him in Dwarvish. He then remembered their fallen companion. "Ipsegar." Vic pointed toward where he had last seen him.

The two dwarves walked off toward their fallen brethren, leaving Vic alone in the rain. He approached the troll and walked along its leg, the top of which was much taller than Vic's head. When he reached the bloodied heel, he found sparks of energy crackling around the wound, his weapon still buried in the monster's flesh. Vic gripped the handle, pulled it free and stood, examining the weapon's head. He touched it tentatively, but nothing happened. Curious, he reached out with it, and when the weapon touched the monster's blood, sparks emitted.

"Interesting." He turned toward the building and remembered his brother.

A bolt of lightning struck across the plains, the flicker of light illuminating the rooftop. The ballista was visible, but there was no sign of Ian. Concerned, Vic ran to the open gate, rushed into the pen, and burst through the doorway at the base of the center column. Panting gasps joined his lunging strides as he covered two steps at a time.

Reaching the top, he charged into the waystop common room and stopped. "Ian!"

From behind him, he heard a groan and turned to find Ian lying on the floor at the foot of the ladder with rain falling on him.

"What happened?"

Ian rose to a sitting position and gestured up. "I fell through the trap door."

"Are you hurt?"

"My feet are sore, but my arse hurts more than anything else."

"Your arse?"

"It sort of broke my fall." Rising to his feet, Ian winced while rubbing his backside.

"Well, it was already cracked," Vic grinned. "And now, it's proven good for something other than stinking up our room at night."

Ian chuckled. "Yours is as talented as mine when it comes to that."

When Vic extended a hand, Ian clasped it and Vic pulled him to his feet. "Let's close that trap door before this place fills with water."

Ian climbed the ladder, pulled the trap closed, and descended. He turned to Vic, his smile gone. "I am afraid that Ipsegar..."

Vic nodded. "He is dead."

The pain in Ian's eyes was obvious. "It could have been me."

"I am glad it was not."

Ian nodded. "And the troll?"

"Dead. Thankfully, the rest of us survived. I just hope nothing like this happens again before we reach Nor'Tahal. We were lucky to live through it once. I'd not like to chance it again." He shook his head. "I can't believe something that big roams these lands."

Korrigan and Vargan emerged from the stairwell, their expressions grim.

Ian said, "That's just it, Vic. Trolls don't belong this far south. Unlike other creatures, they don't come from the Vale."

"Where do they come from?"

"Nobody knows for sure, but they seem to originate somewhere near Talastar."

"The dark elves?"

Ian nodded.

Vic frowned. "It seems we have more reason to dislike them."

"You don't get it."

"Get what?"

"We might have escaped Rysildar and his warriors when we fled Ra'Tahal, but that doesn't mean he gave up. What if this beast was sent after us?"

"Can he do that?'

Ian shook his head. "I have no idea, but it makes me wary of what other dangers lurk on the road ahead."

MORNING BROUGHT the grim task of digging a grave for Ispegar. Beneath gray skies and a falling mist, Ian stood beside the waystop while Vic, with his mattock, and Vargan with his axe, chopped at the wet ground. When the ground was loosened, Korrigan used a spade found in the waystop to shovel chunks aside. Soon, a pit six feet long, three feet wide, and three feet deep waited for its new occupant.

The two surviving dwarves carried their dead comrade and gently laid him in the hole. Dressed in his armor and helmet, his face toward the cloud-covered sky, Ipsegar lay as if taking a peaceful nap. Words were said to honor him, and they began piling dirt on his body. The entire process left their hands and boots covered in mud. When the dirt was replaced, Korrigan placed a rock the size of his own head on the grave. Etched in the face of the rock were the words, *Ipsegar Ironbend*.

The party then returned to the waystop, cleaned up, ate one last hot meal, and finished packing their provisions. With full packs and refilled waterskins, they locked the waystop, so it was ready for the next occupants. Left behind was Ipsegar's sword, so it might be used to defend the building against the next monster attack.

The mist had stopped, for which Ian was thankful. Still, his sandaled feet were cold and mud clung to the soles with each step as he marched north beneath a cloud of melancholy. Rather than walk in silence and dwell on the loss of Ipsegar, he resumed his instructions with Vic. All the while, troubled thoughts lurked in the recesses of his mind.

After many weeks of longing to escape the walls of Ra'Tahal, so he might experience the wonders that he had read about in his studies, he found himself wondering why he had been so eager to leave that safe and comfortable life. Only a few days out, and he had experienced hardship, danger, and loss. Worse, he feared that was only the beginning.

CHAPTER 30
THE DARK ABILITY

D ressed in green, flowing silk with nothing on beneath it, Shria-Li followed High Priestess Valaria out of Havenfall Palace and into the palace garden. The priestess wore the golden robes of her station, her white hair braided with spiraling strands of glowing, golden vines. The priestess was old, some claiming she was over five hundred years old. Still, the lines of age did not touch her face. The afflictions of wrinkles and thinning skin were for other races.

A trail of seven clerics followed her, all female, all wearing robes of white. Nobody spoke – the priestess and her coven out of propriety, Shria-Li out of anxiety.

They followed a path around the tranquil pool in the center of the garden. At the far side, the priestess led them down to the pool's edge, and without hesitation, walked into the water. Each step splashed into the pool but the water depth barely covered her feet. Shria-Li followed and discovered that the water was only a few inches deep. Yet, when she looked down into the clear pool, the bottom was easily four feet down and growing deeper as she advanced. The nine females crossed the gap and reached the island in the pool's center where the Tree of Life grew.

The tree was fifteen feet wide at the base, its trunk stretching up toward the darkening sky like the tallest of towers. The bark, the branches, and the leaves bathed the island and pool in its soft, golden glow.

The priestess approached the tree and placed her hands on it. She made no sound, but Shria-Li knew that Valaria was communicating with the tree as only one of her station could. The tree responded with a minute shudder. The bark split apart to reveal a doorway beyond which was a staircase descending into the bowels of the earth.

With the priestess in the lead, Shria-Li next and the clerics in the rear, the procession descended the curved stairwell, the stairs, walls, and ceiling all made of golden, glowing wood. A dankness filled the air and steadily grew thicker as they descended. After three full revolutions, the stairs opened to an underground cavern illuminated by the roots of the tree above. Those roots wove together to form a complex web that stretched across an earthen ceiling twenty feet above. The walls of the chamber were made of gray rock with golden striations. Water trickled down the walls, and in some areas, dripped from the ceiling.

The floor was carved from granite, the center of which was occupied by a pool. Eight triangular platforms of rock jutted into the pool to create an eight-pointed star of water.

The priestess took position on one of the triangular platforms. The seven clerics split up and walked around the pool, each claiming an empty platform.

"Shria-Li," Valaria announced. "Once the ritual begins, know that it cannot be stopped."

Despite her anxiety, Shria-Li responded with a firm voice. "I am aware."

"Remove your robes, for such restrictions are barriers between yourself and nature."

She untied her sash, opened the robes, and allowed them to fall to the floor. Naked and exposed, she resisted the urge to hide.

"Enter the pool."

With care, uncertain of its depth, Shria-Li lowered her foot into the water. It was cold. Like the pool in the garden, the water depth barely covered her feet. She strode out, her movement disturbing the tranquil surface. When in the middle, she turned to face Valaria.

"Lie down," the priestess said.

Shria-Li squatted, sat, then lay down. The chill water caused a shiver as she settled.

"As the pool calms, you must as well. Relax. Listen to my voice and release all other thoughts." Valaria paused a beat, waiting for Shria-Li to comply and resumed. "It will grow dark. Do not be afraid."

The priestess and the clerics raised their hands above their heads and toward the pool's center. The light from the roots gradually faded until complete, utter darkness surrounded Shria-Li. The trickle of water dulled and her body numbed to the cold water. The world around her slipped away.

A glow appeared above her and drifted closer. Drawn toward it, she raised her arm and reached to touch it. The glow flared to blinding light.

DRESSED IN PLAIN, white robes, Shria-Li stood in a forest but could not recall where she was or how she'd got there in the first place. Massive, towering trees surrounded her, but those trees lacked the magic found in ones groomed by cultivators. A heavy silence hung in the air, not the tweet of a bird nor the rustle of leaves in the wind to be heard. She raised her gaze to the sky to determine the time but only found a thick, dark blue expanse without the sun, moon, or stars visible. Turning slowly, she searched for a sign, something to give her a sense of where she was and why. Then, she spied light through a gap in the trees. She walked toward it, ducking low branches and wading through undergrowth.

Thick tree trunks blocked her view, but the glimpses of light continued to draw her forward. She climbed a small slope, passed between two trees, and emerged in a moonlit field. Knee high grass covered the ground amid massive, cut chunks of stone. Remnants of arches, pillars, and towers littered the ground.

Shria-Li approached what was left of two walls leaning against each other, walked past it, and moved on to a fallen arch. Moss covered one side of the stone, informing her that she walked south...but to where?

An unnatural silence hung over the ruins like a shadow. Soon, it became apparent that she walked through a long-dead city. A fallen spire capped by a cone-shaped roof lay to one side, its design familiar and pleasing, but she could not say why. She came upon a ring of pillars surrounded by broken sections of stone and was again struck by a sense of recollection but could not make the connection.

She moved past the pillars and sighed aloud. "Where am I?"

The ground at her feet shifted and shuddered. She danced aside and then gasped when a boney hand with rotten flesh clinging to it burst through the ground. An arm followed the hand. Another hand snaked into the air as chunks of earth tumbled around it. A scream caught in Shria-Li's throat as she backed from the rising skeleton.

The creature pushed against the ground and a head emerged. Rotten flesh and a single eye dangled from the creature's skull. "You have returned," the creature hissed.

"What?" Shria-Li exclaimed.

The voice was akin to a harsh whisper. "Havenfall was once your home, was it not?"

Uncertain if she should respond, Shria-Li offered a hesitant reply. "It...still is." Confusion and curiosity demanded that she seek answers. "Where am I?"

"As I said. Havenfall."

She looked around. "All I see are trees and ruin."

"The city died long, long ago."

"What about you?"

"I died with the others. Some escaped but they were few and what became of them, I cannot say."

Her brow furrowed. "How is it that I can talk to you if you are dead."

"I should think it obvious. You've the gift."

The gift. The term usually spoke to one's magic ability, something Shria-Li had lacked. Then, she recalled. *The testing. It is why I am here.*

She asked, "This gift. What can it do?"

"You are a death speaker, child."

"I...have never heard of such a thing."

"The Sylvan are one with nature. Death is part of the cycle. Without nature, there is no life. Without life, there is no death. Without death, there is no nature." The skeleton wavered. "I...am tired and must return to sleep." With a rattle of bones, it lay down in the disturbed dirt.

"But I have more questions."

"The answers are within you, Shria-Li," the corpse hissed. "Death surrounds you. Do not flee it. Embrace it, empower it, and it may save you in your time of need."

"I don't know what a death speaker is or what one can do."

"Farewell, Princess."

The body fell still. Silence.

A wave of exhaustion came over Shria-Li, making her feel as if she had run for many miles. Dizziness set in, causing her to stumble to her knee and lean against the remains of a fallen building. Her eyelids grew heavy, her body weak. She staggered, fell to her rear, and settled with her back against the wall. The silence, the stillness, the loneliness of the ruins slipped into her soul. Voices called to her. *Sleep, Shria-Li. Join us. Sleep and never wake again.*

SHRIA-LI'S EYES opened and she sat up in panicked shock. Water dripped from her body, into the pool.

The priestess shrieked and staggered back, her eyes wide and her body shaking. The seven clerics all collapsed simultaneously, two of them falling forward into the water, splashing Shria-Li.

Valaria gasped, her eyes wide. She stared at Shria-Li as if she had seen a ghost. The thought stirred the memory of speaking to a corpse. *It was just a dream*, Shria-Li told herself.

"What is wrong?" Shria-Li asked.

"The dark ability," the priestess gasped.

A chill wracked Shria-Li's body, this one not due to the cold water. For the priestess to be so upset, something bad must have happened. For the clerics to faint, whatever had occurred was likely worse than bad. A dread filled her, and an unanswered question resurfaced.

When she spoke, it emerged as a whisper. "What is a death speaker?"

The priestess stumbled toward the open doorway at the bottom of the tree's main root. "The dark ability has awoken within you."

Bursting to her feet, Shria-Li demanded. "What does it mean?"

The priestess stopped and looked over her shoulder. "With your ability comes the end of our race, as foretold millennia ago. The Sylvan are doomed."

CHAPTER 31
NOR'TAHAL

E arly afternoon, five days after departing from Ra'Tahal, Ian, his brother, and the two dwarves leading them approached a bridge spanning a raging river. Made of alabaster stone with ornate murals carved into the walls along each side, the bridge was a work of splendor. With all four of them walking side by side, they climbed up the arched bridge, crested the peak, and descended to the north side. The rush of water flowing under the bridge filled Ian's ears while another sight held his gaze.

Tree-covered mountains dominated the northern horizon, the range stretching from east to west as far as Ian could see. A narrow gorge waited straight ahead, its walls covered in trees growing amid gray granite. A creek wound along the bottom of the gorge. Above the creek, built into the steep mountainside, was a citadel made of the same, gray granite. Sturdy turrets jutted above the parapets and dwarves dressed in studded, leather armor stood on the wall, monitoring their approach.

The road split in three directions with routes leading east, west, and north, the latter winding up the side of the gorge opposite the citadel. The party climbed along the zig-zagging path, the upslope steady until they came to a sheer drop to the creek, sixty feet down. Across a twenty-foot gap was the citadel gate, blocked by a tall, wooden door laced with thick bolts and strips of iron.

"Ho!" Korrigan shouted. "Lower the drawbridge, so we may enter."

From atop the wall, a dwarf called back, "State your name and your purpose for visiting Nor'Tahal."

Korrigan scowled. "You know who I am, Ogglegon."

"Still, protocol requires it."

"Fine," Korrigan threw his hands in the air in apparent frustration. "I am Korrigan Loadstone, along with Vargan Quartzite. We have come from Ra'Tahal with dire news for Holdmaster Targaron."

"Who are the humans?" Ogglegon demanded.

Korrigan glanced at Ian, his mood obviously sour. "They are refugees and have come seeking shelter."

"Can they speak for themselves?"

Sighing, Korrigan muttered to Ian, "I would like to put my foot in his mouth. However, can you just tell him that you mean no harm, so they will let us in?"

Ian drew in a breath and called out, "My name is Illian Carpenter. This is my brother, Victus. We have come for shelter. You have our word that we will honor your laws and bring you no ill will."

The dwarf on the wall spoke to his companions, one of whom jogged over to the tower rising above the gate. Moments later, a cranking sound arose. The wooden door began to lower, creaking as it descended until it struck the ground on Ian's side of the chasm with a heavy thud. Korrigan and Vargan crossed the drawbridge, so Ian and Vic followed, taking care to remain in the center since a misstep along the edge could result in a deadly fall. They passed beneath the gate tower and into the citadel interior.

A busy square with a fountain in the middle welcomed them. To the left, right, and straight ahead were narrow streets bordered by walls and buildings of gray stone. As they walked down a narrow street and headed deeper into the hold, a variety of smells attacked and tantalized Ian, including freshly baked bread, sweet herbs, and woodsmoke. A subtle muskiness hung in the air, tainted by the odor of manure. The party passed dwarves, goats, chickens, and pigs while on their way to the blocky, daunting keep at the rear of the complex. The keep was a formidable structure, a fortress within a fortress.

Ian and his companions were ushered inside by the two guards posted at the door. They stepped into a grand hall with a high ceiling and a large fireplace. A long table with benches on either side dominated the center of the room. Seated at the far end of the table was a middle-aged dwarf with a thick beard and piercing blue eyes.

"What do you have to say for yourself, Korrigan?" the dwarf growled as he rose to a stance, his fists clenched and shoulders hunched.

Oh, no. Ian glanced at Vic, who appeared worried.

"About what, Holdmaster?" Korrigan asked.

"A full year has passed since you have graced these halls." Targaron stomped across the room, stopped, grinned, and opened his arms. "It is good to see you!"

Korrigan embraced the holdmaster, the two of them enthusiastically thumping each other on the back before letting go. "I have missed you, Uncle."

"Uncle?" Ian muttered.

Turning toward Ian, Korrigan said, "Targaron is the younger brother to my father and was often a bad influence on me during my youth."

Targaron laughed. "You cannot blame me. You'd have found trouble with or without me around, and you know it."

Korrigan shrugged. "That is true. Back then, life was simpler and joy was not so difficult to find."

"Aye," Targaron nodded. "Difficult times come to all at some point, and now they have found the Tahal Clan. But we are dwarves, strong and resilient. We will weather this storm as we have endured others in the past."

"I fear the storm winds blow harder than ever, Uncle. We bring news from Ra'Tahal and none of it good."

The holdmaster narrowed his eyes. "We will discuss it over dinner." He gestured toward the two guards. "Go and inform the cook that we have extra mouths to feed." The two guards disappeared down the corridor and Targaron turned back to Korrigan. "You and your companions are welcome to stay in the keep. The entire fourth floor is vacant, so choose rooms as you wish. Wash up, rest, and meet me back here for dinner at sunset."

Korrigan said, "One more thing. The two humans need new clothing, and the smaller one needs boots."

Targaron glanced toward Ian and gave a firm nod. "Stop by the tailor shop, above the bakery. Tell Evergon that I sent you."

"We will see you at dinner."

The holdmaster walked out of the room, his footsteps fading down the corridor.

"First, let us go upstairs," Korrigan said. "We will drop off our packs and weapons, and then I will take Ian and Vic to see the tailor."

BEHIND A CURTAIN in the back of a tailor shop, Ian slid his legs into a pair of brown breeches. He then pulled a green tunic over his head and laced up the collar. A black leather jerkin followed. Sitting on a bench, he pulled on a pair of black boots. They felt a bit stiff but fit well enough. All dressed, he pulled the curtain aside.

Vic spun toward him and grinned. His outfit was identical to Ian's except his shirt was a dark red instead of green. "You almost look respectable."

"The breeches keep falling down," Ian held the waist in his fist.

"If you ate better..."

"You know..."

A palm held toward Ian, Vic stopped him in mid-sentence. "Easy. I am just giving you a ribbing."

Evergon, an old dwarf with a short, white beard tugged at Ian's pant leg. The waistband slipped from his hand and dropped to his knees. He hastily pulled them back up.

"You need a belt." The tailor turned and rifled through the stacks of material on his workbench. He pulled out a black, studded belt and handed it to Ian. "Use this, so your breeches don't fall down."

"Thank you," Ian slid the belt around his waist, careful to weave it through the loops on his breeches and secured it.

Korrigan walked in the room, looked Ian and Vic over, and then turned to the tailor. "Much better. Do you have any cloaks?"

"Cloaks?"

"Yes. You know. Those things that you wear on your head and shoulders?"

The tailor gave Korrigan a flat stare. "I know what a cloak is."

"Then, why did you ask me?" Korrigan grinned.

The comment elicited a sigh from Evergon, who turned and wove his way through racks of clothing. Moments later, he emerged with an armful of cloth. From the pile, he lifted a gray cloak and tossed it to Vic before handing a dark green one to Ian, matching his shirt. "These are the only two I have that are long enough for these humans."

"Thank you, master tailor." Korrigan glanced toward the window. "The sun has set. We had better go if we want to eat while the food is hot."

They left the room and descended to the ground level, where they stepped out beneath a dark blue sky, the clouds still tinted by the warm hues of sunset. Male, female, and even young dwarves passed them as they returned to the keep. Conversation and even laughter came from the citizens, something Ian noted as a stark contrast to the quiet and serious nature of Ra'Tahal.

Back in the keep, they crossed the entrance hall and followed a short corridor to the dining room, where they had first encountered the holdmaster.

A fire burned in the fireplace. Standing two strides from the hearth while staring into the flames was Targaron, his meaty hands clasped together behind his back. Hearing their approach, the dwarf spun and smiled. "You two look almost presentable, now...for humans."

Ian dipped his head. "Thank you, Holdmaster."

Vargan walked in the room, his beard braided and hair slicked back.

The holdmaster shook his head. "Please, call me Targaron."

"Call me Ian. This is my brother, Vic."

"Were you two among the slaves acquired at summer's turn?"

"We..." Ian frowned, unsure of how to respond until he finally settled on, "Yes."

"As is my cook. She is a skilled chef. I was lucky to get her." He leaned close and whispered, "If Arangar had known, she surely would be cooking for him rather than for me here in Nor'Tahal."

Ian shot Korrigan a questioning look. The dwarf shook his head and turned to Targaron. "We need to discuss something in private, just you, me, and my companions."

"Very well. Let us sit. I just had a barrel tapped. I will have the staff bring a few pitchers of ale and our food. Once they clear, we are free to discuss whatever needs discussing while we eat, and more importantly, while we drink."

The three dwarves took seats first with Targaron at the end, Korrigan and Vargan to one side of him. Ian and Vic sat on the other side. An old dwarf in a dark blue coat entered the room, trailed by two female dwarves. The male held a clay pitcher in each hand. The females each carried a tray filled with bowls and plates of steaming food. With practiced efficiency, the trio set the pitchers, plates and bowls on the table before leaving.

The holdmaster lifted a pitcher and poured frothy liquid into the flagon before him. He then passed the pitcher to Korrigan, who filled his mug before passing it on. When it was Ian's turn, he filled his mug despite his reservations, deciding it was best not to offend the host.

Targaron held his tankard over the table. "To King Arangar. May he live long and rule well."

Korrigan, with sadness in his eyes, shook his head. "It would be… inappropriate for us to join that toast."

The holdmaster frowned. "What is wrong, Korrigan?"

"Much is wrong, beginning with a recent and most cunning betrayal."

Targaron's brow arched. "Betrayal? By whom?"

"The Drow singer, Rysildar. I am sure you heard that he was taken in as a guest near the turn of summer."

"Yes, of course." The holdmaster grimaced. "Whispers of concern haunted these halls for weeks after we heard."

"Well, that concern was well founded. Rather than honor King Arangar's hospitality as a guest, the Drow repaid him with treachery." Korrigan took a drink and set his mug on the table. "Through use of vile magic, he opened a gateway to Talastar and brought dozens of letalis warriors into Ra'Tahal. The king is dead, as are all members of the council. Skilled warriors backed by magic and outnumbering our own defenders led to a rapid capture of the citadel."

Targaron's expression grew dark. "This is dire news indeed."

Korrigan continued, "The Drow control Ra'Tahal and hold its citizens hostage, at least those who survived. We barely escaped with our lives. When clear of the citadel, we made straight for Nor'Tahal."

Targaron leaned back and stared into space before closing his eyes for a long beat. When he opened them, he shook his head. "I thank you for the warning, but even if I sent everyone on the hold, I do not have a force large enough to lay siege to a stronghold like Ra'Tahal."

"In addition to warning you, we came here seeking Arangoli."

Targaron grimaced. "I doubt you will convince him to claim the throne."

"I know that Arangoli will never agree to be king, but he can and will agree to lead a campaign to reclaim what we have lost."

The holdmaster took a swig, wiped the foam from his mouth, and set his tankard on the table. "Although Arangoli is young, his reputation alone is enough to inspire dwarves to fight for him, should he demand it. However, he is not here."

"Where is he?"

"You know Arangoli as well as anyone. Few would call him complacent. Most might say he is restless. He left last winter and made for the free cities, seeking someone to fight. The Head Thumpers left with him."

Ian asked, "What can you tell me about the Head Thumpers?"

Targaron turned toward him. "They are a group of young warriors, who, like Arangoli, seek out trouble. As young warriors, eager to prove themselves in battle, they are bitter at having all but missed Gahagar's war. Unless one chooses to wander about and seek monsters to fight, there has been nothing for a warrior to do during the past three years. The free cities, however, are rarely dull places. Go there and trouble will find you soon enough."

Korrigan nodded. "That is where we are headed, then. With Arangoli leading and the Head Thumpers on our side, we have a chance to retake Ra'Tahal."

"It is still a tall task."

"What would you do?"

The holdmaster chuckled. "The same as you, I suppose."

"Do you know which city Goli was headed for?"

"I heard him mention Greavesport more than once. I would start there."

"Greavesport?" Ian asked. Of any city he had ever heard, the name tugged at his curiosity.

Korrigan nodded. "It lies on the eastern coast of the inner sea, perhaps a hundred fifty miles northwest of Nor'Tahal." He then turned back to Targaron. "Do you have any horses we could borrow?"

"Borrow?" An arched brow and smirk appeared on Targaron's face. "You intend to return them?"

Korrigan chuckled. "It would be unlikely."

"In that case, I can give you two. You will have to share saddles, but it is all I can spare." He gestured toward the food. "Pass that plate of mutton. Let's eat before it gets cold."

CHAPTER 32
REUNION

Plates and dishes were passed around. As always, Ian selected the foods least likely to anger his sensitive stomach and then began to eat. The spiced mutton was tasty, the steamed vegetables soft with just enough crunch remaining, the baked bread moist and warm in the center. But the highlight of the meal were the spiced potatoes. He ate them with a fervor while memories flooded in. When finished, he wiped his mouth and washed the meal down with a pull of ale.

Ian sat back with a sigh, his stomach strained from how much he had eaten. "These spiced potatoes are wonderful," he said in Dwarvish. "They remind me of my mother's cooking."

Targaron grinned. "I told you my new cook was a revelation. I will be sure to tell Zora that you enjoyed her potatoes."

His eyes widening, Ian said, "Her name is Zora?"

"Yes. She is a human woman who came to the hold early this summer."

Ian turned to Vic, speaking in his native tongue. "These are mother's potatoes. She lives here...as Targaron's cook."

Vic blinked. "Mother is here?"

To the holdmaster, Ian asked, "May we speak to this woman?"

"Yes. Of course. She is likely still in the kitchen, on the second floor. Follow the noise of dishes and you'll find it."

Ian hastily pushed his chair back and stood. "Vic. Come with me."

The two of them walked out into the hallway and made for the stairwell, Ian leading with a hurried pace spurred by hope. Once on the second level, he paused and listened for the sound of clanking pots. Following the noise, the two brothers came to a door leading to a long room with worktables down the center, an oven and shelving on one side, a sink, drying rack, and more shelving on the other side. Over the sink stood a middle-aged woman in a pale blue dress and white apron. Her brown hair was tied back in a bun, her attention on a pot she scrubbed. The woman glanced toward the door and froze.

She blinked. "Ian? Vic?"

Ian burst across the room and hugged her. She squeezed him tightly. Then, Vic was there with his arms around both of them. Tears tracked down Ian's cheeks, but he didn't bother to wipe them away. The trio held each other for a time and sobbed in joy and relief before finally stepping back.

Zora dried her eyes. "I worried about what happened to you two and feared I might never see you again."

Vic said, "The dwarves threatened to harm you and the other women if we did not comply with their wishes. We were trapped in Ra'Tahal and held captive under threat of violence against you."

Ian added, "But, we are here, now."

She stared into his eyes while smoothing his hair. "You need a haircut and a shave. Both of you."

Vic rubbed his bearded face. It had grown in much cleaner than Ian's. "I kind of like my new appearance."

"It makes you look older. Tougher."

"I think toughness might be required for what lies ahead, Mother," Vic replied.

"What lies ahead?"

"We are caught up in something dangerous, something I intend to see through."

"What?" Ian asked. "But we just found mother."

"Think, Ian. We both decided we cannot return to Shillings, but we can do something that matters."

Ian recalled the conversation with Vic the night after escaping Ra'Tahal. "By helping the dwarves? I thought you didn't care about them."

Vic shook his head. "By saving our people. Remember, they live in Ra'Tahal as well.

"As slaves."

"For now, but what if we promised to help on the condition that they were released?"

As Ian considered the idea, he realized that the situation in the citadel had altered significantly. "King Arangar and the council were behind our enslavement. With the king and council dead, their influence is gone. Korrigan and many of the others don't believe in slavery. I am sure he would agree, and if he can get Arangoli to buy in, maybe we *can* free the other villagers." He turned toward his mother, her eyes filled with concern. "But what about you?"

She cupped his cheek. "In truth, this life is not so bad. I have always enjoyed cooking, and they treat me well enough. I have my own room and am free to do as I wish when my efforts are not required in the kitchen. I have even made some friends here, so do not worry about me." With her thumb, she stroked Ian's face. "With your father gone and the village destroyed, you two are the only thing that matters. I just want you safe."

Ian shook his head. "You are the one who needs to be safe. If we are to help rescue the other villagers, it will require that we take risks and...more."

"Ian is right, Mother," Vic said. "We are adults, now. You can't protect us, and with others in need, I could not stomach leaving them to a dire fate if I believe I can be of help."

She gave them a sad smile. "Your father would be proud to hear those words come from you."

Ian glanced toward the sink. "Since we are here, we could help you finish the dishes."

"I would like that." Zora tossed a towel to Ian. "You can begin by drying this pot."

AFTER FINISHING THE DISHES, including those brought in by the serving staff, Ian, Vic, and Zora each pulled up a stool, sat around the counter in the middle of the kitchen, and chatted deep into the night. Stories were told, laughter echoed in the room at the funnier memories, and tears blurred eyes when the darker ones were revisited. Somehow, that evening together mended a rent in Ian's heart, one he hadn't even realized was there until it had healed. When exhaustion finally demanded they go to bed, Ian and Vic hugged their mother and wished her a good night with the promise to visit her in the morning. They reached the room they were to share, stripped, and lay down. Sleep claimed Ian within moments.

A HAND SHOOK IAN AWAKE. He opened his eyes to find Korrigan standing over his bed.

"You two need to get up," the dwarf demanded. "Meet me and Vargan at the stables in ten minutes."

"But we haven't even eaten."

Korrigan walked to the door. "Stop by the kitchen on your way out. Get something you can eat while we ride." The dwarf left the room and closed the door.

Ian sighed, climbed out of bed, and began to dress. "I've a feeling we are in for some long days."

Vic slid a foot into the leg of his breeches. "At least we will be riding instead of walking."

"That might be worse. We don't know anything about horses." Ian pulled his tunic over his head.

Standing, Vic hiked his breeches up and buttoned them. "Just do what the dwarves tell us to do and we should be fine."

After securing his belt, Ian slid his sleeveless jerkin on and laced it. He went to the door with his brother a step behind him. Vic stopped and grabbed both cloaks off a hook, handing one to Ian, both of them donning the cloaks to complete their outfits. Ian waited in the corridor while Vic lifted the new harness holding his mattock off the hook and slid it over his shoulder, so the weapon lay across his back at an angle. They descended to the second floor, where noise came from the kitchen at the end of the hall.

Dressed as she was the day prior, Zora bent and reached into the oven before removing a baking sheet filled with flat disks of bread. The scent tantalized Ian's nose and caused his stomach to rumble.

"Good morning, Mother," Ian said.

Zora turned toward the door and smiled. "I am surprised to see you boys up this early, considering how late we stayed up last night."

Vic snorted. "I am surprised as well, but we weren't given a choice."

Ian explained as he crossed the room. "Our companions wish to leave. They headed to the stables, where we are to meet them, so our visit must be brief."

Her smile faded. She reached up and smoothed his hair. "I will miss you boys."

Vic said, "Do not worry about us, Mother. I promise that we will find a way to visit you when this is over."

Sadness lurked in her blue eyes. "Do not make promises you cannot keep, Victus."

He took her hand and matched her sad gaze with one of determination. "We will free the others, and when that happens, you will see us again."

"I pray that the good spirits will let it be true."

Vic hugged her, and when he stepped back, Ian fell into her embrace. She squeezed him as tightly as the day before, but he remained silent and endured it, unwilling to speak lest emotions claim him. When she let him go, she gave him a sad smile. "Have you eaten?"

"No," Ian shook his head. "We were to stop by for something quick and then be off."

Zora turned to the baking sheet she had just removed from the oven. "These biscuits are fresh and hot." Using a hand towel, she wrapped up four biscuits and then pulled an empty sack off a shelf. With the biscuits in the sack, she went to a kettle on the stovetop and used a pair of tongs to remove two sausages, which she wrapped and added to the sack. "Here." She held the sack to Vic. "Take it. You can eat while you ride."

"Thank you, Mother," Vic went to the door. "We should be going, Ian."

Ian backed toward the door, affixing the image of his mother in his head. "We will see you soon, Mother."

He spun and walked out as the tears started falling. A dark stairwell took him to the keep's main level. He paused to dry his eyes before following his brother outside.

Once outside beneath the pale blue sky, they followed a narrow street to an open, gravel yard. Across the yard, the stables backed to the hold's outer wall. There, they found Korrigan, Vargan, and a male dwarf in brown leathers, his black beard braided, his skin tanned. The third dwarf walked two stallions out of the stables, one black, the other a chestnut brown. Both were saddled, the bags on the saddles bulging.

"Here are the steeds the holdmaster promised, Captain," the dwarf said to Korrigan. "Treat them well, and they will do good by you."

"Thank you, Horsemaster." Korrigan climbed on the black horse and nodded to Ian. "Climb on behind me."

Ian walked up to the horse, noting the muscles rippling beneath its dark coat. He eyed the beast warily. "I didn't realize horses were quite so...big. How do I get on?"

"Grip the rear of the saddle, place your foot in the stirrup, and hop up while swinging a leg over."

Ian grabbed onto the back of the seat, lifted a foot, and slid it into the vacated stirrup. He then jumped while pulling himself up. When he swung his leg around, he didn't manage to get it over. He kicked the horse in the arse. The beast released a high-pitched whinny, burst forward, and sent Ian tumbling to the ground.

Vargan and Vic both burst into laughter, the latter bent over with the bag of food still in hand.

Korrigan turned the horse and looked down at Ian while chuckling. "Try not to kick the horse in the arse next time."

Ian rose to his feet, dusted himself off, and scowled at his brother. "I don't know why you are laughing. I could have been hurt."

Vic chuckled. "It serves you right for what you did to that horse."

In return, Ian snapped, "If you think it's so easy, you try it."

"Here." Vic extended the sack of food. "Hold this."

When Ian took the sack, Vic turned toward Vargan's horse, put a foot in the stirrup, and hopped on with ease. This, of course, made Ian look like an even bigger fool.

"I'll take the sack, now," Vic said with a smirk.

Ian shoved it at him. "I hope you choke on that sausage."

"Oh, come on. There is no need to be sore. I had nothing to do with your fall."

Although Ian knew Vic was correct, he was still irritated, mostly at himself. He stomped over to Korrigan's horse and tried again, this time taking care to lift his leg higher. The leg made it over, and he sat, only to find the saddle in front of him rather than beneath him. Again, the horse reacted poorly by bursting into a run and sending Ian tumbling backward, his legs flipping over his head. He landed face-first in the dirt.

Irked at his own ineptitude, Ian scrambled to his feet, dusted himself off, and shot the others a stern grimace. Nobody laughed this time.

The third attempt was successful. Relieved, Ian settled in behind Korrigan, who shifted his horse beside Vargan's, the two of them riding side by side, toward the hold gate. Vic handed Ian a biscuit, which he shoved into his mouth all at once, so he could keep his hands free. The gate opened, the guards there bidding them farewell. Korrigan urged his horse into a trot, which had Ian bouncing in the saddle and holding on tight lest he fall again. Down the curved drive, they rode toward a new destination. Considering what had already occurred during their journey, Ian wondered what surprises awaited them.

CHAPTER 33

A STRANGE ENCOUNTER

It was mid-afternoon after a long day of riding through wooded mountain valleys, canyons, and saddles nestled between two rocky peaks, when the two horses, each carrying a dwarf and a human, crested a rise that offered the first view of the land beyond the mountain range. As the horses stopped at the top of a winding road on the north side of the saddle, Ian stared out into the distance.

A flat expanse of wetlands, thick with green foliage stretched out to the north and west while thick jungle lay to the east. Another mountain range defined the distant northern horizon.

"I don't see any cities," Ian said.

Korrigan snorted. "The Stagnum lies below. You won't find any cities there."

"The Stagnum?" In his studies, Ian had never heard the term.

"Swampland," Vargan said in disgust. "Wet, mosquito-filled swampland. It is a dangerous place."

"Then, why are we going that way?"

Korrigan urged his mount back into motion. "A road runs along the south edge of the swamp, parallel to the Stagnum River. It is the fastest route to Greavesport."

The horse leapt a trickling rivulet, jostling Ian, whose backside was already quite sore. He looked up at the sky. The sun had already dropped halfway to the western horizon.

"It will be night by the time we reach the Stagnum," Ian realized.

Korrigan spoke over his shoulder. "Yes, which is why we will camp just outside it. Tomorrow, we will rise early and ride hard. We will have to camp in the Stagnum one night, but the farther we get from the lake, the better."

"The lake?"

Korrigan pointed north, where a body of water lay nestled amid the greenery. "Lake Raesche. It is named after the witch reported to live there."

Ian blinked. "A witch?" They were often the subject of fireside tales, the kind that elicited nightmares.

"Whether she is real or not, I cannot say. I have only ridden through the Stagnum once, and other than a few dozen mosquito bites, I emerged unharmed."

Despite Korrigan's reassurances, Ian had a bad feeling as he stared out at the distant lake.

They headed down the north side of the saddle on a winding path running along a rocky ridge. The path turned a bend and a person in a black cloak came into view. Like them, the individual followed the downhill trail, his cloak swirling with each step. As Korrigan's horse drew near, the person turned and lowered the cloak hood to reveal a handsome face with blonde hair and gray eyes. The man appeared older than Vic, but not by a great deal. He climbed onto a large rock beside the trail and watched as the two horses and four riders approached.

"Good day," the man said in human before shifting to Dwarvish. "Greetings."

Korrigan stopped his horse beside the man. "You are far from a human settlement."

"Ah." The man nodded. "A very dwarf-like observation. I assume you wish to know where I am headed."

"In truth, I don't care where you are headed. The observation arose because it is rare to find solo travelers on this route and even less common for the traveler to be human."

"Rare is a good description." The man smirked. "I prefer other terms such as handsome or even mysterious, but I will accept rare."

Korrigan frowned, and Ian sensed his mood growing sour, so he chose to interject.

"My name is Ian. This is Korrigan. The dwarf on the horse behind ours is Vargan, and the human is my brother, Vic." Each nodded as their names were said.

The man smiled. "Well, met, Ian. Others often call me Truhan."

Korrigan glanced back at Ian and arched a brow. Ian knew why and asked in human. "Doesn't Truhan mean scoundrel in Dwarvish?"

Truhan's eyes widened. "Does it?" He shook his head. "If so, that explains a few things. I was wondering why Dwarves always look at me like that." He then shrugged. "Oh, well. It is nothing to fret about."

Vargan asked, "Where are you headed?"

The man pointed north and replied in Dwarvish. "I am going that way."

The dwarf rolled his eyes. "And when this trail ends when meeting the road at the bottom of the hillside?"

"Then, I will turn, I suppose. It would be strange to continue on a trail that has ended, especially one that stops at the edge of swampland."

A low growl arose from Korrigan. "Which way will you turn?"

"I have not decided yet. Who knows? I may choose to turn around."

"So, you have no destination in mind?"

"I always have a destination in mind, but I have yet to find the means to reach it."

Korrigan huffed. "I am finished with this conversation. Have a good day." He urged his horse into a walk.

The strange man shook his head and said in Elvish, "Dwarves have little patience."

Over his shoulder, Ian replied, also in Elvish, "I have noticed the same thing."

For a brief moment, Truhan's eyes widened before he said in Dwarvish, "I wish you safe travels. Take care. The Stagnum can be dangerous."

Ian repeatedly glanced backward. The first three times, he found Truhan still standing on the rock and watching the horses navigate the winding trail. On the fourth look over his shoulder, the man was gone, the trail behind Vargan's horse empty.

THE JOURNEY down the mountain side consumed much of the remaining daylight, and as they descended, the temperature and humidity rose. Despite it being deep into autumn, Ian was forced to remove his cloak and loosen the laces on his tunic. The surrounding foliage changed as they rode north, the colors of autumn shifting to both dark and bright greens, the leaves increasing in size, the ferns and undergrowth thickening. As it had for much of the journey out of Nor'Tahal, the winding trail they followed ran above a creek flowing along a ravine floor. The trees surrounding the trail cast it in shadow and provided a modicum of relief against the heat, although the humidity remained. Then, the mosquitoes struck.

Ian found himself slapping at any exposed skin and swatting at the air, but Korrigan appeared unfazed. Instead, the dwarf focused on the trail, guiding his mount along it until the creek made a sharp turn. A bridge constructed of logs bound together spanned the creek. The horses crossed the bridge at an easy walk. The narrow trail followed a rise parallel to the creek before descending yet again. As the ground leveled, they came to a dirt road and turned west.

Flowering vines strangled the trees bordering the road, the swamp bush too thick to see beyond a few strides. Standing water was all around and the road appeared to have been made only a few feet above its level.

Time and again, they crossed wooden bridges spanning pools, the surface often covered in algae. All the while, the sky continued darkening and shadows thickened. The sun set and dusk claimed the sky as they crossed a bridge to a rise covered in long, green grass with flat blades. As an island amid a sea of puddles and foliage, the small hill provided a reasonable place to camp for the night. No dry wood for a fire was in sight but the humidity was too thick anyway for them to need it for warmth, so the party simply ate and slept beside the road, using their cloaks as both pillows and blankets.

Ian lay on his back and stared up at the starry sky, the moon only a thin slice, adding a meager bit of light to the darkness. The stars had long fascinated him, those distant lights like sparkling spirits dancing in the heavens. It was a sight that brought him peace and stirred a bit of wonder at the expanse of the universe. Mosquitoes invaded, chased his musings away, and forced him to cover his head with his cloak. He tried to sleep but the cacophony of croaking frogs around him was so loud, he found it difficult to relax. Despite his weariness, sleep eluded him for hours. A forceful whinny from one of the horses caused him to sit upright and turn toward the animal.

A shadowy form moved near the horse. Ian gasped but did not cry out, thinking it might be one of the dwarves. Another silhouette moved in the darkness, coming toward him.

"Korrigan?" Ian asked.

The silhouettes both froze.

Korrigan's voice came from the long grass near Ian. "Go to sleep."

Vic lay beside Ian, and if neither of the people standing were Korrigan, that meant...

"Wake up!" Ian shoved Vic and burst to his feet. "Someone is..." Something sharp struck his neck. He swatted at it like it was a mosquito, but instead found a dart.

The world tilted as Ian fell backward into the grass. Darkness swallowed him.

VIC JERKED awake to find Ian standing over him. A short, sharp hissing sound came from the direction of the horses, and Ian staggered. Alarmed, Vic reached to his side, his fingers wrapping around the shaft of his mattock. He leapt to his feet to find a half dozen silhouettes standing around him. All were around his height, too tall to be either of the dwarves. Fearing bandits, he roared and swung a broad stroke to keep them away.

"Stay back!" He shouted.

Rather than attack the dark strangers, Vic stood over Ian, intending to protect him.

A cry came from the darkness as Korrigan and Vargan rushed in and attacked. One of the bandits raised a shield, blocking Korrigan's mace. Another ducked low, causing Vargan's axe swipe to miss. A pair of rapid, hissing sounds were followed by exclamations. The two dwarves staggered, fell to their knees, and each made one last, weak attempt at an attack. When their weapons found only grass, the momentum spun them around and they fell on their sides. Neither moved.

Alone, Vic swept his weapon from side to side to keep the others at a distance.

They were in a swampland, with no safe direction in which to flee, other than the road. And even if Vic tried to run, it would mean leaving Ian.

"What do you want?" Vic demanded. "We have no coin and our supplies are only enough for a three-day journey."

A male voice, deep and low, came from the darkness. It spoke in Vic's native language, but with a strange accent. "We have no need for coin. It is you we want. Drop your weapon, and you may survive the night."

Outnumbered and all but blinded by the gloom of weak-mooned night, Vic didn't know what to do. Dropping his weapon would mean giving up his last bit of leverage. As he stood there, struggling to reach a decision, the attackers made it for him.

A sharp sting caused him to slap his neck A dart, which Vic yanked out and tossed aside. Another struck the other side of his neck. He reached for it but his legs gave out and he went down on one knee. The stars began to swirl, and he dropped his mattock as darkness overtook him.

IAN WOKE to daylight and found his wrists and ankles bound to a pole, the rest of his body dangling from it. Ferns and shrubs scraped against his back as he was carried through jungle-like surroundings. The men carrying him were unlike any others he had ever seen. Both were dark-skinned, their arms and legs bare, their bodies otherwise covered in green and brown cloth. Stripes were painted on their faces, their black, curly hair trimmed short. And one was female, her curves modest, her body toned and muscles prominent.

They emerged from the trees, the scene expanding to a lake, many miles across. The party turned and followed the shoreline. With the expanded view, Ian looked around and realized that the dark-skinned strangers carrying him were two of a dozen. Six of the others carried three poles like his with Korrigan, Vargan, and Vic strapped to each pole.

The remaining four walked with spears in both hands, their expressions grim. The captors increased their pace to a jog, each step jostling Ian as he was sped along the lakefront.

He turned his attention toward the sky and found the sun at a low angle above the trees on the far side of the lake. *It must be morning, which means we are heading north on the western bank of the lake.* The information did little for him now, but if the situation changed and he found a means to escape, it would be more than valuable knowledge and might mean the difference between life and death. *First, to find out what is happening.*

"Where are you taking us?" Ian asked.

The female at the back end of his pole replied, "We go to Sacrumi."

"What is Sacrumi?"

"Our home."

Ian didn't know if that was a good or bad thing. "Why? What have we done?"

"You were found."

"I didn't know we were lost."

His response was meant in jest, but she remained serious in her reply.

"We went seeking gifts for our god, so the moon might return. You are the gifts we found."

"Gifts?" Ian had never considered himself a gift and had difficulty determining if she had used the correct word. "For what god?"

"The god of the moon, the god of the night, he who will one day lead our people in the rise above the races of magic."

The woman's explanations did not make sense to Ian. "What does it mean that we are gifts?"

"You are to be sacrificed."

Alarmed, he exclaimed, "What? Why?"

"I told you, so the moon will return."

His breath came in gasps and he argued, "Sacrificing us isn't necessary. The moon always goes dark for two or three days, but it then comes back."

"This we know. The moon returns because of the gifts we give to Urvadan."

Ian blanched. It was a name he had heard before. With that name came another moniker, one used to frighten children into behaving, one that was the stuff of nightmares. *The dark lord. They intend to sacrifice us to the dark lord.*

CHAPTER 34

SACRIFICE

A rhythmic shaking woke Vic. He opened his eyes to a four-inch-thick pole between him and the blue sky. His wrists and ankles were bound to the pole with vines. When he attempted to flex his fingers, he found them to be numb. Raising his head, he discovered a dark-skinned man carrying each end of the pole. Korrigan, Vargan, and Ian dangled from three similar poles, all awake but quiet.

The party ran along a lakefront beneath the mid-morning sun. They came to a narrow stream and turned from the lake to run parallel to the stream while climbing a gentle rise. The tall grass fell away to reveal a village of huts made of clay and thatch. They entered the village and were welcomed by the sound of laughter coming from children running past, their skin dark like that of his captors.

A group of women surrounded a fountain with water bubbling from a pillar of rock in its center. The women were dressed in wraps of bright colors ranging from yellow to red to green to blue. Those women dunked painted clay jugs in the water before placing the filled jugs on their heads and walking away with them balanced there. Men, women, and children were everywhere, going about their daily tasks. It felt shockingly similar to Shillings apart from the huts used instead of log houses and the different skin color and garb of the inhabitants.

At one end of the village was the lake. At the other end stood a tiered, massive structure two hundred feet tall and just as wide. The pyramid had a flat roof and was made of orange-tinted stone covered in vines at the lower reaches. A staircase stood outside the pyramid, leading to a dark opening two stories up. Without pause, the people carrying Vic and his companions headed for the pyramid, slowing as they reached the stairs. Up, they went, and when they reached the top, they entered a dark doorway.

The pyramid interior consisted of one massive, open chamber. A staircase ran down to the chamber floor, three stories below. Tiered seating, three feet tall and three feet deep stood to either side of the stairs. Similar tiers and stairs ran down the far side of the chamber, meeting at a floor made of stone tiles three feet square. Large, stone braziers stood in the four corners of the temple floor, and in the center were eight holes arranged in a circle around an eight-sided altar made of crystal. Sunlight beaming through a glass window in the ceiling's highest tier illuminated the temple interior.

Vic and his companions were carried down the stairs. The man holding the front of Vic's pole approached one of the holes in the floor, lowered his end of the pole, and inserted it into the opening. The one at the rear tilted the other end up until it stood upright. The pole slid three feet down into the floor and left Vic in a standing position, still bound to the pole by his wrists and ankles. Ian's pole was inserted into a hole across from Vic's while the two dwarves were each positioned a quarter way around the circle from him and facing each other.

The captors then jogged across the floor, up the stairs, and out of the building.

Alone in the quiet, empty temple, Vic turned to Ian. "What is happening?"

Ian groaned. "I already explained this to Korrigan and Vargan. You were still asleep."

"I was drugged." Vic recalled the darts and then darkness.

"We were all drugged," Ian said.

"At least they didn't kill us."

"Not yet anyway." Ian said with a note of dread.

Alarmed, Vic asked, "What does that mean?"

"They intend to sacrifice us tonight. They believe our deaths will make the moon return."

"That is silly," Vic scoffed.

"I tried to explain as much, but they think their actions are the reason it comes back after a few nights of darkness."

"What are we going to do?"

"I don't think we can talk our way out of this, so we need to escape. Can you get free?'

Vic pulled at his bonds, which caused the vines to bite into his wrists. The harder he pulled, the more it hurt. He could not break free. "I don't think so."

"We all have tried. Numerous times. My wrists are sore and bloody, but I am still stuck."

Determined to escape, Vic grabbed the pole with both hands and lifted. The pole rose a few inches, but the slack was insufficient for him to clear the three-foot-deep hole. Again, he tried but yielded the same result. Finally, he rested his forehead against the pole. *What are we going to do?*

THE DAY PASSED SLOWLY, the beam of light streaming through the window above moving across the temple as the sun advanced across the sky. Then came a time when daylight darkened and a storm struck. Pouring rain hammered against the skylight, the roar of it echoing in the temple interior. The storm raged for twenty minutes and, just as rapidly as it had come on, it stopped.

On three separate occasions, a trio of warriors consisting of two women and one male visited the captives and poured water from a small pitcher into their mouths. Each time, Ian drank as much as they would allow, and while his thirst was tempered, his hunger raged. But hunger was the least of his problems. Dread of what the night would bring remained at the forefront of his mind. Even if it had not been humid, he would have been covered in sweat from the anxiety.

When the sky above began to darken, a quartet of people in loose, green and red robes entered the chamber. Each carried a torch used to light the four braziers on the temple floor. Rather than leave, they snuffed the torches, climbed up a single tier and stood, waiting with their hands clasped before their chests, their expressions stoic.

The gong beside the temple entrance was sounded, the clang deep and echoing throughout the chamber. A noise arose outside and steadily grew louder until a throng of people poured through the temple entrance. The villagers spread out and began to fill the tiered seating around the temple floor. The seats were soon filled with dark-skinned villagers. The gong rang again and a door at the other end of the temple opened. Through it walked a tall man dressed in garishly bright colors of orange, red, blue, and green. On his head was a strange headdress made of colorful feathers and ivory horns. His dark-skinned face was painted with red, green, blue, and orange lines.

The crowd quieted as the man in the headdress descended to the temple floor. The man spoke as he circled the captives strapped to poles.

"Behold!" the man bellowed in Ian's native language. "We gather to honor Urvadan, god of the moon, god of the night, the god of our people." He gestured toward Ian and the other captives. "To Urvadan, we present the sacrifice. These four shall give their very essence to him, so the moon might return again."

The entire crowd chanted, "Praise Urvadan. May he bless the Crumi, who honor him with this gift."

The man with the headdress turned toward Ian and the others while drawing a massive, nasty-looking hunting knife. He held the blade before his face, twisting it, as firelight from the braziers danced along the sharp edge. Terrified, Ian could not speak. It took everything he had just to not wet himself. He shot a frantic glance toward Vic, but his brother was as helpless as he was. There was nobody to save him this time.

The man stalked toward Ian, who started pulling at his bonds with renewed urgency, but the ropes held fast. Rather than cutting Ian, as he had feared, the man walked past, entered the temple's inner circle and approached the altar at the heart of the room. Standing over the altar, the man laid the edge of the blade across his palm and sliced in one, smooth motion. Blood filled his palm, which he then held over the altar. Drops of blood spilled on the crystal, which began to glow an angry red. The man backed from the altar, out of the circle of poles, and did not stop until he stood beyond a brazier.

The glow from the altar grew brighter and brighter, until it was too bright to look upon. With the glow came heat as magical, red flames spouted from it. Ian turned away and strained against his bonds, attempting to escape the heat. Images of him burning alive filled his mind's eye. *I am going to die.*

The heat receded, and the light filling the chamber died down. Ian turned his head back toward the altar as the flames doused to reveal a figure standing upon it. The man wore black robes, his hood covering his head.

Everyone in the building looked on in shock, most with eyes full of fear.

The dark figure on the altar then spoke in the human tongue, his booming voice echoing throughout the chamber. "Crumi people, hear me! I am your god, Urvadan!" He raised his arms high. "Bow before me!"

Gasps came from the crowd. Beginning with the priest on the temple floor, everyone in the chamber fell to their knees and bowed their heads.

The robed figure announced, "The practice of immolation, as you have long performed it, shall end tonight. No longer will you sacrifice others in my name. If you persist, not only will the moon never return, but I will cast a curse upon your people." He lowered his arms. "Praise Urvadan that it be so."

The audience repeated the phrase, many with tears in their eyes and hands wringing in worry.

"These four innocents are now my chosen. You will treat them with respect, and when they leave the Stagnum, you are never to interfere with their lives again. Now, go! Leave my temple while I anoint my chosen and give them private instruction."

The crowd fled the temple with people pushing, shoving, and many falling down, as they scrambled to escape the wrath of their god. In moments, the building was empty. A beat later, laughter came from the robed figure. He lowered his hood and revealed the handsome face of a young man.

"Truhan?" Ian muttered.

Still chuckling, Truhan jumped off the altar. "I have not had that much fun in years."

Ian looked at Vic before asking, "How did you get in here?"

"I snuck in behind the priest. It was not difficult since the outer portion of the chamber is dark. When the light bloomed from the altar, I rushed in, wiped the blood from the surface, and climbed on." He held up a tan rag covered in blood and grinned. "Clever, wasn't it?"

In his entire life, Ian had never been so happy to see someone, even if the man was strange. "Please, can you free us? My wrists are killing me."

"Of course." Truhan pulled a dagger from his belt as he approached Ian. "But first, I have a question."

"For me?" Ian blinked.

"Yes. When we met, you spoke Dwarvish and Elvish and both quite well. How did you come to know these languages?"

It was an odd question to ask, and Ian could not even guess why it was posed, so he explained, "My people were captured by dwarves at the beginning of summer. Until then, I didn't even know dwarves and elves existed."

"If you won't answer him, Ian, I will." Vic looked at the man. "Ian figured out Dwarvish within days of our capture, all by himself. During the ten-day journey to Ra'Tahal, he learned it well enough that the dwarves made him a translator and apprentice to Chancellor Devigar. The chancellor taught him to read and write and taught him Elvish."

Truhan arched a brow at Ian. "All since summer began?"

Ian shrugged. "Um. Yes."

Narrowing his eyes while rubbing his chin, Truhan nodded. "That is most interesting."

Vic said, "You have your answer. Now, please free us."

"Free, you shall be." Flashing the knife, Truhan approached Ian and began to cut at the rope around his wrists.

When Ian's bonds were severed, he moved on to Vic. In moments, all four were freed.

Truhan sheathed his knife and glanced toward the temple doorway. "I regret that I must sneak out. Having the Crumi see me now would ruin the charade." He nodded to Ian, as if singling him out. "When you walk back into the village, someone will be waiting for you. Be sure to ask for your belongings and some food. I suspect they will treat you well." He then headed up the stairs, toward the rear entrance.

"Truhan," Ian called out. When the man paused to look back at him, he said, "Thank you. We...we owe you our lives."

"I am glad you realize that. Perhaps you can return the favor someday. I suspect we will meet again. Soon." The man flashed a knowing grin before he continued up the stairs and passed through the open doorway.

Vic rubbed his raw wrists. "That is the strangest man I have ever met."

"That might be true, but I am thankful we met him all the same."

Clapping a hand on Ian's back, Vic said, "Me too, little brother. Me, too."

Vargan grimaced. "Why are you two smiling?"

Switching to Dwarvish Ian said, "We were rescued and are free to go, thanks to Truhan."

"I figured that much out myself. Still, I do not see any call for smiling."

Ian snorted. "Why are you so grumpy?"

"I am tired, hungry, and was to be used as kindling for the Dark Lord. In addition, we spent a full day traveling in the wrong direction, which puts us off course. Worse, we lost our horses, so we will have to walk."

Korrigan sighed while rubbing his chafed wrists. "Aye, but at least we survived."

Ian tapped on Vic's arm and headed toward the stairs. "Let's see if we can get our things back. Maybe that will put Vargan in a better mood."

They wearily ascended and stepped outside, halting at the top of the outer staircase, which offered an elevated view of the village.

Torches mounted to poles illuminated the area, but it appeared deserted. At the far end of the village, four Crumi holding spears stood beside the fountain. Two were female and all four were dressed in the same greens and browns as those who had abducted Ian and his companions.

The crew descended, crossed the length of village, and approached the fountain. The four warriors knelt and lowered their heads while still gripping their spears with the tips pointed toward the night sky.

Ian shot a questioning glance at Vic, who shrugged.

One of the women lifted her head. "My name is Ahni. I am to lead the escort to ensure you reach the edge of the Stagnum safely."

"I am Ian. Before we leave, we want our things back."

"And you shall have them, along with food and water. All is being prepared." She stood and the other three rose with her. "Please, follow me."

She turned, approached a torch, and lifted it from the ground with her free hand before walking off, into the darkness. Ian, Vic, Korrigan, and Vargan followed while the other three Crumi warriors trailed them. The ground turned to a downslope, the torchlight illuminating the area in flickering light. They followed a trail through long grass and came to the lake's edge. The three trailing warriors tromped through the grass to the side of the trail. They bent and lifted something before dragging it into the lake. It was an odd boat with a long, narrow hull and two poles connecting a log on one side. Both the hull and the log floated.

"Climb in," Ahni said. "We will be taking the skiff."

Ian looked down at the water and then at the boat, ten feet away. "My boots will get wet."

"Yes. Your clothing as well."

He sighed, waded out into the water, and climbed into the boat, causing it to wobble, but far less than expected. Soon, Vic, Vargan, Korrigan, Ahni, and one other warrior joined them in the craft. A group of villagers appeared in the darkness carrying sacks, water skins, and their confiscated weapons. All were loaded into the boat, and then the two remaining warriors pushed them out of the reeds. The flickering torch and the shoreline slid away. Ahni and the other Crumi each dug a paddle from the craft's hull and began to stroke, taking them out in the darkness. Ian rifled through his pack, found something warm and unwrapped it to discover it was fresh, hot pork. Nothing had ever tasted better.

CHAPTER 35

GREAVESPORT

The watercraft rocked, waking Ian. He opened his eyes to green leaves sprouting from long, thin shoots passing above him. Pale blue sky was visible through gaps in the foliage. He sat up to find himself floating down a river. Ahni, in the front of the boat, and Oghallo, in the back of the boat, paddled with steady, even strokes.

"You are awake," Vic said from behind Ian. "I wondered if you might sleep all day."

"It was just a little nap." Ian rubbed his eyes.

"A three-hour nap?"

He shrugged. "It's not like there is anything else to do."

The boat rocked again, the speed increasing as they came to a small drop. Light came from ahead, giving the immediate impression that the surrounding greenery was about to relax its grip on the waterway.

The river widened, the trees giving way to long shoots of green grass. As the trees leaning over the water slid away, the view opened to reveal a blue sky. White, puffy clouds floated overhead, but to the west, a wall of darkness lurked. Within the darkness, lightning flashed. Ian groaned when he realized a storm was heading in their direction.

Ahni altered her stroke. The craft turned and angled toward shore right before the riverbank increased in height. The nose of the craft slid up onto the dirt. She hopped out, lifted, and pulled the boat forward while Oghallo pushed with his paddle against the river bottom.

"This is as far as we go," Ahni said.

Ian looked around. "Where are we?"

"At the edge of the Stagnum. The city lies an hour walk west of here."

"Greavesport?"

"Yes."

Ian gripped the rails and stood, causing the boat to rock slightly. He eased to the front, put a boot on the prow, and jumped to shore, thankful he hadn't lost his balance or slipped as he half expected himself to do.

Vic, Korrigan, and Vargan climbed out to join him on the bank, all four of them turning back to face the boat.

Ahni handed them their packs, still bulging with provisions, pushed the boat back into the water and climbed aboard, in one fluid motion. She slid her paddle into the water and began to stroke, turning the craft. Soon, the two Crumi warriors were moving upstream without a backward glance.

"They didn't even say goodbye." Ian felt a bit disappointed.

"Nothing personal," Vic said, "But I do hope we never see them again. That was an experience I don't need to repeat."

Korrigan climbed up the bank, waded through the long grass, and shouted. "I found the road. Let's see if we can reach the city before that storm hits."

Ian turned to Vic, "He said…"

Vic stopped him. "No need to translate. I understood it well enough."

"Good to know. It seems that you are finally learning." Ian climbed up the bank.

"Finally?" Vic followed as Ian tromped through the grass.

"Well, you've been around dwarves for half a year, now."

"You do realize I spent most of that time either alone underground while hacking at a wall of rock or sleeping. It's not as if I was involved in conversations until the past week."

Ian was again reminded of how much better his life had been at Ra'Tahal, stoking the guilt he had buried. To lighten his mood and Vic's, he flashed a grin. "It is nice to have the upper hand on you for once."

Vic laughed. "Fair enough. I'll let you have this one."

They walked down the road, heading west with Korrigan and Vargan in the lead.

"Since we have an hour with nothing else to do, let's practice a bit more. Understanding what you hear is not the same as saying it."

Thus, they resumed their practice while the road brought them past long, green grass and lush shrubbery. The time and miles passed quickly, the storm marching toward them at a steady pace. Lightning flashed and thunder boomed, the seconds between the two warning them that the storm was mere miles away. They crested a small rise, and the city came into view.

Greavesport consisted of hundreds, if not thousands, of buildings with peaked roofs clustered along the intersection of the Stagnum River and the Inner Sea. In the distance, beyond the city, whitecaps danced along the open water, driven by the advancing storm. There was no wall for protection, and the buildings were arranged haphazardly along curved streets rather than in the organized rows and columns found in the dwarven holds. The view of the city darkened as a wall of rain passed over it. Soon, the buildings appeared as nothing more than phantom shadows masked by heavy rain, making it clear that Ian and his companions were going to get wet. Again.

They were no more than a quarter mile from the city when the downpour reached them. Ian hurriedly donned his cloak and flipped the hood over his head. The cool rain washed away the heat, which was the only good thing Ian could say about it. Puddles soon dotted the road, and mud clung to the soles of his boots. Still, they marched on and when they entered the city, they were greeted by empty streets, the citizens chased indoors by the rain. Ian could not blame them.

Korrigan led them along a winding lane and turned toward the harbor before coming to a large, three-story building with a covered, elevated porch at the front. The sign above the door depicted a winged mug foaming over with ale. When they climbed onto the porch, Ian pulled his hood back in relief.

The window beside Ian shattered as a dwarf flew through it, landed on the porch decking, and rolled down the stairs before settling in a puddle.

The dwarf staggered to his feet, his eyes bleary as he wobbled and stumbled to one knee. His clothing was stained and torn, his black beard a bushy mess. He righted himself again and stomped back toward the building.

"I will teath thath..." He stopped on the stairs, narrowed his eyes, and leaned forward. "Korrigan? Whath..." He swayed from side to side, appearing ready to fall. "Whath are ya doing here?"

Korrigan pressed his lips together and flared his nostrils. "I have come looking for you, Arangoli."

Arangoli's eyelids drooped, as if too heavy for him to keep open. They drifted closed, and he toppled backward, off the stair, and splashed down into a puddle. There he lay, snoring despite the rain pelting his face.

Ian blinked. "This is the dwarf who is going to rescue your people?"

Korrigan sighed. "Come on Vargan. Let's carry him inside and see if we can sober him up."

IAN STEPPED into the Flying Flagon, the hum of chatter and sprinkles of laughter drowning out the patter of the pouring rain outside. He surveyed the room while Korrigan and Vargan hauled the unconscious dwarf inside.

Men, women, elves, and dwarves filled the inn, many sitting at tables, others standing in clusters, and all with a mug in hand. The taproom was sixty feet wide and just as deep with a bar along the left wall and a stairwell beside it, rising to the upper levels. Three rows of wooden posts were spaced throughout the room, the lanterns mounted to the posts providing light for the interior. Korrigan and Vargan carried Arangoli to the end of the bar, near the base of the staircase.

The barkeep, a middle-aged dwarf with a thick red beard, turned toward them and grimaced. He walked to the end of the bar and pointed. "I want him out of here."

"Hello, Haskabon," Korrigan said. "It is good to see you again."

"I've nothing against you, Korrigan, but Arangoli has overstayed his welcome. In addition to his extensive bar tab, he now owes me for a window as well."

Ian frowned. "It looked like someone tossed him out the window."

Haskabon crossed his arms over his barrel chest. "And I don't blame the men who did it. The blame lands on Arangoli, who seems intent on drinking himself into oblivion."

"What did he do to get tossed out?"

The barkeep grimaced. "He stood on their table and urinated on them."

Ian laughed, which seemed to further sour the barkeep's already bad mood.

Korrigan shot Ian a look to remain quiet before he asked, "Does Arangoli have a room where we can take him?"

"He has a room, but his payment for it is two weeks past due and he owes twice that for the ale he has drank." The innkeeper pointed a finger at the unconscious dwarf and shook it. "I can't extend his tab any further, and the damage he causes with the fights he starts is not worth it, even if he did pay on time."

"We will take responsibility for him. Give us one day to get him sober and speak some sense into him." Korrigan looked over his shoulder, toward the broken window. "It is pouring outside. We just need a room, food for the four of us, and lots of water for this drunken sod."

Haskabon scowled at Korrigan for a long beat before relenting. "Fine. Take him upstairs. Third floor, room twelve. I'll send one of my barmaids up with what you need." He cocked his head. "Mind you, I want the coin he owes me. Tomorrow."

"How much is it?'

The barkeep dug under the bar and pulled out a sheet of paper with numbers scribbled on it. After looking it over, he said, "When I add in the cost of the window, he is up to twenty silver pieces."

Vargan whistled. "Quite a sum."

Korrigan sighed. "Fine. We will settle him up tomorrow."

"Very well then. Go on up. The food will follow shortly." The barkeep waggled his finger. "But I want my coin tomorrow!"

The two dwarves carried the unconscious one up the stairs with Ian and Vic following. Upon reaching the third floor, they traversed a dark corridor and stopped outside of room twelve. Vargan fished a key on a cord from beneath Arangoli's tunic, lifted it over the intoxicated dwarf's head, and unlocked the door.

Ian stepped into the room to find it a total mess. Pieces of armor and clothing lay across the floor, the bed unmade, one of the two chairs in the room tipped on its side. On the small table beside the chairs were a silver pitcher and a cup. Ian approached the pitcher and sniffed, realizing that the liquid inside was water.

Arangoli was set down on the upright chair. Korrigan then lifted the pitcher off the table and unceremoniously emptied the contents over Arangoli's head. The dwarf blinked awake.

"Whath happening?"

"It's me, Korrigan."

Arangoli shook water from his head and raked his fingers down his face. "Why are you here?"

"We came for you. Ra'Tahal has been captured. We need you and the Head Thumpers to lead an assault to retake the citadel."

"Captured?" Arangoli furrowed his brow. "Who?"

"The Drow, led by the singer, Rysildar. I am sorry, but they murdered the king." Korrigan scowled, as if the words were sour to his tongue.

At that, Arangoli's eyes widened then seemed to come into focus. "My father is dead?'

"Aye," Vargan said. "The entire council and Chancellor Devigar fell in the skirmish, along with a fair portion of the remaining city guards."

As Korrigan's words sank in, the dwarf's intoxication seemed to wane. "I heard that Rysildar had been allowed into the city as a bargain between Ra'Tahal and Talastar."

Vargan snarled, "True, but rather than honor the agreement, he repaid Arangar with betrayal."

Arangoli made a fist. "Betrayal." His voice took on a guttural quality, oozing like a threat. "I cannot stomach it."

Korrigan grinned at Vargan. "Now, this is the Arangoli I used to know."

The intoxicated dwarf appeared to wilt. "But I cannot lead this mission. I cannot lead anyone."

"You can," Korrigan insisted. "Your reputation alone will draw others to follow."

He shook his head. "You don't understand. My war hammer...it is gone."

"Gone? What happened to it?"

Arangoli's head dropped in shame. "I...sold it."

"You what?" Vargan exclaimed. "What in the blazes is wrong with you? How could you sell the legendary weapon of your forefathers?"

Refusing to meet anyone's gaze, Arangoli stared at the floor. "I needed coin, so I went to Jarrakan's Trade and Barter and..." He stopped, appearing unable to say the rest.

With his meaty hands, Vargan gripped Arangoli by the tunic and lifted him off the chair. "When did you do this?"

"I don't know. Three or four weeks ago."

With a huff, Vargan shoved Arangoli back into the chair.

Korrigan stroked his beard. "It might still be there."

"But...I have no coin left to buy it."

Vic added, "And he already owes Haskabon."

"In that case, we need to get coin and that hammer, and we need to do it tomorrow." Korrigan walked to the door. "Vargan, I want you to stay with Arangoli. Get him sobered up and then get some rest."

"What about you three?" Vargan asked.

Korrigan crossed the room and stopped at the door. "We are going to solve a problem, and I only know one way to do that."

"Which is?"

"It is time to talk to Revita."

"The thief with the bad attitude?"

Korrigan opened the door. "That's the one."

When the dwarf walked out, Ian and Vic followed.

CHAPTER 36
REVITA

The rain had stopped, for which Ian was thankful. Night had claimed the city, its streets dark and quiet but not empty. A pair of men in dark clothing walked past, both taller and broader of shoulder than even Vic. A tickle on Ian's back had him feeling as if the two strangers had turned and were coming from behind. Although Vic and Korrigan were with Ian, the stillness after the rain had him on edge. Unable to deny his apprehension, he looked over his shoulder, but found the street empty. The paranoia only grew worse as a result, causing his steps to quicken. Another pair of men in cloaks crossed the intersection just ahead, both glancing in Ian's direction as they walked past. Again, he felt as if he were being watched. And yet, when he crossed the intersection and looked down the crossing street, he found the men still walking with their backs to him.

A dozen buildings later, Korrigan turned down a dark alley. He continued until reaching the alley's midpoint, stopped at a door, and knocked. Tense, quiet moments passed until it opened to reveal an old woman. Her gray hair was tied back in a bun, her skin wrinkled, her eyes hazel and kind. She wore a simple, tan dress with a stained apron, on which she wiped her hands.

"Yes?" She said in Dwarvish.

Korrigan spoke in a quiet voice. "I am seeking Revita."

The woman frowned. "I have not seen Revita in years."

"I know who you are," Korrigan said. "She is a friend, one who owes a favor."

"How so?"

"My companion and I saved her from some trouble a few years back. My name is Korrigan. His was Arangoli. We have need of her services."

The old woman narrowed her eyes. "I have heard those names, the latter not always in a positive light."

"Revita," Korrigan said again. "I need to speak with her."

Finally, the woman sighed and moved aside. "Come in."

They stepped inside and the woman closed the door behind them, the four of them crowding the small entryway.

"Back against the door," the woman said in a terse voice.

Ian, Vic, and Korrigan did as she said. The woman crossed the room, stopped a stride into the corridor, and reached for the lantern on the wall. When she pulled down on it, a click resounded followed by a rumble. The floor before Ian began to rise, tilting up until it blocked the hallway completely. In the opening was a staircase leading into darkness.

The old woman's voice came from beyond the raised floor. "Go down. When you reach the door at the bottom, knock thrice, pause, and knock twice more. Do not open the door unless you wish to die."

The ominous warning caused Ian to glance at Vic, who reached for the mattock on his back until Korrigan grabbed his wrist and shook his head. The dwarf began descending. Ian and Vic followed. The trap door began to lower, and by the time they were ten stairs down, darkness surrounded them. With his hand extended before him and the other palm sliding along the cool, stone wall, Ian descended until his boot crunched down on dirt. He took another three blind steps and collided with Korrigan.

"I found the door." The dwarf knocked three times, paused, and added two more knocks.

The door opened to reveal a burly dwarf with a cudgel and a scowl amid his thick, black beard.

Korrigan snorted. "I should have expected you would be here, Morrigan."

"Korrigan Lodestone. I thought you were too righteous for Greavesport."

"No, just too righteous for your kind."

The comment elicited a scowl from Morrigan. "What are you doing here?'

"I am looking for Revita."

Morrigan narrowed his eyes. "If you think to arrest her for something, you'll not make it out of here alive."

"I have need of her skills. Nothing more."

The dwarf stepped aside. "She is in the next room, conducting business. Interrupt her at your own risk."

When they rounded the door, they discovered that the dwarf was not alone.

Three men, one tall and thin, one tall and heavy, and another of modest height and a brawny build sat around a table, each holding cards in their hand. Dressed in patchwork armor, they were all rough looking, their faces covered in stubble and scars, their hair greasy except for the short one, whose head was shorn.

The room was long with two sets of bunks along one side wall and the table positioned in the middle. The wall opposite from the bunks was lined with shelves filled with crates, barrels, sacks, and an assortment of weapons.

Morrigan took the empty seat at the table, set his cudgel down, and picked up the hand of cards that were lying face down on the table. The three men seated at the table watched as Ian, Vic, and Korrigan walked past, heading toward the door at the far end of the room. Upon reaching the door, Korrigan knocked.

A female's voice came from the other side. "I told you, I am busy."

"It is Korrigan. I am here on urgent business. Arangoli needs your help."

The door opened to reveal a woman standing Ian's height, her skin tanned, her raven hair tied back in a tail. She was dressed in dark clothing, all charcoal grays and blacks, including her leather boots and hooded cloak. Her black, leather jacket was padded, adding bulk to her lithe frame. Daggers were strapped to her thighs and knife handles stuck out from the cuffs of her boots. She appeared to be in her early twenties. An intensity filled her dark eyes as she looked from Korrigan to Ian to Vic.

"Hello, Vita," Korrigan said.

"Korrigan. How long has it been?" She wore a smirk, as if she knew something others did not.

"Three years."

"How is captain's life?"

Korrigan sighed. "In truth, not what I expected but better than lacking any direction after seeing what that has done to Arangoli."

"You mentioned that he is in trouble. What does that have to do with me?"

"May I come in and speak in private?"

She stepped aside and gestured toward the room.

Korrigan walked past with Ian and Vic following him into a dimly lit room with a bed, a wardrobe, a nightstand, a vanity, a table, and four chairs, one of which was occupied by a hooded figure with a lean frame.

Revita gestured toward the door. "Sorry, Trystari, but I am going to pass. Another job has come up. You'll have to find help elsewhere."

Trystari stood, the cloak opening enough for Ian to determine her build that of a female. A darkness swirled around her, as she spoke with an accent, her voice little more than a hiss. "You may regret your choice, Revita."

Ian gasped as he realized that she was a dark elf.

Revita said, "My list of regrets is long and seldom worth revisiting. Another joining the mob will make little difference."

With gliding strides, cloak swirling in her wake, Trystari made for the door, stopped and glanced over her shoulder. "Watch your back, Revita. It may have a target upon it."

"I always do. Now, go on. Find another toy to play with." Revita closed the door, using it to push Trystari out. She turned and sighed. "I hate dealing with Drow. Even I do not scheme as they do. They make it difficult to tell where the truth ends and their lies begin. Sometimes, I wonder if they even know." She turned her attention to Ian, scrutinizing him from head to toe before shifting to Vic. Her gaze lingered on him while a smirk turned her lip up. "Who are these two? I have never seen you in the company of humans."

"This is Ian and his brother, Vic. Trouble has come to Ra'Tahal and they were among those caught up in the struggle."

"What sort of trouble?" Revita plopped down in a chair.

"A Drow singer was allowed to live in the city as part of a bargain. The deal went sour when the singer betrayed King Arangar, murdered him, and then killed the council. Caught by surprise, not expecting an attack from within the citadel walls, dozens of citadel guards were killed. The Drow now control Ra'Tahal. We came here seeking Arangoli to lead a mission to retake the city. Unfortunately, we found him in bad shape."

She snorted. "That is an understatement. I saw him at the Breezy Bard Inn a few days back. He was passed out on a table. It wasn't even noon yet. I cannot recall the last time I saw him and he wasn't drunk or unconscious. He seems to have lost himself in his cups."

Korrigan sighed. "He probably spent the night on the table."

"I would not doubt it."

"Which comes to why we are here."

The woman crossed her arms, lifted her legs, and crossed her ankles with her heels on the table. "I am listening."

With a glance toward Ian and Vic, Korrigan explained the situation. "Despite his current state, Arangoli's reputation still carries weight among my people. A big part of that fame comes from the weapon he wields. Unfortunately, that weapon is currently at the Trade and Barter."

"He traded his war hammer for coin?" She burst out laughing. "I hadn't realized that he slid that low."

"Well, we intend to prop him up, so he can save our people. That won't happen without the war hammer."

"Buy it back then."

Korrigan shook his head. "We happen to lack funds right now."

She arched a brow. "You want me to steal it?"

"That and some coin as well. It turns out that Arangoli has taken advantage of Haskabon's hospitality and carved away the last of the barkeep's patience. He owes him four gold pieces. If he is not paid by the end of the day tomorrow, he intends to have Arangoli arrested."

The woman stared at Korrigan for a long, silent moment before replying, "So, you want me to break into the Trade and Barter, procure the hammer and steal enough gold to pay off his debts?

"We do." He nodded firmly.

"And how do you expect to pay me for this service?"

"You could steal gold for yourself as well," Korrigan suggested.

"So, you want me to plan and execute this heist in one day and my only reward is what I can steal for myself in addition to the hammer and gold you need to get Arangoli out of trouble?"

Korrigan shrugged. "I guess."

"There is a situation with the one who owns the Trade and Barter."

"Who?"

"Magistrate Hargrave."

Korrigan held his forehead as if a headache had just come on. "Arangoli, how did you get into such a mess?"

"How, indeed?" Revita agreed.

He dropped his hand and frowned. "Does that mean you won't do it?"

She eyed Ian and Vic again. "You three will need to help pull this off."

Korrigan nodded. "Done."

"And I want one more thing in return."

"This makes me nervous. What is it?"

Revita pointed at Vic. "Him, just for tonight."

Ian frowned. "Vic? What do you want with Vic?"

She smirked, stood, and approached Vic, her hand running up his arm, across his shoulder, and down his torso as she appraised him. "That is between me and him, but he appears to be up to the challenge."

Ian gasped when he realized what she had in mind.

Vic looked at Ian and asked in his native tongue, "I tried to follow the conversation, but gave up until you mentioned my name. Why is she looking at me like that?"

Ian grinned. "She agreed to help us, but you are part of the bargain."

"What does that mean?"

"It means that you are to spend the night with her."

"What?" He jerked in shock. "I am no whore."

Ian leaned closer to his brother and whispered, "Would it really be so bad? She might be brazen and a thief, but she *is* attractive."

Vic frowned. "But it just feels...wrong."

Revita sauntered up to Vic, her hips swaying overtly, her eyes locked with his. She stroked his bearded cheek and crooned, "Do not worry. I won't hurt you...too badly." Without looking away from him, she gestured toward the door. "You two, go. Meet me at the Flying Flagon for breakfast. I will explain our plan and your roles. Until then, leave this one to me."

Ian followed Korrigan to the door and looked back while the dwarf swung it open. Revita had slid a hand around Vic's head, pulled him toward her, and kissed him. He seemed stiff and reluctant at first, but then, his arms wrapped around her, his hands found her backside, and he drew her flush against his body. Ian pulled the door closed and shook his head. *Vic has all the luck.* While Ian was unsure if he was up to the task Revita had in mind, he envied his brother and the night he was about to experience.

IAN DESCENDED to the Flying Flagon's main floor, where he found four tables occupied, one of them by Korrigan, Vargan, and Arangoli. The latter had bloodshot eyes and appeared in better shape than the night before, but that was a low bar to hurdle. Haskabon stood by the broken window, talking to a dwarf with a reel of rope marked with lines. The unknown dwarf unwound the rope, held it to the window opening, and then marked something down on a sheet of parchment. By the time Ian reached the table occupied by his companions, the innkeeper turned and strolled back to the kitchen.

"Good morning," Ian said as he sat on one of the empty chairs. "You three are up early."

Korrigan said, "I couldn't sleep. My neck and shoulder are sore from lying on the floor."

The room Arangoli rented had only one bed and two chairs, leaving one of them relegated to the floor. While thankful for a decent night of sleep, Ian suddenly felt guilty about sleeping on the bed.

Hungry, Ian asked, "I am starved. Did you eat?"

"Not yet. Now that Haskabon is finished with the carpenter, he likely went back to the kitchen to check with the cook."

Footsteps came from the rear of the inn and Ian turned to find Revita and Vic coming towards them. She appeared much as she had the night prior, dressed in blacks and dark grays, her dark hair tied back in a tail, a smirk on her lips as if she privately laughed at everyone else. Vic, on the other hand, had combed his hair, shaved, and looked cleaner than he had in many weeks.

The two of them walked up to the table, Revita taking a seat beside Korrigan, leaving the one beside Ian for Vic.

While Revita began a quiet conversation with the three dwarves, Ian leaned close to his brother and whispered. "How was it?"

Vic gave him a sidelong look. "Don't you know that it is in poor taste to kiss and tell?"

"Even to your brother?"

Vic snorted, "Especially to my brother."

Although he was unsatisfied, Ian shifted topics. "Why did you come in the back door?"

"Vita said it was a precaution in case someone was watching the front door."

Ian smiled. "Vita?"

"She...prefers to be called that...at least in private."

"Do you like her?"

Vic shrugged. "She is not so bad, but she made it quite clear that our night together was merely for fun and that anything more than that was not going to happen."

The information was unlike anything Ian had come to know about women, which wasn't a whole lot. "She sounds almost like...a man."

His brother smiled. "Trust me, she is definitely a woman, and one who is as fit as anyone I have ever met."

Ian's cheeks grew warm at the implication and he shifted topics to avoid his imagination from dwelling upon Vic's evening interlude. "You shaved and cut your hair."

"Actually, she helped me on both counts." Vic stroked his chin. "I'll admit I was nervous to have her blade so close to my face and neck, worried that might nick me, but her hand was steady. In truth, she did a better job than I ever have."

Haskabon and a barmaid appeared at the table with a loaf of hot bread, a bowl of honey, one of apples, and a plate of smoked fish. From the pink hue, Ian knew it was salmon. His history with seafood and allergy to shellfish made his choice easy. He reached for the bread, tore a piece off, and set it on his plate before dropping a scoop of honey beside it. The warm bread and fresh honey were delicious, and the apples were crisp and juicy.

The group ate in silence, the food disappearing swiftly, and when it was gone, Revita leaned over the table and spoke in a quiet voice.

"This thing we are to do begins this afternoon. I have a lot of experience with the Trade and Barter House. Hargrave is a paranoid man, so he pays Jarrakan and his guards well to ensure loyalty. Any thief daring enough to break in when the shop is closed will find more than one enchanted trap, waiting to them. So, we need to get in during the day and, when the shop closes, finish the job."

Korrigan frowned. "How do we do that?"

She reached out and patted Ian's hand. "This pup is the key."

Ian blinked. "Me?" He looked from Revita to the others, all staring at him. He had no idea what was expected of him, but the squirreling in his stomach insisted it was bad.

CHAPTER 37
MISDIRECTION

Revita Shalaan had endured a difficult childhood, growing up on the streets of a city a thousand miles from Greavesport. The streets showed no pity. That was true when she was ten years old and held true when she was twenty-three. Never knowing her father and abandoned by a mother who did not want her, she escaped the cruel confines of the orphanage and set out to live on her own. As it often happens in such situations, she turned to crime as a means of survival.

Her career as a thief began with picking pockets, and when her exceptional skill at doing so began to dull the thrill of it, she turned to more dangerous activities. By the time she reached womanhood, her ability to pick locks, move with stealth, and disarm traps had advanced beyond that of the other thieves in Galfhaddon. Her comely appearance and frame, lithe with enough curves to attract the notice of the opposite sex, became another tool in her arsenal. Manipulating men soon came as naturally as breathing, as long as she had her knives to protect herself should any decide that the fruit was too tempting not to indulge, even if it were against her will. Such an act, committed by the son of Galfhaddon's duke, led to her stabbing him in a distinctly tender location. While the teen survived the wound, his father's wrath resulted in her fleeing the city at the tender age of seventeen.

For six years, Revita had called Greavesport home, building her reputation while taking care not to piss off the wrong people. Most would view her life as one with constant risk while fearing what might happen should she get caught. For Revita, the thrill of the act outweighed the prize at the end. Gold had become a way to keep score, and while she appreciated the things wealth might bring, it was the challenge she sought. The higher the risk and the greater the obstacles that accompanied a heist, the more she enjoyed it.

Thus, when Korrigan came to her with a reason to cross Magistrate Hargrave, she leapt at the chance, but took care to hide the enthusiasm. She could not have the dwarf know that she would have done the job for free. Her reputation required a reward, and a night with a pretty, young man had been long overdue.

She glanced at Vic, who stood beside her while staring at the building across the square with an intense, serious expression. After some coaching on her part, he had performed admirably for someone lacking experience with women. More impressive, he had grown more confident and skilled each time, so after the third go, she was left both exhausted and satisfied. The thought made her smile.

The two of them stood in the shadowed doorway of a cobbler shop while humans, dwarves, and elves crossed the square, some on horseback, others driving wagons or carts, most on foot. The harbor gate stood a hundred feet to the north, thick with traffic passing into and out of the city. The building in question was Jarrakan's Trade and Barter, a three-story structure two hundred feet wide and just as deep, one of the largest buildings in Greavesport and certainly the largest shop.

"Remember your role, Vic," she reminded him.

He turned to her. "I know what to do. Just tell me when."

"Oh, you will know." She spied Ian and Korrigan as they emerged from a shaded street and walked into the square. "Here comes your brother. Once he and Korrigan are inside, I will head across the square. When I am out of sight, count to fifty and follow."

"Got it."

She patted his cheek. "You are such a good pupil." She gave him a naughty smile. "As proven last night."

When Vic blushed, she laughed. "Oh, you are fun. If this works, I may have to invite you to my place for another evening of entertainment."

He pressed his lips together. "What if I decline?"

Revita laughed again. "I find that unlikely."

She walked away, falling in with the foot traffic and slowing to allow a pair of dwarves to walk past before resuming. Across the square from where Vic stood, she passed below the awning in front of the shop and through its open doors. She entered the shadowy interior and paused to survey the scene.

A trio of armed human guards stood just inside the doorway, and a dozen others, some of them dwarves but more human, were visible throughout the space. Men, women, dwarves, and a pair of elves meandered around the space, perusing the wares for sale. Tables, shelves, and racks were spread throughout the shop. Piles of clothing, lanterns, furniture, books, sculptures, and other oddities rested on the tables and shelves. Weapons and pieces of armor occupied the racks, many of the weapons locked behind bars like caged animals. In the center of the shop stood the stone statue of a warrior, ten feet tall and gripping a sword made of stone.

A man dressed in a green coat stood behind the counter at the side of the shop. He wore a turban around his head, his swarthy complexion making it obvious that he originated from Galfhadden, as Revita did. Behind him was a small chest and another pair of armed guards. A woman stood on the other side of the counter, waiting as the man counted out silver pieces. To his side was a cart with a rocking chair and a lute resting on it. When he placed the coins in her hand, she glanced toward the cart for a long beat while a tear tracked down her face. The woman then turned and fled from the building.

Revita sauntered in, pretending to examine the goods displayed as she meandered across the room.

The man at the counter said, "You are not welcome here, Revita."

She turned toward him. "My coin is as good as anyone else's, Jarrakan."

"And your fingers are twice as sticky as well."

She scoffed, "Don't believe the stories you hear in the streets."

The shopkeeper raised his voice. "Tavik. Gorp. Will you please escort this woman out?"

Two of the guards roaming the room came toward her. Revita backed from them and spoke loudly. "Lay a hand on me, and you will regret it."

One of the men drew a cudgel and smacked it against his palm. "If you choose to do this the hard way, you will be the one regretting it."

The other man balled his fist. "If you think we won't hit a woman, you are mistaken."

When she backed another step, a third guard came at her from behind. He wrapped his arms around her, squeezed, and lifted her off her feet. Revita reacted by kicking out, aiming for the groins of the two men in front of her. Both boot toes struck true. The injured guards cried out and doubled over.

"Let me go!" she shouted.

Another guard came in from the side and threw a punch. Revita tilted her head just in time for the blow to glance off her cheek and strike the guard holding her in the face. He loosened his grip and she broke free. Two more guards came rushing toward her.

WITH A MEASURED PACE, while he whistled and pretended to behave as if he were simply on a late afternoon stroll, Vic walked along the square perimeter. Despite his nonchalant outward appearance, beneath his cloak and jerkin, his armpits were damp with sweat. He passed by the broad, awning-covered entrance to the Trade and Barter, glanced inside, and spied Revita in an argument with a guard. Another picked her up and she shouted before kicking two others in the groin. It was time for him to act.

"Leave her alone," he shouted in Dwarvish.

Vic rushed into the shop, darted past tables and shelves, and tackled a burly man holding a cudgel. The two of them sailed past Revita and fell to the floor with Vic on top. He climbed to his feet and turned as another guard rushed in. The guard threw a punch. Vic ducked beneath it and drove his fist into the attacker's stomach. The man doubled over in pain. Vic grabbed him by the hair and shoved the guard's head down while lunging with his knee. It struck the man in the face, bloodying his nose and slicing his lip. As Vic spun around, prepared for the next oncoming foe, Revita leapt and twirled with her leg extended. Her boot struck a guard in the side of the head, and he toppled to the side of Vic.

The shopkeeper bellowed something in Dwarvish, and while the words were unknown to Vic, his tone was not. The remaining guards all raced in, and Vic shifted to defensive mode. He backed up to a rack as four men surrounded him. Two of them drew swords, their expressions lacking humor.

"I surrender." Vic threw his hands up to avoid any misunderstanding.

A man came in from each side, one gripping Vic's right wrist, another gripping his left before twisting his arms behind his back and ushering him toward the entrance. With a shove, the men sent Vic stumbling out into the street. He caught himself short of falling face-first, stopped, and turned back toward the building as Revita was shoved out, her momentum causing her to crash into him. Vic fell backward with his arms around her. She landed on top of him, her weight driving the wind from his lungs.

"Oof!" He lay there, gasping for air while she pushed herself up.

Revita stared down at him, her face above his, her raven tail dangling over him. She smiled and whispered, "You did well. That was fun."

A gasp of air filled his lungs and he coughed before replying, "You are insane."

"Time to finish the charade." She climbed to her feet, turned toward the building, and shook her fist at it while shouting in Dwarvish, "I am going to get you, Jarrakan."

Vic stood and dusted himself off while scowling at the guards standing in the entrance. Korrigan emerged from between the guards and walked off, alone and appearing disinterested.

Remembering his own role, Vic turned and walked off, seemingly done with the entire business. Revita was to head in the opposite direction, so his interference would appear as nothing more than a misguided act of chivalry.

His thoughts shifted to his brother and the role he was to play in their scheme. Everything now relied on Ian. If he failed, the plan was doomed.

CHAPTER 38
HEIST

Ian sat in darkness, his knees against his chest, his forehead resting on his arms. The tiny, cramped space he occupied was hot and stifling. Time advanced slowly, or so it seemed. He longed to escape his confinement, to stretch his legs, to breathe fresh air. Determined not to fail Revita, his brother, and the dwarves, he resisted the urge and sought to focus on something else.

As it often occurred in such moments, his thoughts turned to Rina and the warmth he felt inside when she smiled at him. He worried about what had become of her and wondered if she had fallen prey to Rysildar's dark magic. Worse, he worried that he may never discover the truth behind her disappearance. *Where are you, Rina?* It was a call shouted in his head. There was no reply.

Footsteps approached, drawing Ian's attention. He raised his head and peered through a two-inch diameter knothole. Through the opening, he had a clear view of the dark corridor at the rear of the Trade and Barter.

A male voice came from nearby. "The front doors are closed, bolted, and ready, boss."

The shopkeeper, Jarrakan, replied, "Good. I will arm the enchantment. Wait for me at the back door."

"Will do."

The sound of retreating footsteps was followed by a hum. A person approached Ian's location and walked past, his backside coming into view. It was a tall guard with broad shoulders, his torso covered in studded leather armor, a sword at his side. The man walked down the corridor and stopped at the far end, where he waited in the shadows.

A quiet minute passed before another set of footsteps drew near. The portly shopkeeper walked past Ian. As Jarrakan entered the corridor, the guard opened the door at the far end. The dim light of dusk bled in and allowed Ian a better view. The shopkeeper stopped in front of a bronze panel on the wall and began to press buttons. While Ian noted the location of the first three keypresses, Jarrakan's body blocked the subsequent ones, so Ian counted the clicks he heard. After the sixth click, a humming sound arose. A red light in the heart of the panel began flashing on and off. Jarrakan stepped outside and closed the door while the light continued to flash. A key slid into the lock. The lock clicked. Then...silence.

Ian strained, listening for any signs of movement while wishing he could see beyond the tiny little opening facing the rear entrance. Given his position under the barrel, any attempt to do so would doom him if anyone else remained in the building. So, he waited and prayed that the Trade and Barter had been vacated. Ten minutes became twenty. Twenty became thirty. Finally, he decided to chance it.

He pressed his hands against the curved, wooden wall in front of him and leaned back. The barrel tipped backward and a few inches of dim light seeped in along the floor. He removed one hand from the barrel's inner surface, wedged his fingers beneath the lip, and lifted. The barrel teetered on edge for a beat and then fell over, the inside hitting Ian in the head and taking him with it. A boom echoed in the building as the hollow, wooden barrel bounced off the shop's tiled floor. Ian squeezed his eyes tight and pressed his hand to the wound, certain that his forehead was going to bruise. If anyone was still in the building, it would have been impossible for them not to hear the noise. In fact, he was certain that it was loud enough to alert someone outside.

He lay still, terrified of being discovered, but no cries for alarm were raised, no rush of footsteps came for him. As the pain in his head diminished, Ian eased out of the barrel and into the aisle between a table and a shelf, both covered in an array of goods. Thick shadows dominated the building's interior, the dim light of dusk seeping through the high windows above the front entrance, far across the shop. The vertical iron bars inside those windows prevented them from being targets from would be thieves.

Ian turned toward the rear corridor and crept down it, into darkness. He dug into his tunic and pulled out the amulet Revita had given him. He held it in his palm, pressed his other palm against it, and rubbed his hands together as he had been instructed. The metal amulet began to glow, the more he rubbed, the brighter it became. Ian let the amulet drop against his chest, the glow revealing an open doorway leading to a storage room to one side, a closed door to the other, and a door at the end of the corridor.

The light ate away at the darkness as Ian crept down the corridor. A hum came from ahead, steadily growing louder as he advanced. When he drew near the door at the far end, silver runes marking the doorframe came into view. On the wall beside the door was a circular bronze plaque. Trapezoidal bronze pieces ran along the plaque's circumference. Each piece was two inches wide and marked with a rune. In the plaque's center was a glowing, red jewel. As Ian had been warned, the jewel meant that the enchantment protecting the rear entrance was active. Revita's voice echoed in his head. *Touch the door when it is armed, and you will die a horrible, ugly death.* It was a warning she did not have to give twice.

He stopped in front of the plaque and examined the runes, all of which were familiar and represented words in the dwarven language. Notably, many of them matched runes marking the doorframe. While he had seen Jarrakan press the first three keys and noted their locations, they only solved half of his problem. The runes on those keys represented the words man, power, and fear, but it was up to him to figure out the last three keys. He had been warned that failure might result in a very ugly outcome. So, Ian took a deep breath to calm his nerves as he prepared to solve the mystery of the last three keys required to disarm the trap.

Upon further examination, he realized that the runes around the doorframe told a story when he read them from lower left, up the left side, across the top, and back down the right side.

Talking to himself, Ian recited the tale, "A man who came from nothing rose to power. His enemies feared him. Those who supported him were rewarded. Those who crossed him suffered. Thus, he ruled for many years, and his city thrived."

Ian looked back at the runes marking the small, bronze panels, and relied on his intuition to tell him where to begin. He pressed the button with the symbol for man and leapt back, dreading if he had chosen wrong. Nothing happened. Moving along, he pressed the button representing the word power. Next came fear, followed by reward, followed by suffering. Holding his breath, he pressed the button with the symbol for thrive. The humming stopped, the light in the gem faded, and Ian released his breath. One problem was solved. It was up to Revita to deal with the rest.

He drew a folded piece of parchment from his pocket, squatted, and slid it under the door. When half remained on his side, he gave it a shove.

Revita lay at the edge of a two-story rooftop and peered down into a dark alley. Night had blackened the moonless sky, leaving a sea of twinkling stars as the only light. Over a half an hour had passed since Jarrakan and the last guard locked up the shop and departed for the day. A part of Revita worried that she had asked too much of the boy, but the patient part of her pushed such concerns aside. Patience was a requisite in her profession. Impatient thieves made mistakes – mistakes came at a steep price with either prison or death as payment. So, she kept watch of the quiet, dark alley with her attention fixed upon the Trade and Barter's rear entrance. Then, a pale, rectangular shape emerged from beneath the door. It was time to act.

She gripped the eave, slid over the edge, and dangled with her boots twelve feet above the alley. A kick caused her legs to swing toward the wall. Releasing one hand, she reached for the drainpipe, and gripped the bracket holding it to the wall. With practiced skill, she descended the pipe in seconds and her boots softly touched down on the alley floor. She dusted her hands off and cast a furtive glance in each direction. There was nobody in sight, so she crossed the alley and reached into a hidden coat pocket.

Eight years of picking locks had honed Revita's skills. Two years ago, just when she'd reached the pinnacle of her profession, she came across a prize that made the skill all but irrelevant: A set of picks crafted by a dwarven metal wright and enchanted by a spell wright. The result of the enchantment made even the most complex of locks less than a trivial challenge. She slid the enchanted pick into the lock and a glow emitted from the opening as the tumblers tripped. A turn unlocked the door and she pocketed the pick to keep it safe.

Revita opened the door, stepped over the slip of paper on the ground, and eased the door closed. "Ian?"

A shadow stepped into the corridor's far end. He removed his hand from the amulet, the glow revealing his young face. "Here."

She walked toward him. "You did well. May I have the amulet?"

He lifted it over his head and handed it to her. "I was only able to see the first three keys to disarm the enchantment. I...had to figure out the rest myself."

"Which you did, or the door would still be locked."

"Yeah, but what if I had got it wrong?"

Shrugging, she walked past him. "You'd likely be very dead about now, and I'd be stuck on that rooftop waiting all night."

He frowned. "You don't seem impressed."

She patted his cheek and crooned facetiously, "There's a good boy. Now, I need to get to work."

Holding the amulet up for light, she crossed the room, rounded the counter, and stopped to stare at the barred cage of weapons along the wall. A longsword, a mace, an axe, a shield, a rapier, and a war hammer were displayed inside. The hammer matched the description given to her by the dwarves.

Testing the cage door confirmed that it was locked, but her pick resolved that issue in seconds. Opening the door, she reached in and lifted the hammer from its hooks.

"This thing is heavy." She turned toward Ian and held it over the counter. "Take this, so I can start searching for the safe."

He gripped the shaft, but when she let go, the hammer plummeted. The hammer head struck the counter. A massive thump released, the shockwave passing through Revita like a ripple from a rock tossed into a pool. The marble countertop shattered, sending shards in all directions. The counter itself split down the center, and a panel fell off toppling toward Revita and forcing her to leap backwards lest her toes get crushed.

In a harsh whisper, she snapped, "You clumsy fool! Are you trying to get us caught?"

Contrite, Ian lifted the hammer with both hands and backed away. "I am sorry."

The light of the amulet on her chest shone on a metal box in the newly revealed opening under the counter. Revita squatted and held the light close, curious as to what it was. A dial on the front of the box informed her instantly.

She looked up at Ian. "Sometimes mistakes are a boon. In this case, your accident turned out to be helpful. I'm sorry I yelled at you."

"Helpful?"

"Yes. We found the safe."

Revita reached into another pocket and pulled out a small funnel-shaped object. She turned the collar in the center and held it against the face of the safe. When she turned the dial, the sound was amplified. A paced ticking filled the room until a click resounded. She stopped and began turning the dial in the opposite direction, ignoring the ticking as she awaited the next click. Three clicks in, Revita pulled the lever, and the safe door swung open.

Four sacks occupied the safe's dark interior. The distinct sound of clinking coins sang to her when she lifted the first sack. Moving quickly, she gathered the second and third sack. When she lifted the fourth bag, it revealed a glass-covered opening in the bottom of the safe. A red light bloomed from the opening and began to pulse. Her intuition screamed at her, causing her to urgently back away from the safe. She stood with her back against the wall and stared at it in apprehension while wondering what might happen next.

When seconds passed and nothing happened, Revita glanced up at Ian, who still clutched the war hammer against his chest.

He asked, "What's wrong?"

She shook her head. "I don't know, yet. When I lifted the last sack of coins, it triggered something."

A shadow moved behind Ian – a huge shadow with red, glowing eyes. It burst forward and when the light from her amulet reached it, Revita realized that the stone statue had come to life. The twelve-foot-tall golem was coming at Ian from behind.

"Look out!" she shouted.

When Ian spun around in reaction, his foot slipped on shards of broken marble. He landed on the floor with an oof. The charging golem stepped right over him and smashed through the counter. At the last moment, Revita dove to the side, narrowly avoiding being crushed between the monster and the wall. She released the sacks to catch herself as she hit the floor. Rolling, she scrambled to her feet, drew a throwing blade, and loosed. The blade careened off the monster, not even leaving a mark.

"Oh, crap," she realized her weapons were of no use as the statue turned toward her.

The golem raised its stone sword and swung a downward chop right at Revita. She leapt over the counter. The stone sword struck the floor where she had been standing and shattered, sending shards in all directions. She bent and helped Ian to his feet as the golem stalked around the far end of the counter and took position between them and the rear exit.

"We are trapped in here," she said, now wishing she had brought someone capable of fighting the creature.

VIC STOOD in the dark alley behind the Trade and Barter, listening for signs of trouble while glancing from side to side. Although Revita had assured him that she could execute the heist without his assistance, Ian was in the shop with her, and Vic had promised their mother that he would keep him safe. So, he hid out of sight and waited until Revita entered the building before he snuck down the alley, found a dark recess across from the door, and waited.

A crash came from inside the building, setting him on edge. He tensed and listened. Not long afterward, he heard Revita shout and another, even larger crash came from within. Vic pulled his mattock free from the harness on his back, rushed across the alley, and opened the door. He crept in the darkness, toward a glow at the far end of the corridor. Then, a massive, towering creature made of stone stepped between him and the light. The monster's back faced him, giving Vic an advantage. He burst from the corridor and swung the mattock low. The pick end drove into the monster's calf. Blue sparks danced along the monster's lower leg. The creature staggered and threw a melon-sized backhand, which Vic ducked beneath just in time.

Vic darted to the side, spun, and swung again, aiming for the opposite side of the same calf. The pick hit the mark, angry electricity sparked at impact, and a crack formed. The monster raised a fist and slammed it down, forcing Vic to dive out of the way. The stone fist smashed through the wooden shelving beside Vic, sending splintered wood and shattered pottery in all directions. Vic landed on his side, the impact causing him to lose his grip on the mattock. The weapon skittered under a table ten feet away. He looked up as the statue raised a stone foot the size of a watermelon, ready to stomp his bones into shattered pieces.

IAN STOOD FROZEN, terror holding him captive until Vic appeared and attacked the golem from behind. The creature came after Vic, who struck again, causing the monster's lower leg to crack. When Vic dove to avoid being crushed, Ian realized his brother was in trouble. Alarm overtook his dread and forced him to act.

He gripped the war hammer near the end of the shaft, stepped forward, and wound back as the statue raised its undamaged leg, prepared to crush Vic. With everything Ian had, he swung the hammer. It came around in a broad arc and struck the cracked calf of the creature's supporting leg. At impact, the hammer released a thump Ian felt both in his chest and beneath his feet. The leg shattered below the knee. The monster teetered and then toppled, its towering frame coming at Ian. Revita gripped his arm and yanked him aside so hard that he went stumbling to the floor. The golem crashed down with a tremendous boom that cracked the tile floor and sent shards of rock spraying across the room.

WHEN THE STONE monster crashed to the floor, Vic rose to his hands and feet, scrambled across the floor, and grabbed the handle of his mattock, pulling it out from under the table. He stood and darted toward the monster as it sat up. With a mighty swing, Vic brought the mattock around, straight toward the monster's face. The pick end struck the glowing gem of the monster's eye, which shattered. The monster's head snapped back, and its body began to quake. Vic wound back again, targeting the other eye. The pick struck true, obliterating the gem. As the red glow faded, the golem collapsed and lay still.

Vic wiped the sweat from his brow, his shoulders slumping as he turned toward Revita and Ian, the latter climbing to his feet with a big hammer in his grip. "Are you two alright?"

Ian glanced at Revita before replying, "We are well enough, thanks to you."

"I didn't do it alone," Vic nodded. "You did well with that hammer. I am impressed."

Ian grinned. "Thanks, Vic."

Revita approached Vic, her tone stern. "You were to return to the inn and wait for us."

He stiffened. "My brother was in here. I am responsible for him."

Her expression softened to a smile. "And I am thankful for it. I would be lying if I said I obeyed every command I was given. In truth, I often do as I wish even if it is against the demands of others. In this case, your stubbornness came in handy." She slid a hand around his back and whispered in his ear, the heat of her breath sending a tingle down his spine. "I will show you my appreciation when we get back to the inn...if you have the stamina." Backing from him with a naughty smirk on her face, Revita spun around.

Drawn toward her, Vic watched Revita as she rounded the counter, bent, and gathered four sacks lying on the floor. The woman's aggressive nature put him off balance, but at the same time, he found it alluring and difficult to deny.

She tucked the sacks beneath her coat, pulled it tight, and headed toward the rear exit. "Let's get out of here before someone else shows up."

Vic shared a look with Ian, who shrugged while holding the hammer to his chest. Without a word, the two of them followed her out, along the dark alley, and down the quiet street leading back to the Flying Flagon.

CHAPTER 39
ARANGOLI

Arangoli Handshaw lay curled up in bed, his teeth chattering, his body quaking. A narrow beam of morning light streamed through a gap in the curtains, illuminating his room at the Flying Flagon. That light felt like a knife to his eyes and brought pain to his brain, his head thumping with the beat of his heart.

A knock came from the door, but Arangoli remained silent. He did not feel like answering. He did not want any company. He did not even want to move.

The door opened, and Korrigan walked in. "I worried that you might still be in bed."

Arangoli groaned, "Go away."

Rather than leave, Korrigan crossed the room and drew the curtain aside, the room brightening three-fold. "I found a ship that will take us to Bards Bay. The captain intends to depart in an hour."

"I don't want to go with you. I just want to lie here and die."

Korrigan turned from the window, furrowed his brow at Arangoli, and sighed. "I know that you feel unwell, but that will pass. Less than two days have passed since your last drink. Your body will adjust. It takes time."

While logical, the statement did nothing to make him feel better. "I feel like flattened dung stuck to the bottom of a boot."

Korrigan chuckled. "Be that as it may, we are going to board that ship even if I have to tie you up and haul you to the docks draped over my shoulder."

"Why do you hate me?"

Korrigan sat beside Arangoli. "I do this because I love you like a brother, Goli. You lost your way for a while, but I am here to bring you back to your people, back to me and Vargan, like when we were young."

Memories of a simpler time came flooding in, bringing Arangoli back to his youth, back when the three of them and Ipsegar dreamt of becoming heroes to their people. *Korrigan offers a chance for you to be that hero.* The allure of that dream was the only thing keeping him from running off to a tavern and drowning himself in ale.

"Revita, Ian, and Vic returned last night while you were sleeping." Korrigan reached under the bed and pulled out a war hammer crafted of dwarven metal, the hammer head marked in runes of the enchantment that gave the weapon its name. "They retrieved this for you."

Drawn to the weapon, Arangoli sat up and reached for it. When Korrigan placed it in Arangoli's hands, it felt as if a missing limb had been returned to him, making him whole once again. A tear tracked down his cheek.

His voice thick with shame, Arangoli said, "I...I cannot believe I sank so low as to trade this for gold."

"Nor can I, but the past is the past. Leave it there, Goli. The future awaits, and your people need you." Korrigan stood. "Now, get dressed, don the armor you were meant to wear, and meet me downstairs. We will get some food and water in you before we head down to the docks." He opened the door, stepped out, and closed it behind him, leaving Arangoli alone once again.

Alone. He had spent much of the previous year alone, drowning in any alcohol he could get his hands on. The situation had been of his own making, and now that he was being asked to lead a fight to retake Ra'Tahal, it also meant facing the warriors he had chased off. *Will the Head Thumpers accept me, or will they hold a grudge for how I treated them?* He longed to avoid facing them, but if the mission to save his people was to succeed, he would need their help. Thus, he forced himself to sit up, swing his legs off the bed, and reach for his trousers.

HIS LEGS SHAKING with each step, Arangoli descended the stairs to the main floor of the Flying Flagon. Both of his old friends, Korrigan and Vargan, stood waiting. The two young humans, Vic and Ian, stood with them. All appeared ready for travel, the dwarves in their armor and helmets, the humans in leather jerkins over tunics and cloaks over their shoulders. The older boy, Vic, stared toward the open front door of the inn, yet when Arangoli looked in that direction, he saw nothing but an oxen-drawn wagon rolling down the street.

The kitchen door opened and Haskabon emerged with a basket filled with biscuits and tube-shaped objects wrapped in leather. When the innkeeper turned his gaze toward Arangoli, it lingered, his mouth turning down in a frown.

Haskabon approached Korrigan and held out the basket. "Here are the fresh biscuits and sausages you requested."

Korrigan reached into the basket, grabbed a biscuit and a tube, and stepped back. "Everyone, grab your breakfast. It is likely your last hot meal until tomorrow evening."

Arangoli waited until the others were finished before approaching Haskabon.

The innkeeper scowled at him. "Korrigan paid your debt, so you needn't worry about me calling the city watch. However, unless you have yourself under control, I don't want you here again."

Haskabon's position was valid and understandable. However, the words still hurt.

Pushing his own feelings aside, Arangoli said, "A year back, I considered you a friend and believed you felt the same toward me. Perhaps, given time, I can earn that friendship back."

Haskabon blinked. "I would...like that."

Arangoli forced a smile and clapped the innkeeper on the shoulder. "When this business is finished, I might return to Greavesport."

"If you do, you know where to find me." Haskabon turned and retreated to the kitchen.

"Let's get going, so we don't miss our ship." Korrigan led them toward the exit.

As he reached the doorway, Arangoli glanced back at the empty taproom, bathed in morning light coming through the newly replaced window at the front. Much of his stay at the Flying Flagon was lost in a haze of drunkenness, but it had been his home during the darkest time of his life. Then and there, he vowed to return one day as a hero, able to hold his head up with pride, so that image might erase what the patrons who frequented the tavern currently thought of him.

THE MORNING SUN shone down on Revita, warming her face. She smiled at people she passed, which was unusual. Those who knew her expected nothing more than a knowing smirk and often received a scowl instead. But on this morning, she felt good about herself, her pockets lined with gold coins after a successful heist the night before. To cap it all off, the night spent with Vic in their own rented room at the Flying Flagon had brought her another level of satisfaction.

Having crossed the city while taking numerous unnecessary turns, passing through crowds whenever possible, and ducking into three different shops to throw off anyone who might attempt to follow her, she arrived in the alley leading to her hideout. She reached the backdoor and knocked, waiting for Olga, the old woman who lived in the house above the hideout, to answer.

The door opened a few inches and Olga peered through the opening. "Revita. You are here."

"Yes. This is where I live."

"Just a moment." The old woman closed the door.

Revita frowned, thinking it strange. The door opened, this time swinging wide to reveal a tall, lean man dressed in leather armor with metal plates on the chest and shoulders. He held a sword in his hand, his dark eyes intense despite the smirk on his face.

"Welcome home, Revita. Say goodbye to this place, for you are unlikely to see it again."

"Captain Fessick," she said. "I see Hargrave allowed you out of the kennel."

The captain of the city watch sneered. "Crossing him was a mistake, thief."

"I have no idea what you mean." It was a lie, but Revita was adept at the art.

"Jarrakan said you visited the Trade and Barter yesterday."

She shrugged. "I was seeking a gift for a man, but he wouldn't even allow me to shop there."

"Hours after your visit, the shop was robbed with much of the interior destroyed. Only a thief of great skill could possibly bypass the safeguards Hargrave had installed."

"I am flattered that you think me capable of such a feat, but you will have to look elsewhere for your culprit."

"I don't think so." His eyes narrowed as he cocked his head. "You see, you are under arrest."

Six more men in armor emerged from the corridor behind Fessick. At the same time, the patter of boots came from both ends of the alley as guards rushed in, both groups stopping about twenty strides away and blocking any chance of escape. In mere seconds, Revita found herself trapped and surrounded by two dozen armed members of the city watch.

She held her hands up. "Clearly, you planned this well and leave me with no choice but to surrender."

Fessick grinned. "I am glad you see the sense of it."

Revita stepped into the doorway, turned her back toward Fessick and waited as if to allow him to arrest her. He stepped closer and when he reached for her wrist, she gripped the doorframe, lifted her feet, and placed them against the wall so she straddled the doorway. With a burst, she extended her legs, driving herself backward into Fessick. He fell backward, taking down the line of guards behind him.

She scrambled to her feet, raced out the door, and leapt toward the wall across the alley, where she grabbed ahold of a dangling, broken clothesline. Her weight pulled the line down a few inches, causing the catapult release on the other end to trigger – the catapult arm having been tied to the other end of the rope. Revita shot upward rapidly, the force of the launch arm taking her up two stories, past the eave and well into the air. Her arms and legs flailed as she sailed over the catapult bolted to the rooftop. She passed the chimney, landed just beyond the roof's ridgeline, and tumbled down the other side, her momentum taking her toward the edge.

With an urgent lunge, just before going over the eave, Revita grabbed the coil of rope she had included as part of her escape plan. Her momentum swept her over the edge, and the rope unwound as she fell. The length connected to the chimney drew taut and jerked Revita's entire body to a stop, wrenching her arm and causing her body to swing from side to side. She looked down at the street, a story below. A dozen people stared up at her. With a lunge, Revita swung her other arm up, her fingers wrapping around the rope above the coil. The coil tumbled to the street, allowing her to lower herself down the rope, descending hand over hand.

The moment her feet touched the street, Revita burst into a run. She reached the first intersection just a beat before guards poured out of the alley. Turning in the opposite direction, she raced down the street, weaving through foot traffic and knocking more than one person over. Every time she glanced backward, she found guards trailing less than a block behind.

Vic crossed a plank and stepped on board a ship for the first time. He stopped beside Korrigan, Vargan, and Ian while he surveyed the deck, noting the three masts, the pointed bow at one end, and the raised quarterdeck at the other. Sailors moved about the deck, two of them untying the ropes between the ship and the posts along the pier, others scaling the rigging or gripping lines dangling from above. The crew consisted of two dwarves, two elves, four humans, and one dark elf, all male and all appearing hardened and focused on the task before them.

The ship's captain, a dwarf with a braided, red beard, approached them. Korrigan and he had a brief conversation in Dwarvish of which Vic understood enough to determine that they were about to set sail and could expect to reach their destination late the following day. The captain and the other three dwarves all headed toward the stern and climbed the stairs to the quarterdeck, leaving Vic alone with Ian.

Shouts from the direction of the city caused Vic to spin around just as a woman burst through a crowd of dockworkers. He recognized her immediately. *Revita?* Vic's brow furrowed as he watched her race toward the pier.

A cluster of two dozen guards emerged through the city gate and ran after Revita. She reached the pier at a full sprint and did not slow. As she drew near the ship drifting from the pier, Vic hurried along the rail, toward her. Revita angled toward the ship, gathered herself, and leapt off the pier. He reached over the rail, extending his hand toward her outstretched arm. They clasped each other by the wrist as her body descended. Her boots thumped off the hull as her fall came to a stop, wrenching Vic's shoulder and leaving him bent over the rail at the waist, his feet in the air and her weight threatening to pull him over the edge. Just when he thought he would fall, Ian grabbed him by the legs, stopping the momentum. With his brother's help, Vic pulled backward, and when his feet were firmly anchored, he lifted Revita until she was able to grip the rail with the other hand and pull herself up.

Revita climbed over the rail, her breath coming in gasps. "Thanks. That was close, even for me."

Vic looked at the guards gathered on the pier, watching as the ship drifted into the bay. "Why were they after you?"

She shook her head and panted for air. "Jarrakan thinks I was responsible for the theft at the Trade and Barter. He reported it to Hargrave, who sent his guards to arrest me."

Vic said in a quiet voice, "But you *were* responsible."

Grinning, she said, "But he doesn't know that. He only *thinks* it to be true."

"Isn't that the same thing?"

Revita patted his cheek. "It is a good thing you are so pretty, because it makes your naivety seem cute."

She pulled the ribbon from her hair, releasing it with a shake of her head. Her black mane fell over her shoulders and was instantly caught by the wind. Vic thought she had never looked more beautiful.

The thief glanced toward the stern. "I had better speak with the captain. I suspect he wants me to pay for the voyage and will likely seek double for the trouble he is likely to encounter next time he is in Greavesport."

She walked off, her tight breeches and the swaying of her hips drawing the attention of every sailor she passed.

Vic sighed. "I don't know what to think of that woman."

"How so?" Ian asked.

The sailors in the rigging and those manning the lines unfurled the sails, and the ship picked up speed.

"She is cunning, deceitful, and sees the law as little more than a suggestion. Yet...there is something about her..."

His brother's eyes widened. "You *like* her."

Grimacing, Vic said, "I have spent the last two nights sharing her bed and haven't complained about it, so I think that was implied."

"Yeah, but...you like her for more than the physical stuff."

Vic sighed. "You might be right. However, I don't see her as someone who would settle for one man or any sort of commitment."

The ship passed the breakwater, and the waves increased six-fold, causing the ship to bob.

Ian patted Vic on the back. "You never know what the future holds, brother. A year ago, would you have ever guessed we would be involved in a heist against the ruler of a city halfway across the world from Shillings?"

"I doubt it. In fact, I still find it hard to believe."

The ship dipped and rose as it sailed into the open water. Ian pressed his hand to his stomach, his face turning pale.

"What's wrong?" Vic asked.

"I...I think I am going to be sick."

A beat later, Ian leaned over the rail and emptied the contents of his stomach. Having yet to eat breakfast, that amounted to little more than water and bile.

Vic patted Ian on the back, but his gaze was affixed on Revita as she stood on the quarterdeck, speaking with the ship's captain. He had thought that leaving Greavesport meant he would never see her again. It was to be a clean break, allowing him to avoid dealing with his feelings. Now...

CHAPTER 40

A CURSE

S unbeams streamed through the arched openings lining the fifth-floor palace corridor and created broad strips of light on the stone floor. Shria-Li strode through those patches of light with her chin up to display the external confidence a princess must exude. Inside, troubled thoughts nibbled at that confidence like a host of termites attacking a proud oak tree. She passed through an archway and emerged onto a rooftop terrace overlooking the garden. The Tree of Life loomed above the terrace, its golden leaves reflecting morning sunlight.

Her mother sat alone on the terrace, the wooden table before her filled with bowls of berries, breads, and nuts. Two plates sat on the table, one before the queen, the other across from her.

Shria-Li approached the table and dipped her head in respect. "Good morning, Mother."

"My daughter has decided to come out of her room and see me?" Tora-Li gestured across the table. "Please. Sit. Eat."

Taking a seat, Shria-Li began scooping fruit onto her plate, her mind elsewhere.

"You have been avoiding me for a week." Tora-Li tilted her head. "Tell me you did not avoid your testing."

"I…" She struggled for the right response. Memories of that night had haunted Shria-Li ever since. Although she had done her best to forget it, to pretend it was only a dream, evading the truth was even more difficult than shirking her duty as a princess. "The testing did occur."

"Thank Vandasal." Her mother leaned back and stared at her. "I had hoped Valaria might come to me and share the news, but I have not seen her in days. Perhaps you would care to share with me?"

The testing was the subject of Shria-Li's concerns. She did not understand what had happened or what was to become of her. Fear, as much as anything else, fought to bury the knowledge and never speak of what she learned.

Shria-Li looked away, unwilling to meet her mother's gaze. "I'd rather not talk about it."

Tora-Li frowned. "Surely, you learned something of yourself."

"I…did."

"I sense hesitation."

It was not as if Shria-Li had been hiding it. "Yes."

Tora-Li reached across the table and gripped her hand, forcing Shria-Li to look into her eyes. "Your ability is a part of you, Daughter. There is no shame. Rather, you need to practice it, hone it so you can better serve our people."

"What if…" *A darkness lurks inside of me?* Shria-Li looked down at her plate and sorted through her thoughts as she sought the words to articulate her concerns. "What if my ability is a curse?"

"A curse?" Tora-Li's tone was incredulous. "Don't be ridiculous."

The ominous words of the high priestess echoed in Shria-Li's head. *With your ability comes the end of our race, as foretold millennia ago. The Sylvan are doomed.*

Fighting past her insecurities, she asked the question she feared the most. "What is a death speaker?"

Tora-Li dropped her fork. "Where did you hear that term?"

"That night...the night of the testing. From Valaria."

Her mother stared into Shria-Li's eyes. When she spoke, her words came out as little more than a whisper. "Did Valaria claim you had the... dark ability?"

Shria-Li gave a hesitant nod.

Tora-Li leaned back in her chair. "I see."

"I don't understand, mother. What is this ability? Why was Valaria so frightened?"

The queen stared off toward the Tree of Life. "There is a prophecy from the first age, a foretelling as old as our race itself. It speaks of the end of the Sylvan. In the prophecy..." She frowned. "Perhaps we should pay Pansara a visit?"

"The high scryer? You wish her to peer into my future? We have tried that before. It did not work." Shria-Li barely recalled the visit, for she was quite young when it occurred. Still, the sense of it had haunted her for years. Tales of the scryer circulated throughout Havenfall, each more chilling than the last.

"Scryers study prophecy. She will know more about it than anyone. If your ability truly is...as you say, then we need to better understand the prophecy that foretold your coming." Tora-Li nodded, as if coming to a decision. "To take your mind off your concerns, I shall spend the day with you in the garden. We will go see Pansara tomorrow evening. Eat, and worry about it no longer."

Shria-Li picked at her food, but despite her mother's decree, worry continued to gnaw at her. The dark ability, whatever it was, already stalked her thoughts and dreams like a nebulous shadow, ominous yet unknowable. To add to her anxiety, her mother intended to make her face the most frightening elf in Sylvanar.

RINA WALKED along a corridor bordered by arched openings, the afternoon breeze tugging at her hair. Since her arrival in Havenfall, this was the first day Shria-Li had not required her assistance. It felt odd being left to her own designs, and she found herself wandering the palace without a destination in mind.

She glanced through an arch, into the palace garden, where a pair of females sat near the pool. Curious, she stopped and leaned against the railing. Shria-Li and her mother faced each other on a flagstone shelf beside the water. Both had their legs crossed and hands pressed together before their chests. Their eyes were closed and they remained still, as if turned to statues.

"What are they doing?" Rina muttered.

A male voice replied, "Meditating, it appears."

She turned to find a tall, male elf standing beneath the neighboring arch. He had a lean, lithe build, golden eyes, and was among the most beautiful males Rina had ever seen.

"Your...Majesty..." she stammered. "I did not know..."

"At ease, Safrina." He always called her by her full name, same as the other elves. Until her arrival in Havenfall, nobody had done that since her father's death. "We stand alone. I asked you to call me Fastellan in such situations."

"Very well. Fastellan."

He smiled. Bathed in sunlight, that friendly smile was among the most glorious things Rina could imagine. It filled her with warmth and caused her to smile in return.

The king approached her and held his elbow out. "Would you care to go for a walk?"

"I..." She had nothing else to do, and despite something inside her saying she should find a way out of it, there was something about him she found undeniable. "Would love to."

When Rina looped her arm through his, they set off.

He asked, "I noticed how the griffin encounter upset you. For that, I apologize."

"It was not your fault."

"No, but your presence here is my doing, so I am responsible for your welfare. I have warned my daughter to avoid such risks in the future. I do not expect her or you to venture anywhere near the boundary again."

Rina got the sense that it was an order, although he had not said so directly. "The view of the Vale is breathtaking, and while I would like to see it again, I also understand that it is too dangerous to do so until the barrier is fully functional again."

The elf king guided her to a curved staircase, where they began an ascent. She did not know where they were headed, nor did she care.

He smirked. "You are a smart woman despite your youth. Additional years will bring wisdom to your intelligence. I suspect those years will also further enhance your beauty."

Her cheeks grew warm, and her pulse quickened at the compliment. Coming from him, it felt as if she was lifted, her feet and walking inches above the ground. "You flatter me, Your..." She caught herself. "Fastellan."

"It is not flattery when it is factual." They climbed another flight in silence before he spoke again. "You seem to have adjusted to your new life here."

"Mostly. Shria-Li is friendly and I genuinely like her, so acting as her attendant is better than most other jobs I have endured. As for the city and the palace, I never thought I would live in such a grand, awestriking place, especially after the traumatic events that brought me here."

They reached the top of the stairs and stepped into a small chamber with a high, cone-shaped ceiling. Around them, arched openings faced north, south, east, and west. The wind blew through the openings, ruffling her dress.

Fastellan took her hands and stared into her eyes. "I apologize for any mistreatment you experienced in your transfer from Ra'Tahal to Havenfall. The situation was tenuous, time was short, and I had to see you freed from your servitude beneath Queen Pergoli. There was no time to explain, so I had my guards do what must be done. I assure you, I forbade them from doing you any harm."

"You could have let me go once beyond Ra'Tahal's walls. I still don't understand why you chose to bring me here."

He tilted his head. "Did you not just tell me that you find Havenfall pleasant and your situation improved?"

"I...did." She tried again, seeking an answer. "My feelings are not the issue. Please. Tell me why."

The king turned from her and stared east, toward the Vale. "What do you know of my people?"

The Sylvan were the most graceful, proud, and elegant race Rina could imagine. Yet, they were reserved, mysterious, and difficult to fully understand. "Only what Shria-Li has shared. Until recently, I didn't even know that elves were real and had never heard of the Sylvan."

Still facing away from her, he said, "Did she explain that we Sylvan bond with our mates and it is for life?"

Rina liked the sound of that. "No."

"It is our way...except in my case."

"I don't understand."

"Tora-Li was the daughter of the prior king, Tafallan. His death left my people without a leader. Tora-Li was Shria-Li's age and not fully equipped to rule. I was captain of the Valeguard, respected and known among my people as a skilled warrior and a great leader. To avoid a power struggle or someone unsuitable claiming the crown, I agreed to wed Tora-Li and assume the role of king. That was nigh eighty years ago. We have been together ever since, and while we have figured out how to rule in harmony and show one another respect, she and I have never bonded."

Rina suddenly understood. "You are in a loveless marriage."

He turned toward her. "Loveless, without passion, with little to no affection and rarely of a physical nature."

She reached for his hand. "I am...sorry. I cannot imagine what that is like and for so many years..."

Fastellan stepped close and touched her cheek while staring down into her eyes. "When I first saw you, I felt something I have never experienced. A longing, a desire, a need so powerful, I found myself unable to leave Ra'Tahal without you. I did not understand it and thought it might go away if given time. Yet, each time I see you, and the more I learn about you, the more powerful the longing becomes." His voice lowered to a whisper. "Can you feel it as well?"

The aqua pools in his eyes shimmered and his heart thumped against her palm. She fell into those eyes and found herself drowning but did not care to swim. Her response was little more than a breath. "I do."

His lips met hers. Their softness was a contrast to the firm muscles of his torso. Heavy thumps of her own pulse beat in her ears and a warmth spread from her chest. Too soon, he pulled away but continued to hold her hand against his chest.

He spoke softly with a hint of urgency in his voice. "Tell no one about us. For my people, for my wife, for my daughter, this must be our secret. We are a patient people, Safrina. Time is on our side, yet it flows far more swiftly for humans. You have just begun to bloom into the flower you will one day become. Give me time. Give us time."

The feelings swirling inside of her were overwhelming, her sudden desire for him demanding she act. His request for her to wait was among the most difficult things she could imagine. At that moment, it was approaching impossible. "How long must I wait?"

Fastellan said, "Years ago, I came to an agreement with King Kobblebon of Clan Aeldor. His dwarves labor in the mountains west of here. The castle they are building will become our secret retreat. When the castle is ready, you and I will steal away and indulge in the bliss we were meant to enjoy. Until it is ready, serve my daughter well, and if the opportunity arises, you and I shall capture what limited joy we are able to share."

Again, he kissed her before backing to the staircase. "Remain here for a few minutes, so nobody sees us leaving together. I will do my best to see you again. Soon. Farewell, my Safrina."

She stared after him the entire time, unable to speak, her pulse hammering like irons in a forge. When he was gone, she still felt his touch against her cheek, his hand in hers, and his lips brushing against hers.

CHAPTER 41

THE SCRYER

An escort of palace guards trailed behind Shria-Li as she and her mother crossed Havenfall. Clouds had rolled in from the west, darkening the city to the purple of dusk although the sun had yet to set. They reached the split bridge at the western edge of the city, one path arching over the river to the north bank, the other to the south. The two females and their escorts took the prior.

When they reached the north bank, they followed a road into the shadowy forest, and turned off onto a narrow path. Massive, ancient maple trees surrounded the path, the leaves turned red since autumn had finally reached Sylvanar. As they traveled farther from Havenfall, the forest around them gradually changed, and with that change, Shria-Li's skin began to itch and her mind screamed to turn and flee.

At first, forest undergrowth appeared wilted, the tree leaves curled and dry. Soon, the undergrowth turned to dirt and the trees' bark was cracked and raw. Finally, they found themselves surrounded by trees long dead, their branches twisted and gnarled, the forest floor vacant of life.

The lifeless trunks parted to reveal a winding path climbing a hill in the heart of the dead forest. On the top of the hill stood a singular, cylindrical tower made of white stone covered in dead, leafless ivy, as if the building had been abandoned centuries ago and the forest had reclaimed it, only to then die of whatever affliction the structure endured. At the top of the tower, jutting up over the roof, was a dome made of interwoven, leafless ivy shoots.

They followed the path to the tower's front door, on which Tora-Li knocked.

Long, silent moments followed before the door opened. Inside was the oldest elf Shria-Li had ever seen. Her hair was white as snow, as were her irises. The elf stared into space, her eyes unfocused. *She is blind,* Shria-Li realized.

"My queen. Princess," the old elf croaked. "I knew you would come."

"Greetings, Pansara," Tora-Li said. "Much time has passed since our last meeting."

"Five or six decades, I should think." Pansara spoke slowly, savoring each word that passed her tongue. "They pass so briskly, it is difficult to tell."

"May we come in?"

"I would be honored." The scryer turned and hobbled off.

Tora-Li turned toward the guards. "Captain, you and your warriors are to wait out here."

The elf nodded. "You'll get no complaint from me, Your Majesty. Unless you are in peril, I prefer to remain outside. I suspect the others feel the same."

Shria-Li did not blame the guards. She longed to turn and flee. The dead trees alone were enough to bring chills to any elf. The aura emanating from the tower was even worse.

Darkness clung to the building's interior, as if light was afraid to enter. Shadows lurked in all directions with only the dimmest of outside light seeping through the matrix of twisted ivy branches covering the windows. Even Shria-Li's elven eyes, far sharper than humans, strained to see.

The old woman brought them to a staircase at the outer edge of the chamber and began to climb. The ascent was slow, her pace measured, breathing labored. Shria-Li began to worry that the old elf might die before reaching the top.

They continued past four open doorways before the stairs ended and they stepped out onto the tower rooftop. A circular, complex pattern of silvery runes marked the flat roof, illuminated by an eerie glow from the dome of branches. Above it all was the dome of ivy, which was open in the center.

Pansara turned toward Tora-Li. "You have come because of your daughter."

"Yes." The queen stared at the scryer and, somehow, kept a steady voice.

"You wish to know if she is the one."

"I do."

"With her help, I will peer into the future and discover what it holds."

The future. To know it was said to be against the will of the gods. Shria-Li wondered what that would make the scryer in the eye of Vandasal. The dwarves, Sylvan, and even the Drow prayed to Vandasal. Sharing the god was among the few things they had in common and among the primary things setting them apart from humans.

"You have my permission," Tora-Li gave a firm nod.

The old elf turned to Shria-Li. "Are you prepared to face your fate?"

Despite her desire to flee and do anything else, Shria-Li nodded. "I am."

"Come along." Pansara limped across the rooftop and stopped in the center.

Shria-Li approached Pansara and stopped a stride away The scryer reached out, her cold hands finding Shria-Li's. The old elf's eyes rolled up. Her head snapped back, and something forced Shria-Li's own head to do the same. The two of them lifted off the rooftop and floated up, through the opening in the dome of dead vine shoots.

Still facing the heavens, beams of pale, white light shot out of Pansara's eyes. The light struck the clouds and they began to roil. The clouds shifted, twisted, and swirled, spinning faster and faster. An eye opened in the center, revealing a sea of stars. Shria-Li found it impossible to look away as she was drawn into the eye. The world drifted away. The stars, the elderly elf woman, and Shria-Li were all that existed.

The stars began to spin in the opposite direction of the clouds. Faster and faster, they spun until they were nothing but a swirling blur of light. That light brightened until it became blinding. Then the light faded, and the scene changed.

Shria-Li found herself a thousand feet up, high above Havenfall. Rather than the tranquil scene she was used to, the city was under siege. Elves battled shadowy, unidentifiable enemies. Fireballs rained down, lightning flashed, and the city burned. Just as quickly, the battle ended. The city, while damaged, remained standing. Then, a shift happened in the sky. The ground shuddered. Cracks formed. Lava and geysers burst out, shooting towering fountains of fire and water into the air. Distant mountains burst up from the ground. The sea rushed in, drowning lowlands as it spread unchecked. Massive, destructive waves crashed in and rushed over the land. The ground shuddered again, a hole opened up, and the entirety of Havenfall sank into the abyss. The cataclysm ceased and the world settled.

With horror, Shria-Li looked down upon a land she no longer recognized. Gone were the golden trees, the graceful arches, the towering spires...gone were her people. Where Havenfall once stood, a sea now existed. Her soul shrieked at the immensity of such loss.

The scene faded, the stars returned, and the clouds slowly seeped in to close the hole in the sky.

Shria-Li lowered her gaze and found her feet on the tower roof. The old scryer lay at Shria-Li's feet with her arms and legs splayed out, her empty, white eyes staring toward the heavens.

"Pansara?" She knelt beside the scryer and gently shook her. No movement. Concerned, she leaned down and held a cheek above the old elf's lips. No breath. Sitting upright, she looked toward her mother. "She is dead."

Tora-Li walked over, her eyes narrowed. "What did you see?"

"I saw..." A feeling of horror and loss clung to Shria-Li, the vision beyond disturbing. *Is that our future? Are we doomed? If so, how can I even tell her?*

Her mother gripped Shria-Li by the upper arms and shook her. "Tell me! Tell me what you saw!"

The words came in spurts, drawn out as her mother's demand overcame Shria-Li's hesitancy to say them. "I saw...the end...of everything."

CHAPTER 42

BARD'S BAY

Ian opened the ship's cabin door to a dimly lit, narrow hallway. He followed the corridor to a steep run of stairs, ascended, and flipped open the hatch at the top, where he was greeted by daylight. Gray clouds blanketed the sky, masking the sun and leaving him curious about the time of day. Fresh air filled his lungs as he took a deep breath. He climbed on deck, closed the hatch, and surveyed the ship.

His brother stood at the bow with Revita, the two of them leaning against the rail while staring out into the distance. Ian spun to find open sea to the starboard and stern while land defined the horizon from their heading to the port side. A handful of sailors lounged about the deck, and the first mate, a tall man with a shaved head, stood at the wheel on the quarterdeck. The ship's captain and Ian's dwarf companions were nowhere to be seen. Ian wanted to know what time it was and when they would reach port, so, despite worries that he might interrupt something private between his brother and Revita, he headed toward the bow.

As he drew near, their voices rose above the rush of the sea waters slipping past the hull.

Vic said, "You cannot be serious."

She replied, "I might lie to deceive others to facilitate a heist or to protect myself from arrest, but I only speak truth when I share tales of my exploits."

He laughed. "I can imagine he was quite upset."

"He was so embarrassed, he ended up leaving the city and moving to Sea Gate."

"Where is that?"

"It is one of the free cities, located where the inner sea meets the Horizial Ocean. It is a good four-day voyage west of Greavesport."

Ian decided it was time to interject. "I, for one, would dread four days on a ship. Two is more than enough."

When they turned toward him, Vic said, "Good afternoon, Ian. It is good to see you out of bed. Your skin doesn't even look green anymore."

Lifting his face toward the cloud-covered sky, Ian said, "So, it is afternoon?"

"By a fair margin."

"How soon until we land?"

Revita said, "I spoke with the first mate earlier. He expects us to make port about an hour before sunset."

Ian's stomach growled noisily. "Good. I am starved."

His brother snorted. "I would think so. You haven't eaten a thing since we boarded yesterday."

Ian grimaced. "There is little enjoyment in eating when you know it is going to come spurting back up." A squawk drew Ian's attention to a massive, white bird circling above the ship.

Vic suggested, "Since you are feeling better, you could visit the galley and get something to eat before we make dock."

Ian shook his head, turning his attention back to his brother. "I would rather not chance it."

Revita arched a brow. "Are you intending to remain on deck for a while, Ian?"

"After spending the entire voyage in the cabin dealing with my seasickness, I have no desire to return to that small, dark room now that I am feeling better."

"In that case," Revita turned toward Vic. "The two of us could take advantage of some time alone."

Vic's eyes flicked to Ian. "That would not be fair to my brother."

"Are you suggesting he join us?" She flashed a devious smile.

His eyes rounding in shock, Vic exclaimed, "No! That would be...That is just...wrong."

Revita laughed and patted Vic's cheek. "You are so cute when you're flustered."

"Please, don't mock me."

Her smile melted. "But mocking others is what I do."

In a serious tone, he said, "If you want to spend time with me, I ask you to refrain."

She stared at him for a long beat before nodding. "I will try."

"Thank you."

Her hand found his. "Now, about the cabin..."

When Vic glanced in his direction, Ian said, "Go ahead. I will be fine out here, alone."

"Come along," Revita turned from the rail and pulled Vic with her.

"We'll be back soon," Vic called over his shoulder.

"Don't count on it," Revita said even louder.

The couple soon disappeared down the hatch, and Ian assumed their abandoned position at the rail, where he stared out at the shoreline while leaning on his forearms. Standing there alone, enjoying the fresh air and basking in the fact that his sickness had passed, his mind wandered and time flowed past, like the waves against the ship's hull.

The clouds began to break up with blue skies peeking through in the western sky. The day eased from late afternoon toward evening as the sun approached the western horizon. Over the next hour, the distance between the ship and shore decreased until land was no more than a mile away. The ship eased past a rocky point, and a bay came into view. A strip of white beach lined the southwestern shore. That strip of sand was nestled between the aqua blue waters of the bay and tree covered hills painted in the colors of autumn. The sight was breathtaking.

As the ship rounded the point, the rest of the bay eased into view.

The mouth of a broad river stood at the far end of the beach. Hugging a rocky shoreline to the east side of the river was a city. A trio of long piers thrust out from the shore, into the bay. Walls of pale stone overlooked the docks, beyond which, rows of alabaster buildings with red clay tile rooftops covered a hillside. At the top of the hill stood a castle. It was a glorious sight, but still not the focal point of the vista.

In the center of the river was an island occupied by another castle, its fortifications painted a warm hue in the light of the setting sun. Turrets pointing toward the sky jutted above the castle walls, none taller than the thick tower in the center. It was an ominous, formidable structure that instantly caused Ian to wonder at its purpose.

In the glow of the setting sun, the view was spectacular and Ian suddenly understood the name, Bard's Bay. He was convinced the sight grand enough to inspire a musician to craft a song for the ages.

"You must be feeling better." A gravelly voice stirred Ian from his reverie.

Ian turned as Korrigan crossed the ship's deck, coming toward him. "Much better."

The dwarf leaned against the rail at Ian's side. "Quite a view, is it not?"

"It might be the most beautiful thing I have ever seen."

"Don't let the bay's beauty fool you. Despite its appearance, the city is among the most dangerous in the world and far worse than what we faced in Greavesport."

"How so?"

"Commander Kaden rules Bard's Bay, and while laws exist, they are enforced only when it suits his own desires. The man is craven, conniving, and corrupt. He is rumored to be involved in shady dealings, and his mere presence casts a shadow of depravity across the city. However, cross the wrong line, and you will find yourself on your way to the Carcera.

"What is that?"

"See the castle on the island?"

"Yes."

"They call it The Carcera. It is a prison, where criminals are sent as punishment for crimes committed. The tower in the center is where the most dangerous felons are housed. It is also reputed to be haunted."

"Haunted?" Ian gulped. Tales of ghosts and evil spirits had frightened him when he was younger. As he aged, he began to doubt the validity of such stories. Now that dwarves, dragons, elves and magic had proven to be real, the thought of ghosts seemed far less easy to dismiss.

"Yes," the dwarf said. "By the ghosts of those who died within those halls."

Ian frowned. He did not know if ghosts could harm the living, but he had no intention of visiting the prison to find out. "I feel like there is something you aren't telling me."

"Aye," the dwarf nodded. "Bard's Bay is the home of smugglers, thieves, assassins, whores, and pirates. Speak with care, watch where you tread, and remain outside of any conflict that takes place. It is easy to become caught up in a fight, for they are frequent in Bard's Bay, as are murders. Yet, if you cross the wrong person and are still lucky enough not to end up dead, you are likely to find yourself in shackles and on a ferry to the Carcera, where you will spend the rest of your days."

Ian stared toward the island fortress and noted soldiers stationed upon its outer walls. The central tower stood hundreds of feet tall, and despite its height, it was broad enough to appear squat. He wondered about the rumored ghosts and what it might be like to be imprisoned in a building with restless or even malevolent spirits. His people lacked a god, so he had been taught to pray to good spirits. If there are good spirits, there could be evil ones as well. The thought sent a shiver down his spine, causing him to shake.

Korrigan clapped a hand on his shoulder. "We will soon reach port. Let's retreat to our cabins and fetch our things. Sunset is upon us, and I would prefer we find an inn prior to nightfall. The streets are barely safe during the day. On a dark night...Let's just say I'd rather avoid any unnecessary risk."

Ian turned from the rail and followed the dwarf across the ship's deck while Korrigan's warnings dominated his thoughts. The dwarf opened the hatch and they descended a steep staircase to a dark corridor. Korrigan entered the cabin he shared with Vargan and Arangoli, as Ian opened the door to his own. He stepped into the small room, illuminated by a lantern on the wall, and stopped dead still, his eyes gaping.

Vic lay on his bunk, leaning on his elbow, his bare torso visible while a sheet covered his lower body. Beside the bunk stood Revita, her lean, lithe, yet shapely body stark naked. While Ian remained in a stupefied trance, staring at her bared flesh, she merely arched a brow in challenge.

"I..." Ian stammered, "I am sorry. I forgot..."

She shrugged, a motion that was far more sensual than it had any right to be. "I am not ashamed of my body, so it does not bother me."

The sight of her curvy, naked figure affected Ian's own body instantly. A warm tingling came from his groin, and his trousers suddenly felt far too tight. When her gaze lowered to the region, he spun around to face away from her while covering himself.

Revita laughed. "I see that you and your brother both have the same eagerness."

Ian wanted to hide but sought to change the direction of the conversation instead. "I...um...came to tell you that we are soon to dock."

Vic sighed. "In that case, I suppose we had better get dressed."

She cooed, "Are you certain you would not care for another go, first?"

"I'll be on deck." Ian blurted before he fled from the cabin. Revita's laughter chased him along the corridor and up the stairs.

CONFIDENT, purposeful strides carried Revita down the pier and toward the city walls. Since she had visited Bard's Bay a half dozen times, twice as many as any of her companions, Revita had volunteered to take the lead. More notably, she knew the types of places the Head Thumpers liked to visit and was the most likely to locate them quickly.

Korrigan walked alongside of her, and Vic strolled to her other side while Arangoli, Vargan, and Ian trailed them. The dockworkers they passed worked with renewed fervor, eager to end their day. With the sun below the western horizon, stars and a narrow crescent of the moon emerged in the darkening sky.

When Revita reached the shore, she climbed a staircase and crossed a gravel area, on her way to the city gate where a quartet of human guards stood in a cluster. Another two guards manned the wall above the gate, their faces flickering in the torchlight.

A pair of guards broke off from the others and took position in front of the gate to intercept her.

"Hold," one of them held a palm up. "What is your business in Bard's Bay." Just as in the other Free Cities, even humans spoke Dwarvish, having learned it in the years following Gahagar's army conquering them.

Revita planted a hand on her hip while the other trailed down her chest, hoping to charm the guard. "We are just a simple girl and her friends, come to seek employment at the greatest city in the world."

He frowned, seemingly unaffected. "Employment comes at a price in Bard's Bay."

She frowned. "What kind of price?"

The guard narrowed his eyes for a beat and then said, "One silver piece each."

"And what do I get for this silver piece?" Revita was used to paying bribes, but a silver piece for each was excessive.

"Entrance to the city."

"Why would I pay to enter the city?"

"You don't have to pay, not if you prefer to turn around and return to whence you came."

Arangoli pulled his hammer from his back. "That is extortion, you blazing arse!"

Korrigan leapt in front of Arangoli and put his hands on the other dwarf's chest. "Starting a fight with the city guards will not help our situation."

While Revita wanted to stab the guard, she knew Korrigan was right. She had just escaped trouble in Greavesport and she preferred to avoid a similar situation in Bard's Bay. From her pocket, she withdrew six silver pieces, knowing the others lacked the coin she carried.

"Here are eight silver pieces, giving you two extra to keep for yourself. This had better do more than get us in the door. In fact, I would like to think of it as an investment."

The guard accepted the coins. "How so?"

"Should we cross paths again, I would like to think you will remember our generosity."

The guard grinned. "Fair enough."

Revita led the party through the gates and into the dark streets of Bard's Bay. They followed a broad street to a torchlit plaza with a fountain in the center. Beyond the plaza, stairs carried them up to another street, where a sign above the door displayed a short, bearded dwarf with a tankard in each hand. Raucous chatter and laughter came from inside.

"The Drunken Dwarf," Revita said, "This is one of the taprooms the Head Thumpers frequent. Hopefully, we can find them here."

The door opened, dim light and a cacophony of conversation bled into the street as a pair of toughs emerged. Revita slipped past them, stepped inside, and surveyed the room as her companions clustered around her.

Raised booths surrounded the taproom's exterior and long tables with benches filled the interior. At the heart of it all was a bar that wrapped around a small room. The rafters were open to create a high, vaulted ceiling supported by a network of darkly stained beams. The taproom was busy with nary a seat vacant.

Revita made straight for the bar, her gaze sweeping the thick crowd. Humans, dwarves, and elves filled the taproom, many of them standing, but most seated at a table, a booth, or on a stool along the bar. As she approached the bar, a man dressed in a stained, white apron over a dark blue tunic noticed her.

She leaned against the bar and spoke as he drew near. "Good evening, Borric."

The man was tall and built like an overfed bull. "Revita." He dunked a mug in a tub of soapy water and began to scrub. "What brings you to Bard's Bay? Not enough excitement in Greavesport?"

"Actually, my friends and I have come on business."

The man blanched. "Please don't rob me. The place might be full, but I have no coin to spare. It costs a lot to..."

She reached out and grabbed his wrist. "At ease. I am not here to rob you or anyone else, at least, not yet. I am looking for the Head Thumpers."

The man's gaze shifted to Arangoli. "Are you planning on rejoining them, Goli?"

"We shall see," Arangoli replied. "First, we've something urgent that we must attend to."

The barkeep shifted his attention back to Revita. "I've a bit of bad news."

"How so?"

"One week past, the Head Thumpers got into a bit of trouble."

She groaned inwardly. "What sort of trouble?"

"A man hired them for a job. I don't know the details, but things went sour, and they were caught. Worse, the target turned out to be a smuggler warehouse owned by someone of import."

Korrigan muttered, "Oh, no. Please don't tell me..."

Borric nodded. "Yes. Commander Kaden does not care to be crossed. In a rather public manner, he sentenced them to spend the rest of their days in the Carcera."

Revita shared a look with Korrigan, Arangoli, and the two boys. The warriors they had come seeking were in a prison fortress nobody had ever escaped from.

She voiced the question the others were likely thinking. "Now, what do we do?"

CHAPTER 43
AN ARRESTING DEVELOPMENT

Flickering amber light from the lantern resting on the table illuminated the room, chasing shadows to the corners and the area under the bed.

Vic closed the door and turned to Revita, who stood with her arms crossed over her chest. Her posture and expression told him that she wanted nothing to do with what he was about to request. Despite her projected reluctance, he was determined to change her mind, regardless of the cost.

"We need your help to break the Head Thumpers out of prison."

Her reaction was as he expected. "Listen, I like those dwarves as much as anyone, but what you ask is dangerous and unlikely to succeed. Why would I agree to help when there is nothing in it for me?"

Vic walked up to her and slid his hands onto her hips. "It is not for nothing. We need help if we are to retake Ra'Tahal, and once we do, free my people as Korrigan promised."

"No offense, but I don't know those people. This is not my problem."

Vic frowned. "How can you say that? They are enslaved. How would you feel if you lost your freedom?"

Unswayed, she retorted, "Which is exactly what I risk if I agree, we get caught, and I end up in a prison cell. Do you know what happens to women in those prisons?"

He opened his mouth, prepared to forge ahead, but when he realized that she inferred to the rape and abuse she might have to endure at the hands of dirty, disgusting, murderous male inmates, the words flitted away, unsaid.

After a moment of thought, he tried again. "There must be a way to get them out without putting you at such risk. You've experience with this kind of thing, so you can at least help us plan it."

"When have I ever broken someone free from a prison?"

"No." He shook his head. "I mean breaking into a stronghold and then escaping."

"Well...I suppose you are right about that."

He needed to convince her, and if appealing to her sense of justice would not work, he would try another approach. "There are six of us, and each offers some skill that might be useful. Surely, you can think of some way to utilize those abilities in a way that will work. Besides, if you are able to break them out, just think of what it will do for your reputation."

She sighed. "Fine. I will think on it."

He smiled. "That's my girl."

Her eyes narrowed, her tone hardening. "I am *nobody's* girl."

"I just meant..." The right words would not come. Words were Ian's thing. Vic was a man of action, so he cupped her face and kissed her. She resisted at first but soon gave in. Her lips intertwined with his, her eyes slid to half mast, and her body pressed against his. Revita began to unlace his jerkin, and his heart thumped in a chant, urging her on.

∼

IAN SAT at a table in the corner of the Drunken Dwarf, his mind wandering while Korrigan, Vargan, and Arangoli discussed how they might free the Head Thumpers. Too late for breakfast and too early for lunch, the taproom was empty other than an old couple seated at the other end of the room.

The front door opened and Revita walked in, trailed by Vic. The two of them paused in the doorway, spied Ian and the dwarves, and approached them.

"Where were you two?" Ian asked. "We found your room empty and were worried that something had happened to you."

Vic replied, "We woke early and took a ferry to the river's west bank. The ferry passed close to the Carcera, allowing a closer view of its fortifications."

Korrigan's brow shot up. "What did you find?"

Revita replied, "We passed along the inland side of the island on the first crossing. A dock and a low, rocky shore face south with a path leading uphill, to the prison gate. The gate tower is manned with armed guards. It is open and free of obstructions between the waterline and the gate, making it impossible to approach the fortress without being seen, at least during the day." She glanced at Vic before continuing, "On the return route, we paid the ferryman extra to take us around the sea-facing side of the island. A hundred-foot-tall cliff face defines the shoreline, and the prison's outer wall stands near the edge of that drop. However, while the towers at the corners are guarded, the wall itself is not, so it is likely not thick enough to facilitate a catwalk."

Vic added, "We believe that the steep side of the island offers us an opportunity."

Korrigan asked, "You believe we can break them free?"

Revita said, "I believe there is a chance. However, it requires us getting a few people inside, first."

"What are you suggesting?"

She sighed. "I prefer otherwise, but Vic has convinced me to help, and if we are to succeed, I will need to be on the inside. Two others will need to come with me. Ian, you are one of them."

Ian blinked. "Me?" Memories of the last heist were still fresh in his mind, the worry, the panic, the near-death experience of facing the giant stone golem. "Again?"

"Your thin frame and ability to speak three languages offer possibilities the others lack."

The comment was not dissimilar to the one she had made regarding his involvement in robbing the Trade and Barter. Ian's physical limitations had long been something he wished he could change about himself. He had never found it useful before, but Revita saw it differently. Despite the woman's self-serving nature, her confidence in him made Ian want to be better. Of course, images of her naked body returned to blot out other thoughts, despite his attempt to push those thoughts aside.

Arangoli thumped his fist on the table, startling Ian from his musings. The dwarf declared, "I will go as well. It is my squad, and I will be the one to free them."

Revita shook her head. "No. We will need you and your hammer for another aspect of the plan. I suggest Korrigan join Ian and me inside the prison."

I am going inside a prison. It was something Ian had never considered, but that is what was being asked of him. *It is to save your people,* Ian told himself, but he knew that was only half of the truth. He had decided he would no longer accept the naïve, frail, scared version of himself. It was time to be a man. *I just hope it doesn't get me killed.* He pushed that thought aside, determined to do his part and do it without cowardice.

In his bravest voice, Ian asked, "How do we get inside?"

Grinning, Revita said, "That's easy. We get arrested?"

Despite Ian's brave exterior, a sense of dread settled in, causing his stomach to churn. A cramp had him press a hand to his gut and rise to his feet. "Excuse me. I must go find a privy."

He rushed out so he wouldn't have to hear the others laughing at him.

Ian stood in the shadows among trees along a gravel, hillside road. Below him, the hill dropped down to the clustered buildings of Bard's Bay. Across the bay, the sun clung to the western horizon, soon to retire for the evening. On the hilltop before him stood a castle basking in the warm light of sunset. The structure's ramparts appeared lightly manned with only two guards visible. *Oftentimes, appearances are deceiving*, Ian reminded himself. A rope lay across the gravel road, the far end tied to a tree, the near end held by Revita.

"How long do we have to wait?" he whispered.

"Hush," she replied. "I have no schedule, but he will return for the night. Of that, I am certain."

The rumbling of carriage wheels came from down the road, the distant sound steadily drawing closer.

"This is it, Korrigan." She called out to the dwarf, who stood behind a shrub across the road from them. "Get ready."

From behind the shrub, he replied, "I am ready."

Ian gripped the cudgel he had been given while her instructions replayed in his head, along with her warning. *The difference between being arrested and ending up dead is often a narrow slice that begins with intent and ends with the threat you pose.* Since he had not ever considered himself a daunting or threatening figure, it was an unfamiliar perspective to consider.

The thunder of hooves grew louder. A pair of black horses came into view, the team pulling a carriage driven by a man in black with an armed guard sitting at his side. As the horse drew near, Revita pulled the rope in her hands and wrapped it around the stump beside her. The rope struck the horses near the knee and sent both crashing to the road. The fallen team slid a dozen feet, stirring up a cloud of dust as the carriage came to a stop.

"Now!" Revita burst from the cover of the woods and tore open the carriage door. Just as she had predicted, a guard thrust a sword through the opening, which she sidestepped. Ian, having positioned himself beside the door, brought the cudgel down as hard as he could. It struck the hand gripping the hilt, and the sword fell to the ground.

"Ouch!" the guard in the carriage cried out.

A man dressed in a black doublet with gold trim sat across from the guard. In his thirties, the man was handsome with dark, wavy hair and a trimmed beard. Without a doubt, he was a man of means, as noted by the gold rings on his hand and the thick, gold chain around his neck.

"Commander Kaden." Revita smiled while holding an old, rusty short sword in the doorway. "Give us your gold and we will be on our way. Resist, and you will die."

Kaden made a move to escape out the other door, but it held fast after Korrigan had jammed an iron bar through the handle, preventing it from turning.

The guard in the driver's seat drew his sword, jumped down, and pointed it at Ian, who stepped backward, feigned tripping, and tumbled to the ground, the action knocking the cudgel from his grip and sending it flying into the trees.

Revita shouted. "Get up, you idiot!"

In a flash, one of the guards was standing over him with the sword inches from his throat. "Yield, woman, or the boy dies."

She grimaced at Ian. "I should let you die, you useless pile of rat dung."

"Please, sister..." Posing as brother and sister had been Ian's idea, one which Revita had embraced, stating that it would give her a reason to yield.

"Fine." She dropped her sword. "You made a mess of this one, Isaac."

"Sorry Ava." The fake names had been Revita's idea, both close enough to their real name to remember easily, for which Ian was thankful.

Korrigan circled around the back of the carriage with his hands in the air. A guard stood behind him with a sword at his back. The guard in the carriage climbed out, strode into the undergrowth beside the road, bent, and retrieved his sword. He appeared a decade older than the other two guards, his goatee trimmed to a neat point.

Kaden emerged from the carriage and straightened his coat. He stood tall with broad, athletic shoulders. His gaze swept from Korrigan, to Ian, to Revita before he shook his head. "You three are fools. This is the worst robbery attempt I have ever seen."

The guard from the driver's seat snickered, the driver, who was checking on the horses, echoing him.

Revita replied, "Desperate times require desperate measures." She gestured toward Ian. "Look at him. We've no money for food and if he misses another meal, that might be the end of him."

Kaden snorted. "In that case, you will be fed by the city's taxes. I hope you enjoy gruel. Your meals going forward will consist of nothing else." He gestured toward the third guard. "Captain Essex. Take these three fools up to the castle gate. Shackle them, load them into the carriage, and deliver them to the ferry landing. A year in the Carcera should teach them the folly of attempting to steal from me."

"What?" Revita gasped.

"Yes, Commander," the captain kicked Ian in the leg. "Get up."

Pain flared as the muscle in Ian's thigh knotted up. Still, he forced himself to his feet.

Kaden climbed into the carriage. "Deal with them expeditiously, Captain. I want them locked up by nightfall."

The carriage driver cut the rope strung across the road, hopped back onto the seat, and snapped the reins. A prod from Captain Essex caused his sword tip to bite into Ian's backside, resulting in him hopping forward and slapping a hand to the wound.

"Get moving," Essex demanded. "Before we decide to slice your throats and be done with you."

Ian marched up the hill and realized that it had happened. He had gotten himself arrested by attempting to rob the man who ruled Bard's Bay. He was on his way to prison and he'd brought it on intentionally. *What have I done?*

CHAPTER 44
THE CARCERA

Stars twinkled in the sky while the sea soaked up the last remnants of daylight along the western horizon. A quartet of oars splashed into the water again and again, each manned by a ferryman. The vessel and her passengers eased across the bay while heading toward the dark and foreboding prison. The ferry approached the island, a thumb of rock jutting up from the water where the river met the sea. As the craft drew near, Ian stared up at the fortress with a lump in his throat, his armpits soaked from the anxiety gripping him. The ferry bumped into the dock, causing those on board to stumble. Ian, his wrists in shackles, fell to his hands and knees.

The guard standing beside Ian grabbed a handful of his jerkin and lifted, "Get up, thief. Your new home awaits."

Back on his feet, Ian climbed onto the dock and was soon joined by Revita, Korrigan, and six guards, three of whom held swords at the prisoners' backs. They climbed a long, winding staircase hewn into the rocky ground, the route illuminated by seven-foot-tall torches flickering in the breeze. The fortress loomed above the staircase, illuminated by torches on the battlements. Beyond the walls, amber light visible through narrow windows in the central tower monitored the Carcera like vigilant eyes, watching to ensure none escaped her walls. By the time they reached the top of the staircase, Ian was panting for air, partly from the effort of the climb, partly from fear.

A man shouted from the top of the wall. "Hold!"

The guards and prisoners stopped ten strides from the entrance.

"State your name and purpose."

"It is Captain Essex. We have three new prisoners."

"Why so late?'

Essex grimaced. "Open the blazing door before I have your arse in shackles!"

The man on the wall turned and faded from view. Moments later, a massive door made of wood and metal bands swung open, its hinges groaning in protest. The guard gripping Ian's arm pushed him toward the opening and ushered him inside.

Ian found himself in a chamber wide enough to hold two wagons parked side by side. A single torch on the wall illuminated the space. Walls of gray brick stood to the left and right while a set of double doors stood directly ahead of him, secured by a thick beam. A pair of armed soldiers waited before the doors while two others loitered at the side of the room, bracketing a closed, man-sized door. Torchlight flickered on the high ceiling while shadows gathered in the corners.

One of the prison guards said, "Welcome, Captain."

"Sergeant Wako," Essex replied. "These three are to be locked up for a year."

"What did they do?"

Essex snorted. "They thought to rob Commander Kaden. It was a poor attempt, but incompetence is no excuse."

"One is a woman," Wako noted.

"Aye. A feisty one. I suspect that will either get stamped out during her stay, or she will end up dead. Either would resolve the issue."

"Very well," Wako said. "Leave them to us. We will process them and see them to their cells."

A guard shoved Ian forward. He stumbled and came close to falling before righting himself. Revita and Korrigan joined him as Essex and his soldiers walked back out. A pair of prison guards pushed the outer door closed and then dropped a heavy cross beam into place to secure it. A similar beam was lifted from the other set of heavy doors. A guard pulled the door open, the creak echoing in the chamber. Ian and his companions were escorted through and into the prison yard.

Towers stood at the corners of the yard, and the massive, ominous keep lurked straight ahead. The keep was hundreds of feet wide at the base and over a hundred feet tall. A row of narrow windows ran along each floor except the ground level, where only a heavy wooden door loomed.

They made for the door, stopped before it, and waited while one of the guards produced a ring of keys. With the door unlocked, the guard opened it and led them into a long chamber with a closed door at the far end, an open doorway along the left wall and a staircase on the right. The room lacked furniture other than a long table and four chairs, each occupied by a man in armor. The hum of voices and laughter came from a neighboring room, the sound reminding Ian of a tavern.

They approached the table and one of the men seated leaned forward. "Ah. It looks like we have some new blood."

The man beside him added, "And one is a woman."

A third said, "A pretty one at that."

Revita scowled. "I am warning you. I bite."

The first man chortled. "Feisty. I like that."

"Never mind the woman, Jessup." Sergeant Wako pointed toward the ledger. "Essex just dropped off these three. They are to be incarcerated for theft. One year."

Jessup picked up a quill, dipped it in an inkwell, and began writing. He then looked up at Revita. "I need your name."

"Ava Miller." She thrust her chin toward Ian. "This is my brother, Isaac."

The man recorded the names and then looked at Korrigan. "And the dwarf?"

"Fenric Backwater," Korrigan said.

After recording the names, the man sat back. "All set. The boy and the dwarf can take cell thirty-one on the ninth floor. That one has been empty for a year. The woman can take Bartle's old cell on the third floor." He smiled at Revita. "The body has been removed, but the stench might remain. The man was dead for a few days before anyone took note of it."

She replied, "It can't smell worse than your breath, you flatulent-mouthed pig."

The prison guards laughed except for Jessup, whose lips pressed tightly together before replying. "Your smart mouth is going to get you into trouble. A year is a long time to suffer."

Wako shoved Revita from the table. "Let's get you to your cell."

The guards turned them around and led them to the stairwell. After climbing two flights, a guard unlocked the door and another joined him as they escorted Revita to her cell. Ian and Korrigan continued climbing with the last four guards escorting them. At the ninth floor, after an exhausting climb, they passed beyond a locked door and into a torchlit corridor. The interior wall of the corridor was nothing but solid brick while the outer wall was lined with cells hidden behind thick, iron bars. Some of the cells had a single, occupied bed, while others contained a set of bunks. Many of the inmates lay in bed, unmoving, some snoring. Those who stood at the bars while watching Ian and Korrigan walk past were dirty, their clothing ragged, their eyes lacking any spark of hope. Most of the prisoners were human, but Ian noted one dwarf sitting on the edge of his bed, his elbows on his knees. The dwarf's purple eyes widened upon seeing Korrigan.

They turned a corner and the corridor continued with cells on the outside and torches mounted to the wall on the inner side. They passed by an open door across from the cells to reveal a spacious room filled with tables and benches, all of them empty.

"This is your dining hall," Wako said. "There is one on each floor. Twice a day, you get to visit it for a delicious bowl of gruel. Once a week, we will allow you outside for an hour in the yard." He crossed the corridor and gestured toward an empty cell, its door standing open. "The rest of your time will be spent here. It might not be much, but it is better than where you will end up if you cross me or any of my men."

Again, Ian was shoved forward, the hand gripping the back of his jerkin guiding him into the cell. His shackles were removed and Korrigan joined him. The guards swung the door closed, locked it, and walked off. The sound of their fading footsteps felt like nails being pounded into a coffin with Ian lying in it, still alive.

Korrigan whispered. "The dwarf we passed was Brannigan, one of the Head Thumpers."

"At least we know where to find one of them. I wonder where the others are held."

"I cannot say, but it won't make things easier if we have to search this entire building. We only saw half of this floor and I counted dozens of cells."

Ian sighed and was about to sit on the lower bunk when Korrigan stopped him.

"Don't," the dwarf warned.

"Why not?"

"These places are ridden with lice and bed bugs."

The mere idea of such an infestation caused Ian to back against the opposite wall. "I hope Revita knows what she is doing. I don't want to spend even a single night in this place."

Oars cut into the dark water, the rhythmic strokes urging the longboat forward. Vic sat in the bow, keeping watch for rocks while Arangoli and Vargan rowed. A dark tower of rock loomed ahead, its outline barely visible against the night sky. Dozens of narrow slices of light peered out of the prison high above the bluff it was built upon. His gaze rose to those lights. *Ian is up there, somewhere.* Again, Vic tried to recall exactly how Revita had talked him into her crazy plan. While the last heist had ended successfully, it could have gone very poorly if Vic hadn't decided to go against her orders. With his role cast, placing him in a position outside the prison, there was little he could do if things went wrong before she, Ian, and the others made it outside.

The rush of waves crashing against rock grew louder as the boat neared the backside of the island the prison was built upon.

Spying a boulder jutting above the water, Vic said, "Turn left."

The boat altered course and slid past the boulder. When they neared the base of the cliff, Vic grabbed the rope tied to the bow, stood, and jumped to a rocky ledge three feet above the waterline. He turned the boat while walking along the ledge. Squatting, he tied the bow to a fist of rock. Likewise, Vargan secured the stern. Arangoli handed Vic a coil of rope and then threw a pack over his back, beside his recently returned war hammer.

Vic slid the loop of rope over his head and shoulder and looked up at the wall of rock above him. The sliver of moon in the sky provided just enough light to see outlines and reliefs in the steep surface.

"Ready?" he asked.

Arangoli said, "Aye. Lead the way."

Vic found a handhold and stepped on a lip of rock. He pulled himself up, located another place to grip, and began his climb. When he was six feet up, Arangoli climbed up behind him.

"Whatever you do," the dwarf said. "Don't fall when I am beneath you, or we will both be in trouble."

Looking down, Vic said, "Trust me. Nobody wishes to avoid falling more than I. Besides, you don't look like you'd be too comfortable to land on."

"You have a point. Now, if I were Gortch, you might feel differently."

"Why is that?" Vic pulled himself up and slid his foot out toward another lip.

"You'll see when you meet him. Let's just say he is as wide as he is tall."

Since dwarves already had stout frames, Vic tried to imagine one as heavy as Arangoli inferred but struggled to do so. Concerns about his companions returned to the forefront of his thoughts. "I hope things are going as Revita planned."

"Little chance of that," the dwarf snorted. "Every story I've heard her tell included things taking an unplanned turn and her improvising to make it work. In truth, she might be at her best when that happens."

Vic fell silent and focused on the climb, since there was nothing he could do to help Ian and Revita. Still, it wouldn't hurt to pray for them, so he whispered a request to the good spirits while pulling himself onto a narrow ledge.

REVITA SAT cross-legged on the floor of her cell. She pressed her back to the cool, stone wall, closed her eyes, and listened. Time moved slowly, but she was determined to wait. Success required it.

Footsteps approached, passed her cell, and retreated as the guard on watch made his rounds. She began to count, marking the time. Eight minutes later, the man walked past. Again, she counted. Six minutes passed before he walked by her cell. The next round occurred ten minutes later. By the fifth time, she had established the man's average. All the while, the rumble of snores grew louder as the other inmates slipped deeper into sleep. Still, she waited.

Fifteen times, the guard passed her cell before she moved. The man stopped outside her bars and stared at her as she stood and stretched beside the bed in her cell.

She stopped and arched a brow and spoke in a hushed tone. "Do you mind?"

He whispered back. "I was wondering if you were going to sit on the floor all night."

"I considered it, but frankly I found it too uncomfortable, and I am exhausted." She lifted the covers and sat on the bed, but he continued watching. "Don't get your hopes up. I intend to sleep clothed."

The man sighed. "I thought as much." He continued walking, his pace slow and measured.

Revita immediately pulled her breeches down, retrieved her enchanted lock pick from its hiding place, and pulled them back up. She thrust the pick into the mattress and tore it open. Moving quickly, she pulled stuffing out of the mattress and piled it on the bed. When she deemed the amount sufficient, she pulled the blanket up over the stuffing and stepped back to admire her work. It looked enough like a person sleeping to pass, especially in the dim lighting.

She then went to the cell door, reached through the bars, and inserted the pick into the lock. A glow came from the lock, it clicked, and when she applied pressure, it turned. The door swung open, allowing her to ease through the opening. With care, she pulled the door closed and headed down the corridor in the same direction as the guard. At the corner, she peered around it and found the guard at the far end, his methodical pace taking him around the next corner.

Revita scurried along, counting until she reached the twelfth cell. She stepped up to the barred door and peered inside. A thick, bulky body occupied the bottom bunk, and another one lay on the top. A roaring snore came from inside the cell, the timber nearly rattling the bars. *It is them.* The fact that she had noticed the two dwarves on her way to her cell had been fortuitous.

She unlocked the door and swung it open. The hinge creaked,

causing her to cringe. Easing inside, she nudged the occupant of the bottom bunk.

"Whoa!" He sat up and hit his head on the bunk above him. "Ouch."

"Hush, Gortch," She hissed. "It's Revita."

The heavyset dwarf leaned closer, until his bulbous nose was within inches of her face. "Vita?"

"Yes. It's me, here to break you out."

"You would risk yourself for me?"

She held up a finger. "Not just you. The other Head Thumpers as well. Now, no more questions until we are free."

"Very well. Move aside."

As she stepped back, rustling came from the bed above. "Why are you up at this hour, Gortch?"

Gortch stood, his girth forcing Revita to step back. He then reached up, grabbed the blanket from the upper bunk, and yanked it. The dwarf above rolled with the blanket and tumbled to the floor with an "oof." He had a lean build for a dwarf, his brown beard split and braided, each braid dangling from a cheek rather than his chin.

"That hurt," The dwarf groaned.

"Hush," Gortch growled. "Vita is here to get us out."

The other dwarf stood and eyed Revita. "How'd you get in here?"

She smiled. "Hi, Rax. You know me, always lurking in places I don't belong."

Rax nodded. "You've a knack for it, that much is certain."

She gestured toward the door. "Let's go. We need to set Korrigan free and then find the rest of your crew."

"Korrigan is in the prison?"

"Yes. On the ninth floor."

Gortch grunted. "That's where Brannigan's cell is located."

"Good. We will free him as well." Revita eased past the cell door. "Let's go."

Rax followed, but the opening was too narrow for Gortch, so he swung it open wide, and the door made a mighty squeak.

A voice came from down the corridor. "What was that?" The hammer of footsteps followed.

"Crap." Revita ran toward the footsteps and reached the corner just as the guard rounded it.

She leapt and kicked with both feet, driving her heels into the guard's chest, the force launching him backward. He slammed to the floor, slid, and his helmet-covered head struck the bars of a cell with a massive clang. The guard did not move.

The prisoner in the cell the guard struck pushed his face to the bars while gripping them. It was a human male, his face covered in a scraggly beard, his build gaunt.

"Set me free," he croaked.

She stared at him for a beat.

"Please," he pleaded.

An idea clicked in her head. "I will set you free, but only if you help me release everyone else on this floor. If you all storm out at the same time, maybe you can overwhelm the guards."

A grin stretched across his face to reveal missing teeth and those that remained appearing rotten. "You've a deal, lassie."

Revita knelt beside the unconscious guard, unhooked the key ring from his belt, and handed it to the prisoner. "Free yourself. Unlock all of the cells but tell the others they need to wait. Nobody leaves this floor until all are released, or you won't survive the night."

The prisoner tried a key, but it did not fit. "It will be as you say."

She turned to find Gortch and Rax standing behind her.

"Is that wise?" Gortch asked.

"The distraction might be worth it." She made for the stairwell door. "Let's go."

Her pick made quick work on the door lock leading to the staircase and they climbed up with her counting each door she passed.

IAN SAT ON THE FLOOR, his head leaning against the iron bars while he stared down the corridor. A torch on the wall halfway between him and the far corner provided dim light for the otherwise dark area. The guard making his rounds turned the corner and faded from view. Soon, his footsteps were lost beneath a cacophony of snores.

Korrigan slept on the floor between Ian and the bunks, his breath rumbling with each inhale. How the dwarf was able to sleep, Ian had no idea, but he found himself envious because the time had trickled by at a snail's pace, his stomach churning and armpits damp the entire time.

A minute later, another person rounded the corner, the silhouette lithe, the footsteps silent. Ian leaned forward in anticipation as Revita crept into the torchlight. Two dwarves, one lean for his race, the other heavier than any Ian had ever seen, followed her.

Ian stood and whispered. "Revita!"

"There you are." She scurried to his cell. "Where is the guard?"

"He just walked past a few minutes ago, so I expect he is in the opposite corridor."

She slid something into the cell lock. It clicked and she opened the door.

"Korrigan," Ian nudged his cell mate.

The dwarf jerked and sat up in a burst, blinking as he said, "What's happening?"

"Let's get out of here."

Ian stepped out into the corridor.

Korrigan rose to his feet, emerged, and clapped a hand on the shoulder of the fat dwarf. "It is good to see you, Gortch!"

"You are well, Korrigan."

"And Rax," Korrigan grinned. "You appear even leaner than normal. Don't they feed you in here, or did Gortch steal your meals?"

Rax laughed and clapped Korrigan on the shoulder.

Voices came from the nearby cells. "Let us out." "Help." Have mercy."

The pleas tugged at Ian's heart strings. "Can we free them?"

"Some of these prisoners are murderers. Some are worse than that," Rax said. "Do you want to risk yourself to free all of them?"

"I suppose not."

Korrigan said, "Brannigan's cell is across from the stairwell. I don't know if anyone else is on this level."

Gortch said, "No. The others are on levels seven, six, and four."

A guard came around the corner and stopped with a sudden lurch, his eyes widening. Rather than run toward them, he spun around and raced in the other direction.

"Get him!" Revita raced after the guard.

Ian ran with her. As they turned the corner, the prison guard ducked into the stairwell and slammed the door.

Revita reached the door first and went to unlock it when a gong resounded from the stairwell, the clang echoing throughout the floor and likely the entire prison.

Her head drooped. "Too late. He sounded the alarm."

Ian asked, "What are we going to do?"

Korrigan said, "We are going to free Brannigan and then go find the others, even if we have to fight our way out of here."

Revita nodded. "Agreed. Lead the way."

CHAPTER 45

BREAKOUT

Vic, his fingers sore and arms heavy, pulled himself over the upper edge of the cliff and rolled onto a shadowy ledge. There, he lay, gasping for air and basking in a sense of relief that the long and dangerous ascent was behind him. The urgent nature of his mission pressed him back into action. He rose to his knees in the narrow, four-foot-wide space between the castle wall and the steep drop. With one hand firmly gripping the rocky edge, he extended the other toward Arangoli, who gripped it. Pulling with all his might, Vic helped the dwarf up the last few feet. He then sat and scooted backward to lean his back against the wall behind the prison.

Panting for air, Vic said, "I am glad that cliff was not any higher. My arms are like noodles."

"Aye," Arangoli wiped his brow. "But our work is not done."

Vic sighed and slid the coil of rope over his head and set it aside. "I know. You had better dig out the stake."

The dwarf removed a two-foot-long iron stake and climbed to his feet. "Here. You hold it while I drive it into the ground."

Doing as requested, Vic knelt and held the stake against the rocky surface. The dwarf pulled the hammer off his back, stood over the stake, and raised it high.

"Wait," Vic said. "Won't this alert the guards?"

The dwarf lowered the hammer. "It will, but so will our hammering at the wall."

A gong resounded from inside the prison. Shouts arose, along with cries of alarm.

Arangoli groaned. "It sounds like Revita has stirred up a hornet's nest."

"At least any noise we make won't be so noticeable, now."

"True. Hold the stake." The dwarf raised the hammer high and brought it down.

A clang resounded and a shock of energy shot down the stake. Rock chipped as the stake was driven down. In moments, it was firmly embedded in the rocky ground. Vic tied the rope to it, dropped the coil over the edge, and watched it plummet into darkness.

Reaching over his shoulder, Vic removed the mattock from his back. "Let's see if we can get through this wall."

He and Arangoli moved a few strides from the stake and then separated from each other. Vic wound back and drove the pick end of his mattock into the wall. Sparks sizzled along the rock where the point dug in. As he wound back for another blow, Arangoli's hammer struck the same spot. At impact, a thump released, cracking and splitting stone.

IAN FOLLOWED Revita down the stairs, trailed by ten dwarves, nine of whom were Head Thumpers, leaving only one yet to be rescued. On each of the levels containing Head Thumper members, Revita had rushed from cell to cell, freeing prisoners and urging them to join the others and fight the guards. The growing group of prison escapees would then hurry down the stairs to join the prison break. Shouts, screams and the clash of steel echoed in the stairwell, the fracas growing louder and more urgent as they descended. Finally, Ian and his party arrived on the fourth floor and ran along the corridor while Gortch, Rax, and Korrigan called out the name of the last missing dwarf.

"Pazacar!"

"Pazacar!"

"Where are you, Pazacar?"

Prisoners stood and gripped the bars of each cell they passed, every one of them pleading for release. A voice inside of Ian screamed that he should free them all. Another voice warned that some of the prisoners held evil in their hearts and would do wrong upon innocents.

"Gortch!" A voice called out from ahead.

As they drew near the cell, they found a dwarf with a white beard tied in a single braid. Despite the beard color, his face lacked the wrinkles of age.

The heavyset Gortch stopped before the cell and leaned forward with his thick hands on his knees while gasping for air. "Finally." Gasp. "I cannot run as I used to."

Rax snorted. "When could you ever run?"

Gortch shrugged. "I used to be lighter."

Brannigan replied, "You have been that big since your teen years."

Pazacar gripped the cell bars. "Korrigan? Vita? How did you get in here?"

She replied as she approached the cell door. "Same as you, I suppose."

"You started a brawl that destroyed an inn?"

She inserted her pick into the lock. "While that sounds fun, our crime was more direct." After unlocking the door, she stepped back. "Let's get out of here."

As they began down the corridor, a voice called out, "Ian?"

He turned to find a familiar, handsome face in the cell beside Pazacar's. "Truhan?"

The man grinned. "You remember me."

Although their meeting had been brief, the strange man was difficult to forget. "Of course."

"Take me with you," Truhan said,

Ian glanced toward the others as they continued toward the stairwell door. "I..."

"I am like you, Ian. I do not belong in prison. We humans deserve freedom."

Freedom. The word meant more to Ian than he ever suspected, its value to him rising ten-fold after he and his people had been enslaved.

Although Ian owed Truhan for saving him and his companions from the Crumi sacrifice, he saw an opportunity and decided to act on it. "We head to Ra'Tahal to oust those who wrongly hold it. In doing so, we would free the people from my village. Will you join us in this effort?"

Truhan smiled, his stark white teeth a distant contrast to the nasty, rotting teeth he had seen among other prisoners. "I will fight at your side until every villager is freed."

Ian called out, "Revita!"

She stopped and glanced back.

"Come back and free this man."

Revita groaned. "We don't have time for..."

"His name is Truhan. I know him. He has agreed to join us to help reclaim Ra'Tahal. Besides, Vic, Korrigan, Vargan, and I all owe him our lives."

The woman glanced toward Korrigan, who nodded. "Fine," she walked back to Ian, unlocked the cell, and glared at Truhan. "You had better not cause trouble."

The strange man smiled. "Trouble often follows me, but I'll be sure to direct it away from you."

She frowned at Ian. "I have enough to worry about. This one is your responsibility."

"Agreed." Ian nodded. "Let's go."

They returned to the stairwell and descended, their crew now consisting of three humans and an odd collection of dwarves.

Revita led Ian, Truhan, and the dwarves down the stairs, turning at each landing without pause. While the first two Head Thumpers had been extremes in terms of weight, the other eight all fell somewhere in between, each of them stoutly built except for Pazacar, whose build was not unlike that of Rax. They rapidly descended until reaching the third floor, where corpses and severed limbs littered the stairs. Only one of the dead wore the armor of a prison guard. The grim scene and the sounds of battle below aroused concerns of what they might face once outside. As a result, Revita paused there, thinking.

"What's wrong?" Ian asked.

"We may be forced to fight to get out of here," she replied.

Korrigan said, "We have no weapons. It could go poorly."

"They hold our weapons in the armory," Gortch said. "It is a locked room on the first floor. I don't know about the others, but I do not intend to leave without my mace."

"Are you serious?"

"I am a dwarf. My weapon is a part of me and my family, handed down through generations."

She sighed. "Fine. Let's break into the armory and then we are out of here."

They resumed their descent, stepping over the dead. At each landing they passed, the corpses thickened. When they passed through the door at the bottom, they found no movement in the entrance hall. The guard desk was gone, the chairs nothing but shattered wood. It was a bloody scene, and although two dozen people occupied the room, none moved.

Gortch gestured toward the metal reinforced door at the rear of the room. "The armory is that way."

Revita led them to the door, where she produced her pick, slid it into the lock, and turned it.

"They searched us after we were arrested," Ian said, "How did they not find the pick?"

She snorted. "They did not look where it was hidden." The door swung open with a creak to reveal a dark room. The air was dank and smelled of metal.

Ian's curiosity was apparently not satisfied. "Where did you hide it?"

Turning toward him, she arched a brow. "Do you really want to know?"

His eyes widened and his cheeks reddened. "No. That isn't necessary."

Korrigan lifted a torch off the wall strolled into the armory, the amber light revealing racks and shelving filled with weapons and armor.

The dwarves flooded into the room and spread out in search of their gear. Moments later, Rax called out and the others crowded around him. The Head Thumpers began to don armor, the sound of metal clanking noisily while Revita monitored the door, hoping they would not be discovered before they were ready to fight. The cries and clangs of battle echoing outside were a steady reminder of the danger awaiting them.

Deciding she preferred to be armed, she walked over to a shelf and picked up a dagger.

"What are you doing?" Ian asked.

"You might want to choose a weapon as well."

He swallowed visibly before turning and lifting a cudgel off a shelf.

The other human, the newcomer named Truhan, stood near the door, watching the activity with an arched brow, appearing calm and unconcerned. *He is a handsome one*, Revita thought. *Too handsome.*

Revita approached the man. "Aren't you going to arm yourself?"

Truhan shrugged. "I have little use for weapons."

"What if we have to fight our way out?"

"I will manage."

Revita seldom trusted strikingly attractive men, and the way he responded only served to enhance her distrust. "How do you know Ian?"

"We recently met during my travels." Truhan's gaze remained fixed on Ian during the entire conversation. "It instantly became clear to me that he is...special."

Her eyes narrowed. "How so?"

He smirked. "If you don't see it yet, you will someday soon."

Again, she frowned. "You behave as if you know something I do not."

His smirk fell away, replaced by a serious glare. "I cannot imagine to what you refer."

Gortch clapped a nasty, spiked mace into his gauntlet-covered palm, the noise drawing everyone's attention toward him. "I am ready to break some heads."

Like Ian, Korrigan held a cudgel. Rax wore a rapier on his hip. Pazacar gripped a quarterstaff with metal bands on both ends. Of the other dwarves, two held spears, two wore short swords and shields, one held a hammer, and one carried an axe. Other than Pazacar and Korrigan, all wore armor with a mixture of brown leather and plates crafted of metal with the notable warm tint of dwarven steel.

"Let's get out of here," Revita said. "When we get outside, we need to work our way to the backside of the keep."

Rax grunted. "That doesn't make sense. The gate is out front."

"I know." She walked through the doorway, determined to complete her escape plan.

IAN TRAILED the others as they crossed the entrance hall. Outside, cries, shouts, and the clang of steel on steel continued. *People are dying outside.* The realization frightened him to the core.

Revita eased the front door open, peered out, and gestured for the others to follow. The door swung wide open, and the dwarves poured out. Ian froze, his breath caught in his throat, his palms so slick, he nearly dropped the cudgel.

A friendly voice asked, "Have you no experience with battle?"

He turned to find Truhan standing behind him. The question stirred images of dark elves pouring through a rift and attacking the dwarves of Ra'Tahal. "Only twice. Once, I was injured by a stray arrow. The other time was against a rock troll. I was lucky to survive. One of our party was not so lucky."

"Such things are a risk in battle."

"I..." He looked at the cudgel in his hand. "I don't know how to fight."

"Battles do not always hinge upon strength or physical skill. Quite often, the sharpest minds win the day."

"I can hardly fight by translating or reading."

"No. Not yet anyway." Truhan headed toward the open door. "Let's catch up to the others. I suspect you would rather not be left behind."

The thought terrified Ian even more than facing the battle. He hurried after Truhan and stepped out into a nightmare.

The bodies of prisoners and soldiers lay strewn about the prison yard. A cluster of prisoners stood near the entrance while holding the guard desk. The prisoners rushed toward the closed door and drove the desk into it with a mighty thump. The door held. Other prisoners wielded swords likely taken from fallen guards. Those men acted as a rear guard, trading attacks with soldiers trying to get past them. Guards manning the tower above the gate and the two towers at the front corners of the prison loosed arrows at the prisoners, causing three to cry out and collapse, one of them among those carrying the desk. Another prisoner filled the downed man's place as they drove the desk into the door once again.

Ian searched for Revita and the dwarves, his gaze sweeping the prison yard before finding them near the corner of the keep, engaged in a fight with another cluster of guards. When Truhan strode in that direction, Ian rushed to catch up. They approached the fracas at a purposeful pace as a score of soldiers raced out of the tower in the corner of the yard.

Gortch stomped toward the oncoming guards and began to swing his mace as if gone mad. It clanged off shields, helms, and armor, the force of each blow driving the guards back or causing them to collapse. Rax darted in and out, thrusting his rapier through narrow openings and finding gaps in armor, the tip coming away bloody. Pazacar twirled his staff, blocking attacks and following with thumps to the head, shin, groin, and gut. The others swung, stabbed, and killed with abandon. A guard at the edge of the fight broke off and came at Ian, who froze in fear. The man wound back, his sword prepared to remove Ian's head from his body.

A flash of darkness swept past as Truhan closed on the guard with inhuman speed. Before the prison guard's sword could come around, Truhan thrust a palm at the man's face. The palm struck and launched the guard backward to land six strides away. He did not move.

Another guard broke off and rushed Truhan, who stood rock still until the guard was a stride away. The guard thrust, prepared to drive his sword through Truhan's chest. The sword found only air as Truhan ducked beneath it and thrust his heel. It struck the attacker's midriff, causing the man to fold as he went flying backward and tumbled to the ground a few strides away. He also did not move.

Suddenly, the only guards in the area lay strewn about, wounded, dying, or dead.

"Let's go!" Revita rushed along the narrow gap between the keep and the outer wall, heading toward the rear of the castle.

Ian ran after her and the others trailed him. As the distance increased, the shouts, screams, and other sounds of battle faded. They rounded the back corner of the keep and Ian slowed in surprise.

"Vic!"

His brother and Arangoli stood beside a pile of rubble near the middle of the outer wall.

Ian slowed as he drew near them. "I have never been so glad to see you."

"Same here, but we can celebrate later. Right now, we need to get out of here." Vic gestured toward a four-foot diameter hole in the wall. "Careful when you go through. One step too far, and you'll fall into the night."

Stepping over rubble, Ian ducked and followed Revita through the fresh opening in the two-foot-thick wall. When he reached the other side, he stood upright and found himself on a four-foot-deep ledge. Darkness and the rush of waves came from beyond the edge.

"How do we get down?" Ian asked.

Revita bent and dug through a sack lying a few feet away. She dug out a pile of leather gloves and held out a pair out to Ian. "Put these on."

Ian tossed the cudgel aside and did as requested. "Now, what?"

From the hole in the wall, Vic emerged, walked past Ian, and Revita, and slid his mattock into the sling on his back. He stopped beside a metal stake driven into the rock. A rope tied to the stake dangled over the ledge. "We go down. Follow me when I am out of sight."

Vic gripped the rope with both gloved hands, backed over the edge, and pushed off. After dropping ten feet, his feet struck the wall before he pushed off again. The darkness soon swallowed him.

Revita gestured. "You are next."

"Me?" Ian stared at the rope with trepidation.

"Your brother made me promise you would go second."

The others stared at him, the ledge crowded with dwarves.

Ian swallowed his fears, gripped the rope with his gloved hands, and eased over the edge. He walked his feet down the cliffside while holding onto the rope. His foot slipped, and he fell, the rope sliding through his leather mitts with twenty feet passing before his grip stopped him. His body swung wildly and then slammed into the cliffside, driving the wind from his lungs. He then wound his legs around the rope and began to lower himself hand over hand.

Below him, the whitecaps of waves came into view, along with a longboat.

"Keep coming," Vic's voice came from below. "You are almost to the end."

When Ian drew near the bottom, Vic grabbed his ankles and guided him to the boat. He let go and sat, his arms feeling heavy. The others all descended with an ease that made Ian feel ashamed. Yet, he had survived, and when the boat was full and Vargan and Arangoli began to row them around the island prison, relief drowned out both terror and shame, along with everything else he had endured during the harrowing experience.

Korrigan began to hand out cloaks from a pile in the longboat. Ian wrapped his over his shoulders to protect himself from the damp night air and sat in the bow. Exhaustion soon overcame him, and he drifted off to sleep.

CHAPTER 46
A HARROWING EXPERIENCE

Ian stirred, rolled to his back, and opened his eyes to a pale blue sky. The rumble of snores came from nearby, the gaps between the snores filled by the sound of water flowing against the hull of the longboat. He sat up and looked around. Korrigan and Vic each manned an oar, the two of them rowing in synchronicity. Revita and four dwarves slept in the bow with Ian while the remaining dwarves lay nestled together in the stern.

A voice came from behind him. "You are awake."

Ian turned to find Truhan sitting on the prow. "Where are we?"

The strange man peered toward the tree lined shore. Mountains formed the southern horizon, their slopes covered in the oranges and reds of autumn. "I suspect we are a good fifteen miles upriver from Bard's Bay."

Korrigan spoke over his shoulder. "Watch for a beach on the south bank. We want to land there and should be near it soon."

Others began to wake, starting with Revita and the other dwarves in the bow.

Arangoli sat up and raked his fingers through his beard. "I am starved after a late night of rowing."

"Aye," Vargan agreed.

Gortch stretched, his armor clanking. "I could eat a horse."

Still rowing, Korrigan said, "If we had horses, we would be riding them, not eating them."

"If not a horse, what do you have to eat?"

"Under the seat are packs with provisions."

"Trail rations?" Gortch groaned. "I've been stuck eating gruel for a week. I need a solid meal."

"You will get your hot meal," Korrigan said. "But it will have to wait until we reach Westhold."

"Westhold?" Ian said, "I thought we were returning to Ra'Tahal."

"Westhold is on the way. That route is also safer than trying to cross the Agrosi."

The mention of the grasslands stirred memories of the giant rock troll attack. After barely surviving the encounter, Ian was happy to avoid something of a similar nature. He then spied a pale stripe of sand along the shoreline ahead.

"Is that the beach?"

Korrigan looked over his shoulder. "Aye." He turned to Vic. "Time to angle toward shore."

The craft eased southwest, the shoreline gradually drawing closer until the bow slid up onto the beach. Truhan grabbed the rope tied to the bow and jumped ashore. Vargan, Arangoli, and Revita joined him. The four of them pulled the boat another three feet, beaching it before Ian and the others began to climb out.

As Ian stepped onto the sand, he felt the warmth of the sun on his skin. He stretched his limbs, grateful for the chance to move around after being cramped in the boat. The dwarves set to work, unloading the packs, weapons, and provisions that had been piled in the hull. Ian looked around, taking in his surroundings.

The beach was secluded, with dense forest on one side and a rocky cliff on the other. From the forest side, branches wavered, leaves rustled in the wind, and birds tweeted.

Korrigan shouldered a pack and turned to face the group. "We will make for Westhold trail. I doubt anyone from the prison is following, considering the mess we left them. Watch for wildlife. Our party is large enough to deter most creatures, but that does not mean we are safe from attack." He gestured. "Vargan. You and your axe can lead the way."

Vargan hefted his axe and strode through the long grass above the beach. "Follow me."

With Vargan, Korrigan, and the other dwarves in the fore, the group began to make their way into the forest. The crunching of leaves underfoot and the snapping of branches accompanied the otherwise quiet group of dwarves. Revita and Vic walked together, the two sharing a quiet conversation. Sensing that the discussion was private, Ian kept a gap from Vic. Last came Truhan, and while Ian knew little of the strange man, the way he had fought the prison guards and saved Ian's life gave him the confidence that nothing would sneak up and attack from behind.

After thirty minutes of hiking along a gentle upslope, the undergrowth fell away to reveal a dirt trail with grass growing between a pair of ruts. The trail ran parallel to the river. Korrigan joined Vargan in the lead, the two of them each following a rut as they headed southeast.

Again, the four humans followed the dwarves, their armor clanking in time with their short strides.

Not long into the march, Arangoli turned and walked backward. "What say you to a song?"

Numerous dwarves replied, "Aye!"

Arangoli turned forward and began to sing, the timbre of his deep voice reverberating as if he sang in a wine barrel. "When I was a lad, I knew a lass who brought to her bed any male who walked past, when I say she was quick, I mean she was fast, ya-ho, ya-ho, ya-ho!"

The dwarves echoed in unison, "Ya-ho, ya-ho, ya-ho!"

Revita joined in and sang the next verse, her lyrics even racier than the first. Ian soon found himself blushing. Blessedly, Truhan diverted his attention.

"You keep interesting company, Ian." The man gestured toward the singing crew ahead of them. "A dozen dwarven warriors, a female thief from the north, and a pair of young men from the south all together must make an interesting story. How did you and your brother come to join this motley crew?"

While Ian hadn't really considered the odd collection in that light, he found himself agreeing with the man's assessment. He explained, "Dark elves led by a singer who wields powerful magic have taken control of the dwarven citadel, Ra'Tahal. After Vic and I escaped the citadel with Korrigan and Vargan, we agreed to help them retake the citadel if they promised to release our people in return."

"Your people?'

"Those from the village I call home." Ian frowned. "Although, there is not much left of that home."

"These villagers are held captive?"

"Yes. As slaves."

Truhan grimaced. "While elves, both the Sylvan and the Drow, have long used humans as slaves, I did not realize dwarves had turned to such measures as well. It is bad enough that the elves treat humans as they do."

Ian did not wish Truhan to think poorly of the dwarves in his company. "Not all dwarves believe in treating humans as slaves. Korrigan was always against it, but duty forced him to follow the orders of his king and the council. Now that those former rulers are dead, Korrigan has an opportunity to rectify the situation."

"Still, do you not find it unfair that magic enables elves and dwarves to hold a superior position to humans? It is bad enough that they live far longer lives."

Ian shrugged. "They are creatures of magic. We are not. What else can we do?"

The man posed another question. "If a path opens to alter this inequity, would you take it?"

After considering his response, Ian said, "It depends on the price I must pay, I suppose."

"Price?"

"Everything comes at a cost, at least that is what my father always said."

"Your father was a wise man."

"I used to think otherwise, but the more time passes, the more I realize that I was wrong and he was right about everything."

"Wisdom is earned, Ian, oftentimes the hard way and even more commonly with advanced age. If you can gain wisdom while still young, it can be a powerful asset."

Ian gave Truhan a sidelong glance. The man had stuck to him like a burr on a sweater ever since freeing him from the Carcera. Even in their previous meetings, he had noticed Truhan staring at him with unmasked curiosity. Ian finally asked, "Why do you hold such interest in me?"

The man smirked. "Is it so obvious?"

"To me, it is."

"That is because you are observant, intelligent, and quick to learn from mistakes. Let's just say that those things, along with something unique I see in you are all reasons why I find you intriguing."

Ian was not satisfied. "To what end?"

"We shall see. Something tells me that we will find the answer in your objective to oust the Drow from Ra'Tahal and to free your people."

The dwarves' song ended, but Arangoli was not yet finished. He began singing another, this one about a dwarf with three legs. It took Ian less than a verse to interpret the meaning. Again, his cheeks grew flush.

As the day advanced and the crew marched southeast, the hills to the south gave way to mountains. Amid the thickening shadows of the surrounding trees, a noise arose. It was subtle and low at first. Like the ground cover beneath the trees, the noise settled beneath the rustling of leaves and the crunch of footsteps in the dirt. The sound grew louder until it became clear that it was the rush of water. The ground began to drop away and turn to a steep descent. The trail wound through the trees while providing glimpses of a deep ravine and a hillside on the far side.

The trees opened to reveal a drop of a few hundred feet. To the south, a waterfall roared down a steep drop to the bottom of the ravine, where a rushing creek flowed north. Mist from the waterfall swirled in the air and cooled the travelers, who had grown warm from exertion.

The dwarves gathered at the edge of the drop while Arangoli approached a drooping bridge spanning the ravine. Secured to thick posts sticking up from the ground on both sides, the bridge was made of parallel ropes spanned by strips of wood.

As Arangoli began crossing, Korrigan turned and spoke to the crew. "We cross one at a time. Wait until the dwarf or human in front of you reaches the other side before you begin. While the bridge appears intact, it ages and it would be best if we do not stress it."

Rax said, "What about Gortch? Should half of him cross at a time since he weighs twice as much as any of the others?"

Laughter echoed across the ravine.

Gortch said, "You are lucky I did not eat you when we shared that cell, Rax. It is unwise to anger a fat, hungry dwarf."

"I never called you fat."

"Which is why you are still standing."

Ian looked up at the sky. The tree-covered hillside behind them blocked the sun. "It'll be dark soon."

"Aye," Korrigan agreed. "Which is why we must cross and climb the far hillside in short order."

Ian turned his attention back on Arangoli, watching as he crossed the bridge. The dwarf appeared cautious, keeping one hand on the rope at all times and testing each step before advancing. Time seemed to slow, the minutes ticking by slowly until he finally reached the far side and waved for the next dwarf to follow. One by one, they crossed until only the four humans remained. Revita went first, and of any thus far, crossed the most quickly, her steps confident, her arms always moving along the two ropes. Vic followed and crossed just a tad slower than Revita. That left only Ian and Truhan.

"Do you want me to go first?" Truhan asked.

While Ian wanted to say yes, he realized that would leave him alone on the west side of the ravine, which would be even worse. "No. I will go and will see you on the other side."

Ian walked up to the edge, his fingers wrapped around the rope to each side. He stepped onto the first board and felt his boot slip slightly, the wood slick from the mist. His empty stomach churned with anxiety, but the others had crossed without a problem, so he was determined to do so as well. With cautious strides and careful foot placement, he continued down the drooping bridge. It wiggled and shook with each step, and as he drew close to the middle, he realized that it swayed in the breeze. After what seemed like forever, Ian finally reached the low point in the center. Even then, the bottom of the gorge waited hundreds of feet below, a drop he could not survive.

A cry came from the direction of the waterfall, high pitched and far too loud for anything human. He turned in that direction as a bird flew into view, its wingspan a hundred feet across, its beak larger than a man. Shocked at the sheer size of the winged, feathered, creature, Ian froze. At the same time, his bestiary research informed him of what he saw.

"A roc," he muttered in awe.

From the far side of the ravine, Vic shouted. "Ian. Run!"

The giant bird passed over the waterfall and dove, straight toward Ian, still frozen in shock. The bridge began to shake with a violence, stirring Ian from his trance. He glanced over his shoulder to find Truhan running toward him. His attention turned back to the giant bird coming toward him, its wagon-sized talons extended.

Truhan shouted. "Ian. Get down!"

Finally, Ian reacted. He dove onto his stomach just as the giant bird reached the bridge. The talons caught in the ropes and the giant monstrous bird tore the ropes loose from the post on the west side. The bridge swung out with the momentum of the bird, twisted, and then plummeted. Ian held on tight as the ravine twirled around him. He and the bridge fell and then began to swing toward the eastern wall. The bridge crashed against the wall, the impact shaking Ian loose. He fell, his arms flailing as he tried to reach the boards, but they were too far to reach. *I am going to die.* It was his last thought before his fall suddenly stopped.

Ian's arm was nearly jerked from its socket, his body flinging wildly as Truhan gripped him by the wrist. He swung toward the bridge and grabbed ahold of the boards. In the distance, the roc soared, heading, away from Ian and his companions. With both hands clutching the boards, the toes of his boots found purchase in a gap, and he closed his eyes, his heart racing.

Truhan's voice came from above. "Can you climb?" Truhan asked.

Ian opened his eyes. "I think so." *Climb or die, Ian,* a voice inside his head said. "Yes."

"Let's go before the roc returns." Truhan began scaling the bridge as if it were a ladder and he an expert climber.

With more care and at a slower pace, Ian followed while trying not to look down. Twice, he made that mistake, both times causing his anxiety to climb up his throat and threaten to overcome him. As Ian neared the top, he heard his brother urging him on. Then, a hand gripped each wrist as Vic and Arangoli hauled him up the last few feet.

Gasping for air, he backed from the ravine and fell to his rear before lying back on the trail. Relief overcame him, and he began to laugh. At first, it was just a chuckle, but the laughter grew louder and he soon had to curl on his side and clutch his stomach as he continued to laugh uncontrollably.

Gortch arched a brow. "Has he gone mad?"

Rax shrugged. "Who knows what brings on madness?"

His brother knelt beside him and placed a hand on Ian's shoulder. "Are you well?"

Ian finally got control of himself. "I am fine...somehow."

"Why are you laughing?"

"Because I almost died. Again."

Vic frowned. "I fail to see humor in that."

Ian explained, "I am weak, uncoordinated, and useless in a fight. Yet, I somehow keep surviving when I should be dead six times over."

"And...this is funny?"

The others stared at Ian with concern in their eyes.

He climbed to his feet and dusted his hands off. "It's just that I keep freezing when I should act. When I do act, it is only just before it is too late. You'd think I would get over my fear, but it continues to haunt me and comes close to getting me killed every time."

Vic glanced toward the others. "I still don't understand your laughter."

"You don't find it funny?" Ian asked.

"No. Frankly, I thought you were going to die and...I promised mother."

"I know what you promised mother." Ian clapped a hand on Vic's shoulder. "But you are only responsible for yourself. You cannot protect me from the world, Vic. Only I can figure out how to protect myself."

Truhan said, "What Ian says is true. It is best that he realizes as much now, before it is too late."

Vic frowned. "What does that mean?"

"Only the future knows, Vic. Somehow, I suspect fate has plans for Ian, plans that he does not yet comprehend."

Korrigan looked up at the darkening sky. "Night is fast approaching. Let's climb this hillside and get out of the ravine before it is too dark. We need a level spot to make camp, and this certainly will not do."

The dwarves all began up the winding, wooded, hillside trail.

Revita paused as she passed Ian. "I am glad you did not die. I have become fond of you and your brother, and I would be sad to see your life come to an end when you are still so young."

Vic followed her, leaving Ian and Truhan alone.

Ian turned to the man. "Thank you for what you did. I...I would be dead without you."

"Perhaps there will come a time when you can return the favor. Until then, let's go."

They began up the hillside while shadows thickened around them.

CHAPTER 47
WESTHOLD

L ate the next day, dark, gray clouds rolled in from the west. The wind picked up until it bent trees and tossed thick branches around as if they were twigs. Heavy gusts tugged at Vic's cloak as he climbed a rocky hillside.

Korrigan, Arangoli, and the other dwarves led the way, following a series of switchbacks at the foot of a mountain. As they had the day prior, Ian and Truhan walked behind him in silence. Driven by the desire to outrace the approaching storm, the party had not stopped to rest for hours. The quickened pace and steady incline left Vic feeling like he was wading through mud, his legs heavy and his muscles weary. Complaining would do no good, so he kept such thoughts to himself and just marched on.

They crested a rise to reveal a gorge draped in shadow. With the sun masked by thick storm clouds, their surroundings were darkened as if nightfall had come early. Lightning flashed, the flickering light briefly chasing shadows away to reveal a stream at the bottom of the gorge. A fortress lay nestled at the uphill end of the gorge, the stream flowing out of an opening beneath its ramparts. The boom of thunder rumbled across the sky, the brief gap between the flash and boom informing Vic that the storm was stalking them like a rabid wolf.

"Westhold," Korrigan said. "The storm approaches. Let's see if we can reach her walls before it hits."

The trail turned southeast and ran along the inside of the ridge, toward the waiting hold. They made it only a few hundred feet before the skies opened up and it began to pour.

Vic raised his hood and pulled his cloak tight around his shoulders, and while the wool helped shed the water, the deluge was so heavy that he could barely see Revita walking in front of him. Onward, they trudged, the dirt turning to mud that stuck to his boots. He stepped on a rock to avoid the mud, but his foot slipped, his boot stopping at the lip of the gorge. Learning from that mistake, he treaded carefully and kept his gaze on the ground to avoid any misstep. With his attention committed to his footsteps, Vic didn't notice when the others stopped, so he bumped into Revita's back.

He looked up to find the hold walls towering above him. Korrigan approached a darkly stained, wooden door and pounded on it with his mace. Moments later, a small panel in the door slid open. He and the dwarf on the other side of the door exchanged words, and the small panel closed. The door swung open and Korrigan led the party inside.

With his head down to keep the rain off his face, Vic followed. A dozen strides later, rain was suddenly no longer falling on him although the patter of it said otherwise. He lifted his gaze and looked up at a rock shelf hanging over the hold, leaving only the front quarter of the citadel open to the elements.

They stood in the heart of a plaza surrounded by buildings, all of which backed up to a cliff. The buildings were cut from stone and timber, built to last generations. All structures stood two stories tall or taller, with timber frames and slate roofs, complete with parapets on top. On the lower levels, they had buttresses and windows which framed views out onto the plaza.

Near the rear of the citadel, water spilled down from an opening in the rocky overhang and splashed into a pool. A gushing stream ran from the pool and flowed down the middle of the plaza before disappearing into an underground cave. Vic instantly connected the stream to the one flowing through the gorge. *It must go underground and flow beneath the wall.*

A dozen armored dwarves poured out of a building to one side of the plaza. They marched in pairs, the one in the lead sporting a thick, black beard and wearing a helm with a crest down the center.

"Korrigan? Arangoli?" The dwarf stopped, his gaze sweeping across the party. "I see you brought your crew, Goli, but who are the humans?"

Arangoli stepped forward and gripped the dwarf's forearm. "It is good to see you, cousin."

"Don't cousin me and think you can avoid answering my questions."

Korrigan said, "Well met, Holdmaster Orsagar. We thank you for the shelter and for your support. The humans have joined us on an urgent mission."

"What mission?"

"To reclaim Ra'Tahal."

Orsagar's expression darkened. "I know what occurred there." He shook his head. "But your numbers are not sufficient to retake the citadel."

"Against a singer and two dozen letalis warriors?" Korrigan asked.

"Two dozen?" The holdmaster snorted. "Just yesterday, Cantacar returned from there and reported that a hundred Drow now hold the citadel."

Korrigan's smile fell away. "A hundred?"

"As you know, Ra'Tahal is impenetrable. Even if you found a way beyond its fortifications, they outnumber you eight to one. Your mission is doomed." Orsagar glanced toward the pouring rain. "Perhaps we should head inside and sit by the fire, so you can dry off. I suspect you are hungry as well."

"We are starved!" Gortch replied.

Orsagar clapped the big dwarf on the shoulder. "Now, that is the Gortch I remember. Come. Let's see if we can fill you up."

VIC SAT at a long table positioned before a roaring fire. Tapestries and weapons adorned the walls of the dining hall. Darkness loomed outside the window, the interior illuminated only by an iron chandelier above the table.

He finished his plate of spiced lamb, potatoes, and buttered brussels sprouts, the latter being a vegetable he rarely ate, but a hot meal after two days of trail rations made anything sound good. The food was chased down by a swig of pumpkin ale, something he found to be a revelation. The sweet, spiced aftertaste was akin to drinking a pie for dessert.

As everyone finished eating, and the clanking of silverware on clay plates settled, Korrigan turned to Orsagar. "We need your help."

Orsagar wiped his mouth and dropped his napkin on his empty plate. "I fed you and will house you for the evening. What else would you have of me?"

Korrigan leaned forward and stared intently at the holdmaster. "Help us retake Ra'Tahal."

The request caused Orsagar to snort. "You must be daft. It is not possible."

"What if I told you we could get inside without a siege?"

Orsagar narrowed his eyes. "How?"

"Trust me. It can be done."

Orsagar stroked his beard. "If the lot of you could open the gate and allow my warriors in, perhaps it could work. But what of the singer? How do we counter his magic?"

Korrigan leaned back with a frown. "Rysildar's magic does present a problem."

Vic suggested, "What if we removed him before opening the gate?"

Revita nodded. "If we can get inside the citadel without notice, we could split into two teams. One team could go after Rysildar before he is aware of the breach. The other team would be responsible for overwhelming the Drow holding the gate and opening it for the rest of our force to enter."

Arangoli thumped his fist on the table. "I like it!"

Korrigan turned to Revita. "Will you lead the assassination team, Vita?"

"Assassination?" Vic muttered, the word tasting bitter on his tongue.

She snorted. "What did you think we would do with Rysildar? Ask him to leave?"

"I don't know. I guess I..." Vic realized she was right. While he did not like the thought of murder, if anyone deserved such an end, Rysildar's actions had earned him as much.

After a moment of quiet contemplation, Revita arched a brow. "I will lead a team, but what is in it for me?"

Vic scowled at her. "This again, Vita?"

"You are asking me to risk my life. Such risk requires reward."

He glared at her, but she returned the look with her jaw set in a challenge. "Other than it being the right thing to do?"

"Yes."

Korrigan leaned over the table and stared at her. "If you do this, Vita, I will offer you your pick of weapons from the citadel armory."

She narrowed her eyes. "What makes you think the Drow have not already raided the armory?"

"Oh, I am certain they have cleaned out the shelves of the citadel armory," Korrigan grinned. "But there is a hidden, underground chamber where we store additional weapons, armor, and enchanted relics. They do not know about that store. Even if they discover its entrance, they do not possess the key to enter it."

She arched a brow. "This armory contains items crafted of dwarven steel?"

"Always."

"It is a deal." She looked Vic in the eye. "I want you with me."

A warmth filled his chest. While proud that she would request him personally, he felt that there was more to it than that, but he was unable to identify what exactly.

She added, "I'll also need someone who is familiar with the citadel."

Vic glanced at his brother and realized that her request gave him a reason to keep Ian close during what would surely be a dangerous mission. "Ian knows it well after living there for half a year."

Revita stared at Vic for a silent beat before she nodded. "Fine. He is with us."

Truhan spoke for the first time the entire day. "Then, I am with you as well."

Vic still didn't know what to think of the strange man. "Can we trust you?"

"I will follow your orders, so long as they do not conflict with me keeping the three of you alive."

After a long, tense pause, Revita smiled. "I can live with that."

Korrigan turned to Orsagar. "How many soldiers can you spare?"

The holdmaster leaned back in his seat and crossed his arms over his chest. "There is one remaining thing we must address before I commit."

"Which is?" Korrigan arched a brow.

"I place my entire hold at risk to retake another. Some sort of compensation seems appropriate."

"Now, you sound like Revita."

"She appears to be an intelligent woman, so I will take that as a compliment."

"It was not." Korrigan sighed. "However, should you do this, West-hold will receive first claim on all weapons and armor forged at Ra'Tahal for one year."

Orsagar grinned. "I always liked you, Korrigan."

"Now that is settled, how many dwarves can you spare?"

"I can field four dozen and still leave a skeleton crew behind to protect the hold."

Arangoli blurted, "Ha! That brings our total beyond sixty against a hundred Drow warriors." He grinned. "I like those odds."

Logs burned in the fireplace at the end of the small room, the flames providing heat and dim, flickering light. Vic draped his damp cloak over a hook near the fireplace and removed his jerkin. An hour had passed since entering the hold, and even his tunic remained damp. He was about to remove it, but paused, his thoughts occupied by Revita. The woman was self-centered, coy, and frustrating, often demanding much of others while focused on her own desires. Yet, he could not stop thinking about her.

Ian undressed, stripping down to his smallclothes before hanging his clothing up to dry. He slid into one of the two beds in the room while Vic kept staring into the fire.

"What are you doing?" Ian asked.

"I..." Vic turned toward the door. "I need to step away for a bit."

Before he reached for the knob, Ian said, "You are going to see Revita, aren't you?"

Stopped before the door, his hand on the knob, Vic replied without turning around. "Is it that obvious?"

"I see how you watch her. You are never far from her side."

And what does that get me? Vic needed an answer. "That is why I need to talk to her." He opened the door. "Rest while you can. Tomorrow will be another long day."

The door clicked shut behind him. He lingered in the dimly lit corridor for a full minute before walking along it and stopping at the last door on the right. The rapping of his knuckles on the wood echoed in the silence.

"It's me," Vic said just loud enough.

"Come in," her voice came from inside.

He opened the door to a room similar to his own, the fire burning, her clothing draped over hooks near the fireplace. Propped up on one elbow, she lay in one of the two beds, her dark hair spilling over her bare shoulders. A blanket covered her body from the chest down and clung to her curves just enough to tease his memory as to what hid beneath.

She smirked. "Have you come to seduce me?"

His pulse quickened at the thought, although that was not the purpose behind his visit. *You tempt me, woman.* Still, he remained resolute. "I came to talk."

Her lip turned down in a pout. "You are no fun."

Vic crossed the room and stood over the fire. "What are we doing?"

"Talking. I thought you just established that."

"No. Me. You. This thing between us." The words seemed to flit away as he grappled for them. "What is it?"

"I thought we had an understanding. You certainly have been eager enough."

He struggled to figure out what to say, how to articulate his feelings. Ian had always been better with words, while Vic did better with actions. *Actions are what got you to this point, you idiot. It is time for words. You need to say something so she understands.* He cast his mind back, seeking the answer. It came in the form of the impressions laid upon him while growing up. His parents.

Vic spoke while staring into the fire. "My father doted on my mother, and she loved him dearly. He did anything she asked. In return, she cooked for him, washed and mended his clothing, and performed a dozen other menial tasks. When either of them needed to discuss what troubled them, the other was there to lend an ear and a shoulder. They frequently would go for walks together, and laughter often filled our small home." Turning, he found her looking up at him with a furrowed brow. "I want what they had."

"You want a woman who cooks and cleans for you?" She huffed. "I am never going to be that person."

"No," he shook his head. "I can't imagine you doing those things. The tasks are not relevant. It is the love behind them."

"I don't understand."

Vic sighed and rubbed his eyes. "I like you, Revita. Even when we are apart, I find myself thinking of you, your eyes, your laughter, your body..."

She pulled the blanket away to reveal tawny skin and not a shred of clothing. "This body?"

The tingling returned with a vengeance, his body reacting and demanding he take action. Yet, he had taken a stand and would remain vigilant until the situation between them was resolved. "As much as I would like to join you, my heart requires something more than the taste of flesh."

"What are you saying?"

"I am saying that you are going to sleep alone unless you are willing to give us a chance."

"Us?" She frowned. "What us?"

"You and me." His tone was earnest and stopped just short of pleading. "Together for more than a night at a time."

"I have been with you for the past ten days."

"Which is why I find myself needing more. I need to know you won't just disappear the moment this mission is finished. I need to know that you will let me in. That you will try to feel more than my touch or the brush of my lips against yours. If it doesn't work out, at least we will have tried."

Revita sighed. "I do not do relationships, Vic. I wouldn't even know where to begin."

"You begin by opening yourself to the idea. You follow that up with trust."

"I have always taken care of myself. Trust opens yourself up for betrayal."

"If you think I will betray you, you don't know me at all." Vic walked to the door. "Sleep well, Revita. I will see you in the morning."

He tore the door open, stepped out, and closed it behind him. In the flickering torchlight, he stood in the corridor for a long time, wishing she would open the door and pull him back inside. His wish went unfulfilled.

CHAPTER 48

INFILTRATION

The journey from Westhold to Ra'Tahal took longer than Ian had expected. After two full days of marching southwest, they set out early on the third morning with the anticipation of reaching the citadel by day's end.

The forest road connecting the two Tahal Clan holds was worn and easy to follow despite the thick forest bordering it. For the bulk of the journey, the road ran parallel to the Wellspring River, giving them a steady source of fresh water. A snaking line of sixty dwarves led the way, followed by Ian, Truhan, Vic, and Revita, the latter two strangely quiet since leaving Westhold. Something had occurred between them, and whatever it was, it left Vic in an uncharacteristically sullen mood. Ian had tried on numerous occasions to engage his brother in conversation in the hope of lifting his spirits. Vic had replied with nothing but one-word sentences and made no attempt to continue the discussion.

A trio of wagons carrying provisions brought up the rear of the procession, each towed by a pair of oxen. Considering the mess the oxen left in their wake, Ian was thankful for walking ahead of them.

It was near midday when the road turned, the trees opened, and a bridge came into view. Made of tan stone, hewn to perfection and mortared together with barely perceptible seams, it was a thing to behold. Statues of winged, humanoid creatures bracketed the bridge entrance, and as Ian passed between them, he noted the feathers covering their bodies and their pointed ears. He had no idea what kind of being they represented, but the imagery was striking. The bridge arched over the Wellspring River, spanning a gap of two hundred feet. Thick brick pillars supported the center of the bridge, built upon a small island in the middle of the river. As they passed over the peak of the arch, a fortress positioned on the lip of a bluff came into view. Near the structure, a waterfall shimmered in the afternoon sunlight.

"There it is," Ian said. "Ra'Tahal."

Vic and Revita both looked in that direction, but neither spoke.

When they descended the bridge's far side and passed another set of statues, the forest thinned. There, the dwarves gathered beneath the shade of a trio of giant oaks.

Korrigan and Arangoli hopped onto a pair of stumps and clanged their weapons against their armor. The hum of conversation settled as all eyes turned in their direction.

"We approach the citadel," Korrigan said in a loud voice. "This is where we unload the wagons and split into groups. The soldiers from Westhold will hide beneath the tarps in the wagons. Those who cannot fit in the wagons will act as an escort that the Drow are certain to keep out of the citadel, and that distraction will allow those hidden to pass through the gate.

"Orsagar and I will lead that team as we retake the lower hold and then scale the bluff," Korrigan announced. "Arangoli will lead the team who opens the bluff gate while Revita takes the fight to Rysildar. Timing is critical here. Rysildar must be dealt with by the time the bluff gate has fallen. The bluff gate must fall by the time the lower hold is recaptured and the first team reaches the top of the bluff. All must occur before nightfall. If we fail to reclaim the city before then, the entire plan is in jeopardy. Darkness gives the Drow an advantage we wish to avoid."

Arangoli clanged his hammer against his breastplate. "The dark elves have taken our city. They are vermin and must be exterminated. The Tahal Clan will not be enslaved by the likes of Drow. We are a free people. We are strong. We will fight, and we will win!"

A cheer came from the dwarves as they thrust weapons in the air. It was loud enough that Ian wondered if it could be heard in the citadel, three miles away.

"Fight at my side!" Arangoli bellowed. "Make your ancestors proud. Become the heroes our children and grandchildren honor for centuries to come!"

Again, they cheered. Even Ian found himself drawn into it, and he cheered with them. His name would be among those who rescued Ra'Tahal from the clutches of the dark elves, and he would free his own people in the process.

THE GROUP SPLIT UP, and Ian joined the team led by Arangoli. While the wagons and main force continued down the road leading to Ra'Tahal's lower hold, the humans and the Head Thumpers crossed the bridge back to the south side of the river before turning east and following a lightly tread trail running parallel to the river. A rising sense of anxiety and anticipation simmered in Ian's stomach as he hiked along the wooded trail. An hour passed before the rush of the falls rose above the crunching of leaves beneath their feet. A quarter mile from the falls, the trail turned sharply away from the river and began ascending the steep bluff.

Dozens of switchbacks had them winding as they ascended. Ian found himself repeatedly looking north, toward the fortress perched on the edge of the bluff. Although he saw no movement, it felt as if the structure watched with vigilance, wary of any approach. Much of the bluff was wooded and provided cover, but occasional gaps left them exposed to possible notice. Through those areas, they moved swiftly and did not slow until they were once again safely hidden in the shadow of the trees. A thirty-minute climb brought them to the top, where they joined another trail.

As they made their way through the forest, a palpable tension hung in the air. They walked in silence, everyone alert, weapons holstered yet ready to draw at a moment's notice.

They circled east around the field outside the citadel before stopping at the forest edge, careful to remain in the shadows of the trees while staring out at the sunlit field surrounding the citadel. The rock outcropping that hid the secret passage entrance jutted up in the middle of the open space. To reach it, they must risk possible discovery. While the gate was off to the side and barely visible from their location, they would need to hurry and minimize exposure. As Ian stared toward the quiet citadel walls, he felt a sense of dread wash over him. A difficult journey and deadly trials had brought him to this point. Somehow, he had endured them all, yet those risks paled in comparison to what he was about to face. Rysildar's dark magic and his warriors' swift and deadly efficiency remained at the forefront of his thoughts. His stomach recoiled, he turned, and vomited.

"Are you well?" Truhan asked.

Ian wiped his mouth, the aftertaste bitter and acidic. "I will be fine." He took a drink from his waterskin and turned back toward the field. Determined to rise above his fears, he said, "Let's do this."

Arangoli peered across the field. "Are you certain you can find this hidden passage?"

Pointing across the field, Ian said, "It is located on this side of that rock outcropping, behind that shrubbery."

"Very well. Lead the way. Vita, Vic, and Truhan will be on your heels.

The Head Thumpers and I will wait a beat before following. Everyone be sure to move quickly and quietly."

Both humans and dwarves nodded, their expressions resolute.

Ian took a deep breath, burst out from the forest, and ran straight toward the rocks. Although he ran as fast as he could, time seemed to slow, his gaze repeatedly going to the top of the citadel wall, searching for movement or any sign of alarm. His breath came in gasps, his heart thumping like a hammer in a forge. Finally, he drew near the shrub, slowed, and dropped to a crouch. He pulled the branches aside, eased past them, and scurried into a shadowy recess.

To Ian's relief, the hidden entrance remained open and gave him the hope that nobody had used the passage in the weeks since their escape. He held a hand in front of him and shuffled forward, into the darkness. His brother came behind him, joined by Revita. She activated her amulet and a glow illuminated their surroundings as Truhan joined them.

They stood in a small chamber at the top of a staircase, its ceiling high enough for even Vic to stand upright, but not by much.

"We go down." Ian began descending with Revita following, her hand held up to provide light. A few stairs later, the clanking of armor drew near. He glanced over his shoulder, peering past the other humans. Dwarves began to fill the chamber above, so he continued down. Soon, the entire party filled the stairwell.

At the bottom, they passed through a doorway and into a circular chamber where Ian paused, recalling the time he had followed the Drow singer and caught him working his magic with the strange crystal. *Had I done something to stop him then, the king and council would remain alive.* Another voice in his head said, *but then, Vic would still be working in the mine and you would not have the influence to set your people free.* It suddenly occurred to him how his own actions and the events surrounding him had impacted his life. Despite his own free will driving his decisions, he now had the overwhelming feeling that fate had played a hand in the outcome of each event. *Were my choices really of my own volition?* Nobody had told him what to do, where to go, or how to react, but it all had come together in a way that seemed preordained. He had read about a term to describe such outcomes. *Prophecy.* However, he never understood if a prophecy simply foretold future events or if it possessed the power to dictate the outcome.

Revita stood between Vic and his brother as the latter stared into space. "Ian?'

No response. She frowned. *Is something wrong with him?*

Arangoli pointed toward the door across the chamber. "I assume we go that way."

Vic replied "Yes. It leads to a staircase that emerges from the citadel wall."

The dwarf crossed the chamber. "In that case, I will lead from here."

The other dwarves followed, and soon, the four humans stood in the chamber alone.

Vic glanced toward Revita, his brow furrowed in concern. He put a hand on Ian's shoulder. "What's wrong?"

Ian shook his head. "I don't know. I just feel like something is going to happen."

Revita snorted. "Considering the circumstances, I certainly hope so."

"No. I mean..." His tone sounded wistful, detached. "It feels like something momentous is drawing near."

Truhan said, "Listen to your instincts, Ian. Let them guide you."

"I..."

Cries of alarm came from down the corridor, followed by silence. The four humans spun toward the corridor entrance, where darkness loomed beyond the doorframe.

Revita stepped up to the doorway, held up her charm, and peered down the corridor. Gortch stood at the rear of the group, his hand raised, his mouth open in a roar. Frozen.

She asked, "What happened to them?"

Vic appeared at her side "They aren't moving."

She rolled her eyes. "I can see that myself. The question is *why?*"

Truhan, standing at Revita's other shoulder, said, "I have seen this before. It is a trap crafted by singer magic."

"What do we do about it?" She asked.

"Find the source of the trap and undo it."

Revita frowned. "If we head down the corridor, we are likely to be caught in the spell as well."

"Very likely, yes."

Magical traps were nothing new to Revita. Determining the trigger was the first aspect of bypassing them. While angry red sparks sizzled around the dwarves' feet, nothing like that appeared where they touched the walls. "The floor appears to be connected to the effect holding them, yet the trap did not trigger until they reached the far end. What if I can bypass the floor, traverse the corridor, and disarm the trap from the other end?"

Truhan rubbed his chin. "That might work."

"I am going to try it."

Vic asked, "Try what?"

"Crossing the corridor. If I can get beyond Arangoli, I might be able to figure out what triggered the trap."

He gripped her shoulder and stared into her eyes. "Are you certain it is safe?"

"Safe is a luxury those in my profession rarely enjoy. In truth, I enjoy the challenge."

Rather than reply, he continued to hold her gaze while his hand rested on her arm.

Her tone softened. "I am flattered by your concern for me, Vic, but I trust my abilities."

In contrast, his tone hardened. "At least you trust something." He stepped back, clearly unhappy.

Revita turned and focused on the task before her. Reaching through the doorframe, she pressed her palms against the corridor walls, jumped, and spread her legs out, shifting her boots until her feet found purchase. The uneven rock of the walls offered a better grip than anticipated. She hopped forward and up with each lunging movement. By the time she reached Gortch, her crotch was inches above the dwarf's head. She continued past the dwarves, each frozen a stride behind the next, her muscles straining to maintain constant pressure. As she neared Pazacar, a burnt doorframe came into view. With lunging movement, her hands slapping against the walls, her boots finding purchase on the rough surface, she continued until reaching the doorframe. Just beyond the door stood Arangoli with one foot on the bottom step of a long staircase, his hammer in his grip.

Getting past the doorframe required her to get a solid foothold and reach through. She pressed her hands firmly against the walls and swung her legs forward before spreading them again. One last lunge brought her past Arangoli. Her hand slipped and she fell, landing with one foot on the second stair. She held her breath, concerned about the trap's magic. Nothing happened.

Then, she felt a tingle as sparks of crimson danced along the sole of Arangoli's boot where it touched the bottom step. She climbed another stair, brought her knee up, and kicked out, so her heel struck his breastplate. The dwarf tipped backward, his foot came off the bottom stair, and he stumbled into the door frame.

All at once, the dwarves in the party came to life.

"What the blazes?" Arangoli exclaimed.

She smiled. "Hello, Goli."

"Where did you come from?"

Relieved, Revita wiped sweat from her brow. "You triggered a trap.

The entire lot of you were frozen until I removed your foot from the bottom stair."

The dwarf narrowed his eyes, looked down at the stairs, and nodded. Over his shoulder, he said, "Be sure to avoid touching the bottom step."

Arangoli jumped to the second stair and climbed past Revita.

Rax, Pazacar, and others followed, none saying a word until Gortch reached the staircase.

"I always liked you, Vita," the big dwarf said. "You are not a bad lot for a human."

She arched a brow. "For a human?"

He chuckled. "You know what I mean. In fact, when this is over, you and I are waging war on a barrel of ale."

Revita grinned. "I look forward to it."

Gortch climbed over the bottom step and followed the others up, into darkness.

ARANGOLI STEPPED through the hidden door and into the streets of Ra'Tahal for the first time in years. With nobody in sight, he gestured toward the others. Dwarves burst from the opening, each holding a weapon while they glanced left and right, seeking a target.

Rax said, "There is no way we are going to make it to the gate without notice.

Stealth had gotten them inside the citadel, but with the sunlit, empty streets to traverse and an open square to cross, they would never reach the gate without notice. Arangoli nodded as he made his decision. "Since we cannot sneak up to the gate, let's use haste as our means of surprising them. Are you ready to bash some Drow heads?"

The response was a resounding "Aye!"

"Go!"

He burst into a run down the street and led his squad past the central keep, on their way to the bluff gate.

KORRIGAN RODE in the front of the wagon with a cloak over his shoulders. His mace and Orsagar's axe were both hidden under the seat and the wagon driver rode at his side, bracketed by him and Orsagar. The lower hold appeared as it had always been with smoke rising from the forges, the walls protecting the farms and dwarves who lived and worked there from the animals and monsters that roamed the forest. Despite the hold's placid appearance, he felt a sullenness emanating from the walls, as if they were saddened by the Drow infestation. *We have come to exterminate the vermin.* The thought came with a surge of anger and vitriol Korrigan was unused to. His ability to remain calm and to govern his emotions were both undwarvish and useful assets. Those traits had helped him rise in the estimation of King Arangar and had been the reason the king had placed trust in him. Quiet. Thoughtful. Balanced. Analytical. Trustworthy. Reliable. They were all terms others used to describe Korrigan. Bitter. Angry, Outraged. Vengeful. Those words described his new reality, one he sought to rectify with every bone in his body.

A train of four wagons rode behind his own. Matching the pace of the wagons, dwarven warriors marched in single file, twenty to each side. The lead wagon approached the closed portcullis, made of spiked iron bars. A half dozen dark elf archers stood on the wall above the gate. Twice that number, all armed with naginatas, blocked the way beyond the bars.

"Hold!" a Drow bellowed in Dwarvish.

The driver stopped the oxen, the noise of hooves and wheels settling as dust from the gravel swirled in the breeze.

"Why do you wish to enter Ra'Tahal?" the Drow demanded.

Orsagar spoke in a loud voice. "I am Holdmaster Orsagar from West-hold. Who are you?"

"My name is Hexadal. I am a Drow captain and lead the sixteenth phalanx of letalis warriors. Why have you come, Holdmaster?"

"These wagons are filled with chromium, required to forge dwarven steel."

"Is it usual for the holdmaster to deliver chromium himself?"

"No" Orsagar snorted. "In truth, I have never done so before. However, our last shipment was beset upon by rebel dwarves from Nor'-Tahal." Orsagar growled. "Our economy is based upon our ability to provide chromium to the Ra'Tahal forges. My people are poor, and we cannot afford another incident like the last. The warriors you see here accompany me to ensure the delivery arrives safely. I have come to offer apologies for the delay and to guarantee it will not happen again."

A quiet moment followed as the warriors behind the gates conversed.

Finally, Hexadal said, "The wagons may enter, but your escort remains outside. Have them back up a hundred strides. If any take even one step toward the wall, my archers are instructed to attack."

Orsagar stood and relayed the command. The dwarven warrior escort turned and jogged back the way they had come before assembling beyond the last wagon. The portcullis began to rise, and the holdmaster reclaimed his seat. Chains clanked as the dark elves inside the tower gate cranked the lift mechanism. When the portcullis reached the top and only the barbed spikes at the bottom remained visible, the clanking ceased. The wagon driver snapped the reins and the oxen pulled the wagon into the hold.

Additional Drow warriors emerged from the gate tower, the numbers on the ground exceeding twenty. Those warriors formed a half-circle, cutting off the wagon's advance. The driver stopped the lead wagon while the ones trailing came to a halt to its left and right, which placed all five wagons inside the gate.

Hexadal approached Korrigan's wagon. "We will inspect the wagons before you advance any farther."

Orsagar shrugged. "If you wish. It certainly doesn't matter to me."

The elf captain barked out commands and five of the soldiers broke off from the others, each one of them approaching a wagon. Korrigan tensed, ready to take action. The Drow beside him lifted the tarp and leaned in to peer beneath it. A blade flashed and pierced his eye. The injured dark elf staggered and collapsed. The tarp pulled free and six dwarves leapt from the wagon bed, armed with axes, spears, and swords. Similar groups emerged from the other wagon beds.

Hexadal bellowed something in Elvish while rushing Orsagar. Korrigan reached beneath the wagon seat, gripped his mace handle, and leapt while swinging. The mace met an enemy blade with a clang, deflecting it. Korrigan landed and brought his mace around with a low to high swing. The Drow danced backward and another warrior darted in from the side. Rather than attempt to pull back, which would take too long, Korrigan jumped forward, allowing the momentum of his swing to assist him. The enemy's naginata blade missed him by inches. Before the attacker could pull back, Korrigan came around with a downward attack. The mace smashed into the hand gripping the naginata shaft, causing the Drow to drop his weapon. A back hand swing brought Skull-crusher straight into the enemy's face, shattering bone in a killing blow. With one down, Korrigan spun to block another attack as the portcullis crashed to the ground, separating the dwarven warriors outside the walls from those within.

Orsagar shouted. "We need to take the gate tower."

Korrigan replied, "I know, but I'm busy right now." He blocked an attack from Hexadal and countered with a kick to the side of the Drow's leg, causing it to buckle. As Hexadal fell to one knee, Korrigan delivered an overhead strike, cracking the elf captain's skull. Hexadal crumpled to the ground and another Drow rushed in.

CHAPTER 49
CONFRONTATION

Ian emerged from the hidden door as Arangoli and the other dwarves rushed down a narrow street with their weapons brandished. He found himself jealous of their courage, eagerness, and confidence. All three emotions seemed so elusive to him, yet, here he was, inside a fortress held by enemy warriors and led by one who could wield powerful magic.

Vic stood at his side. "Something tells me our presence will no longer be a surprise."

"Not true," Revita said, "The dark elves don't know the four of us are here. Goli and his team will draw the attention, so we can operate in the shadows until we find Rysildar. The question is: Where do we begin?"

"I have been thinking about that." Ian pulled the hidden door closed. It clicked shut, the seams impossible to see despite the direct light of the afternoon sun. He turned from it with a destination in mind, one where he would find the answer to the question. "Follow me."

Ian scurried along the street the dwarves had just sped down with Vic, Revita, and Truhan following. He slowed and ducked into a shadow-filled alley. At the alley's far end, he leaned out and frowned when he spied Devigar's Tower. Two Drow holding naginatas bracketed the entrance.

He pulled back and said, "I don't know what to do, now."

Vic frowned. "What's wrong?"

"I wanted to visit Winnie and ask her where we can find Rysildar, but Devigar's tower is guarded."

Revita peered around the corner and pulled back. "Why would they guard it? Are they holding Devigar captive?"

Ian recalled the blood oozing out of his old master, the light in his eyes dying out. "I saw him die."

Vic asked, "Then why secure the door?"

Revita ventured, "What if it is to keep others out?"

"To protect what?" Vic asked.

"Rysildar himself."

"You think he lives in the tower?"

Unlike the central keep, the tower was a private space, separate from others. It was ideal for someone who preferred secrecy. Ian nodded. "I agree. He is in there."

Truhan drew himself up. "In that case, it is time for me to act."

"What do you intend to do?" Ian asked.

"I intend to get you inside. Be ready." The strange man walked around the corner, his cloak swirling as he strode across the open space, straight toward the two elves.

"Hold," one said in Elvish.

Truhan responded in their language. "I have come with an urgent message for Rysildar."

The two Drow crossed their weapons, barring access to the door. "None are to pass, human. Give the message here and now, and we will determine its urgency before delivering it to Master Rysildar."

Rather than reply, Truhan continued toward them. When he was two strides away, he launched himself and kicked with both feet, driving a heel into the chest of each guard. The Drow stumbled back into the door frame, snarled, and thrust. The blades on the ends of their weapons found only air as Truhan bolted.

One of the guards chased after the man while the other walked a dozen strides in the same direction and watched.

Revita burst past Ian, raced across the open space, and wound back with her dagger ready. She leapt and slammed the dagger down, driving it into the base of the dark elf's neck. The Drow collapsed in a heap.

"Vic!" She knelt and pulled the dagger free before wiping it on the Drow's leather vest. "Help me carry him inside."

Ian ran over with his brother and stopped next to the downed dark elf. His eyes were closed, his body unmoving. "You killed him."

Revita scowled at Ian. "What would you have me do? Ask him to dance?"

Vic grabbed the Drow beneath the arms while Revita lifted him by the ankles. "Open the door, Ian."

Ian opened the tower door and stepped in to find the interior much as he remembered. Despite the same furniture and décor, the building felt different, as if darkness lurked around every corner.

Revita nudged the door closed as she and Vic carried the corpse into the sitting room and placed it on a sofa. "There. If anyone comes in, they will think he is sleeping."

"Until they try to wake him," Vic said.

"True."

Ian crossed to the staircase at the edge of the room. "We need to take the stairs. He is up there...somewhere."

Vic pulled the mattock off his back, his expression grim. "Let's do this."

Revita drew a knife from her hip and handed it to Ian. "Use this to protect yourself." She then unsheathed her dagger and pulled a throwing knife from the leather band on her forearm. "Ian, take the lead. If you see the singer or anyone else, get out of the way."

" Why should Ian be in the lead?" Vic asked.

"It only makes sense, allowing us to react and fight."

"Revita is correct, Vic." Despite the churning of his stomach, Ian ascended.

The second level was dark, the kitchen, dining room, and pantry empty. Rising to the third floor, Ian found the door to his old room open, the room unoccupied and appearing no different than when he had left it weeks earlier. He approached the door to Winnie's room and knocked softly. A beat later, the door opened a crack. She peered through the opening and then yanked the door wide.

Winnie burst from the room and hugged Ian. "Thank the good spirits, you are alive."

He hesitated a beat before stroking her cinnamon hair. "I am fine, but I need you to remain quiet."

She pulled back and glanced toward Vic and Revita. "What is happening?"

Vic said, "We are here for Rysildar."

The mention of the Drow singer caused her to visibly wilt and back toward her room. In a whisper, she said, "He is a frightful, terrible person. I worry that he will do something horrible to me should I make another mistake."

Ian asked, "Where is he?"

"Upstairs."

"We will deal with him." He tried to sound confident, hoping to reassure her. "Go back in your room and remain there. This will be dangerous."

"What are you going to do to him?"

"We..." Ian struggled to say the words. "Will find a way to rid the city of him and his ilk."

She gripped his hand. "Be careful, Ian. Some dwarves thought to cross him. They gathered us into the square and forced us to watch." Her voice dropped to barely more than a ragged breath. "He burned them alive with his magic."

Ian had felt the effect of that particular spell, and the incident had scared him more than anything else he'd gone through since then. "We must do this, Winnie. Just stay out of the way. I don't want anything to happen to you."

Winnie slid back into her room. "I pray that the good spirits watch over you." The door closed and the landing fell silent.

After a deep breath, Ian turned back to the staircase. "Let's do this." With the knife held in his sweat-slicked palm, he resumed his ascent.

ARANGOLI RAN with fury filling his chest and adrenaline pumping through his veins. More importantly, he ran with purpose. Lacking purpose had caused him to languish, to drown himself in his cups, and to wallow in the shame that followed. A battle was to be fought. Fighting was in his blood. He excelled at one thing – killing the enemy. Now that he had an enemy to focus his rage upon, he found himself grinning.

He charged toward the gate, the eight dark elves posted there turning to face him. Those on the wall drew arrows and took aim. An arrow sailed at him but he lifted his arm and the buckler strapped to it deflected the shot. Another arrow loosed and Arangoli reacted, his speed and agility both exceptional for a dwarf. The arrow shattered off the buckler in a spray of splinters and feathers.

As he closed in on enemy warriors, he came to a sudden stop and launched a massive, overhead attack. His hammer crashed down and struck the plaza floor. A thump released, the ground cracked, and the enemies stumbled. A blink later, he burst forward and swung. The dark elf he had targeted raised his naginata to block the blow. The effect was akin to a twig attempting to stop an avalanche. Tremor blasted through the naginata shaft and struck the dark elf in the head, caving his skull in.

As Arangoli turned toward the next enemy, Rax loosed an arrow that pierced the Drow's arm, causing him to twist and leave himself open to attack. Arangoli's hammer struck the elf in the chest, a concussion released, and the elf launched backward, into the gate before slumping to the ground.

The gate tower door opened, and Drow poured out. Arangoli roared and charged the new batch of enemies with a mighty swing. The Drow in the lead ducked the blow, but Arangoli had expected as much. He ducked as well while spinning around another full turn. The enemy's blade sliced over him and when he came around, his hammer shattered the enemy's lower leg, causing him to collapse.

The Head Thumpers engaged. Gortch swung left and right with fury, his mace crushing bones and tossing dark elf warriors aside. Pazacar darted in and out, his staff spinning, jabbing, sweeping legs, and blocking attacks. Axes removed limbs, spears skewered bodies, and crossbow bolts downed enemies perched on the wall. The shields and armor made of dwarven steel repelled and deflected attacks, and soon, the numbers shifted in the dwarves' favor.

As quickly as it began, the fight ended when Arangoli tossed a Drow backward, into the spear held by Brannigan. The Drow fell limp, slid off the spear, and lay still.

Arangoli spun around, seeking another enemy, and disappointment set in, at seeing them all dead.. His weapon dropped to his side, his shoulders slumping as he sighed.

"What's wrong?" Gortch asked.

"That was over too quick."

The big dwarf clapped Arangoli on the shoulder. "Do not worry. These were merely the enemies guarding the gate. There are dozens of Drow to kill yet."

A grin spread across Arangoli's face. "That's right. Let's charge the tower and get this gate opened, so Korrigan and Orsagar aren't upset about missing the fun."

THE FIGHTING inside the lower hold gate was fast and frantic. Equal numbers of dwarves and dark elves soon lay on the ground around Korrigan and Orsagar, but the dwarves within the walls outnumbered the elves in the fight.

Suddenly, no enemies stood near Korrigan. He turned toward the gate tower and found the path open.

"The tower!"

Orsagar hefted his axe. "Allow me."

The holdmaster ran toward the door, wound back, and swung. The axe bit deep into the wood and wedged into place. He pressed a foot against the frame, yanked the axe free, and chopped again. The wood split. Targeting the weak point, Korrigan swung. His mace struck the door and blasted through it, leaving a hole. He peered through and saw nobody inside, so he reached in, pulled the bolt, and the door creaked open.

"Let's go," Korrigan charged into the tower and up the staircase.

Five turns and three flights up, he emerged into the tower winch room. Between him and the winch, a pair of dark elves stood ready, each gripping a naginata while blocking the way.

Korrigan growled, spun around with his mace extended, and released his grip. The mace sped across the gap, drove into an enemy's chest, and sent him stumbling back against the winch. The Drow fell to his knees, dropped his weapon, and leaned forward onto his hands as he attempted to take a breath. Orsagar charged past Korrigan and swung. His axe passed over one Drow, who ducked and thrust. The naginata blade plunged into Orsagar's stomach and out his back. The dwarven holdmaster staggered, but when the enemy tried to pull the weapon free, it remained stuck in Orsagar's body. Korrigan charged past, drove his shoulder into the Drow's midriff, and lifted him up while his legs continued to pump. The dark elf stopped with a lurch as the winch crank handle thrust into his back. Korrigan felt a crack and the Drow went limp. He dropped the enemy, who landed on the floor beside his dead comrade. Neither moved.

Korrigan pulled the lock lever and hurriedly cranked the winch. When the portcullis was halfway raised, he threw the lever again, locking it open. A roar sounded from outside as the rest of the dwarven warriors charged the lower hold.

He then turned toward Orsagar, who remained on one knee with the naginata pole sticking out from his stomach. It was a fatal wound.

"Oh, Isa." Korrigan knelt before the holdmaster, so they were both eye level.

Orsagar groaned and spoke between clenched teeth. "Don't let me die with a dirty, dark elf weapon in me."

Korrigan leaned forward and peered around Orsagar. The entire blade was coated in blood and visible behind his back. "I'll have to pull it through."

"Do it," Orsagar replied between clenched teeth.

Korrigan stood, circled the wounded dwarf, and gripped the slick shaft just below the blade. He put a boot against Orsagar's back and pulled. As the four-foot shaft slid through Orsagar, he released an agonizing howl. The weapon came free, and Korrigan tossed it aside.

Orsagar toppled over and lay on his side, his breath coming in short, shallow gasps.

Squatting beside Orsagar, Korrigan gripped the wounded dwarf's hand. "I am sorry, Orsa."

"See it through, Korri." Orsagar gasped. "Make my death count for something."

A tear tracked down Korrigan's cheek and settled in his beard. "May Vandasal grant you a seat beside him in the hall of champions."

"I...will...see you there..." the last word came out with his final breath, and then, he fell still.

〜

On the fourth level, Ian listened at the closed door but heard nothing. He gripped the knob, turned it, and eased it open. Devigar's old bedroom waited within. Although it was mid-afternoon, a gloom held the room captive, the windows covered by black curtains that had not been there when Ian lived in the tower. It was too dark to see if anyone lay in the bed, so Ian opened the door wide and moved aside. Revita crept past and made for the bed. When she reached it, she nudged the pile of covers with a knife point. No noise or reaction meant that the bed was empty.

Ian peered into the bathing room and found it also vacant. He met Revita and Vic in the middle of the room.

"There is one more floor above," Ian whispered.

"What is up there?" She asked.

"Devigar's study."

"Then, that is where we go."

Steeling himself, Ian returned to the stairwell and climbed. He turned at the landing, looked up at the door at the top of the stairs, and paused. The knife in his hand slipped, struck the step in front of him, and red sparks danced along its hilt and blade.

He jumped back in alarm. "A trap."

Revita squatted and held her hand over the blade. "It is like the one in the passage. Leave the knife and skip the bottom step."

Ian stared up at the study door, praying it would remain closed. He whispered, "What if he heard me?"

"Then, you had best be careful."

A deep breath of courage later, Ian stepped over the first stair. When his boot touched down on the second stair and nothing happened, he climbed up and continued his ascent. At the top, he pressed his ear against the door but no noise came from inside. Preparing himself, he reached for the knob and glanced back. Vic stood two stairs below with Revita just behind him. Dread filled Ian's chest, causing it to constrict so much it was difficult to draw a breath. He turned the knob, swung the door open, and stepped to the side, as he had been instructed. A blade flashed and raked across his midriff. Searing pain caused him to stagger as the blade tore him wide open. He urgently pressed his hand to the wound to hold his entrails in place. His brother shouted his name, but Vic may as well have been a thousand miles away. Ian slid down the wall, fell to a sitting position, and stared into space. The shock of receiving a horrifying, mortal wound consumed all other thoughts.

CHAPTER 50
THE GIFT

"Ian!" Vic exclaimed as his brother slid to the floor, his stomach covered in blood.

A dark elf gripping a naginata stood beyond the doorway, the blade at the end of its shaft slick with Ian's blood. Rage clouded Vic's vision, and the target of his blind hatred stood before him.

He bellowed a wordless cry and leapt forward with a wild swing. The Drow raised his weapon and blocked the blow. While Vic wound back for another, the enemy thrust, forcing Vic to twist lest he be skewered. A blade thrown by Revita sailed past and struck the dark elf in the shoulder, causing him to jerk and twist. Vic swung again, this time aiming for the enemy's exposed side. His mattock buried in the Drow's back near his armpit. The dark elf cried out and dropped his weapon. Vic pulled hard on the shaft of his mattock while the pick end remained hooked in the enemy. The Drow stumbled forward and Vic extended a leg, tripping him. The enemy sailed into the stairwell.

≈

Revita drew another throwing blade while her dagger remained ready in her other hand. She stood two strides behind Vic, perched on the upper two stairs, waiting for another opening. Then, Vic sent the enemy warrior stumbling through the doorway and straight toward her. She twisted, pressed her back against the wall and slashed as the dark elf sailed past. Her dagger bit into the enemy's neck with a spurt of blood, and then, the Drow was beyond her. He crashed to the stairs, tumbled, and settled on the landing, bloodied and unmoving.

When she turned back toward the doorway, her gaze fell to Ian, who sat with his back against the wall. One hand was pressed against his stomach while he stared into space. The wound was bad and she suspected he was moments from passing. *There is nothing you can do for him...except to make his death matter.*

She strode through the doorway and stood at Vic's side.

Like the other levels in the tower, the windows had been covered, leaving the room dark and gloomy. On the desk in the center of the study, the flickering flames of a dozen candles provided the only light. A hooded figure in black robes stood across the room, shadows swirling around him.

"I suspected you would come," the figure hissed in the human language.

Vic glanced back at Ian, who sat at the top of the stairs, just beyond the open door. His brother still breathed, but he had lost too much blood. The wound was beyond repair, his brother beyond saving. His sorrow turned to anger, the grip on his mattock tightening as he turned back to the dark elf.

Between tight lips, Vic warned, "Your evil ways will cost you."

"Evil?" Rysildar shook his head. "You misunderstand if you think my actions are evil. They are nothing but a means to a necessary end."

Despite his rage, Vic asked, "Which is?"

"We need dwarven steel to save our people."

"Save your people from what?"

"Creatures from the deep. They threaten to destroy the Drow. If that occurs, they will sweep across the land. Elves and humans will fall to them. It is only a matter of time. So, you see, I am trying to save the world."

Vic frowned and muttered, "What is this nonsense?"

Revita shrugged and whispered back, "I have no idea."

"Let's end this."

"I agree."

With a measured pace, his gaze glued on Rysildar, Vic shifted to one side. Mirroring his actions, Revita moved to the other.

I need to distract him. To do so, Vic asked "Why should we believe you?"

The singer remained still, his hood covering his face. "I speak the truth. A darkness threatens, and my people are the only thing keeping this darkness at bay."

"So, you ask us to just leave and allow you to control Ra'Tahal?"

"As long as we hold the city, we retain a steady supply of the weapons we require. Perhaps, given time, we can defeat this enemy, and the city can revert to the Tahal Clan."

Without turning his head, Vic glanced at Revita, who stood ready with a knife in each hand.

Gathering himself, Vic readied himself for an attack and charged.

Revita drew her hand back and threw. Her blade spun toward Rysildar. The singer opened his mouth and bellowed a high-pitched note in her direction. The blade stopped an arm's length away and fell. Revita froze with her arm cocked back for another throw. Like a column collapsing from a quake, she toppled to the floor as the thrown blade clattered off the stone tiles.

Rysildar turned toward Vic, now a few strides away. Again, the Drow singer released a shrieking call. Vic's body locked up, his muscles frozen in mid-stride, his momentum causing him to fall and slide past Rysildar before coming to a stop.

Rysildar lowered his hood and approached Vic, who stared into space, paralyzed and helpless. "I gave you a chance." The dark elf drew a hooked knife from his robes. "Now, you die."

SHARP, throbbing pain consumed Ian's thoughts, leaving him in a cloud of agony. Slowly, that ache dwindled, along with his strength. A numbness settled in and his surroundings eased back into focus.

He sat at the top of a staircase with his back against the wall. To one side, beyond the open doorway, his brother and Revita exchanged words with Rysildar. To his other side, a Drow warrior lay on the landing below. A cloaked figure stepped over the dark elf corpse, climbed the stairs, and knelt beside Ian.

"Truhan?" Ian asked, unsure if the man was real or if his pain had tricked his mind into a delusion.

The man gripped Ian by the wrist and pulled his hand from his midriff. "Your wound is fatal."

Ian looked down at his hand, coated in crimson. Blood matted his clothing...far too much blood. *I didn't know I had that much blood in me.* "I feel weak," he muttered. "Tired."

Truhan reached into his coat and pulled out a leather wallet. "I can save you, but it will come at a cost."

"A cost?" Thoughts were difficult to hold, like a wet fish squirming to escape his grip.

From the wallet, the man pulled out a narrow shard of red crystal. The crystal seemed to pulse, but that might have been Ian's imagination. *Is any of this real? Am I already dead?*

Truhan held out his hand while pinching the crystal between two fingers with the other. He made a quick movement, pricking his finger with the sharp point. A bead of blood appeared on his fingertip. Like the crystal, the blood seemed to shimmer with energy.

"If I do this, you and I are forever connected." Truhan warned. "You will owe me a debt. One which I will collect for many, many years."

Ian's eye lids were heavy. So heavy. "Please. I need to help my brother."

"Pledge yourself to me."

"I...do."

The man reached toward Ian's wound and thrust his bloodied finger into Ian's lacerated flesh.

Raging pain flared from Ian's midriff, the agony blinding him. A fire spread from his wound, searing through his veins and causing his heart to pump so hard, he thought it might burst from his chest. He writhed as if burning alive, the flames contained by his own flesh. Just as rapidly as the pain overtook him, it receded. His vision returned, but everything had changed.

Sparks of amber light flickered along Ian's skin. He raised his gaze to Truhan crouched before him, his gaze intense as he stared into Ian's eyes.

The man spoke softly. "Use your new gift, Ian. Save your brother."

"My gift?"

"Open yourself to it. Let it in."

Ian relaxed a tension he hadn't realized he had been holding. Energy flowed into him, seemingly boundless, until he thought he might explode. A glorious sensation washed over him, even more intoxicating than how he felt when Rina smiled or graced him with her touch. Sights, scents, and sounds all were heightened, the world strikingly more vibrant with him perfectly attuned to the endless song it sang. Never before had he felt so alive. He looked down at his hands, surrounded by an intense aura.

"Listen to me, Ian." Truhan held his hand up. A disk of light encircled it. "Look at it. Memorize it. Project it around your own hand."

Ian stared at the disk and its design spoke to him, the twisting lines forming a complex matrix surrounded by runes. It instantly felt like a language he had once known but had not used in years, so its knowledge languished in the back of his head. Seeing it, was akin to recollection, and it immediately made sense. With a thought, that same construct appeared around Ian's own hand.

"Let your power flow through it," Truhan pointed toward Devigar's study. "It is the only way to save your brother.

At the mention of his brother, Ian glanced toward the open doorway. Vic lay on the floor, unmoving. The Drow singer stood over him with a hooked dagger in his hand. Across the room, Revita lay frozen and helpless. When the dark elf squatted beside Vic and brought the dagger toward his throat, Ian reacted.

Buoyed by the power flowing through his veins, he burst to his feet and rushed through the doorway. Rysildar looked up and when his gaze met Ian's he opened his mouth and released a high note. Time seemed to slow as a burst of crimson energy shot across the room. Ian held his arm out and allowed the energy surging through his veins to flow out of him and through the construct of light surrounding his hand.

A semi-transparent shield burst from his hands, deflecting the Drow singer's attack and sending red sparks out toward the chamber walls.

Rage burned inside of Ian, fed by the power surging through his body. So much had gone wrong over the past two seasons and much of it was due to the dark elf he faced. *He killed Devigar, Arangar, and dozens of others with his actions. I nearly died, and he would have slain Vic had I not intervened. He must pay.*

With a thrust, both mental and physical, the shield burst forward, struck the dark elf, and launched him across the room. The dark curtains wrapped around Rysildar's body as he was driven into them and crashed through the window. The tinkling of shattered glass joined Rysildar's scream, which grew fainter as he plummeted. The scream stopped and silence settled over the chamber. Afternoon sunlight streamed through the broken, curtainless window, brightening the room tenfold.

Still holding onto the tingling, euphoric power, Ian strode across the room and peered through the window. Rysildar's body lay across the square, his limbs akimbo, his neck bent in an unnatural way. To Ian's enhanced vision, the body appeared dull, vacant...lifeless.

"Ian?" Vic's voice came from behind. "How?"

Ian turned to find both Vic and Revita climbing to their feet. He followed Vic's gaze to his own stomach. His clothing remained torn and matted with blood, but the wound had healed. Rather than answer, his attention turned to the man standing in the doorway.

Truhan spoke softly, his voice soothing Ian's rage. "Let it go, Ian. Should you hold it too long, especially when you are still learning, you could burn yourself out."

Simultaneously, Ian released the power he was holding while also replacing the block that allowed it to flow in the first place.

The man continued, "You three should go. Free your people, which can only happen when the citadel is cleansed of the Drow infection."

"What about you?" Ian asked.

"You and I are connected, Ian. Do not worry about me. Finish what must be done. When all is well, return here. I will be waiting."

While still confused by everything that happened, Ian felt compelled to obey. He headed toward the door and when he reached it, Truhan grabbed his arm, stopping him.

"Remember the spell you used, Ian." Even without Truhan's warning, the strange yet compelling construct remained fixed in Ian's vision. "Use it if you face trouble. For now, it will be enough to keep you safe."

Ian nodded numbly, still confused by what had occurred. He began down the stairs, stepped over the dead Drow warrior, and turned at the landing. Rapid footsteps followed, his brother and Revita catching up to him.

"What was that about, Ian?" his brother asked.

"And how are you alive?" Revita added.

Ian continued down the stairs. "I am not certain on either account."

Vic grabbed his arm, stopping him on the third-floor landing. "What you did to Rysildar...I saw him go flying out the window as if launched by a catapult, but you were still strides away when it happened."

"I know."

"How did you do it?"

"I don't know." Ian struggled to explain it, so he did so in the simplest of terms. "It was some sort of...magic."

Revita snorted. "Humans don't control magic."

"I am aware, but I did it all the same."

"Can you do it again?" she asked.

Without removing the block holding it at bay, Ian felt the wellspring of energy trying to get in. "Yes." He knew it with certainty.

"Well, that could come in handy."

Vic frowned at her. "My brother almost died up there."

"Your point?"

"I..."

Ian shook his head. "I am not your responsibility, Vic. I told you this before, and I'll say it again. If I place myself at risk, it is my choice. I am your brother, not your child or your slave."

After a long beat, Vic nodded. "I know."

"Let's go tell Winnie that the building is safe. Then, we will see if the dwarves need help securing the city."

CHAPTER 51

SURRENDER

With the lower hold under the dwarves' control, Korrigan led the remaining Westhold warriors into the mines. They came upon a cluster of four dark elves and attacked, taking two by surprise and overwhelming the others with sheer numbers. Determination had taken hold, and in Korrigan's mind, there would be no option for the usurpers to surrender. The Drow would be exterminated like vermin after an intolerable infestation.

They reached the forges, where metal wrights and spell wrights worked their magic beneath the watchful eyes of Drow warriors. Crossbow bolts took out the dark elves posted on the ledge overlooking the workspace, and those stationed on the workshop floor were slain by dwarven warriors armed with spears, swords, and axes. The dwarves working in the forge area were freed before Korrigan moved along.

When his party reached the lift, Korrigan issued orders, sending a squad of dwarves deeper into the mine to free the humans working there and kill any Drow still lurking in the tunnels. He stepped onto the lift while dwarves gathered around him, their expressions grim. In moments, the platform was crowded, he and twenty-four warriors packed tightly together while the lift climbed a shaft of smooth rock. Nobody spoke. Among them, every spear, axe, or sword blade was coated in crimson. It had already been a bloody affair and the main Drow force still waited in the upper hold.

The lift stopped. They stepped off, walked out of the tunnel, and began ascending the staircase carved into the cliffside. *I pray Arangoli has control of the gate,* Korrigan thought. If not, he and the other dwarves in his party would be ripe targets, exposed with nowhere to hide.

A FRANTIC BATTLE took place in the bluff gate tower as dwarves and dark elves fought for control of the winch chamber.

Arangoli swung a broad swipe, and the Drow opposite from him leapt back. His war hammer struck the wall and sent shattered rock spraying out. The enemy thrust, but a backhand swipe with Arangoli's buckler deflected the attack. With a one-handed swing, Arangoli brought the hammer down on the dark elf's forearm, breaking bones and causing the enemy to drop his naginata. Leaping forward while delivering another backhand blow, Arangoli's buckler smacked the enemy in the side of the head with enough force to take him off his feet. The Drow hit the floor hard and slid into the wall.

Spinning around, Arangoli stood ready for another attack. None came. Pazacar stood over a downed elf while Rax pulled his rapier from the chest of another. Gortch lifted two fallen enemies by the hair and smacked their heads against the floor with a resounding crack. When he released his grip of their hair, they lay still.

"Was that really necessary?" Arangoli asked.

The big dwarf shrugged. "Can't be too sure with these vermin. Dead is not as good as really dead when it comes to a Drow."

"You'll hear no argument from me on that account." Arangoli pointed across the room. "Gortch, I need you to open the gate while Rax and Pazacar hold the room. Bar the door leading out to the top of the wall, so nobody comes in that way. When you are finished, come back down."

"Where are you going?" Gortch asked as he began to crank the winch.

"I am going to meet Korrigan and Orsagar. Since the lift limits how many soldiers he can bring at a time, there will be another wave. When the first force is inside, I will lead them toward the keep. You three can follow with the next group."

The heat of battle still raged in Arangoli's veins and the intoxication of it all buzzed his head while he descended to the ground level. He emerged from the tower door as Korrigan and two dozen ragged and bloody dwarven warriors strolled through the gate.

Arangoli met Korrigan with a nod. "It is good to see you made it."

"It is even better to see that you hold the gate."

"Where is Orsagar?"

Korrigan's face darkened. "Dead."

While Arangoli had never been close to his cousin, the loss still stung, but the time for mourning would come later. "I see two dozen came with you. How many others survived?"

"Perhaps fifteen in addition to eight who are too wounded to fight."

"Gortch, Rax, and Pazacar are holding the winch room and will wait to ensure the remaining warriors reach the upper hold safely. In the meantime, let's make for the keep."

"Aye." Korrigan waved. "To the keep!"

Arangoli gestured and the Head Thumpers joined him as he and Korrigan strode purposefully across the square. The central keep loomed ahead, blocking the end of the street. No movement was visible until Drow archers emerged in pairs and soon occupied the keep's lower balconies. In moments, two dozen archers were in position. The front door opened and dark elves gripping naginatas stormed out. Far more than expected.

Both Arangoli and Korrigan stopped halfway between the gate and the keep, the warriors behind them doing likewise.

"How many Drow did Orsagar say occupied the citadel?"

"A hundred."

"We killed two dozen already," Arangoli noted.

"And we slayed at least as many," Korrigan said.

"Then, why do I count more than a hundred enemies remaining?"

"It appears Orsagar got the numbers wrong."

"Too bad he is dead, because I'd like to wring his neck about now." Arangoli hefted his hammer, its weight a reassurance that instilled him with confidence. "The odds don't look good."

"No, they don't," Korrigan agreed in an even tone.

"Do you suggest we surrender?"

The reply came out as a growl. "Never."

"So, we are going to fight them anyway?"

His expression grim, Korrigan nodded. "We must. They cannot be allowed to hold our city any longer."

Arangoli grinned. "I was hoping you would say that." He raised his hammer high and roared. "For Clan Tahal!"

The dwarves behind him echoed his cry. With Arangoli in the lead, they charged toward the enemy force.

IAN OPENED the door to Devigar's tower and stepped outside, where he was met by the cries of battles. Down the street from where he stood, a frantic confrontation took place outside of the central keep. The square adjacent to the building was thick with dark elves and dwarves engaged in battle. The clash of steel on steel echoed from the crowd. While every dwarf in sight fought furiously, half of the dark elves had yet to engage. A contingent of Drow broke off from the main force and circled the battle.

Vic said, "They are surrounding the dwarves."

Revita added, "Who are outnumbered."

When Vic strode toward the battle, Revita gripped his arm, stopping him.

"What are you doing?" she asked.

"I need to help them."

"The dwarven warriors are too few. One more weapon on our side won't make a difference."

"You expect me to just let them be slaughtered? They are our friends, and if they die, my people will never be freed. We did not come this far to fail."

During the conversation, Ian stared at the battle while flexing his hand. His body still tingled with the memory of the magic that had coursed through him. He longed to experience that euphoria again. Rather than continue to resist, he opened himself to the power. It flooded in, warmed his blood, enhanced his vision, and made his head buzz as if he had just downed three tankards of ale.

With a thought he recalled an image he had committed to memory. The construct of light reappeared around his outstretched hand – the same construct he had used against Rysildar. The magic flowed out of Ian, through the construct, and a shield formed. Confident, defiant strides carried Ian and his shield across the square and toward the enemy. He spread his hands and applied thought, his will altering the shape of the shield until it formed a ridge down the center, creating a wedge. As the shield reached the rear of the enemy force, it pushed them aside. Dark elves stumbled and turned toward Ian with confusion on their faces as the shield forced them backward. Numerous Drow hacked, slashed, and stabbed at the invisible shield, to no avail.

The front of the wedge reached the dwarves, and Ian stopped. He then flipped his palms so they faced away from each other and spread his arms slowly. In reaction, the shield split and the separate sections pushed the dark elves away from the dwarves. One by one, they stopped fighting, backing away instead, with confused expressions.

Ian shouted in Elvish. "Throw down your weapons! Surrender or suffer!"

When the enemy warriors did not respond, Ian gathered himself and released a burst of energy. In rapid succession, the two shields blasted into the Drow warriors, knocking dozens off their feet and creating two piles of twisted limbs and weapons. He then pointed toward the ground, formed another shield beneath his feet, and added depth to it. His feet, standing on the expanding shield, lifted off the ground. In moments, he was ten feet up, appearing as if he were hovering in the air to anyone else. The last of those fighting stopped and, like the others, turned their attention toward Ian. Confusion, dropped jaws, and gaping eyes marked the faces of dwarf and elf alike.

"Withdraw. This battle is over," Ian demanded. "Rysildar is dead, and his plans now die with him. This citadel belongs to Clan Tahal. All Drow will surrender, or you will die as well."

The dark elves exchanged looks in a long, tense moment. Whispers of wonder and a word Ian had never heard before came from many of the Drow. Then, one knelt. Another joined him. Soon, all were kneeling.

Arangoli, standing amid a dozen dead dwarves and twice that number of elf corpses furrowed his brow. "I don't get to smash any more heads?"

Ian shook his head and replied in Dwarvish, "Not today." He gestured. "Confiscate their weapons. We will walk them to the gate and send them on their way."

The dwarves began collecting weapons as the thunder of footsteps came from down the street. Gortch, Rax, Pazacar and fifteen other dwarves rushed into the square and came to a stop.

Gortch dropped his mace to his side and frowned. "Are you flying Ian?"

His mood still sour, Ian ignored the question. "I am ending this conflict. Too many have died already."

"We missed the fight?"

"You did," Ian replied. "Now, help the others to disarm the Drow from their weapons."

The big dwarf sighed. "You are no fun."

Ian relaxed his spell and lowered himself to the ground before snuffing his magic. The world dulled in every sense and left him an empty shell.

Vic appeared at Ian's side. "What happened to you Ian? First, you destroy Rysildar, and now this."

"I did what I had to do, Vic. Nothing more."

His brother frowned, unhappy with Ian's response, but he did not press further. Instead, he asked, "What was that word the Drow used when they saw you?"

"Barsequa," Ian said.

"What does that mean?"

"It means," Ian translated in his head before speaking it aloud, "One who is gifted."

Pazacar approached Ian. "We dwarves have a word with the same meaning."

"Which is?" Vic asked.

"Wizard."

"Wizard," Ian repeated the word before testing the elvish translation. "Barsequa."

Vic's question then replayed in Ian's head. *What happened to you Ian?* The true answer to that question was one he had not wanted to share. Truhan had done more than save his life. Somehow, the gift of his blood had changed something inside Ian, something significant. Nothing would ever be the same.

CHAPTER 52

SACRIFICE

Shria-Li cracked the bedroom door open and peered inside. Soft, golden light seeping through the gap in the curtains illuminated the room to reveal Safrina lying in bed. Quietly, Shria-Li crept into the room and stared down at the sleeping woman with sadness in her heart.

Over the weeks since her arrival in Havenfall, the young human woman and she had formed a bond of sisterhood. For the first time in her life, Shria-Li had gotten a taste of what it would be like to have a sibling, albeit one who was required to act as her attendant. To know she may never see Safrina again filled her with sorrow and regret. Such feelings did not alter the facts. Raised as an heir to the throne, Shria-Li had always known she would be required to make sacrifices for the good of her people. She just never expected the sacrifice to hurt so much and to happen when she was so young. *The truth has no agenda*, she reminded herself. *All you can do is face it and respond as required.* Although Shria-Li had decided otherwise, she briefly considered waking Safrina and begging her to come with her. It would be a selfish act, and one she promised herself she would avoid. Thus, she bent, brushed her lips against Safrina's forehead, and turned to the door. With care, she snuck out, crossed her apartment, and stepped out onto the balcony.

The palace had been Shria-Li's home her entire life. Growing up in such splendor came with a price. It had been her prison as well. As a result, she had often dreamed of escaping and how it might be done. For years, she had watched the guards, their movements, their posts, and their rotations. The result was a plan formed years earlier, one she never thought she would test. Until now.

Standing beside a rope tied to the rail, she peered over the balcony and surveyed the garden, bathed in the soft, golden light emitted by the Tree of Life. Minutes passed with nothing moving until a pair of armored guards emerged from an arch to her left. The guards moved at a measured pace as they circled the garden, following paths through the flowering tree before fading beneath another arch on the opposite side.

Hurriedly, Shria-Li squatted, lifted the coil of rope from the balcony floor, and tossed it over the rail. The rope unwound and it plummeted, the knotted end beside her holding firm. The far end fell into a shrub with a rustle of leaves and snapping of twigs. Shria-Li froze and strained to hear if any had taken notice. Moments passed without movement or any cry of alarm. She exhaled, scooped up the pack of provisions, and slipped it over her shoulder. With the rope in her grip, she lifted one leg over the railing and then the other. Fifty feet below her, the shrub-covered ground waited. She stepped off, wrapped her ankles around the rope, and began lowering herself hand over hand. A rapid descent was needed to avoid notice. Moments later, she slid between two shrubs and her feet touched down. The rope would be a telling sign as to what became of her, but with any luck, it would not be found until morning. She slipped between the shrubs, reached the paved path, and scurried after the guards.

Two sets of arches brought her to the palace exterior. She stepped out and then hurriedly ducked back behind the wall upon seeing the guards continuing their round, their backs facing her. After waiting for a few beats, she hurried out, ducked behind a hedge, and followed it to the palace's outer wall.

The wall stood three stories tall with ancient oaks, over a hundred feet tall, growing alongside it. Like the other trees in Havenfall, the bark and leaves shone with a golden aura. That light increased the risk of discovery, and her window of opportunity would be small. She peered through the hedges as another pair of guards approached. At the hedges, they turned and followed the path leading back toward the palace garden. As soon as their backs faced her, Shria-Li crept over to the base of the nearest tree spread her arms and gripped the thick bark of the giant oak. Her fingers found purchase and she pulled herself up. The going was slow, and it took several minutes to reach the first branch, twenty feet up. She pulled herself onto the branch and scrambled to the next. When she was thirty feet up and above the palace wall, she shimmied along a branch, took a breath of courage, and leapt.

Shria-Li landed on the wall, stumbled a step, and her momentum took her over the far edge. She twisted as she fell and slapped her hands at the top of the wall, getting a grip just in time. Her legs swung against the wall and she hung there for a breath before letting go.

The drop was far enough for her to be injured if anything went wrong. Curling up as she plummeted, she landed on her back in a shrub, snapping branches before her momentum stopped, the pack on her back taking the brunt of the fall. The noise was far louder than she would have wished.

A voice came from the other side of the wall. "Did you hear something? It was that way."

Rapid footsteps came toward Shria-Li, who remained still. The footsteps slowed just strides from where she lay. Tense moments passed as two guards crept toward her, the concern of being caught causing Shria-Li to hold her breath.

A hoot echoed in the quiet night just before an owl burst from the branches of the oak she had just vacated. The giant bird soared over where she lay and drifted out of sight.

"I don't see anything," a male voice said.

The female guard replied, "It must have been that owl. Perhaps it snatched a rodent from some shrubs."

The guards turned and walked off. Only when they were a dozen strides away did Shria-Li gasp for air.

Blessed by such fortune, Shria-Li said a prayer of thanks to Vandasal before slowly rising from the shrub. The sleeve of her coat was torn and there was a small rip in her breeches. Other than scratches, she was unharmed. In a crouch, she slunk off, away from the palace and toward the city outskirts.

CRAWLING to stay out of sight, Shria-Li carefully peered up over the surrounding shrubs. The branchless trees that made the barrier protecting Havenfall stood fifty feet away, across the open expanse of rock. Beyond the tree line was the cliff edge and then darkness.

A trio of guards walked along the trees in quiet conversation. They passed her position and continued on. The moment they were far enough from where she hid, Shria-Li rose to a crouch and ran, taking care to step lightly, as only elves can do. She repeatedly glanced in the guards' direction, fearing one might look backward. None did.

The cliff edge drew near, so she slowed until she could peer over it. A frightening drop waited just a stride from where she stood. She walked along it until she came to a crevice, its angle steep but not impossible to climb. Turning to her stomach, she eased into the crevice, and began her descent. In seconds, she was hidden from view and the only remaining risks lay in falling or some creature in the Vale deciding she was prey.

The climb down would consume the rest of the night and likely last well into the morning, but by then, Shria-Li would be masked by the cliffside and be beyond discovery. She was free from her palace prison and the life prescribed for her, but those were not the reasons for her desperate escape. Such an act was driven by duty to her subjects. Prophecy told her that her curse would destroy her city and bring a dark end to the Sylvan people. The dark ability lurked inside her. The only way to prevent it from bringing doom to Havenfall was to remove it and herself with it.

She continued down the crevice until it came to a ledge. Shuffling along it while descending at an angle, she reached a tree growing on the cliffside. The tree provided hand holds while the jagged cliff face offered footing as she continued her descent.

Soon, I will be far away and will no longer threaten Havenfall with my presence. Where she would go, she was uncertain. She only knew that when her disappearance was discovered, her father and his guards would conduct an exhaustive search, first in the city and then the lands beyond. They would never look in the Vale, which is why she chose to go where no sane elf ever ventured.

CHAPTER 53
ANSWERS

Morning sunlight streamed through the stained-glass windows in the wall above the statue of Vandasal, bathing the temple interior with a myriad of colors. The skylight above the temple dais remained broken. Through it, scattered, wispy, white clouds were visible in the pale blue sky.

The building teemed with conversation. Dwarves filled half of the recessed seating as every surviving member of Clan Tahal was in attendance. Not long ago, every seat would have been occupied with little effort. Gahagar's war remained the primary cause of most of those vacancies, but the situation had only grown worse with Rysildar's betrayal. When those seats would ever be filled again, Vic was uncertain. Secretly, he worried that it might never happen.

Vic stood to the side of the dais, at the front of the temple, dressed in a new coat especially crafted for him by a dwarven tailor. The coat was made of black fabric, trimmed out with gold buttons and red and gold dragons on the shoulders. A narrow stream of flames ran down the arms of the coat, appearing like stripes with extra flair. The coat seemed ostentatious, but Vic had to admit he cut a dashing figure in it.

To his side stood his brother. Instead of a new coat, Ian had requested robes, as he had worn during his time as Devigar's apprentice. Draped in black with silver and red on the cuffs, hem, and lapel, Ian also appeared distinguished. In his brother, Vic sensed a gravity he had lacked before. With a serious expression, Ian stared into space, his thoughts elsewhere. The magic he had displayed the prior day remained affixed in Vic's mind. He had found it stunning, bewildering, and a little frightening and suspected others felt the same.

Revita hovered at Vic's other side, still dressed in her old leather coat. Beneath the coat, she wore a newly crafted, dark red tunic. The tunic was loosely laced and left enough cleavage visible to tug at Vic's attention. She had said little to him since their argument in Westhold and even less since the battle. That left Vic with a twisted mess of emotions, ranging from desire to frustration, bound up inside of him.

In an effort to think of anything besides her, he recalled his first visit to the temple, when his people were sentenced to a life of slavery. Two seasons and more had passed since then, including his harrowing escape from the deep and sweltering lava pit far below the temple. Death and destruction had taken root in the holy building that day, and he hoped nothing like that would come again, especially on this day.

Drums began to beat, the steady thumping, as if the temple itself had come to life and those inside were listening to the beat of its heart. The chatter quieted, and the priest of Vandasal emerged from the antechamber at the other side of the dais from where Vic stood. The dwarven priest wore white robes with a gold and red stole, his pointed white hat covered in shimmering, golden symbols. He stopped on the dais and the drums fell silent.

"We gather today to mourn the loss of many. A cloud darkened the halls of this citadel for weeks. Some would say that the cloud arrived years or even decades ago and the bleakness merely attained a new level with the Drow occupation. From the deaths of King Arangar and the council, to those who gave their lives yesterday to regain our freedom, the Drow have much for which they must answer. Yet, I beg you to resist going after them in a quest for vengeance. Such a choice would only begin another war. The last persisted for five decades, and over that time, our race gradually dwindled until only a pale shadow remained of what it once was. Now is not the time for war. It is the time for rebirth, renewal, and renewed hope. For today, we crown a new king.

"Captain Korrigan, come forward."

Korrigan, dressed in full armor with his helm under his arm and his mace on his hip, strode down the raised center catwalk. He circled the pit opening and stopped before the dais. A cleric in gold robes walked in from the side of the chamber with a pillow upon which rested a crown, the same crown recently worn by Kind Arangar. The high priest lifted the crown from the pillow and held it up to the statue behind the dais,

"Oh, Vandasal. We pray that you will watch over and guide our new king, so he may govern with wisdom and lead Clan Tahal to a glorious future." He turned toward Korrigan. "Kneel."

Korrigan bent to one knee.

"Korrigan the first, by the grace of Vandasal, I crown you King of Clan Tahal and ruler of all her lands."

The crown nestled on Korrigan's head. He rose to his feet and turned to the crowd.

The high priest shouted. "Long live the king!"

A thousand dwarves bellowed the sentiment. When the crowd quieted, the high priest retreated to the back of the dais and Korrigan took his spot in the center. Facing the audience with his chest thrust out proudly, he addressed his subjects.

"Welcome, Clan Tahal. Once again, you are free people. As long as I wear the crown, no dwarf shall suffer the control of another." The crowd cheered. When it quieted, Korrigan continued. "Now that you have experienced the distaste of enslavement, I suspect you will agree with my first decree." He took a deep breath and spoke with a bold tone. "From this moment, all human slaves in the control of our clan are to be set free. Those humans are welcome to remain members of our society... as equals. If they so choose, they are free to leave and will be given provisions including clothing, food, and water to aid them in their journey to wherever they wish to live."

When Korrigan looked in his direction, Vic nodded, acknowledging that the dwarf turned king had lived up to his promise.

The king resumed his speech. "As you know, I was in the citadel when it was captured by Rysildar and his letalis warriors. I escaped with Vargan Quartzite and Ipsegar Ironbend, and we set off to find help to free our people. However, we did not leave the citadel alone. Two humans were involved in our quest from the start, and a third joined along the way. Without these three heroes, the quest would have failed. Today, we honor Victus Carpenter, Revita Shalaan, and," Korrigan frowned. "Barsequa Illian."

The name seemed to taste strange on the dwarf's lips. Vic could not blame him. He might never get used to it, even though Ian now insisted his old name would no longer do when it came to public interaction.

The king continued, "Not only have these humans earned a permanent place among our clan, but they will each receive a medal forged of dwarven steel and enhanced by a spell wright." He turned toward them. "Vic. Ian. Revita, please come forward."

The trio crossed the floor and stopped before the dais while the cleric carried a small wooden chest out and stopped beside the king. Korrigan opened the chest and removed an amulet. He spread the cord and slipped it over Vic's head before letting it drop against his chest. The dwarven king repeated the act with Revita and Ian.

Korrigan then said, "I hope you will consider dining with me this evening."

"I would be honored," Vic replied.

"I as well," said Revita.

"Thank you, Korrigan," Ian replied, "But I must follow through on a promise that requires otherwise of me."

The dwarf king's brow furrowed. "You are leaving?"

Ian gave a firm nod. "I am."

Vic began to ask, "Where are you..." He stopped in mid-question. Although he wanted an explanation, he realized it was not the time for such a discussion.

Korrigan gripped Ian's forearm and gave it a friendly shake. "We will miss you, Ian."

"I may be back. Who knows what the future holds?"

"Indeed. Now, if you three will step aside, I have additional announcements to make."

As requested, Vic, Ian, and Revita reclaimed their positions to the side of the dais while Korrigan called for Arangoli and the other Head Thumpers to come forward. All the while, Vic repeatedly glanced at his brother, whose mind seemed to be elsewhere.

IAN WALKED out of the temple and looked up at the sky to find the sun nearing its apex. *It is almost time.*

His brother stopped beside him while dwarves headed down the streets in all directions as they returned to their shops and homes.

"Why are you leaving?" Vic asked.

He turned to Vic. "I am sorry I didn't tell you. I didn't want you to try to talk me out of it. If it makes you feel better, I will not be alone. Truhan will be with me."

"Truhan?" Vic furrowed his brow. "Where are you two headed?"

"In truth, I don't know." The lack of knowing irritated Ian, but he did his best to hide that irritation.

"I don't understand."

"There is much we don't understand, but that does not make it any less real."

"Now you are speaking in riddles."

Ian smiled. "I know. Infuriating, isn't it?"

Vic laughed.

When his brother's laughter subsided, Ian began his explanation. "As you know, I came within a breath of dying yesterday."

With concern in his eyes, Vic nodded. "I thought I had lost you."

"It was a close thing. When I thought I might slip into sleep and never wake, Truhan appeared and saved me."

"How?"

"I...can't explain it." *How does one explain the impossible?* Ian didn't understand it himself, but he had a sense that the details needed to remain private. He continued, "However, when he did so, he made me promise I would commit myself to him. I am to meet him at noon. We are leaving together."

Vic's brow furrowed at Ian. After a long, silent beat, he asked. "And you don't know where you are going?"

"He would not say."

"How long will you be gone?"

"I don't know." Since Ian did not have answers for Vic's questions and wished to be finished with them, he asked one of his own. "What about you?"

Vic glanced toward Revita, who stood a dozen strides away while speaking with Arangoli. "I..." The sentence remained incomplete.

"Do you love her?" Ian asked.

"I...don't know yet." With his gaze still affixed on Revita, Vic added, "I think I could, if she would allow herself to feel the same."

"You should talk to her."

"I have."

Ian patted his brother on the shoulder. "Do it again. Life is too short to wait."

Vic turned toward him and nodded. "I will try."

"If you decide to leave Ra'Tahal, tell Korrigan. If I return here and find you are gone, he will guide me, so I can find you again."

"I will do that."

Ian peered toward Devigar's tower. The broken window on the top floor was a reminder of what he had done. Rysildar deserved to die, but the weight of the Drow's death wore heavily on Ian's soul.

Vic clapped a hand on Ian's shoulder. "Be well, Ian. No matter what happens, we are brothers, and I have your back."

"Thank you, Vic. Tell Revita I said goodbye. If you see mother, let her know that I am well and that I will find a way to visit her when I am...allowed."

Ian walked off, refusing to look backward, afraid that he might cry. *You are no longer that scared boy. You are a man. You are a...wizard.* Even in his own mind, the term felt strange. He still didn't understand what his newfound power would bring or what was possible, but the change had been significant. His only worry, at what cost?

Devigar's tower loomed above him as he approached the door. The door swung open just before he touched the knob. A shapely redhead stood inside the entrance, her eyes lighting up when she saw him.

"Hello, Winnie," he said.

"Welcome back, Ian." She smiled. "Master Truhan said you were to arrive now."

"He knew?"

"Yes. He seems to know...much." Winnie backed up to allow him past.

Ian stepped inside. "If you have not heard, the dwarves have a new king who decreed that everyone from our village was to be set free."

"Free?" Her green eyes blinked in surprise.

His voice took on a tone of encouragement. "You can go and live where you like."

She frowned. "I have no family. Where would I go?"

"That is up to you. Of course, you can choose to remain here if you like."

"Here?"

"This tower..." Ian still could not believe it. "Has been promised to me by King Korrigan. I must leave for a while, but while I am away, you could remain here and take care of it for me. The food and provision needed will be supplied by the citadel, there will be no charge for room or board."

She smiled. While not equal to Rina's, her smile was nice and made her eyes sparkle. "I would like that."

He placed a hand on her arm. "I know I can trust you."

Her brow furrowed. "You said that you are leaving. Where do you go?"

"Somewhere with Truhan. For how long, I do not know."

"He is upstairs, waiting for you."

A deep voice came from the stairwell as Truhan descended to the main floor. "He is right here, ready to leave."

Ian dipped his head, "Hello, master."

Truhan smiled. "Respect. Very nice. It has been far too long." The man gestured toward a pack leaning against the wall. "Is that it?"

Winnie said, "Yes. I packed it with provisions as you requested."

"Well done." He turned to Ian. "You will carry the pack. We need to strengthen your body and that begins with you acting as a pack mule."

"My body?"

"Your new ability requires a strong mind, but if your body fails, what good is your mind?"

Ian sighed. "Fine."

"You have said your goodbyes?"

"To Korrigan, Arangoli, and my brother, yes."

"Good. Then, let's be off."

Ian turned to Winnie and saw the sadness in her eyes. "I must go."

She stepped closer to him and rubbed his arm. "I never thanked you for getting rid of the Drow. Working for Rysildar..." A tear tracked down her cheek. "Every day was worse than the last. I feared he might kill me a dozen times over."

"Well, he is dead and his ilk were chased out of the citadel. I highly doubt they will ever return."

Winnie burst forward and wrapped her arms around him, squeezing tightly. Her body pressed against his caused his pulse to race. She bent her neck back, peered at him with tears in her eyes, and then pressed her lips against his. Her soft, wet lips suckled on his for a moment that ended all too soon.

"Goodbye," she croaked through the tears in her voice before turning, lifting the hem of her skirts, and racing up the stairs.

The room fell silent.

"What was that?" Ian muttered as a confused mess of emotions roiled inside him.

Truhan snorted. "If you must ask, then you are not as observant as I thought. Do not worry about her. Humans are resilient, and she will be safe here in this tower." He gestured. "Grab the pack and waterskins. It is time we departed."

Ian bent and hoisted the pack over one shoulder. Over the other, he draped the waterskins before following his new master out the door and pulling it closed. He stopped outside the tower in a moment of reflection. It felt as if one chapter in his life had just ended and another was about to begin.

He turned to Truhan. "Now, can you tell me where we are going?'

"First, we go to the lower hold." Truhan walked down the street.

Ian scurried to catch up to his master. "Then what?"

"We head west." The man said it as if it were such an obvious fact, it needed no further explanation.

Despite the evasive answers, Ian was unwilling to give up. "For how long must we travel west?"

"Until we reach our destination."

Ian rolled his eyes and fought to corral his patience. "Which is?"

"You ask a lot of questions."

"That is because you are poor at answering them."

"Actually, I consider myself quite skilled at it."

"But you keep avoiding a direct answer."

"Exactly."

Ian sighed. "Is everything going to be this difficult?"

"No. Most of what you will soon face will be far more complex. I suspect the trials to come will push you beyond anything you thought possible."

The east gate came into view, the portcullis raised and a half dozen dwarven warriors guarding it.

"I have been meaning to ask you something," Ian said.

"It seems you ask something every time you open your mouth," Truhan noted.

"This is something specific."

"And the other somethings have been random? How odd."

Resisting another sigh, Ian asked, "Why me?"

Truhan waved at the guards as they passed through the gate and continued down the platform overlooking the lower hold. Beyond its walls, forest stretched out with distant peaks defining much of the horizon. The man stopped at the top of the staircase and peered into the distance. Ian settled at Truhan's side and waited, sensing an answer was coming.

When Truhan spoke, his typical smirk was nowhere to be found. "Your gift for language proves that your mind is suited for comprehending and memorizing things beyond what is possible among most humans."

While the response gave Ian a sliver of insight, he remained unsatisfied. "What about elves? They seem intelligent."

"Elves cannot do what is required. Only humans are capable." He turned to Ian and arched a brow. "Do you truly wish to know where we are headed?"

Ian suspected a trick. "It would be nice, but I suspect a catch."

"There is always a catch." Truhan pointed toward the horizon. "Do you see that solitary peak?"

It was the tallest mountain in sight, positioned to the northwest with a significant gap between it and the next mountain to the north or south.

"Yes."

"It will be your new home."

"I am to live on a mountain?"

"*In* the mountain would be more accurate."

Ian had spent time in caverns and tunnels, and while he would miss the sun and the beauty of nature, it hardly seemed like a horrible life. "What is the catch?"

"Well, we must first cross the length of the Agrosi to reach it."

Images of the troll battle flashed in Ian's mind, followed by the herd of horses led by a unicorn and its confrontation against a trio of were-cats. The Agrosi had proven a wild and dangerous place, yet during his last visit, he did not wield the power he now controlled. Also, he had not met Truhan until after he had crossed the plains and visited Nor'Tahal.

"Let's be off," Truhan said. "We have a long way to go and must walk the entire way." The man began down the staircase.

Ian hurried after him. "Can we not purchase a horse or something?"

"Horses are expensive." Truhan paused. "Do you have gold?"

"I have no coin," Ian realized.

"Then, we walk."

Down the staircase they went. The pack on Ian's back already felt heavy and he worried it would only grow heavier as the day advanced.

CHAPTER 54
A PRIZE FOR THE FUTURE

Vic finished the roasted pork, swallowed, and popped the last piece of baked bread into his mouth. Traces of beans and potatoes remained on his otherwise clean plate. A deep swig of ale helped the food slide down his throat, the bubbles tingling his tongue. A burst of air came back up, and he belched. The result was far louder than anticipated.

"Good one," Arangoli slapped Vic on the back. "We will make a dwarf out of you yet."

Despite himself, Vic grinned. He genuinely liked the boisterous, brash, and headstrong dwarf. "You may be a bad influence, but if you can turn me into a dwarf, you wield some mighty powerful magic."

All twelve dwarves seated around the table laughed. Even Revita smirked. Smiles had been rare from her over the recent days, and Vic found that he had missed them.

Korrigan sipped his ale and leaned back, his plate clean as well. "If nothing else, I will eat well as king."

Revita smirked. "Careful, or you'll end up larger than Gortch."

"Ho!" Arangoli exclaimed. "If so, we would have to enlarge the doorways and roll him into the throne room in order to hold court!"

Again, laughter filled the room, lifting spirits and reinforcing the sense of camaraderie among the group.

When the laughter calmed, Korrigan turned to Vic. "I was wondering if you would consider staying in Ra'Tahal."

Vic glanced at Revita. "I don't know. I was thinking I might try life in one of the free cities."

She arched a brow. "You know nothing of the big city. I suspect you might get chewed up, spit out, and stepped upon in short order."

Deciding he was willing to chance it in front of the others, Vic suggested, "That is why I was hoping you would come with me."

Through narrowed eyes, she stared at him while he smiled expectantly, hoping to disguise the anxiety brought on by posing the question. If she denied him now, it would be the end of them as a couple.

Her gaze lowered to the table as she rubbed her tankard handle. "I probably should avoid Greavesport for a while, or until Hargrave is replaced by someone else."

Not one to give up, Vic tried again. "Bard's Bay?"

She shook her head, "Too many of the prison guards have seen my face. If any survived the prison break, it could lead to trouble."

Crestfallen, Vic's smile melted, the castle of hope he had built up crumbling to dust. "I had hoped…"

"Now," she continued as if she hadn't heard him speak. "Hooked Point is a place I have yet to visit. I hear it is gorgeous, especially when the sun is setting over the Inner Sea."

"Hooked Point?"

"It is on the north shore."

With a sliver of hope remaining, he asked, "And, we could go there together?"

She rolled her eyes. "Don't make me say it."

"Say what?"

Revita sighed, ran her hand through her dark hair, and took a firm breath. "I..." She frowned and swept a hard gaze from one end of the table to the other. "I will stab anyone who laughs or even makes a comment."

More than one dwarf jerked in surprise. A few covered their mouths. Nobody spoke.

Seemingly satisfied, Revita tried again. "I like having you around, Vic. If you join me, we will see if there is something between us...." She smiled. "Or if I just end up getting tired of having you around."

Vic smiled. "I am willing to chance it."

"Good. Now that is settled," she lifted her mug and tipped it, a single drop of ale falling to the table. "What does a woman have to do to get another tankard of ale? I am parched."

Korrigan laughed. "Right you are." He raised his voice. "Ale! Send in more ale and tap a new barrel!"

THE NEXT MORNING, Revita waited while Korrigan approached the giant stone door in the heart of the central keep. She remained very aware of Vic standing at her side with his hand resting on her hip as he gently held her against him. He seemed to touch her whenever possible. Surprisingly, she found herself enjoying the contact. Their night together, the first in a week, had been both spirited and fulfilling.

Korrigan produced a bronze disk with an array of oddly cut teeth on its outer edge, making it appear like a gear crafted by a drunkard. An array of metal pegs stuck up from the face of the disk, each a different length. He pressed the disk into the sunburst carving on the stone door. It clicked into place so only a three-inch diameter portion remained above the stone surface. When turned, the disk caused the sunburst to turn with it. A heavy click resounded and the door swung open to reveal a ramp leading down into darkness.

"The Drow emptied the primary armory. Thankfully, it was only a quarter full at the time, so the loss is not so great. This armory, however, is a well-kept secret. They may have discovered the door and wondered what hid behind it, but I find it unlikely that they located the key. Without it, there is no entering, not with the protections we have in place."

Curious, Revita asked, "Where was the key kept?"

"Oh, no," Korrigan shook his head. "The fact that you even know it exists is enough of a risk. There is no way I am telling you where we hide the key."

"You don't trust me." She said in an accusatory tone.

"I mean no offense, Revita, but that is not without good reason. Were I forced to rely on you in a fight, I would have no qualms. When it comes to giving you access to what might be the greatest treasure in the world, and certainly among my clan, I prefer to take the cautious route."

"You can't fault his logic, Vita." Vic noted, "You *do* have a reputation."

She nodded. "Damn right, I do. It is a reputation I worked hard to build in Greavesport. A new city means starting over. You do realize that is your fault, don't you, Korrigan?"

Korrigan stepped through the doorway, and when he crossed an ornate, gilded seal marking the floor of the ramp, light bloomed from a series of globes down the center of the angled ceiling. "How is it my fault?"

She walked alongside him. "My problem with Hargrave stemmed from the heist you forced me into."

"I hardly forced you to do it. I doubt anyone could force you into anything."

Revita could not disagree with the last comment. "Well, if it wasn't for you, I'd never have tried to rob the Trade and Barter, and I would still be living in Greavesport with my reputation intact."

"But then, you would not have come with us." Vic chose to add a compliment. "And without your help, we likely would have failed in freeing the Head Thumpers from prison or recapturing Ra'Tahal."

She stopped and patted his cheek. "It is sweet for you to say that, but I feel like my role in ousting the Drow from the citadel was minor at best."

He took her hand from his face and held it as he resumed walking down the ramp. "Well, I am glad you ran into trouble at Greavesport, or you and I would not be together."

Revita smiled but refrained from replying in kind. *He knows how I feel about him. I should not have to say it.*

As the ramp leveled, they came to an intersection where a wall blocked the route ahead but openings to other rooms stood on both sides of the tunnel. The dwarf king led Revita around the corner and stopped. She gasped and stared in awe.

The central keep was a large building, and the armory hidden beneath it had an identical footprint. As in the sloping corridor, globes mounted to the ceiling illuminated the long space. Rows and rows of racks, shelving, and barrels held thousands of pieces of armor, weapons, tools, and more, all forged of dwarven steel.

"This is...overwhelming." Revita allowed the awe she felt into her tone.

"What you see is less than half of what we have stored." Korrigan gestured toward the doorway they had just walked through. "The other side of the armory is much like this one. However, this merely shows the volume of the works we hold."

"What else is there?"

"The prized pieces." He headed down a path between rows of racks. "Follow me."

They walked the length of the room, Revita's attention flitting from item to item like an eager butterfly in a sunlit field of flowers. They drew near the far end and Korrigan stopped before a stone door much like the one in the hall above. Again, he placed the disk into the sunburst carved into the door, turned it, and the door swung open. They entered a smaller chamber placed below the ramp entrance. In the chamber were more weapons, amulets, staffs, helms, shields, and various oddities. Again, everything was crafted of metal cast in the warm tint of Dwarven steel.

Vic shrugged. "This stuff is nice, but these hardly seem better than the other items."

"Ah." Korrigan nodded. "Until you realize that these items all have been granted a magical ability by one of our own spell wrights."

Revita looked around. "I can choose one of these?"

"I promised you as much."

She wandered into the chamber, her gaze sweeping her surroundings. A rack to her left held a great sword far too big for a dwarf to wield. She was unsure if she could even lift the massive blade. Beside it were a spear, a halberd, and other polearms. On the table to her right rested helms, one of which stood out for the disk-shaped sapphire on the front, the blue shimmering in the light.

Korrigan reached for the helm. "Ah. I was wondering what became of this."

"Are you going to claim it for yourself?" she asked.

"Nay. I now wear a crown, and it is best if I focused on governing our people. Instead, I will gift this to Arangoli. It once belonged to Gahagar, before they crafted the armor that allowed him to wield the Caelum Edge. Goli is the greatest warrior in our clan, and he deserves a helm like this to help keep him alive."

"What does it do? Vic asked.

"The sapphire blooms with light when a creature with evil in its heart is nearby. The light is reputed to cause such monsters pain. If true, it might come in handy in the future." The dwarf gestured. "We are waiting on your selection, Vita."

Resuming her search, Revita passed the shelf filled with exotic trinkets and a pedestal came into view, the object on top of it drawing her attention. It was a foot long, its core made of leather, including the straps. Thin, bent metal plates covered much of the leather from the outside.

"What is this?"

Korrigan appeared at her side. "That is a bracer with special abilities. The plates flip out and curl into spikes when you clench your fist. If you fling your arm and open your fist, the spikes launch from the bracer."

Revita picked up the object and rotated it in her hands. It was far lighter than expected. The strap that wound around the palm included a button and tiny linkage that ran up the inside of the arm. "So, it is purely mechanical?"

"The magical element is unique and has never been successfully replicated." He pointed to a pair of gems on the inside of the bracer. "The person wearing it can recall the spikes by pressing fingers against these gems. When the spikes reattach to the bracer, they lay back down into place as plates."

There had been times when Revita wished she had additional physical protection to help defend herself, but armor was at best an inconvenience to a thief. More often, it was a major hinderance. This, on the other hand, was compact, light, and did not clank when she shook it.

"I will take it."

Korrigan nodded. "Interesting choice. It is yours. Use it wisely." He then turned to Vic. "What will you choose?"

Vic blinked. "Me? Vita is the one who asked for a reward. I only requested that my people be free, and that request has been granted."

"Nonetheless, you deserve it."

"Korrigan is correct," Revita said. "Besides, look at all this stuff. Surely, you can find something of interest."

He wandered among the items and examined each shelf, table, and pedestal he passed. When reaching the chamber's far end, he rounded the corner and came back on the opposite aisle, not stopping until he stood directly across from her with shelving and pieces of armor blocking her view.

Revita turned her attention back to her new prize. She slid the bracer over her hand and strapped it to her forearm while strolling back toward the chamber entrance. The sound of rummaging through metal objects came from Vic's direction. As she turned back toward him, he emerged with something in his hand.

"What did you choose?" Revita asked.

He approached her. "There is nothing in here I want...except for you." He opened his palm and revealed a brooch in the shape of a dragon. The brooch was made of gold and red metal with tiny gems for eyes and gems along the spikes on the spine. "I chose it for you." He handed it to her.

"For me?" It was a gorgeous piece of jewelry, the metal edges and gems glittering in the light. She had no idea what it was worth, but she knew it was a lot. "Does it do anything?"

Korrigan shrugged. "I have no idea. It...does not look like anything I read about in the inventory journal."

"I can choose this?" Vic asked.

"It is your choice, Vic."

He nodded. "I want Vita to have it."

She lifted her gaze and peered into his eyes as something stirred inside her. "What are you doing to me?" she muttered.

"I thought it might make you happy."

"I..." Her mouth turned down into a frown. "Are you trying to manipulate me?"

He sighed. "If you think that, you don't know me at all."

When Vic walked past her as if to leave, she caught him by the arm and stopped him.

"It isn't you," she explained. "It is everyone else who has passed through my life."

He still didn't turn toward her. "What does that mean?"

"I have been on my own for a long time, Vic. In that span, others have tried to manipulate me at every turn."

"Not me."

"I...realize that...now."

Vic turned toward her. "What would you have of me?"

She eased up to him. "As I said last night, I want you to come with me. Let's spend time together and see what comes of it."

"I would like that." He took her hand and held it in his. "When do we leave?"

"I was thinking...now."

"Give me an hour." Korrigan said from behind Revita. "As a farewell gift, I will ensure you are set with the provisions and coin required to get you to Hooked Point."

Revita nodded. "We accept."

Vic stood at the bluff gate, waiting while Revita chatted with the gate guards. She laughed and flicked her hair, her flirting obvious, but Vic knew it was not that she wanted to bed the dwarven guards. Such behavior had become engrained in her after years of manipulating others toward her own ends. One moment, she was sugar, smiles, and as pleasant as they came. The next, she was sharp, guarded, and full of bite. Either side suited her needs based on her own perception of the audience. What hid beneath the two personas was the true woman, the one he felt drawn toward, the one he sought to bring out more often.

Korrigan and an escort of guards emerged from the shadowy street and crossed the square inside the gate. All wore armor and helms except for the new king, whose crown glittered in the morning sun.

"Vic, Vita. I apologize if I am a few minutes late. Are you ready to go down?"

Revita gave a firm nod. "More than ready."

"Let's go."

Vic walked at Korrigan's side, Revita at the other side and the escort of ten dwarven guards trailing. They passed through the gate, crossed the stone bulwark that jutted out over the lower hold, and began down the stairs.

The descent was quick and without conversation. They then reached the lift and rode it down to the mine. Its tunnels were vacant, the forges cold, which felt odd to Vic who was used to the constant activity during his time working there.

They emerged to the open yard of the lower hold and followed the gravel road toward the outer gate. As they approached the bunkhouse Vic had called home for two seasons, memories of that time resurfaced. It had been a difficult and challenging life but not one without cama-raderie or satisfaction. To Vic's surprise, Korrigan walked up to the bunkhouse door and addressed the two guards posted there. One opened the door and shouted for those inside to come out.

Out came the familiar faces of the men from Vic's village, all of whom were miners, half of which worked the day shift with him.

The men blinked in the sunlight and looked around, appearing confused. Then, Brady's eyes fell on Vic and patted Henrick, who stood beside him. Soon, all were staring at Vic with shock on their faces.

Korrigan walked back to Vic. "Go on. Tell them."

Vic's brow furrowed. "Tell them what?"

"That they are free men."

"Me?" He blinked in surprise.

"I thought you might want to be the one to do it, since their freedom was your doing."

Vic argued, "Ian, Revita, and many others had as much to do with it as I."

Korrigan clapped a hand on Vic's shoulder. "You, alone, worked among these men. You deserve to tell them, and they will appreciate it most when coming from you."

Vic nodded, gathered himself, and crossed the space. Thirty-one men, all unshaven, their clothing stained and ragged, stared at him expectantly.

In his native language, Vic spoke in a loud, firm voice. "Much has occurred over recent weeks. Your lives were already hard, then catastrophe struck, the mine caved in, and dark elves captured Ra'Tahal." Vic then realized that the other miners likely thought him buried and dead somewhere in those tunnels. "You might be wondering how I survived the tunnel collapse. My escape was narrow, both from the tunnels and from the city itself, but I was not alone. My brother Ian and I joined King Korrigan on a quest to find help, infiltrate the citadel, and drive out the Drow. Much was sacrificed to reclaim Ra'Tahal, but we succeeded. As part of the bargain for our assistance in the quest, King Korrigan has agreed to grant your unfettered freedom."

The miners stared at Vic as if he was speaking a foreign tongue.

"Did you hear me? You are free men."

"Free?" Brady repeated it as if tasting the word to see whether or not he liked it.

"Yes. You can leave and go anywhere you like."

"Or," Korrigan spoke in Dwarvish. "You are welcome to remain here and be paid for any work you perform."

Brady strode forward, opened his arms wide, and hugged Vic. "Thank you!"

Henrick bellowed a cheer and the others joined in. In moments, Vic was surrounded by men clapping him on the back, hugging him, and shaking his hand. Their comments came at a flurry and he hardly heard half of them over the ruckus. When everyone settled and stepped back, he turned to find Revita watching him.

"Oh," he walked up to her and slid an arm around her back. "And this slice of beauty is Revita. While a thief by trade, she is more likely to steal your heart judging by my experience."

Again, the men surrounded Vic, this time focused on Revita as an idea struck.

"I suspect you men are undecided as to what to do next. You may choose to return to Shillings and see if you can resume your lives there. Some may decide to remain here or even venture out on their own and see the world.

"If your inclination is the latter, I have an offer. Revita and I are off to a distant, seaside city called Hooked Point. You are welcome to join us, but you must decide now. We are leaving in the next few minutes."

The men looked at one another, breaking into a dozen different conversations. Minutes passed and then, Brady and Henrick separated from the others and approached Vic.

Brady said, "A few of the men have decided to remain in Ra'Tahal. The rest wish to return to Shillings."

Vic nodded. "Very well. I wish you the..."

Henrick interrupted, "But Brady and I want to go with you."

"You do?"

"Had it not been for you, we wouldn't have survived the mines," Henrick said.

"We believe in you, Vic." Brady patted him on the shoulder. "You have proven to be a good friend and a better man. Our families are gone, so there is nothing left for us in Shillings. We would rather bet on you than wander the world while blindly seeking a future for ourselves."

Vic arched a brow. "What do you think, Vita?"

She tapped her finger on her lips while looking the two young men up and down. "They seem strong enough and are not totally unattractive. I suppose I could allow them into bed with us."

"What?" Vic exclaimed while the other two gaped.

Revita laughed. "Oh, that was worth it, just for the look on your faces."

Vic exhaled. "You can be cruel at times."

She put her hand on his arm, the warmth of her palm a familiar connection. "I never said I was nice."

He admitted, "In truth, I prefer your edge anyway."

"On that, we can agree." She looked at Brady and Henrick. "I would be happy to have your friends join us, so long as you and I have our own room. What they do in theirs is their business."

Vic laughed. "I agree on both counts." He then turned to Korrigan. "We are ready, but we might need more supplies."

"I anticipated a few of the villagers might go with you," Korrigan said. "That is why I sent a wagon filled with provisions to wait at the gate. That wagon will take you to Ferdig's Landing, which is a few hours downriver from here. There, a boat will be waiting. Two days on the river will take you to Bard's Bay. From there, you are on your own."

Vic clapped a hand on the king's shoulder. "Thank you, Korrigan."

"Technically, it is Your Majesty, but I am unused to such things yet."

"You will be a fine king," Vic said in earnest. "Just don't let power go to your head, and all will be well."

"I will try." Korrigan gestured. "My guards and I will escort these men to the upper hold, so they can bathe, get fresh clothing, and a good meal. You had better get to the gate. The wagon is waiting."

The dwarves led the remaining villagers away, Vic briefly watching them retreat before he turned and headed toward the outer gate. When the gate came into view, a wagon pulled by two oxen waited there. The driver gave them a friendly greeting, told them to climb into the wagon bed and sit among the packs piled there. Once everyone was settled, the driver snapped the reins and the oxen pulled them through the open gate.

Soon, Vic found himself watching Ra'Tahal fade into the distance. The citadel remained a place of both good and bad memories, and despite the harsh beginning Vic had endured, he felt a sense of loss when leaving it.

Putting such thoughts aside, he turned and looked west while wondering what surprises the future might hold.

EPILOGUE

Gray clouds blanketed the evening sky, the layer so thick that shadows were imperceptible despite it being an hour until sunset. The land surrounding Talastar, capital city of the Drow, appeared bleak and barren, a notable reminder of the war that had come to her doorstep before faltering.

Gryzaal, Captain of the Letalis Elite Legion, jogged across open, life-less plains while heading toward the dark, foreboding city walls. The fifty warriors trailing him were unarmed, their weapons confiscated. Giving up his naginata felt akin to losing a limb. Gryzaal suspected the other warriors experienced the same sense of loss and regret. A letalis warrior and his or her chosen weapon were said to bond for life. *Would we have been better off fighting to the death?* It was a question he had asked himself a dozen times over since leaving Ra'Tahal. As they had frequently during the journey north, his thoughts turned to the urgent quest that had sent him south in the first place.

Circumstances had required subterfuge, the situation dire. When Rysildar approached him with his scheme, Gryzaal had agreed and firmly believed it would succeed, especially when backed by singer magic. Yet, Gryzaal now found himself returning home without three quarters of his force and little gained to compensate for the lives lost. Even the singer had fallen in the ill begotten mission. It was unlike any Drow to admit defeat, but when Gryzaal and his warriors fought against the dwarves and found themselves facing something unexpected, something with untold power, it had become clear that the situation had become untenable. So, he surrendered and fled, believing that doing so would better serve his queen than allowing the rest of his squad to die a meaningless death.

With the city walls drawing near, he vanquished his musings and locked them away in a corner of his mind. Too soon, he would have to face them and what they meant to his people.

The column of warriors headed toward Black Gate, the massive door made of petrified wood named for its dark hue. Just like the walls of dread surrounding the city, it had stood intact for thousands of years. Even Gahagar had not been able to crack its shell when the dwarves sought to rule the world. The dwarf overlord's death had ended that campaign, but the scars it left upon the world remained raw and unhealed.

Gryzaal, slowed to a stop, approached Black Gate, and thumped knuckles against the door while shouting in Elvish. "I have returned and demand entrance, so I may speak with her eminence, Queen Liloth."

A Drow warrior appeared on top of the wall. "State your name."

"It is Gryzaal, Captain of her majesty's Letalis Elite."

Another dark elf peered over the wall before disappearing. Shouts echoed and the gate began receding. As the gate creaked open, a sense of uneasiness oozed out. It was as though an intangible shroud of darkness had descended upon Talastar, and Gryzaal dreaded what lurked in the city's shadows.

The warriors followed him inside and across an empty square as they made their way to Castle Umbria. The streets were eerily quiet, the only sign of life being the few scattered merchants who hurriedly retreated into their shops. Gryzaal thought back to the time when the city thrived, before the dwarves brought war to her walls, before his own people made the mistake of delving too far into the depths beneath the city. Their desire for Vartanium had pressed them beyond reason, and the veins in the mine below Talastar ran vertical. When the upper portions were exhausted, they dug deeper and continued, until it was too late.

He led his squad to the castle gate. The warriors posted there watched them pass in silence. A grand welcome was not expected, nor would they dare to turn him away. The tension among his people had never been higher. With the news he was to deliver, he worried that the situation would only grow worse.

The castle was made of the same dark, dreary stone as the city walls. Its towers and crenelations loomed over him like the darkness coming for his people. The front door stood open, and he led his squad inside while imagining them entering the mouth of a giant golem, eager to consume them.

The building's interior was even emptier than the streets. He strode across the entrance hall with the throne room in sight, the doors standing open and quiet voices coming from inside. A deep breath of courage was required to maintain his pace and not turn away. As he entered the great hall, the beat of his strides did not waver, nor did his determination.

Twisted columns lined the hall's center aisle. Those columns supported a cathedral ceiling sixty feet above him. Torches mounted to the columns illuminated the path to the dais at the far end. Upon the dais, Queen Liloth sat on her obsidian throne, speaking to Arieldar, her personal advisor. Arieldar whispered one last thing to Liloth and then turned toward Gryzaal, while assuming his accustomed place beside the throne. The queen held up a palm and beckoned Gryzaal toward her with the stroke of a finger. Alone, he advanced down the center aisle. The other warriors in his squad remained in the shadows near the entrance. He did not blame them. Liloth had a history of harshly responding to bad news. Anyone standing nearby was likely to be caught in the tempest of her fury.

Gryzaal reached the fore of the throne room and dropped to one knee before the dais. "Your Majesty," he began hesitantly. "We have failed."

Liloth's face remained stoic but behind those penetrating eyes lay a hardened soul, cold, and calculating. Worse, he knew he was being judged for the mistakes of another.

"Where is Rysildar? Your quest was his to lead." A crown made of blackened wood with an oval-shaped onyx gracing the front rested on her head. The dark crown was a stark contrast to her white hair and pale flesh. Yet, as dark as the crown appeared, her eyes were darker.

Gryzaal replied, "The singer is dead, as are all of the letalis warriors who joined this mission, save for those who stand behind me."

She raised her gaze to peer across the hall. "I see no more than two squads. Four times that number were sent with you."

"Yes, my queen."

The queen arched a painted brow. "What of the dwarven steel, the weapons, the armor?"

He hesitated only a beat before responding. "Did the shipment we sent not arrive?"

"The shipment arrived a week ago, but it was not even enough to outfit a single squad."

"That was the entirety of what we found in the citadel armory, the one the dwarves admitted existed. We then discovered what we believe to be a secret armory beneath Ra'Tahal's central keep, but the chamber resides behind magical and physical barriers we were unable to penetrate. Rysildar claimed that he had devised a means into this armory and had nearly completed forming the spell, but he died before it was ready. Thus...what we sent is all we could recover."

"And what of the mine?"

"We had taken control of the mine, but an explosion caused the tunnels to collapse while also damaging the crusher. The clean up after the collapse consumed weeks before the crusher and tunnels were safe to resume operations. The dwarven metalwrights and spellwrights were finally producing again for us when the attack came."

She pressed her black lips together, her nostrils flaring, but her voice remained even. "Attack from whom?"

"A squad of dwarves aided by a handful of humans."

"I thought you had control of the citadel and those within."

"We did. The attack came from outsiders."

She arched a brow. "How did they breach a fortress that was reputed to be impenetrable?"

He shrugged. "They found a means to infiltrate the citadel by stealth. Once inside, the invaders attacked and killed Rysildar and then over-whelmed the warriors I had posted at the city gate. With the dwarves in control of the gate, they opened it and allowed a larger force inside. That was when I was alerted to the infiltration. I assembled my remaining warriors outside of the central keep and met the dwarves head on. A frantic battle ensued, and just when we were about to surround the enemy force and crush them, something unexpected occurred." The battle replayed in Gryzaal's mind, ending with a human intervening in a most unanticipated manner.

After a long beat of silence, the queen urged him forward. "Go on. Say it."

How do you explain the impossible? He was uncertain, but his queen needed to know. "There was a human among them, a young male. He used magic against us, making our attacks futile while tossing us around by some powerful, invisible force. With this magic, he threatened to destroy us lest we cease fighting and flee the citadel. When nothing could harm this boy, be it weapons or arrows, I did not know how to face him. Rather than waste the lives of my remaining warriors, I thought it prudent to ensure that some of us survive so we might return, report what occurred, and be able to fight another day."

486

The queen leaned back in her throne, her black fingernails tapping on the obsidian arm. The tapping echoed in the otherwise silent throne room like a countdown to an unfortunate fate. As the moments trickled past, Gryzaal imagined her bursting to her feet, opening her mouth in song, her magic causing him and the other soldiers to burst into flames, the burning warriors flailing and screaming as they died. Her voice pulled him from this nightmare.

"Our situation has grown dire. At best we have weeks before the orcs break through our defenses. When that occurs, I fear they will flood the city. Their numbers appear endless while ours have dwindled to a mere shadow of what they once were. If we remain here, we will perish. Thus, you will devise an evacuation plan, so we may relocate. It is the only way."

Gryzaal released the breath he had been holding. "Thank you, Your Majesty."

"Do not think you have avoided punishment for your failures," she snapped. Leaning back, she looked down her nose at him. "In order to execute this plan, you and your team will replace those who hold the mines in check. While the miners flee, you are to act as our rear guard. You will be the last one out of the city...if you survive."

He had feared worse, but death still stalked him. *At least this will give me and my squad a chance at redemption.* "I will begin planning our evacuation immediately. When ready, we will flee the city. So long as a single living Drow remains within Talastar, I will as well. Of that, you have my word."

While Talastar was lost, the Drow would survive, but only if he could find a means to slow the horde's advance.

The story continues in
Paragon of Solitude

NOTE FROM THE AUTHOR

I hope you enjoyed the first book in a series that peers into the distant and legendary past of the world of Wizardoms. More books are in the works, the first of which is **Paragon of Solitude**, releasing in early 2024.

I am thankful to have you joining me on this grand adventure.

Best Wishes,
Jeff

Follow me on:
Amazon
Bookbub
Facebook

Also by Jeffrey L. Kohanek

Fate of Wizardoms

Eye of Obscurance

Balance of Magic

Temple of the Oracle

Objects of Power

Rise of a Wizard Queen

A Contest of Gods

* * *

Fate of Wizardoms Boxed Set: Books 1-3

Fate of Wizardoms Box Set: Books 4-6

Fall of Wizardoms

God King Rising

Legend of the Sky Sword

Curse of the Elf Queen

Shadow of a Dragon Priest

Advent of the Drow

A Sundered Realm

Fall of Wizardoms Boxed Set: Books 1-3

Fall of Wizardoms Box Set: Books 4-6

Wizardom Legends

The Outrageous Exploits of Jerrell Landish

Thief for Hire

Trickster for Hire

Charlatan for Hire

Tor the Dungeon Crawler

Temple of the Unknown

Castles of Legend

Shrine of the Undead

Runes of Issalia

The Buried Symbol

The Emblem Throne

An Empire in Runes

* * *

Runes of Issalia Bonus Box

Wardens of Issalia

A Warden's Purpose

The Arcane Ward:

An Imperial Gambit

A Kingdom Under Siege

* * *

Wardens of Issalia Boxed Set

Made in United States
Troutdale, OR
04/12/2024